In June 2011, September was weeks away, and the full dread of the approaching anniversary hadn't yet settled on New York City's residents. But from One Police Plaza to the FBI's grim headquarters in Washington, D.C., the top brass harbor a rumbling in the gut. Each person who works for them down the line shares their unease, from every rookie cop walking the beat to the lowliest surveillance specialist. And Archer Landis is about to get caught up in their fixation.

Landis is not one of his city's guardians, and a different sort of electricity runs under his skin on this warm Thursday evening. A highly successful Manhattan architect—a man you'd say has his life totally, enviably, in order—Landis works the room at a Midtown reception, shaking hands, being seen, accompanying his cheerful greetings with the convivial clinking of ice in an untouched glass of single malt.

When the noisy crowd becomes sufficiently dense and everyone present can say they've seen him, he will slip away. Out on Fifth Avenue, he will grab a cab for the run south to Julia's Chelsea apartment. It's a trip that will hurtle him into deadly danger. Everyone and everything he cares about most will be threatened, and he will have to discover whether he has the courage to fight his way clear.

ARCHITECT
OF COURAGE

Dear Ann —
Happy Reading!

Victoria Weisfeld

—V

A Black Opal Books Publication

Black Opal Books
BECAUSE SOME STORIES JUST HAVE TO BE TOLD

GENRE: MURDER MYSTERY

This is a work of fiction. Names, places, characters and incidents are either the product of the author's imagination or are used fictitiously, and any resemblance to any actual persons, living or dead, businesses, organizations, events or locales is entirely coincidental. All trademarks, service marks, registered trademarks, and registered service marks are the property of their respective owners and are used herein for identification purposes only. The publisher does not have any control over or assume any responsibility for author or third-party websites or their contents.

ARCHITECT OF COURAGE
Copyright © 2022 by Victoria Weisfeld
Cover Design by Transformational Concepts
All cover art copyright © 2022
All Rights Reserved
Print ISBN: 9781953434814

First Publication: JUNE 2022

All rights reserved under the International and Pan-American Copyright Conventions. No part of this book may be reproduced or transmitted in any form or by any means, electronic or mechanical, including photocopying, recording, or by any information storage and retrieval system, without permission in writing from the publisher.

WARNING: The unauthorized reproduction or distribution of this copyrighted work is illegal. Criminal copyright infringement, including infringement without monetary gain, is investigated by the FBI and is punishable by up to 5 years in federal prison and a fine of $250,000. Anyone pirating our eBooks will be prosecuted to the fullest extent of the law and may be liable for each individual download resulting therefrom.

ABOUT THE PRINT VERSION: If you purchased a print version of this book without a cover, you should be aware that the book is stolen property. It was reported as "unsold and destroyed" to the publisher, and neither the author nor the publisher has received any payment for this "stripped book."

IF YOU FIND AN EBOOK OR PRINT VERSION OF THIS BOOK BEING SOLD OR SHARED ILLEGALLY, PLEASE REPORT IT TO:
skh@blackopalbooks.com

Published by Black Opal Books **http://www.blackopalbooks.com**

Chapter 1

When Manhattan architect Archer Landis let himself into Julia's apartment, he was surprised to find it dark. He strode down the short entry hall to the living room and felt for the light switch. The heavy draperies were closed, and thick blackness pressed in on him. A trace of her perfume teased the air, along with another smell—elemental, evoking... something.

"Julia? I'm here."

For Landis, this second-floor apartment was a treasure-house, its sangria-colored walls crowded with portraits and huge mirrors with carved, gold-painted frames. Deeply fringed paisley shawls draped chaises upholstered in carmine velvet. It would require all his French curves and a full palette of rose and violet pigments to reproduce the effect.

His glance traveled the room, skipping past something he didn't want to see, something his brain didn't at first accept that he *had* seen, until it reached the farthest corner and unwillingly returned to settle on the room's one discordant object: Julia sprawled on a chaise, the white lace ruffle of her shirtfront soaked with blood.

For a moment, Landis's heart stopped. He stood frozen at the edge of the room, yet he saw himself rushing to her, kissing her hands, grabbing her shoulders and shaking her, soothing her, calling her. She didn't move, and neither did he. He choked before he could create a single word.

Now he identified the strange smell. Blood. Blood that had oozed from a huge wound in her chest. Blood that drenched the crocheted lace of her shirt and darkened the crimson velvet of the chaise. A stray drop, spattering upward, had left a dot on her chin. He took two halting steps toward her.

Shouldn't he wipe off that spot? Couldn't he put all the blood back? Couldn't he press his hands on her ravaged chest and seal life inside? Her dark eyes, wide open and fixed, gazed blankly toward him and told him he could not.

He stepped backward to sag against the wall and slowly collapsed to the floor. His head drooped. He sobbed into the hands that had held her hands, caressed her face. Hands that should be holding her now. When he raised his head, tears blurred the contours of her pale face, the empty black pools of her eyes. All else washed by a tide of red.

He couldn't bear to think about the terror of her final moments. What was the last thing she did? What did she see? *Who did she see? Who?* A dark cloud of vengeance rose in him like smoke from a bonfire. He had to call the police, make them come immediately. Set the hounds of the law on the scent of her killer.

Yet.

Yet he shouldn't—he couldn't—be found in her apartment. His presence would damage his reputation and ruin Julia's. The lie he'd told his wife Marjorie about his evening dinner plans rolled like a boulder through his tumbling thoughts. His associates, his team, the people he spent every day with, considered Julia a colleague, and they'd never trust him again. He wasn't on easy terms with betrayal—not enough practice. Nor was he clever with lies and excuses. He couldn't conjure up a plausible reason for being in her apartment when he was so clearly supposed to be elsewhere.

He had to leave, to escape the awful sight of Julia's body, the awful reality of it. *What did I touch?* He scanned the room. At one time or another, he'd touched furniture, switches, faucets, dishes, glassware, books, and more. He'd have to explain those fingerprints, eventually.

Evidence of *this* visit, though, could disappear. If only he'd never come tonight; if only he'd never made this awful discovery. He pulled out a handkerchief and wiped his presence away, scrubbing around the light switch. His back was to her, his eyes were squeezed shut, and still he saw Julia's broken body.

With a final look at the face he loved, Landis promised her she wouldn't be alone and in the dark for long and retreated down the hall. He wrapped his hand in the handkerchief, quietly opened the apartment door, wiped the outside knob, and hurried downstairs to the lobby.

He hadn't seen any of her neighbors when he came in, would one of them be there now and see him leave? He ran his hand through his long and distinctive white hair, straightened the collar of his suit, and paused to compose his face. No, the lobby was clear. He exhaled.

He'd walk east to Eighth Avenue to hail an uptown cab. A few cars were parked on the opposite side of the street, and he didn't see any pedestrians. *Except there.* Up ahead, across the street, an elderly woman turned the corner, heading his way, led by yappy wirehaired terrier. Tall as he was, Landis was hard to miss. The dog looked straight at him, barking furiously.

"Toby!" the woman admonished in her brittle voice. Her arm strained forward with the pull of the leash. Her attention was on the dog, and Landis still hoped he could slip away.

"Toby!" she screamed. "Come back!" Dragging his leash, Toby darted between parked cars. An SUV hissed toward them from the next corner.

Landis stepped into the street and waved both arms. The SUV squealed to a stop. He scooped Toby up and handed him to his quivering mistress. "No harm done."

She hugged the rambunctious terrier, a little plastic bag of poop flapping in her hand. "Toby, you naughty boy. You mustn't run from Mama like that."

Landis edged away, but she wasn't finished thanking him. She opened her handbag.

Was she fumbling for a tip, for Christ's sake? No, she pulled out a tissue and wiped her eyes. He put a few feet between them. "Now, Toby, you be good," and to her, "Are you all right now?"

"We're fine. You go on. You've done your good deed for this evening."

ᴄ⁄ᴐᴇ⁄ᴐ

All the way up Eighth Avenue Landis huddled in a corner of the sour-smelling cab, breathing hard. The swarthy driver stared at him in the rearview mirror. Under the man's suspicious gaze, he returned his phone to his pocket instead of calling 911.

The sticky breath of the early June night blew in through the cab's half-open window. This ride felt completely different from the one he'd taken—what? forty minutes before?—when he'd slipped out of the Plaza Hotel, past the line of malodorous horse-drawn carriages waiting for tourists, and toward the honking melee of Fifth Avenue. There, he hailed a bright yellow cab and climbed inside, full of thoughts of Julia. A buzzing energy had him drumming the leather seats, willing the traffic lights ahead to turn green.

Off the rails, heading straight into the abyss.

Before that earlier ride, Landis believed himself securely moving forward, on track and at speed, in full control of his considerable professional talents and personal powers. He'd worked the room at the Plaza, a reception for his peers, the city's most talented magicians in glass and steel and stone.

They sought him out, and he laughed with them, shook hands and patted backs, accompanying his good cheer with the convivial clink of ice in a glass of single malt. He bear-hugged the evening's honoree, Phil Prinz. He brushed off praise and bestowed it on others. Accomplishment haloed him, and because he was generous in his success, it did not breed resentment, but drew the light to him.

He made sure everyone would remember greeting him, touching him. When the noisy crowd became sufficiently dense, he'd made his discreet escape. Now his reentry into that world had to be just as smooth.

⌒⌒

The dinner was under way when he arrived, and he had to find his seat, leaving no time to place the call right then. He'd missed the salad.

"What's wrong, Arch? Where've you been?" a colleague asked. "You look awful."

Landis adjusted the knot of his tie. "Touch of a bug. Killed my appetite." He cringed at how easily the lie came. It was what he'd planned to say if anyone asked why he didn't appear at dinner. At least now they wouldn't question it if he jumped up later and went out for a few minutes. He'd call the police from a hotel phone, not his cell. Much better. He'd do it between the main course and dessert.

The men at the table commiserated. "It's going around," one said. "Three of my people are out."

As his tablemates ate and shared shoptalk, Landis frowned at his plate. *Who would kill Julia? What possible reason could there be?* Nothing in her world explained it. Her working life was his office, and her social life was him.

He was confident of that, of her. *Was it a random, sense-less, act? Or did some secret peril lurk close by?* If so, it could be as close as his own skin.

When the servers came to clear, the food on his plate was rearranged but uneaten. The evening's introductions and accolades began. The words of the welcoming speeches jumbled meaninglessly. He rested his head on his hand and mapped out what he'd say to the police. Dial 911, give the address, disconnect. *Don't answer questions. Don't give them time to ask anything. How long does it take to trace a call?* He'd stay on the phone for seconds. Only the facts, no context. Hang up.

Here came dessert. He'd lost another chance to make his call. The server set a collapsing strawberry pavlova in front of him. Frothy white meringue shell, a lake of red juice. Landis's stomach turned over. He pushed the dish away and took a great gulp from his water glass.

Now he was stuck. It would be too awkward to step out during the commendations, especially since Landis's long-time friend and fellow Yale alumnus, Phil Prinz, was re-ceiving the main prize—the 2011 Calder Award for Integrity in Architectural Practice. Called to the lectern, Phil's first words were to ask the award's previous recipients to stand. Landis wobbled to his feet, waved—*my God, did I just smile?* His other hand gripped the rim of the table so tightly he could hardly pry his fingers loose.

Prinz's high-minded theme was courage: physical, men-tal, emotional, and moral. He might have been speaking di-rectly to Landis, chiding him.

"Physical courage," Prinz said, "is the kind people think of most often, the kind that lets us ski black diamond runs, compete in marathons, and drive the Jersey Turnpike. A misstep can end with a trip to the emergency department, but any physical damage is visible, treatable, and often heals completely."

Not when a hole has been blown through your chest. Landis fingered the stem of his water glass.

"Mental courage—being brave enough to rally your mental faculties, make critical decisions, and not be paralyzed into inaction—demands more," Prinz said, citing race car drivers and soldiers in battle. Landis saw himself in Julia's apartment, stunned, panicked, choking on tears. *Direct hit.*

"Emotional courage is when you put your inner self, your core being, in harm's way, when you risk sustaining wounds people may never see and that may never heal, when you face truths you'd rather ignore. It's when you risk the very essence of yourself."

Of course Landis had initial reservations about an affair with one of his employees; of course he'd worried his wife Marjorie might discover it. But he'd left those concerns behind. Instead, he'd followed the single shiny track that appeared in front of him: he fell in love. Unexpected, unlikely, unwise. Julia had opened his heart, revealed to him his true self.

Finally, Prinz said, "there's moral courage—when you stick your neck out for some cause not your own simply because it's the right thing to do."

The white noise inside Landis's head drowned out the rest. Although the speech wasn't especially profound, it earned a standing ovation that precipitated a rush for the doors. Clamoring colleagues swarmed the lobby. A discreet telephone call was impossible.

Moment after moment, he put off calling the police until not calling became inevitable. He simply could not speak the words that would make Julia's death real, that would pierce his chest like arrows. His life had a hole in the middle of it, and he felt its razor edges. Unless he grabbed onto something, he would fall through. What he clutched tight was his shameful secret.

Chapter 2

Landis's penthouse with its dramatic window walls was an aerie of straight lines and right angles. The sparsely furnished interior was gray and white—his wife's taste a stark contrast to Julia's. Only the Miró hanging on a far wall provided a restrained confetti of color. He was too drained to appreciate the apartment's muted comforts, however; wherever he looked, he saw the red blur of Julia's apartment.

His son lay in wait. At age 28, Hawkins Landis was bent on living in comfort while he launched his own architectural career at his own leisurely pace. After spending a couple of years knocking around Europe's capitals, he'd returned to the States in March, three long months ago. He manipulated his father into hiring him and took up residence in his old room. Tonight, Landis was hardly in the door when Hawk resumed an argument from earlier that evening.

"While you were at Phil's dinner, I thought more about my situation, and all I can say is you don't get it, Dad. No matter what I do at Landis + Porter, people will knock me down. They'll say I'm nothing without your help. It doesn't matter how good I am."

"That's baloney, and you know it." Landis desperately wanted not to have this conversation. Not tonight. His head was pounding. "The projects will speak for themselves.

Eventually."

"I'm not designing real buildings. I'm doing scut work. The other associates have real projects."

Hawk's whining tone hit the sensitized spot in Landis's brain like a dentist's drill. "For Christ's sake, you're starting out. My lead people—Ty, Charleston, Julia"—he caught his breath—"have been with me for years. Always up for any assignment. Pay your dues, Hawk." His throat tightened; he needed air. He reached up to loosen his tie.

"Not Julia. She's new." When Landis didn't answer, Hawk said, "You think they're so perfect. Well, they're not. They get special treatment. I've seen it. You're not giving me a chance."

Landis glared. "I'm confused. You say people will criticize you because they'll think I gave you unfair advantages, and now you're asking for one?" With a grunt, he pulled off the tie and flung it on the sofa.

"That's so like you. You make everything my fault. I'm not important to you."

"Now, hold on—" His voice logjammed with jostling emotions, but Hawk cut him off.

"I need to be where I have friends."

Marjorie walked into the living room. A long-knit skirt and tunic in some pale color draped her thin frame. "What's going on? Archer? What did you say to him?" She walked to Hawk's side and put her arm around their son's waist. "What's happening here?"

Landis waited for Hawk to explain himself, knowing his own version of the argument would make matters worse. Hawk jerked away from her and left the room. At the end of the hall, the bathroom door slammed. Landis winced.

Throat aching, he said, "Don't ask *me*."

"Is he unhappy? At work?"

"He wants bigger projects, but he's a neophyte."

"Well, of course he's ambitious, he's your son." It

didn't sound like a compliment.

"But he doesn't want people to think he's had any special breaks. He gets the same treatment all the associates do." All except Julia, exceptional Julia.

"But he's your son. That *should* be special."

"Marjorie, think about it. That would be the worst thing for him." He put his hand to his forehead. "To tell you the truth, I wish he'd move out. When is he ever in a good mood?"

"How can you say that? I like having him here. We talk. We have good conversations. The minute you come home, an argument starts."

"His constant hostility is my fault?"

"Anyway, he can't afford a decent place. This is where he belongs. I'd worry about him if he weren't here."

"That was a long time ago, Marjorie. He's had a lot of help since then." *Since his teenage rebellion. His suicide attempts. His acting out.* Landis had never taken any of that as seriously as she had.

"He's right, you know—you shouldn't treat the others better than you do him."

"What others? What the hell—"

"Hawk says they're out to get him, that they're nothing but back-stabbing sycophants." Her voice rose, betraying her anxiety the way it did every time she had to defend Hawk.

"That's not true, Marjorie. They've been nothing but helpful to him. They've never said a word—not one hint of criticism."

"They're not stupid. There's more than one way for them—and you—to undermine a young person with talent and chip away at his confidence."

"I don't know what he's told you, but neither of you knows what you're talking about."

"Hawk knows, and that's why he's threatening to leave

you."

"That's what he meant by being somewhere he has friends? He would leave Landis + Porter?"

"That's right," said Hawk, strolling back into the room. "Starting Monday, I'll be working at BLK. Ivan Karsch made me a very generous offer."

"Oh." Marjorie slumped to the sofa, stunned.

"BLK?" Landis snorted. "According to reputation, they eat their young. And Ivan Karsch, who sued L + P a couple years ago? Great role model." He stood behind Marjorie and grabbed the back of the sofa. "So this is decided? And tonight's the first I hear about it?"

Hawk shrugged.

Landis recalled encountering Karsch at the reception, back-slapping as always, flattering Landis. Now that he thought about it, the man's smug expression had been even more self-satisfied than usual.

So many things were wrong with this conversation. The ball of misery filling his chest now had a red-hot coal at its core. He was in no position to accuse Hawk of betrayal. Nor should he fight with Marjorie, the innocent in all this.

Lately Marjorie was increasingly opaque—distant and preoccupied. She was planning a big fundraiser called the Gala for Peace and Understanding, taking place in early July, the highlight of an international conference of think-ers and talkers—Muslims, Christians, Jews—in every un-happy sociopolitical combination the organizers could con-ceive. The difficulties involved kept her distracted, he'd told himself.

What he hoped was that when the gala was behind her, they could sort themselves out, and he could face up to what Julia meant to him—to them. He'd been gradually getting used to the overwhelming possibility that he might leave Marjorie. Marjorie, who was as essential to him as his pulse.

Leaving her wasn't an idea he could entertain for more than a minute or so, but he'd been working on it, waiting until he was sure. In his career, he'd negotiated his way out of a lot of tight situations, but this wasn't going to be one of them. He was in the wrong. He had done wrong. He'd have to step up to the responsibility. The conversation would be devastating for them both. Even so, with his growing certainty about Julia, it had loomed nearer and nearer. Now, he realized, he'd never have to have that conversation. The flash of relief was brief, but it squeezed his heart like another betrayal.

He glanced at his watch, not seeing the time. "I'm going to bed. I have an early morning."

What he needed was to think. Could he also be a target for some reason? It didn't make sense that he would be, but killing Julia didn't make sense either. What about Marjorie and Hawk, were they safe? Would the old woman mention she'd seen him near Julia's building? Might he be a suspect? How would he explain his visit? All his secrets would come out. His feelings for Julia might end his marriage, even though she was gone. Until the police knew about Julia, he had a little time, maybe. And maybe he'd think of something.

Behind the closed door of the master bathroom, he brushed his teeth with his back to the mirror, unable to bear the sight of his coward's face. With no combination of analysis and imagination could he explain what events, mistakes, connections, and bad timing had brought Julia into contact with her killer. The rushing water from sink taps on full barely masked his crying.

Chapter 3

In Landis + Porter's Flatiron District office the next morning, thirty young architecture associates sat at long tables in a large, daylit loft, glued to their computer monitors, CAD programs humming. On their screens, lines and grids subtly pulsed, skeletons of the buildings they might one day be. Landis observed his staff from his cantilevered mezzanine office, its front glass wall overlooking their bullpen. A few staff huddled around a workstation, another chatted with Deshondra, the firm's receptionist.

It looked like a normal Friday. So normal it gave Archer Landis physical pain. Only he knew the significance of the two empty workstations. Julia and Hawk. Gone.

His young associates typically wore colors akin to the building facades they designed—black and gray and beige. Onyx, steel, stone. Julia had been a brilliantly painted bird in their midst. She wore juicy watermelon, lime, and saffron linen dresses, garnished with African beads and wide, ever-present bracelets. A giant paprika-colored clip had only moderate success in corralling her long black hair. Her exotic foreign education shimmered around her. As Landis stared at her empty place, the images of the young men and women below flowed into each other, their individuality blurred. He walked away from the wall of glass.

They have no idea what's coming. Or did one of them

know? He shook his head sharply. *That's unthinkable.*

All morning, the missing employees' absence went un-explained. To various staff members, he professed mild concern. Was Julia sick? He asked Deshondra to call. No answer. Of course. No one asked about Hawk.

⊱⊰

By lunchtime, the suspense coiled around his heart like barbed wire was the only thing holding it together. He couldn't believe Julia's body and its bloody, indecipherable Rorschach still lay undiscovered—*abandoned by him*—in her apartment, four city blocks and all eternity between them. He still hadn't called the police. He hadn't started them looking for her murderer. His rage and disappointment with himself felt bottomless. The consequences of his failure had settled in, he was stuck in it, and he couldn't think past it.

Deshondra brought him a bag from the deli around the corner. He ate a bite of the corned beef sandwich and threw the rest in the trash. As he pretended to busy himself in his office in full view of everyone working below, his gaze was drawn again and again to Julia's empty workstation, to Hawk's vacant place on the periphery.

It was time for the early afternoon staff meeting. Today, his words came fast to hide the unaccustomed cracks in his self-assurance. He told them about Hawk's new job at BLK, news greeted with surprise.

Most of the meeting involved discussion of a major project they were bidding on—against stiff U.S. and foreign competition—to build a supertall skyscraper in Dubai. Winning it would put them on track for a banner year, in both prestige and fees. Not quite as tall as Burj Khalifa, which had opened the previous year and was the world's tallest, this new building would have a larger footprint and afford as much hotel, residential, office, and shopping space as the taller structure and have a similar twenty-five-acre park setting. The project had sat on hold during the worldwide economic slowdown, but now the Al Maktoum family was anxious to move forward.

Burj Khalifa had cost some $1.5 billion to build, and the investment group funding the new building expected to spend at least as much. Ty Geller, the project point person, expressed several safety concerns: fire suppression and vulnerability of the HVAC system to a terrorist attack that could spread a chemical or biological agent throughout the building. To encourage the Emiratis to support the expense of disaster prevention measures, he was pushing for permission to name the tower Burj Maktoum. The family would not want its name associated with a calamity. That's what Landis's staff called it too—Burj Maktoum, or Maktoum, so much easier than saying "that outrageously tall thing in Dubai that could make or break us."

Then Charleston Lee, in his careful Southern drawl, described initial concepts for the Brussels train station in his portfolio.

"Where's Julia? What does she say?" Landis asked, knowing she'd loathe these uninspired suggestions and disliking them all the more for it. Pretending Julia was alive and could still contribute to their work offered surprising relief. If only he could create some alternative universe where that could happen.

Get it together.

Charleston shifted in his chair. Landis guessed he and Julia disagreed about the approach and, without her presence, he'd neglected to convey her opinions.

"Has anyone heard from her?" Landis's disappointment that no one had was unfeigned. "Ty"—he addressed the man he'd picked to do the dirty work, as hard-edged and steely as the buildings he designed—"call her apartment

again. Maybe she's sick. If you don't reach her..." Landis
sought a suggestion in the blank white sky outside the conference room windows.

"I'll run over to her apartment and check."

Ty was a bright boy. Ambitious.

"Good idea. Yes, do that." Landis gave his attention to
the station plans. Under the table he pressed his thumbnail
into the palm of his hand so hard he broke the skin. The
physical pain helped him refocus. "This needs work," he
said, managing to sound confident, in control. "First, we
couldn't build it on budget, and second, it needs some
juice."

Charleston's face pinked. "Yes, sir."

Landis gave him a way forward. "Go back through the
community and user discussions we've sponsored. See
what we may have missed. We've designed train stations
all over the world. Study them, what made them unique in
their settings." He gestured toward a tower of shallow-
drawered file cabinets that held renderings of many recent
projects. His strength was fading. "Articulate a vision.
Bring it back when you've rethought it. I know you can."

"Yes, sir. We're on it." Charleston said, his drawl thick-
ening.

The associates gathered their materials from the conference room table. "Ty, keep me posted?" A precisely titrated
dose of boss-employee concern.

Back upstairs in his office Landis sat at the round oak
table and faced the office's rear wall. Its brick was the color
of a wound, and it was crowded with photographs and
drawings of Landis + Porter's major buildings. Polished
wood outcroppings among the bricks created shelves for
the firm's many awards. Landis regarded the older structures as monuments to his long friendship and collabora-
tion with the late Terry Porter. The firm's most recent
buildings lacked Terry's touch, and, he thought, were

poorer for it. On a normal day, studying these photos provided intense satisfaction. Today, they were all but invisible.

A few minutes before three, Deshondra forwarded a call from Geller.

"Arch? I'm at the police station." Ty's voice shook.

"What's the matter?" Landis's insides liquefied.

"I had the building super open up Julia's apartment. We found her, all right—"

Landis gave Geller a moment to compose himself. "Yes?" His own voice broke, but Geller didn't seem to hear.

"She's dead, Arch. For a day? Or more? They don't know yet…It's hot…"

Geller confirmed what Landis knew to be true, but still his words encountered a resistant mind. *It can't be.*

"My god! Was she sick? Why didn't she go to the hospital?" Landis hated himself for dragging the story out of the stricken young man.

"Worse. She was shot. Murdered."

Silence. Then, "Tell me you're kidding. Please. One of my people? Are you sure?"

"Oh, I'm sure. We called the police, and they brought me to the 10th Precinct station. I'm there now. I had to answer a lot of questions. I think they suspected me at first. But when the medical examiner said she probably died sometime yesterday, early evening—and I had an alibi— an alibi, can you fucking believe it? I went to Poughkeepsie to have dinner with my aunt yesterday. Remember I left early to catch the 4:30?—and didn't get home until late. I had the ticket stubs in my wallet. They called my aunt too…When I think how, most nights, I'm in my apartment alone or grabbing a beer somewhere, it was so lucky I could—oh, Arch, you should've seen her! No, no, you shouldn't. No one should." He sounded like he might cry, might be crying. Geller, of all people.

"I'm so, so sorry. It sounds…awf…unimaginable."

Unfortunately, he could imagine it, exactly. He clutched his head in one hand, phone pressed to his ear, seeing what Geller had seen, afraid he might be sick.

Geller's tone was flat, exhausted. "The crime scene people are still at the apartment, I guess. I haven't seen them come back, and two detectives are on the way to our office." He paused. "I need to go home."

"Go. This was rough duty. I'm so sorry—sorry about Julia and sorry you had to go through that. Horrible." His voice was rough with emotion. "I'll call this evening, see how you're doing."

Two men in wrinkled summer suits talking to the receptionist glanced up to his glass perch. "The police just walked in. Go home, Ty." He disconnected.

Deshondra buzzed, and he told her to send the detectives up.

"Ty Geller called me," Landis greeted them. He hoped the shock of the call would explain his trembling. "It's unbelievable." So far, he hadn't lied.

The three men sat at Landis's round table. The older detective, Edward Fowler, was from the Manhattan South homicide squad, detailed to work with Detective Lou Gennaro from the 10th Precinct. Clearly, Fowler was in charge. He wore his gray hair military short—for simplicity more than style, Landis guessed—and ran his hand over his stubbled scalp at least three times before he began speaking. The youthful Gennaro pulled out a notebook and waited right leg jiggling.

"Geller was helpful," Fowler said. "He identified the deceased as one of your employees, Julia Fernández."

The moment he'd dreaded, here now. People who didn't know Julia would be talking about her, speculating, digging into her life. Fowler asked predictable questions about

her job at Landis + Porter, her co-workers, her family—
about which Landis knew next to nothing, he realized—
and received replies that were thoughtful and truthful, as
far as they went.

"Social life?" Fowler asked.

"Other than with these guys?" Landis swept his arm to
indicate the busy associates below. "They go out together
after work fairly often. Her apartment's close by, convenient. They've all been there for birthdays and pizza,
TGIFs…Me too, sometimes. Other than that, I wouldn't
know. I don't know. Who do you think—"

"We don't think anything yet. Not much in the way of
clues."

Gennaro gave his colleague a quick look.

"No weapon on the premises, so we can rule out suicide."

"Suicide!" Landis went white.

"Neighbors were out. Quiet building. Nice apartment."

Landis cleared his throat and said, "She has a valuable
painting over the mantel. A Velázquez. Too valuable to
abandon."

"Thanks. We'll secure it." Gennaro jotted a note.

A memory crowded out the detectives' presence. The
remarkable painting, dimly lit, over Julia's fireplace. "Is
that—?" He'd squinted at the stiffly dressed seventeenth-
century family, the women's wide brocade skirts.

"A Velázquez? Oh, yes," she said. "The *maestro* painted
it for my father's ancestor, twelve generations ago. The
man on the left, with the curling mustache? That's my
many-greats grandfather. I'm the last, so the painting is
mine now."

"There's a resemblance—"

"Genes like conquistadors." Her laugh came from deep
inside, causing him to look from the figures in the painting
to their living, breathing descendant. Julia had shortened

her richly genealogical name for American consumption, stripping away the many *de*'s and *y*'s linking her to them, yet they remained.

Fowler was talking. "Two places set at the table and carryout in the refrigerator. She was expecting someone for dinner."

Landis came back to the present. *Not "someone." Me.* Afraid he might reveal too much, he said nothing.

The one unexpected question came when Fowler asked about Terry Porter. The firm continued to bear the Porter name for the sake of its history, Landis said, not mentioning his deep sense of loyalty. And because the mystery surrounding Terry's freak auto accident remained unsolved. The Essex County Sheriff's department gave up long ago, and he'd stopped bugging them about it. Still, it haunted Landis and, as far as he was concerned, the firm. Three years had elapsed, yet Landis missed Terry every day—business partner, tennis coach, drinking buddy, ace poker player. Best friend.

Chapter 4

As soon as the police left Friday afternoon, Landis gathered his staff. He told them about Julia, asked for their cooperation with the police investigation, and sent them home amid a great many tears and questions. Nothing useful could have been accomplished at the office after a shock like that.

The detectives, however, must have worked over the weekend, but from what Landis could glean Monday morning, they had no solid leads. Fowler and Gennaro were at the office again, Fowler with something on his tie that looked like powdered sugar and running his hand over his scalp, Gennaro taking sparse notes. They were telling him what he already knew: Julia's life was circumscribed by her work, her friends from work, and her apartment. They'd found lots of fingerprints, but no matches in any criminal databases.

"Recognize this?" Fowler tossed a pair of photographs onto Landis's table. He needed a minute to figure out what the faintly blue branching lines were. Wrists. Someone's wrists. Someone whose wrists bore long vertical scars.

"Who? Not Julia," Landis said.

"Yes, Julia. A serious attempt, the medical examiner says."

"So, why would she try to kill herself?" Gennaro asked.

"It can't be. She's the most grounded person I know."

Knew.

"You never saw these scars?" Gennaro's pen quivered above the notebook, eager to make a dash for the truth.

"Never. Except—" Landis pictured her so clearly. He rubbed his four-day beard "—her bracelets. She always wore so many bracelets. I suppose I never saw her wrists."

His gaze traveled to the workroom below. Several of the associates glanced away. They were keeping an eye on him and his interactions with the police. Having an office overlooking his staff's space gave their workplace an intimacy, but it required him to exert iron control over his emotions. He always had an audience. For that reason, Julia rarely visited him there, and, for that reason, he couldn't reveal how shaken he was to see those scars.

"Remind us," Fowler asked, "how long did she work here?"

"Six months." Landis could hardly believe the time had been so short, given how she'd filled his life. "I interviewed her in late October. I liked her portfolio. We had an opening a few weeks later, and I hired her. She came on board in early December. My CFO can give you the exact date."

Fowler gathered the photos. "That's not all. The Velázquez you had us pick up? A phony."

"No," he said, his voice faint. He had hoped to arrange things—he had no idea how—so that prim Spanish family could hang on one of his apartment's blank walls. His piece of the family that produced Julia.

"When we found that out, we looked closer. The long and the short of it, Mr. Landis, she wasn't who she said she was."

Genuine surprise washed over Landis's face.

"Her story doesn't check out," Fowler continued. "You followed up on her references? Tell me."

"Of course." *Where is this going?* "She studied abroad—American University of Beirut. Very well-respected school—chartered by the State of New York back in the 1860s, by the way. We have an increasing number of clients in the Middle East, and we're competing for a huge contract there. So, I thought—" Landis reined in his response. "She had a mentor here—a close friend of mine from Yale, Oskar Chuikov. He died of a heart attack last August, a month or two before she appeared, so I couldn't...He'd met her over there during a guest lectureship, saw her work, met her professors. He wrote a recommendation letter, which he wouldn't have done unless she was extremely competent, which she was." He flushed. These questions struck at his firm's integrity.

"She *said* he was her mentor. Maybe she knew you were friends."

"No secret there. Though he knew everybody. The term 'starchitect' was first used about Oskar and m—about him."

"And he was six feet under." Gennaro clicked his pen. "Convenient."

"Well, of course our human resources people checked her other credentials. She had her degrees—architecture, master's in urban planning—and she needed to add a couple years' experience before taking the different components of the A-R-E."

"The what?" Gennaro asked.

"The Architect Registration Exam. Getting an architect's license involves a long process of education, experience—"

"I need to see that letter." Fowler cut him off.

"Human resources has it. I'll have it sent to you." Landis looked away. This conversation was deeply, unexpectedly troubling. For Julia his lover to lie to him about the painting and possibly her family background was bad. Awkward and disappointing to him. But if Julia his employee had lied about her credentials, that was unforgivable, and affected them all.

"Maybe her degree was phony too," Gennaro said.

Stop. Just stop. "I don't believe that for one second."

Fowler intervened. "Mr. Landis, something's not right, and we're trying to determine what that is."

Landis lifted both hands. "She was a talented designer with a degree from a respected university, every bit as skilled as any young architect we have here, if not more so."

"And she was hot." Gennaro again.

"I'm not such a fool as that." Landis's reddening face belied the words. "She was a brilliant designer, and she knew what she was doing. A hard worker, a solid team member. Why would she need phony credentials?"

"What kind of buildings do you design?" Fowler asked.

"Everything. Office buildings, sports facilities, apartment complexes, private homes. Right now, we're working on athletes' housing for the Brazil Olympics, train stations in Brussels and Krakow, a communications tower in Beijing, a 1,000-room hotel-resort in the Caribbean. Other projects. Manhattan is our headquarters, but we have much larger offices in White Plains, Chicago, Miami, Los Angeles. A small outpost in Dubai."

"How old is this firm?"

"Nearly seventy-five years. Terry Porter's father launched it despite the looming war. Inauspicious timing, but it worked out." He gestured vaguely to the brick wall's display. "After, there was much new building."

Fowler strolled along the wall, hands in his pockets, taking in the photographs. A puzzled expression corrugated his forehead. "You had a bunch of awards here before?" Group photographs of staff now occupied those shelves.

"Too much bric-a-brac," Landis said. He gave a dismissive wave. He'd put them in his closet. Prestige, accomplishment. They'd mocked him.

"What's this?" Fowler asked.

Seemingly out of place in the middle of the display was a colored-pencil drawing of the floor plan and elevation of a modest house. Visitors inevitably asked about it. Landis as a rule feigned reluctance to tell, though he'd eventually describe how none of the late 1950s housing developments had the right scale, the right aesthetic, the right sense of place to suit his parents. So, eight-year-old Archer Landis drew what he thought was the perfect house, they had it built, and they lived in it the rest of their lives. He told the story with self-deprecating humor, hinting his parents were perhaps too indulgent of their only child. He never uttered the words "boy genius" and didn't need to. In response to Fowler, though, all he could mutter was, "Silly memorabilia."

"So, the company files," Fowler said. "If I wanted to know how, say, a building from the 1970s or 1990s was constructed, you have the plans?"

"Of course. It would help if you also had the engineering drawings. We usually have those as well. Between the two, you'd have a good idea of how the thing was put together." Landis shifted in his chair. "Originally, anyway."

"Those plans are all in those skinny-drawer cabinets?" Fowler gestured to the workroom below.

"Only the current ones, actually. We rent climate-controlled space in Queens. Hanging files, flat files, tube storage, it's all there. These days, a lot of archival materials are electronic. On hard disks. I don't get—"

The detective held up a hand. "She work at night, this Julia? Here alone?"

"All our architects work late many nights. Our kind of detailed creative work doesn't stop when the clock says five."

"Do you have a record of when people come and go?"

Landis considered the question. "We use entry-access

card keys. I think there's a record. Deshondra at the front desk will know how to get it."

"Do you have a list of the buildings the company has worked on?"

"My god, that would be a huge job!" Landis massaged his scalp, lifting his long silver hair. "Wait, we did a report for our fiftieth that cataloged them to that point. Deshondra can give you a copy. Since then we've gone electronic, and she should be able to put together the more recent work fairly easily."

"Did Julia Fernández make a lot of after-hours phone calls? Send Fed Exes or packages on the company account?"

"As far as I know, only normal business stuff. I can't imagine what else." He planned to look into that question himself.

Someone had pointed a gun at Julia and pulled the trigger. From Fowler's questions about her background and her work at Landis + Porter, he sensed the barrel of a much different kind of gun swinging around to point at him.

"We'll need to check."

"Deshondra and the CFO have the records."

The detectives were leaving, and Fowler paused in Landis's doorway. "Oh, and your associate wasn't Spanish. Her real name was Alia Said, and she was born in Dearborn, Michigan. Raised in the Arab American community there. *Her* fingerprints—for reasons I cannot disclose to you—the FBI had."

They sat on this during our whole meeting? Un-fucking-believable. "She wasn't—? I don't—? *What*—?"

"Not Spanish. Alia Said. Michigan," Gennaro summarized.

No way. "You found this out, how? Fingerprints?" Landis couldn't keep the skepticism out of his voice.

"Even easier. A name change form was attached to her

registration paperwork with the state education department. She was Alia Said when she first wrote them last
summer. She became Julia in September."

Then the letter from his old friend Oskar must be a fake,
written about a woman who didn't yet exist. And the police
knew it.

"The form included her parents' address," Fowler
added. "Her body is being shipped to Dearborn in a day or
two."

Landis would rather not have known that, but guessed
Fowler said it to observe his reaction. He muttered,
"Wow," and let it go. "Tell Deshondra what you need." The
circular stairs clanged as they descended. "Wow."

He took their NYPD business cards and, out of habit,
tapped their numbers into his phone. *Not that I'll need these
again.*

On a blank piece of paper, he made a few notes. Pulling
together his thoughts, most of which were questions. Oskar's supposed letter troubled him, especially since a long-
ago letter from that same man helped launch his own career. Writing persuasively about the young architect's potential, he guaranteed Landis would receive a prestigious
fellowship. The competition was fierce. Phil Prinz was in
the running, as were several students he knew only slightly,
including Ivan Karsch.

Funny, how things turn out.

His notes memorialized the stunning depth of Julia's deception, how she'd evidently planned all along to mislead
him, the reasons the FBI might have her fingerprints, the
incomprehensible fact of her body leaving New York air
space and reentering another life, her real life. His neat
printing grew shaky.

The dead woman—he should try to stop thinking of her
as "Julia"—had wormed her way into his confidence. Her
degrees weren't phony, though. He'd called her advisor at

the University. He remembered the conversation. They'd certainly responded to the name Julia Fernández. Could the police be wrong about that, or had she covered all the angles? Persuaded her professors to go along with her scheme—was it a scheme? Or something harmless?

What did it matter, though? She obviously had design training and knew the CAD software. She also sketched a lot by hand, a habit that endeared her to him, a shared talent.

Eventually she would have been found out. Or would she? Why would she? He hadn't probed for cracks in her story; he'd seen what he wanted to see. Had he been blinded by the flash of her black eyes, the fall of lustrous hair down her back when he unclenched the red hairclip? He surreptitiously rubbed his eyes to wipe away that image.

Dearborn. What did he know about it? Company town—L + P had done work for Ford Motor Company. The Rouge—a touchstone of industrial architecture. He remembered his surprise to see the Arabic-language billboards along Michigan Avenue, the Lebanese restaurant where he and the Ford men ate lunch.

But who killed her and why? She wasn't crumpled inside her doorway, so she must have let the killer in, had known him—or her—or them. His gaze shifted to the bull pen of associates. Was it one of them? Ty? Charleston? Any of them? They were competitive—"to a fault," he once said to Marjorie. Did one of them discover the fakery? Did the lies themselves trip her up, leave her vulnerable?

Or had Marjorie shot Julia? *Not a chance.* Marjorie wasn't the type. She'd never handled a gun in her life. Or had she? He squinted at her picture on his desk. If he could have been so completely wrong about Julia, could he have been wrong about Marjorie on that one vital point?

Or had Hawk seen something? Had that caused his irrational hostility? His outbursts? Was it why he fled the firm so precipitously?

Truly, he was more comfortable believing the killer was part of some life unknown to him. Except it would mean that life was more important, more consequential, than the one she shared with him.

He shredded the page of scribbled questions. They had mired him deeper in confusion without yielding up a single useful idea.

Chapter 5

The police were returning to the Landis + Porter office early Monday afternoon to interview and fingerprint the staff. On their first visit, last Friday, he'd been so unsure of what he might say he was reluctant to say anything. Maybe his newfound numbness would make his interactions with the detectives easier. Easier, that is, until they discovered Julia's apartment was full of his fingerprints, in all kinds of hard-to-explain places.

Before they arrived, Landis gathered the associates, who teased him good-naturedly about his prickly silver-and-black stubble. He tried to sound jovial. "You keep me so damn busy I don't have time to shave." As long as shaving meant looking at himself in the mirror, he wasn't sure when he'd be able to shave again.

They laughed, as they were meant to, and Landis began the meeting, turning serious. He told them about Julia's real identity. They were as puzzled as he was. They'd liked her, respected her as a colleague. Omitting mention of Oskar's letter, he reassured them regarding her professional integrity. Her credentials had been real.

He said he hoped they'd agree to be fingerprinted, so the police could focus on any prints in the apartment they couldn't identify. He watched for hints of unwillingness. But no, everyone appeared eager to cooperate.

Landis was talking to Deshondra when Detective

Fowler and his team arrived. He invited Fowler up to his office to have his own prints registered first, in full view of the associates below.

As the technician worked, Detective Fowler observed Landis's slightly trembling hands, and said, "Don't be nervous."

"I'm not," he lied.

"We need to find out who was close to her. Any reason your prints would be in the apartment?"

"Every reason," Landis said. "Julia gave me a tour. She had interesting art. I probably handled—touched—a lot of her things."

"Bed?" Fowler asked, his tone flat.

"Perhaps."

"I see."

"Most of us have been to her apartment." Landis gestured to the associates lining up in front of three technicians below. "She had parties—a Friday tradition. All our prints will be there."

"Uh-huh."

Landis knew to stop talking.

"There's something you're not telling me," Fowler said, studying him. "If you *can* help, I hope you will. Otherwise, we don't have much to go on."

"I've got nothing." *The whole truth this time.*

෪෧෪

The police lab must have worked hard overnight because a call from Fowler interrupted the Tuesday staff briefing and Ty Geller's update on the Burj Maktoum. "Your prints were everywhere, Mr. Landis. Kitchen. Bathroom. Bedroom. Bed." Fowler's tone would freeze gin.

"As I said, I'd been to several parties there. I appreciated Julia's taste—her artistic choices. I helped out in the kitchen. These young people…" He let the comment fade into nothingness. His insides felt dry as paper.

"They were in places a casual visitor wouldn't have touched. Are you sure you don't need to tell me more?"

"Not without my lawyer."

"Bring him then. 10th Precinct. After three o'clock."

∽∾∽∾

Landis arranged to meet Colm O'Hanlon for lunch at a quiet bistro near Houston Street. While he waited for the lawyer, he studied the black-and-white photographs covering the walls—minor celebrities mugging with the owner, her cotton candy hair in a 1960s bouffant, dark eyeliner and lipstick like a child's drawing of a face. The pictures might give the impression of simpler times, he thought, but that was wrong. Those grinning people would have had their own secrets and shames.

By the time O'Hanlon arrived, most of the lunch tables had emptied. The lawyer dropped his briefcase on a chair and threw his dripping raincoat over its back. When he removed his hat, wiry red hair stood up, defiant as a stubborn witness. He was a scrapper. Landis enjoyed watching him take on a room of three-piece suits; their impeccable legal positions versus O'Hanlon's street smarts. They always underestimated him, first time out.

O'Hanlon gestured toward Landis's chin. "So, what's this then?" Although O'Hanlon's great-grandparents immigrated to the United States more than a century before, it amused him to salt his speech with his in-your-face patrimony.

"Time for a change." Landis's beard was coming in darker than his hair, and it gave him an unexpectedly youthful look.

The lawyer took in the rest of Landis's appearance, his

slumped posture and bloodshot eyes betraying his recent lack of sleep. "Looks like you had a bold night."

"How are the wife and kids, Colm?"

"Jeannie's grand. The girls are grand. Marjorie and Hawk?"

"Marjorie can't think about anything except her gala, and Hawk packed up his massive talents and strutted off to BLK."

"Ouch."

"I can't say I'm sorry. It was awkward having him in the office, though BLK is about the last place I wish he'd gone. That's a tough environment, and he's not up to it. The only thing worse would have been if he'd joined the United Brotherhood of Carpenters or the IBEW."

"You sparring with the unions again?"

"They're unbelievable. They'll never forgive me for winning that last fight."

"Their case was bollix, and they knew it."

"That didn't make them like the result any better."

"Course not. And the firm?" O'Hanlon represented Landis + Porter too, guiding it through its ups and downs. Mostly ups, but the downs had been painful, with Terry Porter's accident the worst, never adequately explained. By contrast, Landis's high-profile quarrel with BLK over the master plan for developing Governors Island had been a brief, if intense, legal unpleasantness. Landis put it behind him as part of the cost of doing business, but he hadn't forgotten O'Hanlon's deft salvaging of the situation.

"Couple of hefty proposals out. The Burj Maktoum project is alive again, and it looks like a firm will be picked this summer. It's a tough fight, and some of my competitors are promising more than they can deliver. This fiasco with Julia Fernández may affect whether we get any of these jobs."

Landis ordered steak and potatoes with a side of coleslaw, and O'Hanlon said, "The same. Thanks, boyo." He handed the waiter his menu without opening it.

Landis had given him the bare facts about Julia's murder over the phone. Now he told him what the police had learned about her background. He omitted the one key point—that he'd discovered the body and run out on her and, it occurred to him now for the first time, destroyed evidence in the process. No way he could justify any of it, least of all to himself. He twisted sideways in his chair to cross his long legs.

O'Hanlon jumped ahead. "They found your prints."

"Mine and everyone else's. We'd all been to the apartment. Julia's books and objects, all very touchable."

"The lady herself?"

Landis refolded his napkin and shook it out again, delaying. "They found my fingerprints in the bedroom. Now they want to talk about it."

"Is there something to talk about?"

"There is."

"Ah. We won't explain how they got there. Not yet. If they stumble onto some piece-of-shite corner boy who shot her, we may never have to. Is Marjorie onto this?"

They stopped talking as the waiter approached with their meals. O'Hanlon dug in, but Landis stared at the bloody juices, unable to pick up his knife. He had a vision of the early days of his marriage, of how open he and Marjorie used to be. They'd sit together, leaning into each other, sharing everything, he believed—their hopes for his career, her writing, their son. She'd turn his wedding ring around and around, kiss his wrists, and he'd take the barrettes out of her long hair and comb it with his fingers. "I'm sorry, what?"

"Marjorie? Suspicious?"

"Marjorie? No, I'm sure not. She's amazingly busy right now, stretched awfully thin. If something's eating her, I'd guess it has to do with Hawk. She of course says she likes having him at the apartment. To me, it's like living with Vesuvius. There's smoke, but is he letting off steam or about to blow?"

"When he worked in your office, those few months, d'you think he stumbled onto it? You and Julia?"

Landis pursed his bottom lip. "Nah. Too busy making excuses for himself, and Julia and I were very discreet. No emails, no texts. None of the associates know."

O'Hanlon sounded unconvinced. "If they did, might they blather to the cops?"

Landis ran his mind's eye over the faces of his staff. While they'd admired Julia and her lively style, all of them would feel betrayed by their boss. Picking favorites. "I'd say, we can count on it. *If* they knew."

"How'd they react when you brought Hawk in?"

"Wary. But he didn't get special treatment. Ironically, that's his big complaint."

"They saw it that way?"

"Who knows? People are so…what difference does it make? He's out." Landis picked up the steak knife and put it to work.

"Assessing your vulnerabilities, Arch."

"And?" He shoved a bite of steak into his mouth and chewed aggressively.

"You've got a right bag of 'em." O'Hanlon wiped his mouth and forked some slaw. "Here's what I advise. This afternoon, we're mum about the affair. They're already be-lieving there was one, but we'll not give them any free aid and comfort. I won't let you answer those questions. What we'll try to find out is, are you a suspect?"

"Really? That's a catastrophe."

O'Hanlon held up a hand. "It could get a lot worse." He gnawed on his last steak fry. "What was she up to? That could put you *and* the firm in the bull's-eye. Bleedin' awful public relations, whether she was after something specific or an off-her-nut chancer. Seducing you could have been part of her game."

"Now, wait—I'll look like a middle-aged fool."

"That's better than a lot of other cow piss they might rain down on you. Take my advice. We sit tight for now."

❦❦❦

O'Hanlon walked up to where Landis waited outside the 10th Precinct station, his face shadowed by a two-person black umbrella. They entered together and soon were escorted to a room with half-partitions where Fowler and Gennaro worked. There was barely space for Landis and O'Hanlon's chairs.

Landis made introductions, and Fowler looked at O'Hanlon skeptically. "We're not charging your client with anything, you know."

"Today," Gennaro added.

"My client has the impression he's a suspect in the death of Julia Fernández."

"Alia Said," Gennaro corrected.

"At this point, everyone's a suspect," Fowler said. "As I told him earlier, he needs to explain why we found his fingerprints all over her bed."

Landis started to repeat his explanation, but O'Hanlon silenced him, sticking to the script they'd agreed on. The back-and-forth over this issue soon convinced them that, contrary to what Fowler had said and at least for the moment, he was in fact their only suspect. O'Hanlon called this line of thinking preposterous.

"I only know what the evidence tells me," said Fowler.

"Aye, right," O'Hanlon said. "Then you lot need to keep looking."

Chapter 6

The meeting with Fowler and Gennaro persuaded Landis he'd had enough surprises. That evening and the next morning, he became better informed about Julia and what she'd done for L + P. Taking care not to raise staff suspicions, he poked around the office records. To his CFO's consternation, he asked general questions about who'd been sending Fed Exes and reviewed six months of telephone bills. He found nothing suspicious. If only he could get into Julia's apartment again. Perhaps it held some clue the police didn't know to look for.

The foray into office operations made him feel pretty secure until late morning, when representatives of the FBI-led Joint Terrorism Task Force appeared unannounced. He told himself he should have realized their visit was inevitable. Alia Said was an Arab and a Muslim, educated in Lebanon, living and working with a false identity, murdered in mysterious circumstances. She had to be "a person of interest."

The older, shorter man, who did most of the talking, was an FBI agent named Roger Friend. The other, from the NYPD, claimed to be a colleague of Fowler's. He slightly lifted an eyebrow as he mentioned Fowler, and Landis wondered how much they'd discussed. The detective's card indicated his last name was "Wojcik," which Landis heard as "Woe, Jack."

From the outset, they were more interested in Alia Said's politics than in Julia Fernández's death.

"NYPD is handling the murder investigation," Agent Friend said. "That's not what concerns us."

Did they know about the affair? Possibly. Probably. Would Fowler have shared that? Wasn't sharing what the JTTF was for? This crew would see potential security breaches coming out of the woodwork.

"We have people reviewing her phone records and emails," Friend continued.

They wouldn't find out about his relationship with Julia that way. Neither of them put anything compromising in the electronic record. Phone calls were easily explained. She was hardly the only associate he talked to outside working hours.

"That school she went to. In Beirut. What do you know about it?" Wojcik asked.

Landis explained the solid qualifications of the American University.

"Did she meet up with any jihadis or other radicals there?"

"How would I know that?" His bafflement was genuine. "We never talked politics of any kind. As far as I know, she had no radical friends or views or inclinations. She wanted to be an architect—someone who builds, not someone who destroys. I don't get this whole line of questions." A wave of anger surged inside him.

"Don't be naïve, Mr. Landis. Working for a firm like this"—Friend gestured toward the photos of prominent Landis + Porter buildings displayed on the brick wall—"who knows what a terrorist could learn?"

Landis fired back. "She was a young architect, gaining experience so she could take her licensure examinations. She was hardly working unsupervised. She wouldn't have had time or opportunity to study building plans and documents at random." He hated the defensive tone that had entered his voice. Especially since there was nothing to defend. Julia was blameless, he was sure of it.

"What about working late at night, weekends, by herself?"

"No. Never." He could say this with confidence because he had checked. It was frustrating. The JTTF's fixation on spying was every bit as absurd as Fowler's suspicion he was a murderer. "If she was such a useful spy, why did they kill her?"

"Who?"

"Exactly right. Who?" Landis said. *Get off my back.* But he knew that if the JTTF decided it was interested in Julia, in him, in Landis + Porter, they'd be like black mold spreading through the office, contaminating projects, unnerving the staff, alarming clients.

Friend sighed. "Once again, the NYPD—"

"I know, I know. But as far as I can tell, you are all spinning your wheels."

∽∾∽∾

After the unnerving session with the JTTF, Landis asked O'Hanlon to meet him for lunch again, this time at a twelve-table Italian place two blocks from his office. He arrived a few minutes early and studied the menu, but couldn't have recited three things on it, the words obliterated by the buzzing in his head.

"What's the problem?" O'Hanlon asked, pulling out a chair, skipping his usual banter.

"The JTTF. I don't like what they're implying. It's insulting. It'll be bad for business, my business." He described the visit and the kinds of questions they'd asked.

"The NYPD has a right list of questions of their own," O'Hanlon told him. "My sources say the homicide detectives are bloody stuck. That leaves you their prime suspect."

The architects' dinner at the Plaza was an alibi of sorts. But if the police found his cab drivers, if the hotel doorman remembered his leaving and coming back, he'd be worse off. Or if they found Toby and his mistress. "What possible motive would I have?"

"They heard you're up for the Pritzker, and they're wondering if you'd kill Julia to avoid a scandal."

Landis snorted. In his mind, architecture's most prestigious award and this situation were so far apart, they were on different planets. "That's nuts." He slapped the menu down.

"Agreed, but you're all they've got. Your Julia was a loner. No boyfriend. No friends they've found in New York. Family halfway across the country. University thousands of miles away. Neighbors report no visitors, except the L + P crowd. And you, of course. In your next life, Arch, come back with less distinctive hair."

"Thanks, counselor."

"Kept the meter off for that bit." O'Hanlon grinned.

After the waiter took their order, O'Hanlon's expression grew serious. "Unfortunately, other than Julia's, the only fingerprints in the bedroom, on the actual bed, are yours. They see access, opportunity. Now that they've bagged the bright idea about the Pritzker, they see motive. The JTTF likes you in this too." O'Hanlon tore off a piece of bread and dipped it in olive oil.

Landis recoiled, then hissed, "You've got to be fucking kidding. Where does that come from?"

"The FBI can't get past the Middle East connection. So, a love affair with a beautiful woman scheming to blow up buildings? Would knock you so far out of the Pritzker game you'd never get back in the effin ballpark. You'd do a lot to keep the lid on that. So they think."

"The Pritzker wouldn't do me much good if I were hiring—criminals." He couldn't say the word "terrorist." Not in connection with Julia. "The hundred thousand it pays wouldn't cover your bill."

"They know it's the prestige. Future commissions." O'Hanlon chewed. "The Pritzker's a men's club, isn't it?"

Landis studied the salad the waiter had put in front of him. "There was Zaha Hadid, and that Japanese woman shared it one year. But that's the profession. Architecture isn't kind to its female practitioners. What's your point? Colm, you know I don't have a problem working with women."

"No particular point. Though Alia Said was a bit of a feminist. Did you know that?"

"God, no."

"A feminist and political."

"Meaning?"

"Back in Michigan. In high school. Protesting, writing letters to the editor, organizing committees."

"On feminism?" Landis tried to wrap his mind around this.

"You Googled her, right? No? Good man. Our investigator uncovered it. The feminism. And she was against media bias. Specifically, anti-Palestinian coverage." O'Hanlon crunched his salad.

"She never mentioned any of that to me." Landis arrayed this last fact against Landis + Porter's roster of important buildings. "Any particular—?" He stopped himself before he said "targets."

"The usual. Fox, CNN. Bloody BBC," O'Hanlon said, his mouth full of lettuce.

A cherry tomato rolled off Landis's suspended fork. "BBC?"

"Always. Those fuckers."

"We designed the building where they have their

commercial arm. Which brings in over a billion pounds a year for them. Their offices—" He remembered the arguments vividly, shouting matches with the union rep that were legendary among the associates. Julia definitely would have heard about them. "There's floor-by-floor security in that building. Front desk manned 24/7, cameras everywhere…"

"Can the architect get in? Say to discuss some problem with the building operations director?"

"Sure, one of us was over there a lot in the beginning when there were issues they needed a consult on. Us or the engineers, or both. Less often now. The shakedown period is over."

"What about the architect's beautiful young assistant?"

Landis moved his salad aside, no longer hungry. Since the murder, he'd lost two pounds at least. "You're saying Julia could have used that access."

"I'm not saying anything. I'm thinking about potential scenarios. Things the cops might blaggard you with. There's a right barrel of such things, Arch."

Landis recalled Fowler's questions about his files. Could it be that Julia came to work for Landis + Porter to grab the specs of a specific building, or was she trolling for a target? Those drawings would be gold for terrorists. They described entrances, basements, subbasements, HVAC and electrical systems, hardwired security measures. How many times had he proudly said his firm had designed many of the world's most important buildings? Now that assertion could whip around and bite him. But what he'd said to Friend and Wojcik was true. Julia *was* supervised. Plus, he'd had his eye on her. But maybe he'd been looking for the wrong thing.

"What you're saying, Colm, threatens my entire business. If I go down, a lot of good people go with me." His staff in offices across the country and the world, hundreds of projects in some state of coming into being—they all depended on him.

"I'm well aware of that, Arch. As counselor to the firm, doing my duty here. But at some point, we have to talk succession plan."

Landis jerked to attention, his face hardening into a mask.

"Don't be offended." The lawyer raised a calming hand. "We should have done it when Terry died. Life has too many uncertainties to rest a big, important firm like L + P on the shoulders of one person. This current shite is a reminder."

Landis leaned across the table and looked directly into O'Hanlon's face. "I can't keep on like this. We've got to know who killed Julia and put all this speculation to rest."

"You're not considering looking into her murder yourself, now, are you, Arch?"

Landis sat back. "That's ridiculous. I have a business to run. People depending on me. Right now, there's some risks there, as you so clearly pointed out. Priorities, Colm."

If only I knew how and where, I'd start looking today.

ཀ྄ཇྍ

A power nap was in order, Landis thought, dragging himself home late Wednesday afternoon. That simple desire was frustrated by the discovery of the JTTF men settled in his living room, occupying his sofa, drinking his coffee out of his china cups, and talking to his wife and son. Agent Friend and Detective Wojcik, the very last people in the city he wanted to see.

Marjorie's pale face matched her colorless silk blouse, while Hawk perched on the arm of a sofa, gleaming with cooperation.

"There you are!" she said as Landis appeared. The tight

line of her jaw told him the investigators' visit irritated her, she held him responsible, and now she expected him to handle it. He sensed a quarrel on the horizon. No wonder Hawk was enjoying himself.

"Well, this is a surprise. What's going on?" Landis didn't pour coffee for himself. A rattling cup would betray his nerves, and everyone in the room had him under their own particular microscope.

"Your office said you were out for the afternoon. We thought you might be here, and we have a few more questions."

"Shoot." Landis winced.

"Did you know the dead woman was an Arab American?" Agent Friend—*a misnomer if there ever was one*—addressed this information to Marjorie and Hawk.

"Oh, really?" they both said. They didn't know. Landis hadn't shared. He wished he'd suggested they leave him alone with the JTTF investigators. Now their curiosity was up, and he'd get pushback if he asked them to go.

"She said she was Spanish. From Spain," Hawk said.

"She was a political activist from Michigan," said Wojcik.

In high school. Grateful for O'Hanlon's heads-up, Landis didn't react.

"Wow, Dad, you can sure pick 'em."

Landis hoped Marjorie missed Hawk's sly ambiguity. "We stay out of politics in my office," he said. "We have clients all over the world. We can't be calling balls and strikes on their governments or their opinions. Not unless they affect our own work."

"So, you think it was a political murder? Was Julia a terrorist?" Hawk voiced Landis's worst and secret fear.

Landis couldn't stop himself. "Just because she was an Arab American doesn't mean she had anything to do with terrorists." His glance darted to Marjorie, who was staring at him. *Peace and understanding,* he tried sending telepathically.

Agent Friend consulted his notes. "What was she working on?"

"Mostly a train station in Brussels. A few other projects, smaller ones."

"Weren't you planning to have her work on the Burj Maktoum, that megaproject in Dubai?" Hawk asked, grabbing Wojcik and Friend's attention. "Didn't she help with the embassy in Abu Dhabi?"

Landis glared at his son. The investigators might not detect the malicious undercurrent, but Hawk was up to something. He shook his head. "We don't have the Dubai project yet. It's a competition."

"Which embassy in Abu Dhabi?" Friend asked.

"Ours, of course." Hawk sat up straighter. Landis wouldn't have been surprised if he'd put his hand over his heart.

"When was that?"

Landis stepped in. "It was about complete when she joined the firm, and she had very little to do with it."

"She worked on the Coppersmith Building, didn't she? So she said," Hawk added.

"Nothing substantial. Only as the interior work was finishing. Office building on Sixth," he said for the investigators' benefit. He couldn't tell whether they attached any significance to this last revelation, whether they had any idea who the tenants of that building were—"Bloody BBC," as O'Hanlon so colorfully put it. He didn't believe Julia was a terrorist, and he wasn't going to point them down that road.

Hawk's steady undermining of his late colleague surprised Landis. Had he been that jealous of her? Or was he trying to discredit Landis + Porter, him? The investigators were probably wondering why so much information was coming from the son, not the father, while Hawk acted oblivious to any potential downsides of this conversation.

In the calmest, most authoritative voice Landis could muster, he said, "My firm uses a team approach on major projects. The interns and associates work on discrete aspects. That's how they learn." He gave Hawk a look, but his son gazed out the window, studying the nebulous reaches of Queens.

"NYPD gave us a list of Landis + Porter buildings." Friend didn't say what they planned to do with that list. Landis could envision checks on security systems, debriefings of their managements' private security services, threat assessments. A huge job. A significant investment they would try to assure led to prosecutable outcomes.

"Don't you screen your people?" Marjorie said, belatedly realizing the seriousness of the inquiry and assuming the worst. Already she'd judged him guilty of something.

Landis held his tongue. He didn't need to mount a defense, not yet, and not to her.

"Who's your contact in Brussels?" Friend asked. "Our legat there will talk to him."

And if you lose my client for me? "Your—?"

"Our legat. Our office."

"Short for legal attaché," Wojcik said.

"I'll have my associate call you with that information in the morning."

"We'll call you," Friend said, staying in charge. He looked inquiringly at Wojcik, who shook his head. They closed their notebooks and prepared to leave. "No more questions for now." Friend's gaze lingered on Hawk. "Thank you."

When they were gone, Landis lit into his son. "What are you up to?"

"What do you mean, Dad? I want to help them get to the bottom of all this, same as you. So we can put it behind us."

"Us?"

"Us as a family."

"Hawk's right, Archer," Marjorie broke in, right on cue. "Any help we can give, we obviously have to provide it. An investigation could drag on for months. It's terribly inconvenient having the police show up here at all hours."

"Five p.m. doesn't qualify as 'all hours,' and you've hardly been inconvenienced like the people in my office, one of whom was greatly inconvenienced by being shot dead."

"Exactly my point," Hawk said.

"What point is that?"

"We need to put this problem to bed."

Landis squinted at his son. He couldn't tell whether the constant innuendoes were real or his guilty imaginings. Marjorie was quick. If there was something there, she'd catch on. He sucked in the anger billowing out of him. For once, he wasn't soothed by the penthouse view of Queens stretching far and away into the golden haze of late afternoon. It reminded him how high up in the world he was and, consequently, how far he could fall.

And that fall looks more and more likely, with Hawk's help. Landis glanced over his shoulder at his son. *I can't stand to be in the room with him right now.*

But he couldn't escape the implications of the JTTF's questions. Maybe, maybe, there were vulnerabilities he hadn't recognized. He needed to deal with them before the FBI and the JTTF and the NYPD and Friend and Wojcik and whoever-the-hell-else was looking might find them-.

"Marjorie, I'm heading back to the office. These men wasted too much of my time today. You and Hawk have dinner without me."

"Arch, please—" But he was gone.

Chapter 7

Landis arrived at his office in time to exchange a few words with Henry, the building's afternoon security guard, who was closing the reception desk for the day.

"Watch your step there." Henry indicated thick power cords strung across the lobby floor.

"What's up?" Landis asked.

"Larry's fixing up the storage space behind the elevators, to make hisself an office over here. In a hurry—you know how he is—so he's got them bustin' ass six-to-midnight."

Landis grunted. The landlord's whims were hard to figure, but always put into immediate execution. Landis pushed the elevator button.

"They'll be in and out until late, unloading stuff, making a godawful racket. You probably won't hear them up where you are." Henry sighed as a man pushed a wheelbarrow full of broken wallboard across the lobby, leaving a dusty white trail. "People gonna step in that and leave shoe prints all over," he muttered.

A power saw whined. It was loud. Henry was right about that. As the elevator door closed, he hollered after Landis. "Front door's unlocked til they leave."

The high keen of the saw receded as he rode the elevator up to five, where Landis + Porter occupied the entire floor.

He was glad all the associates had gone. Small talk came hard these days. Late afternoon sun streamed through the office's large windows, and he didn't bother with the overheads. The screen savers of a few computers bounced lazily in front of empty chairs.

He appreciated the next generation's skill and speed on the computer, but for him, trained in a different era, architecture was a tactile discipline, a process that began with pencil in hand. Understanding a structure meant drawing it, its shapes and volumes, then creating a clay rendering or white-paper models. A few paper cuts, clay packed under his fingernails proved he was engaged in construction, creation. He and Julia had shared that passion for making a space take form under their fingertips. Now the 3-D printer did that job, and one of them hummed away in the back room, left to work overnight. It wasn't the same.

On a table in one of the conference rooms lay the Brussels train station plans, neatly stacked in the bright light of the west-facing windows. For the last few days Charleston and his team had camped out in here, reworking the design. Landis draped his jacket over a chair.

He fanned through the large sheets until he found the site plan. As designed, the train station would occupy two rectangular city blocks, a slight expansion of its current footprint that required demolishing several modest shops and cafés. Protests involving one of these structures—something about a gay rights historical site—were slowing the inevitable. The site would be clear with time to spare.

"Context," Landis emphasized to his staff. "Context makes a building work." A train station was a building that absolutely had to work.

Charleston's revised design created graceful visual transitions between an ugly web of overpasses, the area's few remaining nineteenth-century buildings, and the dominant modern and postmodern facades of nearby office buildings housing the European Union and the international banking community.

"Oh lord," Landis said under his breath. The EU buildings were so close. Much closer than he remembered. In fact, right across the street. Is this what the terrorists were after?

Fucking FBI, messing with my brain.

Yet it was true: a bomb or poison gas in that station during rush hour would decimate the EU staffs. A biological exposure could reach into the offices themselves, could be carried in on coats and bags, on hands and hair, not sparing the high-ranking officials who didn't use the train or the subway—the Metro. International leaders driven to work in shiny black automobiles would be as much at risk as the most junior secretary. From news coverage of the anthrax exposures after 9/11, he vaguely recalled it was difficult to turn anthrax into an aerosol. That was a decade ago. Technology moves on.

"Goddammit!" he muttered to the empty air. "Goddammit."

He picked up another sheet, queasy as the horrible potential washed over him. The drawing resembled the circulatory system of the human body, with the station its heart. It showed how the existing train and Metro lines connected and how visitors and thousands of daily commuters flowed through the station to access taxis and buses, to bike or walk to their jobs. They would penetrate every office building in the European District as efficiently as the human bloodstream reaches each cell of the body.

A sharp noise jolted him into the present. The plate glass window in front of him cracked. A bullet furrowed his left arm. Erupting blood spattered the careful drawings. Reflexes from his time in Vietnam revived, and he dove to the floor. As he hit the carpet, a second bullet buried itself in the wall behind where he'd stood seconds before.

"Holy Christ!"

Where's that coming from? More concerned about catching the gunman than the burning pain in his arm, he grabbed his phone and called Fowler. He clenched the phone between ear and shoulder so he could grip his injured arm.

Miraculously, the detective was still in his office and picked up. "Fowler."

"Archer Landis. I've been shot." Tight as he squeezed, his sleeve was already soaked.

"Where are you?"

"My office."

"On my way. Need an ambulance?"

"Haven't called one. Flesh wound." He spoke through clenched teeth. What his tone revealed was "hurts like hell."

"I'll get you one. Are you safe?"

"Who knows? The shots came from across the street."

"Anyone else there?"

"No, I'm alone," Landis said.

"Is the office secure?"

Landis hadn't thought of this. "Downstairs is wide open. Up here, the shooter has to get past the card reader."

"He might have a card. Can you shut it down?"

"I can cut the power," Landis said, though at that moment crossing the bright sunlit space between where he crouched and the electrical panel, in the coat closet by the front door, seemed impossible.

"Do it. We'll be there in ten." Fowler clicked off.

The shooter might have a card key? Then all he has to do is cross the street and ride the elevator up. "Front door's unlocked…" Henry had said. *He could be on his way right now.*

Leaving the protection of the table required an act of faith. A gunman with a good scope could see him easily.

One who had barely missed twice. *Stay or make a run?* A vision of being found cowering under the table got him moving.

Fiery pain traveled up his arm as he crawled out of the conference room. With a backward kick, he slammed the door behind him, partially blocking the view from across the street. He bent at the waist and ran an irregular path to the first row of associates tables. Shielded by them, he took a few seconds to catch his breath. In the jungle, he'd been a lot younger.

No shot came. He dodged past the rows of tables. Now twenty feet of open space lay before him. If the shooter was still across the street, he had to hustle. *Give him a target and you're a dead man.* He hustled.

Clutching his arm, he covered the distance in a crouch, flung open the closet door, and flipped the main power switch. The closet went dark. Returning to the reception area, he pushed the closet door closed. Farthest from the wall of windows, this part of the office was dim. Dim and safe.

The solid wood front door had long glass panels on either side. They weren't a problem. He'd foreseen that vulnerability long ago and designed decorative metal screens installed behind the glass. He stumbled over to peer through one of them. The elevator bell chimed. No time to hide. He flattened himself against the door.

Footsteps tapped on the marble floor of the elevator lobby. *Is it him?* The visitor hummed an eerie tune. A man's voice. Landis shivered. A card key swiped, swiped again. The humming stopped. A shadow appeared at the glass panel as the man peered inside. Landis barely dared breathe. Blood dripped on the carpet in sharp plops. To Landis's horror, dots of red marked the gray carpeting. They led from the closet straight to the front door. He couldn't squeeze his arm any tighter.

"I know you there," the man called in a high-pitched sing-song mere inches from Landis's ear. When he banged on the door, it shook against his spine. "OK," he yelled, "I shoot this fucker." *Can he? Does he mean the door lock? The card reader? The door is strong, but it can't stop a bullet.*

A street sound, coming closer. Sirens. Lots of them. The man's cell phone rang. "OK," he said, "I come." The sirens stopped, very close. Another yell, from across the fifth floor lobby: "We *will* meet again."

Footsteps diminished and the stairwell door clanged. Landis pressed against the office door until, through the roaring in his ears, Fowler called his name. He swung the door open.

"He was up here two minutes ago. Then he got a warning call and took off down the stairs." Landis struggled to say this much, as Fowler strode in, trailed by Gennaro.

Fowler spoke into his radio. "Watch that street, and send a man around to the alley. He has a lookout. Check the stairwells. If you don't find him, we'll have to search floor-by-floor." He noted the blood seeping between Landis's fingers. "You OK?"

"I—" Landis was suddenly light-headed.

Fowler steered him to a chair. "Medics will be here any minute. Tell me."

"I turned off the power, like you said. Then I went to the door to look out, and the elevator arrived. I was there"— Landis pointed to a bloody spot on the carpet in front of the door, the size of a silver dollar—"my back to the door. He tried an access card, all right. He peered in through the screen, but couldn't see me. Bad angle. Then I heard your sirens."

"Will your system tell us whose card that was?"

"Not with the power off."

"Shit," Gennaro said.

"Who did this? Why?" Landis was asking himself, more than them. He knew they didn't have answers, not then. Not yet.

Fowler said, "With all that's happened, I'd ramp up your security. Cameras." To Gennaro, he said, "Have them try to get prints on that stairwell door, the glass, elevator buttons, anything he might have touched. And check the building across the street."

"He was humming," Landis said.

Gennaro stopped scribbling in his notebook. "Huh?"

"Humming."

"Weird."

"Did he say anything?" Fowler asked.

Landis recounted the words. "He had an accent, and his voice was high-pitched, like he'd been watching too many cartoons."

"Any idea who he is?"

"None."

"If he has a card key, why the hell didn't he come up here to begin with?" Gennaro asked.

Landis considered. "He might run into other people in this office? It's easier to keep watch from over there? He's less likely to be spotted? How do I know? A few of those offices across the way are empty. He's a good shot. Judging."

Fowler motioned to the emergency medical team that appeared at the door. "Get him out of here." As they dealt with Landis, Fowler added, "You were alone and wounded. He could take a chance on using that card key."

What Fowler meant was, Landis couldn't identify him if he were dead.

❧❧❧

From the emergency room doorway, Marjorie's searching eyes flitted across the crowded waiting room, pausing a nanosecond on each person. Hawk trailed behind, looking unsure what facial expression to adopt for a parental shooting, but determined to be cool. There was Arch, at the end of a long row of stained and thinly padded chairs. She rushed to him and gave him a gentle embrace.

"What happened?" she cried. "Where are you hurt? How bad is it?"

As she rested her head on his uninjured side, he gave her the details, emphasizing that his injury wasn't serious. The possibility he could have been killed escaped neither of them, and Arch's reassurances were meant as much for himself as for her.

The call from his father had short-circuited Hawk's usual plans for dinner and bar-hopping. Now he yawned and paced, avoiding the few empty chairs among the derelicts, the bruised and bloodied young, the sour-smelling elderly. Time passed slowly.

Marjorie rubbed her husband's uninjured arm and rested her head on his shoulder. "That beard, or stubble, or whatever you call it makes you look like one more homeless person." She indicated the room at large.

"My brethren." He stared at the far wall, trying not to flinch. With every heartbeat, the wound pulsed with pain. At last they were called into a consultation room. He was given pain relievers and a fresh dressing. "We've examined the X ray. No damage to any bones," an emergency department doctor assured him before sending them on their way.

Back at home, Hawk spoke up. "With all due respect," his tone suggesting the amount due was rather small, "why would anyone try to kill *you*?"

Marjorie spoke up. "Hawkins, please. We've had a terrible scare. Please don't make things worse."

It was an intriguing question that made Landis briefly wonder whether the intended target might have been someone else—Charleston or one of the other associates who usually worked late in that same conference room. On those plans for the Brussels station. Smack in the middle of European Union headquarters. A prime terrorism target.

He thought not. Hesitatingly, he said, "We do need to consider that he—or they—may try again." Hawk snorted. "I know you think I'm a boring target," Landis said to his son, "but the man did say he'd be back."

"What do the police say?" Marjorie asked, bringing him a cup of tea. "Will they help?"

"They advised me to take precautions," he said. "Coming on top of…you know, what happened to Julia."

"Yes, there's that." Marjorie set the cup down, perhaps a little harder than necessary, and left the room.

Chapter 8

Detective Fowler arrived around noon Thursday, amid the commotion of glaziers replacing the conference room window and cleaners working on the bloodstained carpet. The associates were going about their work, but their darting glances revealed they were on edge. First Julia, now this.

"Glad to find you here." Fowler gestured to the architect's arm in a dark blue sling.

"A security consultant is coming in this afternoon to review our system," Landis said, acknowledging Fowler's recent advice. "Deshondra says we've handed out eighty-three card keys since the current system was put in, and we can't account for fourteen of them. One of them belonged to Julia." *Alia Said.*

Lax card key controls apparently were no surprise to Fowler, and he collapsed into one of the chairs at Landis's worktable and pulled a candy bar out of his pocket. "After you left, we searched the building, top to bottom. Didn't find your guy. Like you thought, he shot from an empty office across the street. Scuffmarks in the dust in front of one of the windows—windows that actually open. Shitty locks. The bullets we dug out of your wall will be useful if we find the gun."

"It was a rifle, right? How'd he carry it around in this neighborhood?"

"We've found them hidden in golf bags, mailing tubes, trombone cases, fabric rolls."

"Sounds like a scene from a bad movie."

Fowler snorted. "A bit of acting helps. If the gunman looks the part, nobody notices what he's carrying." He glanced down at the associates trying to work. "Gennaro and I have to ask your people more questions."

"Could one of them have been the target? Someone who usually works late?"

"I'll think about that." Fowler glanced at Landis's distinctive silver-white hair and pursed his lips, "but the view from that window is pretty clear, especially with the afternoon sun lighting up the place."

Landis sensed relations between him and Fowler had changed, a lessening of tension he couldn't explain. His guilty secret sat on his shoulder like a chattering monkey, so the change had to be in Fowler. The detective rested both forearms on the table and leaned into them.

"You're no longer a suspect in Alia Said's murder, by the way. I'm sorry it's taken the prosecutor nearly a week to make a final decision on that."

"But why? What's changed? What have you found out?"

Fowler scanned his face. "I'm only telling you because it's definite. Otherwise, I wouldn't. But half a bloody fingerprint on the toilet seat saved you. Such a trace amount of blood it took time to analyze—it was hers—and such a small partial we had to work hard to rule out other possibilities. As you may remember, he'd wiped the most likely sites for prints—light switch, door handle—"

"I remember." The monkey tightened its grip, and Landis coughed. "I thought you said she was shot from a distance. How'd he get blood on his hands?"

"Arranging the body."

Landis's stomach lurched. Even the monkey shut up.

"We knew from day one that finding the toilet seat up would be important," Fowler continued.

"You hadn't mentioned it."

"You're not totally in the clear. The JTTF is all over the terrorism angle, and they don't tell me much. I'm guessing they're coming up empty. But they have a lot of questions about her and about whoever that fingerprint belongs to." He glanced down into the staff bull pen. "Not any of their prints, either."

"That whole idea is off base." A frustrating mix of emotions stirred in Landis. While he couldn't believe Julia had been mixed up with terrorists, studying the Schuman Station plans brought home how vulnerable L + P's work was.

"You know a man named Yusuf Zardari?" Fowler pulled out a notebook.

"Sure. Why?"

"His name keeps coming up. The JTTF is watching him, and they've asked me questions about your phone records."

"Zardari is in charge of the big fundraising gala my wife's organizing. I'm sure she talks to him several times a day."

"What's this event?"

"It's called the Gala for Peace and Understanding—part of a huge international conference. One of my wife's charities." Did it sound like he was trying to implicate Marjorie in some way? His eyebrows pulled together.

"Can she get out of it?"

"Of course not. Why should she?"

"It's scuttlebutt. Zardari seems to be a bright red flag. We don't have him in our system, so that's all I know. But you haven't been calling him?"

"Never. I don't understand how they can think I'm any kind of a suspect after...last night?" Landis raised the sling.

"The guy missed, didn't he?"

Landis's eyebrows shot up.

"I'm only saying."

❧❧❧

This conversation required another call to Colm O'Hanlon.

"Stay calm, Arch. Christ's sake. People will be all over the investigators' asses to solve any kind of terrorism plot faster than—"

"*What* terrorism plot? *I'm* the victim here! They have no proof of terrorism, and they sure as hell can come stick their goddamn fingers through the goddamn holes in my goddamn office window. They're real! The other? Terrorism? It's just paranoia running amok!" His impulse to defend Julia flared.

O'Hanlon was posing another question, when Landis interrupted. "I have to put you off. A meeting in a few minutes." He glanced at his empty schedule for the afternoon. "I'll catch up with you later—at your office, six o'clock. That work?"

"Sure. See you then."

O'Hanlon's "six o'clock office" was McSweeney's Pub, around the corner from his law firm's offices on Fifty-Second Street. O'Hanlon would guess Landis might be worried his phone calls were monitored. It didn't take imagination to know by whom and why.

❧❧❧

In the long walk north, aside from glancing over his shoulder, he thought about how far Landis + Porter had come since the early days, and, checking behind him once again, wondered where it was headed. Terry Porter had been a great business partner, always ready to turn an impending disaster into something positive. Ever since Terry's death, whenever Landis encountered a difficult situation, he asked himself how Terry would have handled it. *WWTD?* After the shooting the night before and the innuendoes about Julia, his response this time was quick.

By the end of the afternoon, he and his CFO had worked out a way to put together a team on "antiterror design." His people already followed published guidances, but they treated them like fire safety or disability design standards. Meet the code, move on. From now on, heightened security would be a few associates' main work.

Their first challenge would be the Schuman Station project, studying past events—the 1980 bombing at the Bologna central railway station, the 7/7 London Underground bombings, Madrid in 2004, the sarin attack in Tokyo's subway—learning all they could. Then they would pick apart Charleston's plans looking for vulnerabilities, as O'Hanlon called them. They would learn to think like terrorists.

Chapter 9

O'Hanlon was in a rear booth at McSweeney's. With him was a man Landis hadn't met, who wore a black polo shirt, its short sleeves tight around impressive "I work out" biceps.

"How long d'you have to wear *that* flatterin' thing?" O'Hanlon greeted Landis, pointing to the ugly blue sling.

"Couple more days. Flesh wound." He stuck out his right hand to the stranger. "Archer Landis."

"Carlos Salvadore."

O'Hanlon indicated his colleague. "Carlos works the criminal side, and—What *is* your job description, man?"

"Investigations, security, heavy lifting."

Landis's eyebrows danced. Several of O'Hanlon's more entertaining workplace tales had hinted at the kinds of heavy lifting Carlos had performed and the creativity he put into it. When O'Hanlon suggested bringing him onto their team, Landis agreed without hesitation. Extreme situations, extreme measures.

O'Hanlon and Carlos each had a beer in front of them. As Landis slid the sport coat off his good arm, a green-clad server delivered an encouraging amount of single malt.

"Thanks." He lifted his glass to his friend.

"So, Arch, what's on your mind? Other than harboring terrorists and getting shot at for your trouble?"

"Jesus." Only O'Hanlon could have gotten away with

that. "How much time do you have? The one piece of good news: I'm off the list of suspects for Julia's murder." He choked on the thought he'd been on such a list in the first place.

"About bloody time they got one thing right."

Landis described the JTTF's visit to the apartment and the rest of his conversation with Fowler. "Unbelievably"— and he repeated the word with rising anger in his voice— "unbelievably, Fowler says the Task Force is still interested in me. Even after this." He raised his left arm awkwardly.

"D'you know why at all?"

He explained about Zardari.

"Simple enough then," O'Hanlon said. "He's Marjorie's boss."

"Why didn't they ask about him yesterday?" Landis asked. He couldn't keep the peevish note out of his voice.

"Maybe they did."

"Before I got home, you mean?" The possibility Marjorie had any kind of information exchange with the JTTF investigators needled him. "What'll they dream up next? If they're checking phone records, they could be monitoring our calls, following me."

"Are they?" Carlos asked.

"Am I getting paranoid, you mean? People are shooting at me, for Christ's sake!"

"I've been waiting for you to talk about that," O'Hanlon said. "I'm accustomed to your cool affect, Arch, but aren't you overdoing it a wee bit? Avoiding the obvious?"

"Lesson learned. I won't leave myself vulnerable like that again."

"How'd you get here? To McSweeney's?" Carlos asked.

"I walked. Takes a half-hour. On the street, I'm safe, right? Crowds?" He didn't mention the jolt of panic every

time a Times Square tourist bumped him or how he kept
checking the people behind him.

Carlos raised an eyebrow.

"Pretty safe," Landis amended. "Maybe the authorities
are right. Maybe the hit man *was* trying to miss. To scare
me. You'll say this is irrational, but I'm more worried
about Friend and Wojcik. At least we know they weren't
shadowing me late yesterday."

"Maybe," Carlos said.

"I mean, when I—" Landis raised his wounded arm
again. "If they'd been there, they would have stepped in...
helped...got the guy."

Carlos's silence was more unsettling than anything he
might have said.

Landis sat back and took a pull of the scotch. "Oh, no,
man." Angry as he was at the investigators and their accusations and assumptions, he couldn't go there. He couldn't
believe his government would stand by while someone
took a shot at him.

O'Hanlon changed the subject. "Suppose they *are* monitoring those calls between Marjorie and Zardari, what are
they hearing?"

"Plans for a whopping party—menu, guest list—stuff
like that."

"You sure?"

"Am I sure of Marjorie? Of course." Landis said this
automatically, though the idea sparked further thought. Her
strange distance, her change in behavior, too tired for sex.
She was a beautiful woman. Kind, smart, compassionate.
Had he taken her for granted? Too preoccupied with Julia
to notice the little things? His frown of concentration deep-
ened, and he rolled the bottom edge of his glass in small
circles on the tabletop.

"Let's tackle the nub of this bloody business,"
O'Hanlon said. "Could it be a random thing that Alia Said

came to work for you, or did she have Landis + Porter in her sights?"

"I've thought about that. Day and night this past week." His last words disappeared into the void where feelings go to drown. He was grateful O'Hanlon used that other name, her real name. Hearing anyone call her "Julia" reopened unhealed, guilt-inflected wounds. He pushed those thoughts into a corner of his mind and doused them with scotch. At last, he said, "I don't believe it was random."

"Because...?"

Carlos pulled out a notebook and pen.

"Because one of her credentials was a glowing letter from Oskar Chuikov, her supposed mentor and my close friend for thirty years."

"Died shortly before she showed up," O'Hanlon muttered to Carlos. "So...?"

"So, because of that, I didn't check so thoroughly. Oskar's signature on that letter was like seeing my own. I didn't need to know more."

"Anything else?"

"At our first interview, she was so open, so enthusiastic, so..." Landis reddened. "OK, call me an old fool, but I thought she might be interested in me. Then after I hired her, we got close, and I gave her good assignments. She was talented and practical-minded, a team player. We're busy. I had every legitimate reason to move her forward, like I do all my strongest people." Landis set his glass down hard enough that Carlos glanced up from his notes.

"Tell Carlos what she was working on."

"Train station in Brussels. It's replacing an existing station that will keep operating during construction, so it's a complicated project."

Carlos asked, "Did you get that job—"

"Commission." Thinking about the station and its prime position cranked up the worry machine all over again.

"—that commission before or after Said came to work for you?"

"There was a competition, and we were waiting for the winning firm to be announced. I knew it would entail a lot of coordination and quite a bit of travel, and I wasn't sure whom I could free up to provide support to the lead architect. Then when we got it, I hired her." What a mistake that had been! For Julia, for himself, for the firm.

"Any difficulties with the project?" Carlos's pen was poised.

O'Hanlon signaled their server for another round of drinks.

"Minor disagreement among the staff about how to maximize pedestrian flow." He might as well drop the bomb, the one wrecking his sleep. "Here's the thing. The station is in the heart of the city's European district. EU offices are all over, and the main headquarters building is right across the street."

Carlos stopped writing again.

"Holy shite! A bomb…that cow powder."

"Anthrax," Carlos said.

"Does the JTTF know this?" O'Hanlon asked, leaning across the table, his voice low.

"They have maps." Landis knew he sounded defensive and knew that wouldn't help. "I haven't mentioned it. Because I don't believe it. I'm hoping…" They waited for him. "I'm hoping…we figure it out before they go off the deep end. Slap my ass in jail or whatever." Landis made fists of his hands to hide their shaking. "It's an awful possibility, but no way was—" he tried to think what to call her "—was Julia involved in anything like that."

Their drinks arrived.

"The pachyderm in the pub," O'Hanlon muttered.

"Any problems with the project on the ground—union troubles, archeologists in a sweat, anything?" Carlos asked.

"No. We have good partners over there, so, nothing." Landis sipped the scotch. "Nearly."

"Let's hear it."

"A few existing structures have to come down. One is the former headquarters of a gay rights group that organized Belgium's Pink Saturday marches. About fifteen years ago, a gang of right-wingers attacked the office and beat a teenager to death. That makes it kind of their Stonewall, so there have been protests, or rather, rumblings."

"Interesting."

"That connection seems so unlikely," Landis said.

"These days, nothing is too far-fetched," Carlos said, writing.

"Makes me long for the Cold War, time to time." O'Hanlon called the server over and ordered a burger. Carlos asked for the same. "Why are they so much better here?" He grinned up at the young woman in her green apron.

"It's the horse meat," she said and winked. They watched her go, chuckling.

"Say more about the staff disagreement you mentioned. Pedestrian flow," Carlos said.

Landis thought. "No blood in the water, if that's what you're asking. Regarding the other two leading associates—Julia's potential 'rivals,' once she had her license—one of them doesn't have the killer instinct, and the other, well, it wouldn't occur to him he *had* competition. They were fine with her. Counting all our offices, it's a large firm. There's room for everybody to grow."

"Names?"

"Ty Geller and Charleston Lee. Ty's the super-confident one. He graduated from the University of Michigan and Charleston from the Savannah College of Art and Design."

"Carlos should check them out, if you don't mind,"

O'Hanlon said.

"If it's discreet. They're no more suspects than anyone else."

Carlos continued, "You said L + P competed for the train station job—commission. Is that common?"

"With government-funded projects, especially."

"Any bad blood with your competitors?"

"Firms put a lot into their entries. So, sure, there can be hard feelings. We get over it. Architects in general are a very long-lived bunch. We don't get that way by carrying grudges and shooting each other." Arch's confidence that many more peak career years lay ahead of him came through clearly. "Or are you thinking corporate espionage?"

"What are *you* thinking?"

"Part of the business. We're involved in a high-stakes competition right now for a cluster of buildings in Dubai. Involving some overseas firms and our chief competitors here in the States. Including a familiar name to you, Colm."

"Fucking Ivan Karsch. Can't forget him."

"I've always tried to get along with the guy, but something about me has bugged him for years. Coincidentally—" Landis stopped a moment "—I take that back, it probably isn't a coincidence. My son recently joined his firm. BLK."

"Not a coincidence?" Carlos asked.

"I supposed Hawk went there to annoy me. But it's also possible Karsch recruited him. Hawk isn't ambitious enough to be out job hunting." Landis rubbed his beard with his good hand. "He wasn't hired for his architectural talent—he's untested. I wonder what Ivan is up to."

As long ago as architecture school, Landis said, he'd pegged Karsch as someone with an agenda. At that time, he was more clearly the son of Russian immigrants struggling to send him to university. The family lived in an insular Brighton Beach community where tar-like resentments bound people together and where any hint of failure tainted someone forever. Word was he still spent every Sunday with his parents, a weekly booster shot of greasy stews and Russian garlic that trailed him like a ghost. Landis actually admired his family commitment, he admitted.

O'Hanlon had a more jaundiced view. "His years of moderate success must have validated his parents' investment."

"You think so? That claustrophobic background distorted his view of the world. He always believed the rest of us had it easy. Not true, of course. It's a shame he's never made many friends in the business. Other firms accuse him of lowballing his bids. I've seen that myself. It's also true his people don't stick with him. Sad state of affairs, really."

"Food for thought," O'Hanlon said, contemplating the overflowing french fries on the platter plunked in front of him. "Want one?" He pushed his plate toward Landis.

"Thanks, no. Have a dinner later." He didn't say he hadn't been eating much.

Landis's injured arm ached. Meetings with O'Hanlon usually gave him a boost. Not tonight. The vulnerabilities kept piling up. He watched Carlos grab the massive burger with one hand. Heavy lifting. Yes, he needed that.

Chapter 10

Landis left McSweeney's and hurried home to change clothes. Tonight was the opening dinner for the AIA Committee on Design summer conference. In his jacket pocket was a list of architects Marjorie wanted him to hit up for gala contributions. He dreaded another evening in the company of his colleagues, pretending to be filled with bonhomie. Asking them for money was another blight on the affair, but he'd do it.

To keep her on my side, he told himself, then thought, What side? When had sides come into it? Marjorie had always been on his side and he on hers. Until Julia, she was his only real love. He still loved her.

"Your tie is a mess," she said. Her face hovered inches from his, every line and plane of it so familiar and so precious. For a nanosecond a burden lifted—the burden of having to choose between them—before he clenched his eyes shut. That betrayal again.

"Sorry," she said, squeezing her fingers between his collar and neck. "Didn't you look in the mirror?" she asked, buttoning his collar. Of course he hadn't. "I can't decide whether I like that beard."

"Hawk's out, and you'll be alone all evening. It isn't too late to go with me. You can promote your conference much better than I can."

"You know how your dinners bore me."

"What if we leave before the speeches?"

"I've heard that before, but it never works out." She gave his shirt front a finishing pat. "I have lots to do here. Friday—tomorrow—we have another big planning session."

As he left the apartment, her phone was plugged into a speaker and she made notes on her iPad. Barely looking up, she waved.

~~~

At the Plaza, he was directed to a familiar ballroom. Though a little frayed around the edges, it was holding up bravely. *Like me.* His colleagues and rivals clustered around two bars set up along the rear wall, bobbing and jostling like swarming bees.

Landis dove into one of these crowds, squeezed to the front, protecting his injured arm as best he could, and asked for a scotch. Drink in hand, he turned and found himself looking down on pockmarked Ivan Karsch, a good six inches shorter than he, who'd tried to enlarge his presence this evening with a bare-knuckle aftershave.

"We've got your son." Karsch said, blunt as ever.

"So you have." Landis tried not to inhale.

"Glad of it too."

Landis grunted noncommittally.

A third man jammed against them placed his request with the barman. "You hired Hawk?" he asked Karsch.

Landis looked past them and gave an upward nod, as if acknowledging someone at the edge of the crowd, and excused himself. He shouldered through, needing air, holding his drink high in his good right hand. Before he moved out of earshot, Karsch muttered something involving the word "useless." He flushed, an angry retort a burr in his throat, but he kept going, certain Karsch had *some* use for Hawk, or he wouldn't have hired him.

Three of Landis's best professional friends, all on Marjorie's list, clustered around a high-top table where they huddled, stretching forward to hear themselves above the din, jovially radiating success.

Landis walked up to them. "Drunk yet?"

"No, goddammit," said Theo Gregg, his frequent tennis partner. The thing Landis most admired about Theo was he was a gracious loser, though it was a skill he rarely had need to practice.

"Too bad. I'm about to ask for money."

"Landis + Porter on the skids, eh?" said Phil Prinz, recipient of the award the night Julia was killed. A short man, he wore a flamboyant paisley tie only one shade redder than his perennially cheerful face.

"Don't get your hopes up," Landis pulled out his pen. "No, my wife's gala is next month—" he rolled his eyes, and they all groaned "—no, wait. It's connected to an international conference called Peace and Understanding"— they groaned again—"come on, it's a charming thought. Muslims, Jews—your people, Irv. Marjorie thinks with the construction boom in the Middle East, the city's rich architectural firms," he drew the words out encouragingly, "in addition to Landis + Porter, might want to grease the wheels of understanding."

"What about peace?" Prinz asked.

"Sure. Ten thousand a table. Cheap for peace."

Prinz gave him a thumbs up. "I'll hold you to it."

"OK, OK, put us down for one," said Gregg.

"Me too," grunted Irving Davidoff. Unlike the others, he had some skin in the game—several new projects in Israel. "Talk to my assistant."

"Thanks, guys, really," Landis said, checking off three names. Seven more to go.

"What happened?" Davidoff asked, waving his glass in

the direction of Landis's sling. "Hurt your pitching arm?"

"Didn't you hear? Somebody took a potshot at our friend here," Prinz said. "Really, Irv. Get your nose out of the *Times* and read the *Post* once in a while. That's where you find the juicy stuff."

In the stewpot of New York calamities, the shooting hadn't excited more than a minor bubble of media attention. L + P's public relations counsel had done his job, keeping the story on the inside pages and off the television news, away from general notice.

"I think he was aiming at New Jersey," Landis said. "Got turned around."

"Yeah?" said Davidoff. "And?"

"The police say there's nothing to it. Random urban craziness."

The men chuckled. Davidoff flapped his trademark Yankees tie.

"Beard's coming in nice," Gregg said. "Why the new look?"

"You used to have one," Landis said.

A sudden crash of shattering glass. All conversation stopped. *Not again!* Landis yelped and ducked under the skimpy table. A waiter had dropped a tray of empty glassware. His companions, looking to the source of the noise, missed his reaction. By the time they turned back to each other, Landis had straightened and manufactured a calm expression. It took longer for his heartbeat to slow.

"So," Prinz said, "I hear BLK hired Hawk."

"Yep."

"What's he up to?"

"Hawk?"

"No, Karsch."

"He'll give Hawk a different experience than I can. Hawk's so green, it hardly counts as poaching."

"Well, we always knew he wanted Terry," Davidoff

said. A moment of reflection followed, as they remembered the awful accident.

"Terry wouldn't leave Arch," Gregg said.

But Hawk would. The men studied their drinks, the melting ice.

"I need a refill," Landis said. "Anyone?"

"Not me," said Davidoff. The others shook their heads. "See you inside."

Landis circulated through the crowd, and by the time a discreet chime summoned them to dinner, he had Marjorie's ten tables, plus two more, and felt lousy about it. Now Landis + Porter would be on the hook for donations to assist the pet charities of all of them.

He followed the crowd to the dining room, troubled as well by thoughts of Hawk's erratic behavior. The previous evening he'd fled the dinner table again, claiming nausea. The kid was a bundle of nerves. He saw Davidoff waving and angled through the crowd toward his friends' table.

∽∾∽∾

When Landis arrived home, Marjorie was pasting sheets from an easel pad to their living room windows. On them was a web of names, arrows, scribbled-out lines, and empty boxes drawn with different-colored markers.

"You've been busy," Landis said, peering over her shoulder.

"Figuring out who sits with whom," she said, the cap of a marker between her teeth.

Landis shuddered. All those personalities. The unstable chemistry of human interaction. "I'm giving you a new card key for the office. We've changed security systems. Use one of my conference rooms for this, if you want to spread out. Oh, and I got your tables." He put the list and the card key on her desk.

"I knew you would. Thank you." She walked to the dining table and picked up another large sheet, sticking it next to the ones already there. Landis gazed thoughtfully at her back, trying to read from her posture whether things had changed between them. In his professional life he had a natural sense of spatial relationships, of the volume of structures, but what lay between people was always shifting, revealing hidden spaces, invisible barriers, never more so than the last few weeks.

"I hope Zardari knows how lucky he is," he said. "I don't know anyone else who could pull this off so beautifully. After the gala, you can move right into the diplomatic corps." Marjorie had always had that talent, reading people. Over the years, it had made her a valuable ally, but she'd missed one critical thing. She'd missed Julia. Or had she? He reached out, wanting to hold her close.

She moved away, laughing. "We know who the most important guests will be, and if I can sort them out, I can plug in other people as they respond. If we have any empty seats at the end, Yusuf will fill them with students."

She scribbled out another line and drew a new box, writing in the name of an Israeli academic—Tamara Dagan— a name Landis recognized. A decade ago, Landis + Porter had designed several buildings for Ben-Gurion University of the Negev, and Dagan was on the faculty advisory group. Opinions prickled out of her as if she were a desert thorn bush. She wasn't the typical sort—the "advisors" who never speak up until the job is half-built, then erupt with criticisms. You knew where you stood with Tamara from the get-go. He'd admired her.

"Marjorie, in August, when all this is behind you, why don't we take a trip?" She looked skeptical.

"We're doing a train station in Brussels, and I'd like to see the site, make sure everything's good there. Then you and I can go on to northern France." Her expression didn't change. Wasn't she hearing him? "Paris, Brittany. We haven't had a vacation in years. It's time." He was practically pleading. This trip could reopen a door she hadn't known was closing.

"You'll spend the whole time in Brussels poking around in a pit of dirt." She studied her cryptic seating charts. "No thanks."

"Not this trip. We haven't broken ground yet."

"The only thing more boring than staring at a big hole in the ground is staring at the place where a big hole will be."

"I've always wanted to see Picardy."

"Where is that again, exactly?"

"Between Brussels and Paris. Amiens cathedral, chateaus, the Somme. Lots of history."

"Depressing history."

"But Paris? Jolly Parisians?" An old joke between them.

"Maybe." She sounded doubtful, but she looked at him warmly.

He hoped it meant she too remembered their Paris honeymoon.

ewen

Marjorie's "maybe" was more enthusiastic than Charleston's response when he mentioned this trip during the Friday 9 a.m. staff meeting. The staff packed the conference room, and no one commented on the new venetian blinds closing off the view.

After a couple of beats, Charleston said, "You're going to do what, sir?"

"Take a look at the site myself. I need a better sense of the surroundings."

"I have hundreds of photos on my computer. I could show them to you again."

"I know you do. But I can't quite—*smell* the place yet."

"Yes, sir."

Charleston had a way of hesitating before he spoke, framing his words carefully. This worked well with the younger associates. He didn't jump on their comments or short-circuit their half-formed ideas. Yet Landis sensed there was some piece of himself that Charleston refused to show anyone. This morning he couldn't tell whether he was seeing the man's usual caution or whether he really didn't want his boss in Brussels.

Chapter 11

Landis's idea for the new security team met with a much warmer reception than his proposed site visit. Developing a security team would be a fresh way to channel his associates' energies. He clearly intended this team to be high profile, and Ty Geller volunteered to lead it. Two savvy associates volunteered to join him. Combined with the firm's usual efforts to seek input from communities affected by their projects, they would develop a new generation of security measures. They'd be effective, but also aesthetically pleasing to people who used, worked in, or lived near a new building. "No ugly bollards!" Ty enthused.

Landis moved on to a social topic. Every year around the fourth of July, L + P sponsored a family picnic at his Fire Island cottage. Because of the gala, Marjorie had begged off the planning this year, her annual contribution to office morale, and he gave the assignment to Deshondra.

"Put it on your calendars," he said. "Sunday, July 3."

"If you have ideas? Food, drink, entertainment?" Deshondra said to the group, "Spill."

That ended the meeting on a positive note, and later Landis gratefully handed her Marjorie's file of past catering contracts and phone numbers.

"Everything more or less like before?" Deshondra asked and pushed the door buzzer for the mail carrier to enter.

She flashed her smile at the young man, and he cut Landis a quick look. If the boss weren't standing there, he'd doubtless linger.

"Make it easy on yourself. But if you want to change anything, I'm open," Landis said.

The man deposited a haphazard pile in the inbox and took the short stack she handed him.

"Mojitos," she said, grabbing the day's letters before they slid off the slick catalogs and magazines.

"Vitamin C. Fine by me."

She riffled through the envelopes, pulled out one marked "personal" and handed it to him. The lightweight blue envelope was hand addressed, unusual in an era of email and instant messages. Fundraiser, Landis supposed, the first payback for Marjorie's gala contributions. He trudged up the steps to his office.

The handwriting was unfamiliar and clear—too clear, Landis thought twenty minutes later, as he considered the contents. In perfectly formed cursive, as if the writer were copying from a penmanship chart, his anonymous correspondent ordered him to go to Julia's apartment and retrieve a particular wooden box. Landis knew at once which one the writer meant. About four inches by seven, it was an ebony puzzle box inlaid with tiny pieces of yellowing ivory and mother-of-pearl in a complex Moorish geometric. He and other staff members had tried to open it, unsuccessfully. It was a good-humored contest every time they visited her.

"There's a trick to it," Julia said, when she saw him struggling, but she didn't reveal it. She said it was from Granada and belonged to her grandmother. He longed to think some bit of that was true. Surely everything hadn't been a lie.

He raked the thin soil of the letter again, trying to uncover the logic behind the request. The writer wanted the box, or, more likely, what was in it. Was that why she never opened it? Was something incriminating inside? Apparently, the letter-writer couldn't get police permission to visit the apartment or couldn't ask for it, but believed Landis could. Of course, if he were caught taking the box, he could be implicated further in Julia's activities, whatever those were. Or, rather, whatever the JTTF thought they were. The writer may have counted on that too.

If the reasons for wanting the box were ambiguous, the threats were not. They touched Landis in all the places that sent his anxieties spiking. "Remember Thursday," the letter said.

Landis glowered. *Which Thursday is that?* Julia was murdered two Thursdays back. This past Thursday, he'd dealt with the aftermath of being shot. Thor had brought his ringing hammer down pretty damn regularly on Thursdays of late.

Right on cue, a pulse of lightning crackled outside, followed by a deafening percussion of thunder. A midsummer storm had crept up on the city and exploded with rain and noise. Landis took one glance at the tumult outside and picked up the phone to call Fowler.

He was tempted to come clean about the letter, tell the detective what it said, and let the police deal with it. But "Remember Thursday" wasn't the end of the threat. The letter also said, "You have a wife. Talk to the police and she is next." He couldn't—he wouldn't—risk adding Marjorie to the summer's casualties. Now, waiting for Fowler to pick up, he crossed his injured left arm over his waist, gripping tightly, holding himself together.

He told Fowler he needed to retrieve some books Alia Said had borrowed. Fowler put him on hold and, after a moment, clicked back on. "OK, Gennaro says a uniform will let you into the apartment at eleven. You can retrieve your books. We're done there, but we're keeping the scene closed another few days, just in case."

"Thanks." Landis hesitated. "I should tell you—" The threat on the blue page appeared in front of his eyes as if written in flashing lights.

"Tell me what?"

Landis crumpled the blue sheet. He had no illusions he could protect Marjorie perfectly, but he had to do at least this much for her. "Nothing. Thanks."

❧❧❧

Much about Julia's apartment remained the same. The furniture and belongings were in place. At the tall windows, between the heavy draperies, the black lace curtains hung like mantillas for a race of giant women. Squat silvered lamps created more shadow than illumination.

Landis brought along a canvas bag to hold the books borrowed from the L + P library, which he truly did want back. He distracted the policeman by pointing out the sparkling gold matador suit in its glass-fronted display case and slipped the inlaid box into the bottom of the bag. He kept his back to the chaise where her body had lain. *Had been arranged.* The chaise now rested upside down. Not seeing the bloodstains didn't mean they weren't there. The hint of a terrible smell permeated the room. Perspiration beaded his hairline.

"Here they are," he said. "*Gio Ponti. Fast-Forward Urbanism.* My language of flowers dictionary. Glad to have these again. They cost a small fortune." He crowded the oversized books into the bag, the box a hard lump in the bottom. "Done."

❧❧❧

Up in his office, Landis tore off the sling and flung it into the wastebasket, disgusted at how helpless it had made him, wrangling the books and his umbrella, having to accept the officer's help, risking discovery of the box.

He fiddled with it on his desk, trying once more to persuade it to give up its secrets.

Hopeless.

Maybe he was better off not knowing the contents, if they'd make Julia guilty of something.

You don't believe that!

Yet, whoever had written that letter wanted the box badly. He grabbed a sheet of heavy paper, wrapped and taped it tightly around the box, and left the package with Deshondra, marked "For Pickup." He didn't give her any special instructions, hoping she wouldn't pay the claimant any special attention. *Keep it low-key.*

He'd been instructed to tape the blue envelope to the conference room window as a signal the box was ready. This was the window through which someone with a rifle had spied on him, taken aim, and fired. Twice. He moved quickly. No large and tempting target this time. He closed the blinds so the staff wouldn't notice that unexpected blue rectangle.

Around one o'clock, two associates came to his office to consult about a contractor's question, and when he glanced down at Deshondra's desk a few minutes later, the package was gone. He was disappointed not to see who took it, but at least he'd done exactly what the letter told him to do. He lied his way into the apartment and stole the box. He wrapped it and left it on the reception desk. He taped the envelope to the window. Now the box was gone. Done.

His relief was cut short by the insistent chime of his cell phone. A muffled male voice, vaguely foreign, speaking through a screen of background music said, "Where it is?"

"What are you talking about?"

"The box, motherfucker. It is mine." The voice was a rasping growl.

"But you have the box."

"No. You have it. Is not at the apartment."

"How do you know?"

"Is not here. And I saw you leave with something." The pulsing background music and the man's aggressive tone made it hard for Landis to think. This conversation made no sense.

"How did you get in? And if you could get in, why didn't you get the box yourself?"

"I want your fingerprints on it. So where it is?"

Shit, shit, shit. "Look, sir, you sent someone to pick it up. Here at my office."

"What the fuck you talking?"

"I did what you said in the letter. You sent the letter, right?" Landis prayed it was so. It had to be. The phone nearly slipped from his grasp. "Look, we should talk." Maybe this stranger could help him figure out what was going on.

"What letter? I don' know any fucking letter. I want the box. I *will have* it."

"I don't have it. I got a letter—" He rubbed his forehead "C'mon, man, let's talk."

"Who sent letter?"

"Hell if I know. I'm guessing it was you."

The man made a noise like a buzzer. "Wrong."

"You told me to fetch the box from the apartment and bring it here for someone to pick up. Someone did. It's gone."

"Then get it back."

"I don't know who—"

"Bzzzzzt. Wrong again."

"I can't—"

"Forget excuses. I am coming five o'clock, and I want the box. Get it by then, or…well, I won't miss second time. If not today, I will have other chances. Don' call police." He hung up.

Landis put his hand over his eyes, which failed to obscure the vision of an AK-47-toting foreigner bursting into the office and slaughtering every last one of them. Laying waste to tremendous architectural talent, sixty or more university degrees, parents of at least twenty children.

Why? For what?

He couldn't sort it out—the letter, the box, the phone call. None of it made sense. He dry-swallowed a couple of pain pills from his desk and punched in Deshondra's extension. "Did you see who picked up that package?" he asked.

"Ty let a messenger in and told him to wait. He was gone when I got back to my desk. He must have taken it. They don't stick around."

Landis thought a moment. "Do you know how our new security system works?" They'd gone from bare bones to the other extreme, and now a camera watched the front door, the emergency exit they never used, and the hallway to the restrooms.

"Sure. The installer spent hours explaining it to me."

I'll bet he did.

Deshondra tilted her head to Landis in his office overhead and gave him the benefit of her smile. He realized that if someone broke in, she'd be his first victim.

"Can you find the messenger's picture in the tape— DVD, whatever?"

"Sure. I can play it on my computer."

While he waited for Deshondra to cue up the video, he went downstairs and retrieved the blue envelope.

Then, over her shoulder, he watched the twelve seconds of action, hoping to see something useful. The front door opened, a bicycle messenger in head-to-toe spandex and fingerless gloves entered, muttered "pickup" to Ty, who walked away. Helmet and sunglasses obscured his face. He marched to Deshondra's desk, slipped the package into his backpack, zipped it closed, and walked out the front door. His gait was stiff and artificial, but he was featureless. Unidentifiable.

"Again, please."

The messenger walked in. He said a word. He took the package and zipped it away. He walked out.

"Again."

He came in, took the package, left.

"Again."

In. Out.

"Get what you needed?" Deshondra asked.

"No." Landis's voice was sad. He abruptly stiffened. "We're closing early today. Tell the staff *no one* stays past three."

"OoooKaaay." She drew the syllables out, inviting clarification that didn't come.

"TGIF."

Chapter 12

Initially, every instinct told Landis to run. Last one out, shut off the lights, dash to the elevator. That impulse was thwarted by deeper fears that kept him at his desk. He had to stay and face this problem. In truth, where could he go? This man—whoever he was—could pursue him no matter where he hid. Just as he said, if not today, another day.

The hole he'd dug for himself by stealing the box was too deep to climb out of now. He'd been an idiot to think that would be the end of it. These people—whoever they were—were leeches. He had to get rid of them.

But how?

Foolishly, he'd skipped his chance to unload to Fowler before he stole the puzzle box. Thought that would have just delayed the inevitable. For sure, in the two days since he was shot, he'd learned one thing: he wasn't equipped to live in constant anxiety. Looking over his shoulder. Jumping at every noise.

The arguments for staying and for going chased each other around and around like Indy cars. When his mind at last held up the yellow caution flag, signaling it would be cowardly to leave, that fleeting warning settled it. He'd stay.

Get it the hell over with.

Alone in his office, Landis didn't have guns or knives,

but he did possess certain weapons. He was armed with a sharp intellect and high-caliber persuasive powers. Briefly he longed for his old M16, could feel its heft, smell the hot metal barrel steaming in the rain. Long gone. Another life. Words were his weapon now. He'd talk to this man, figure out his problem, and try to come to some resolution that didn't leave him dead. Sure he would. One thing he'd gleaned from their interactions so far, the man was not a negotiator.

As the minutes crawled by, he wasn't certain he could save himself. He flipped through the calendar Deshondra kept for him, saw all his appointments for the next week, the next month, to the end of the year. Would he be able to keep any of them?

He jerked off his tie and tossed it into the wastebasket on top of the sling, which sent him into a wild fantasy of taking off *all* his clothes and meeting the man that way, naked as a Vietcong sapper slipping through the American camp's barbed wire perimeter. He laughed bitterly. As if he wouldn't be wearing layer upon layer of the lifelong camouflage he'd diligently stitched to hide his insecurities, his mistakes, his blindness to those close to him. He'd wrapped on another layer of these thick garments to insulate himself from the pain of Julia's death and, crucially, his loss of nerve when he ran out on her. He could never be naked.

The caller had said he was practically a dead man, and now, waiting, Landis believed it.

As the clock pointed out four-fifteen, his cell phone chimed. "When are you coming home?" Marjorie asked.

"About six, I hope." He cleared his throat.

"Can't you leave early? Now?" Her voice shook. "I'd feel better if you were here."

"Why, what's wrong?"

"Those antiterrorism people were here again. Asking

about Yusuf."

"What's to know?"

"Nothing, I think." She paused. "Something's not right." She sounded confused. "Hawk…"

"Hawk what?"

"Never mind. I'll tell you later."

"I'll be home soon as I can." Landis's voice thinned. Could this be the last conversation they would ever have? "I love you, Marjorie. Don't worry."

"Come home." Her words were barely audible.

"I can't." So were his.

After he ended the call, Marjorie's ghost reached out to him from behind the phone's black screen, showing him the things he needed to do that mattered. What Marjorie should know, the sentences he couldn't speak out loud, he wrote in a letter and sealed in an envelope with her name on it. He wrote encouraging words to Hawk, forcing himself to look beyond his son's current anger and back to the promising boy he had been.

O'Hanlon got a note too, asking him to sell the business to Ty and Charleston, if they wanted it. The generous terms he suggested meant they'd probably accept; the price would keep Marjorie comfortable for her lifetime. Of a personal nature, he wrote only, "Thank you, old friend."

A short note to Detective Fowler too, who'd probably have to deal with the aftermath, and a plea for him to continue the search for Julia's killer. Landis studied the words he'd written. This distorted version of his usual neat printing was barely recognizable.

All four envelopes went into a nine-by-twelve. He carried it downstairs and put it in the middle drawer of Deshondra's desk—the first place she'd look. To make room, he shoved a few papers aside, uncovering an envelope marked "photos," one of which had slid partway out. It was a snapshot of him and Julia and Charleston at the holiday party, all of them grinning for the camera, happy.

God. So long ago.

He pushed it back in the envelope, closed the drawer, and hid Deshondra's desk key in their secret place. He made two circuits of the workroom floor, pausing behind Ty's table and Charleston's and the stations of a couple of the others he especially admired, saying good-bye to their absent selves. He stopped for several minutes at Hawk's empty place and rested his arms on the back of the chair. His mercurial son.

How did I go so wrong with him?

At Julia's station, he fingered her keyboard, her pens and pencils, things she'd touched. No one had guessed how many secrets she protected.

He came to rest at Deshondra's desk and sat in her chair, facing the entry door twenty feet in front of him. He studied the crowded photographs on her desk—girlfriends, cousins, and Deshondra herself, lighting each picture with her non-stop grin. Among the photos and mementos, a lucite block with a spoonful of dirt from a recent groundbreaking ceremony and an eighteen-inch stainless steel model of one of the firm's award-winning skyscrapers. Deshondra displayed these mementos, proud to be part of L + P. Her loyalty mattered a great deal, and he hoped he'd never taken it for granted.

A quarter to five, and he hadn't decided yet what to do or say to his visitor. L + P won commissions because of Landis's absolute commitment to managing every detail, leaving nothing to chance. Another jungle survival skill. In this encounter, he'd have to wing it. He was terrified that when the moment came, he would reach inside himself and find empty space.

One minute to five. Adrenaline coursed through him. Millions of years of fight-or-flight evolution, and here he was, stuck in a chair, unarmed.

Five o'clock. His ears strained. Deshondra's clock ticked. Its minute hand moved in super-slow motion. 5:04. 5:07. 5:12. He thought he heard something, but it was the lack of something, the rain stopping at last. 5:15. 5:16. 5:19.

Is it all a tease? They're not coming. THEY??? OR HE????

The elevator bell dinged. The doors swished open. A shadow approached the office door, and someone peered through the grillwork. Landis pressed the entry buzzer. A man wearing a voluminous trench coat pushed the door open.

What? It can't be.

Landis forgot to breathe. In the shock of the moment, every assumption blown, he hesitated, rapidly reassessing, his gaze fixed on the handgun pointed at him. Trying to keep his voice level, he said, "If you're my appointment, you're late."

"Here alone?" Hawk stepped forward. "Too bad. I would have liked to say a last good-bye to Charleston, that mealy-mouthed prick." The gun drifted toward the work-room, in the general direction of Charleston's table. Hawk stepped closer, crossing the reception area halfway. The gun swung around again to point at Landis.

"Let me guess. Your being here right now is no coincidence."

"Thaaaat's right." Hawk's tone was off, like he spoke through a wad of cotton.

"Put the gun down, and let's talk about it."

"Uh-uh."

"Hawk, put it down."

"No way."

Despite his words, Hawk looked confused, uncertain. Asking questions might help him focus. "So, what's in the box you had me steal?" Landis asked.

"Dunno. Pretty, though, isn't it?"

"So, you have it."

"Yeah." Not interested. "I do."

Another piece fell into place. "That was you who called. Disguised your voice. Pretended to be in the apartment."

"Don't you make yourself sick, being right? Every. Fucking. Time."

"What are you playing at? What's wrong with you?"

Hawk's head bobbed; he was only half-listening. "Just playing."

"Seems like a dangerous game to me. Was it you who killed Julia? Is that the gun?"

Hawk appeared to wake, his eyes suddenly wide, and grinned. "Yes, sirree. I wanted to kill them all." He took several more steps, stopping about six feet in front of the desk.

The incongruity of his expression repelled Landis. "It was you who shot at me."

Hawk shrugged. "Like you said, if you hadn't reacted so fast, you'd be dead. You'd be in your comfy satin-padded room. Forever." He cackled, and again he corrected his aim.

"Since when do you know anything about guns?"

"There's a lot you don't know about me, Dad." Hawk slapped his left ear, as if trying to dislodge something stuck inside. He didn't react to the faint click of the security system. Perhaps he didn't hear it. The front door of the office eased open, but Hawk blocked Landis's view of whoever came in behind him. Beset with so many conflicting emotions, his son's face wobbled like a rubber mask.

"When you sent me away to Europe, I made friends, and my friends had interests. One of them took me shooting. Lots of times. Turns out I'm good at it. So, I have you to thank for this…skill." With the last word, his attention appeared to focus.

"Who *are* your friends these days, Hawkins? Why haven't I met them?"

Hawk cocked his head, apparently listening to noises only he could hear.

"You're right," Landis said, prolonging the moment. "There's a lot I don't know. What else? Lay it on me."

The barrel of the gun sagged a few degrees. "You never paid any attention to me." The pitch of Hawk's voice escalated. "You put everything and everybody else in front of me. Poor Hawk, always at the end of the…end of the line. Admit it, you were useless as a father."

From behind him, Marjorie's tiny figure emerged. "It's not Hawk's fault. It's—"

Startled, Hawk whirled and fired. Marjorie hugged her chest and gasped. Blood flowed through her fingers. Hawk screamed.

"No!" Landis shouted. He sprang across the desk, grabbing the steel building model.

Gazing at his dying mother, Hawk sagged. Landis couldn't correct his swing fast enough, and the model crashed not into Hawk's shoulder, but into his left temple. His skull shattered with a sickening sound.

"Oh," he said, his eyes rolling back into his head. He sank to the floor, his mouth forming a second, silent "Oh."

Landis leapt past Hawk's falling body to reach Marjorie. He held her and crooned softly, but she was beyond hearing him. Meanwhile, his darting glance sought the gun. Hawk had dropped it, and it lay on the floor partly hidden by his splayed legs. Landis reached out his foot and kicked it away.

He didn't believe he could bear this. He couldn't see or hear or think. He couldn't move. *Marjorie.*

The best idea would be to retrieve that gun and shoot himself. Complete the carnage. But then he'd never know *why*. Why all this destruction? A quick death would be too easy. What would be hard, the punishment he deserved, was living with himself.

Chapter 13

Landis swiveled the chair away from the scene in front of Deshondra's desk—the bodies, the hovering medical examiner's staff. He bent forward, elbows on knees, head buried in his hands. The long silver hair fell over his fingers, a thin screen of privacy.

He responded to Detective Fowler's questions, though Fowler had to pull his chair close to hear him. They were practically knee-to-knee. Behind Fowler, Detective Gennaro slapped the security camera disk against his hand, undoubtedly eager to play it. Fowler gave him a warning look.

"Where was your staff? Nobody working late?" Fowler asked.

"I sent them home. After the phone call, I couldn't take the chance…There might be a confrontation, some weirdness, but I never…" He struggled to stick to the truth, if not the whole truth. Fowler was helpful, supportive. That would change if he learned Landis was hiding information.

"Was the kid some kind of nut job?" Gennaro asked. Fowler made an irritated sound.

Landis raised his head, his shoulders curled in on himself like a dried leaf, "I thought he was…hostile. Toward me. He wasn't under treatment, as far as I know…" At that moment, Hawk's life was a blank to him. He couldn't explain any of it, he didn't know who Hawk's friends were or what was going on at his work. If only they'd let him sit on the floor beside his son and cradle his poor mixed-up head, embrace Marjorie, pull her into his lap. That he'd done so before the police arrived was clear from the bloody smears on his shirtfront and the prickle of blood drying on his face where he'd rested his head on her chest, sobbing.

"I wanted to stop him from shooting her…" He said it over and over.

"Was his confession real, do you think?" Gennaro stumbled on. "Did he kill Julia?"

Long pauses preceded all Landis's replies. "He didn't know what he was saying…but I don't know. Everything was so wrong. Maybe that was why."

The M.E. team finished its on-site work and moved the bodies to the waiting gurneys. Landis heard Gennaro talking to them, then the gurneys squeaking and the team's voices fading as they reached the elevator. Fowler joined Gennaro across the room for a brief conversation.

Head still resting in his hands, Landis appreciated the sudden stillness. He couldn't bear another minute of the M.E. team's constant chatter, their measuring, probing, and flashing cameras.

Fowler returned, saying, "What they found so far confirms your story. We'll have the evidence from the security camera and the weapons. We know how to find you. Go home. Is there someone who can be with you?"

Landis shook his head. He thought of Prinz, Davidoff, O'Hanlon, and that reminded him of the letters. He retrieved Deshondra's key and opened the desk drawer, pulled out the manila envelope.

"Letters to Marjorie, my lawyer, you—in case…" Landis's voice had no power behind it.

"You expected the worst?"

"If not today, eventually, maybe."

"May I?" Fowler held out his hand.

Landis handed over the note intended for him, but kept

the others, and Fowler didn't ask for them. Instead, he said, "I'll drive you home."

For the first time since the police arrived, Landis let himself look where the bodies had lain. The carpet shocked him. "So much blood," he whispered. "I didn't ex-..."

"Yeah."

Shakily, Landis rose and found he couldn't move. He could not approach the door, could not walk near those bloody stains. He steadied himself with a hand on Deshondra's desk.

"We'll go out the back way," Fowler said.

∽∾∽

Alone in the apartment, Landis embraced the sting of Marjorie's last words, her half-formed accusation. She was right; it wasn't Hawk's fault, it was his. He was not a good father. He'd never get over it, the truth of it.

No time for that, too much to do.

He began a list, but stopped writing after the first item.

One thing at a time. Do this one thing.

This would be the most difficult call—Marjorie's brother, John. Landis had been an outsider to the Hawkins family's wealthy and socially prominent Connecticut circle, and they'd never let him forget it. His mother-in-law, especially, didn't warm to him, even when he and Marjorie wasted no time giving her a grandson—one who everyone said looked like the Hawkins side of the family—or when Landis achieved unequivocal professional success. To her, he was never more than an *arriviste* of undistinguished origins. Her generation was gone, but in Marjorie's older brother, the habit of chilly distance was too solid to melt now.

With difficulty, Landis held his own emotions in check and described Marjorie's death as an accident, which he believed it was. When he tried to stop Hawk, he said, their son had died too.

"I'm shocked," John Hawkins said, followed by a lengthy pause that suggested he needed time to think of what else to say, how to respond. When at last he spoke, it was with weary resignation, as if he'd expected a call like this for years. "And so very sorry. Hawk. Really quite remarkable. Was he deranged?"

"It appears so."

Another long silence ensued, in which Landis imagined John reviewing the Hawkins family tree in order to rule out any genetic guilt on their side. "All right. I'll notify the family, our parents' friends, the Greenwich crowd. Let me know when you have the funeral arrangements in hand. We can bury them in our plot here, if you like. There's room."

A flush that began in his toes surged to the roots of his hair. The family taking over, asserting its priority. As always. His anger was pointless. John's suggestions were practical and useful, which further infuriated him. John would give the family his own opinion of events, Landis could count on that. Those calls were one less task for him, though, and what the aunts and cousins and country club set thought of him mattered not an iota. He agreed to John's offers and, at the last moment, remembered to thank him.

One step at a time. Square away the office.

He called Deshondra at home. She cried, but immediately her good sense told her what he'd need. Without his asking, she said she would let the staff know not to come in on Monday. She'd check with Fowler to make sure it was all right to find a crime scene clean-up service to deal with "whatever." New flooring, for a start. No one would want to set foot on that carpet again. First, though, she would call O'Hanlon and Landis + Porter's public relations advisor and ask them to come to the apartment. He needed their counsel, obviously, but Deshondra also made it clear he shouldn't be alone.

Landis sat on his and Marjorie's bed a long while, shivering. Julia was dead only eight days and, unbelievably, he'd now lost Marjorie and Hawk too. He wrestled a thick wool sweater over his head. The effort exhausted him.

O'Hanlon arrived, followed a few minutes later by the firm's P.R. consultant, Ben Silk. O'Hanlon and Silk had worked as a team on tricky Landis + Porter issues for a decade. They knew Marjorie, and they knew Hawk. The three of them sat silently a while, lost in memory and reflection. Then O'Hanlon and Silk gradually took charge.

e/se/s

"Jeannie and I will make calls, if you like," O'Hanlon said. "She'll help with the funeral arrangements too, if you tell her what you want. Did Marjorie leave any instructions?"

Silk came from the kitchen, carrying a pot of coffee. He listened.

"We never talked about it. No. I don't think so." Landis raised his head to glance at her desk. He didn't get up.

"Mind if I look?" O'Hanlon asked, checking Landis's expression for permission. "If she didn't specify, everything's up to you."

Landis was deep inside himself, still shivering despite the sweater, when the telephone rang. Silk waved him in place and picked up the phone. He'd managed to keep Landis + Porter mostly out of the stories about Julia. This would be different.

"He's resting. I won't disturb him," he said after the caller's long preamble. "He'll have a statement tomorrow afternoon." Too late for Saturday's early editions and the dinnertime news, if they timed it right. His statement would make the 11 p.m. television news and the Sunday papers.

By midweek, interest in the tragedy might have moved on. Of course, some version of the story would be all over the Internet soon, if it wasn't already. Silk hung up. "*Post*," he said. "We don't need that right now."

After an hour spent making plans and lists, Landis sagged. O'Hanlon and Silk stopped writing.

"We've covered most of it," O'Hanlon said. "We can pick up again in the morning."

Landis stared at his hands, the ones that had held Hawk as a baby, guided his tiny hands when he made his first drawings, helped him pack his bags for college, then Europe. Hands that wielded the weapon that killed his boy. *How had he let things go so far?*

"Unplug the bedroom phone," Silk advised. "And leave your cell phone out here. Reporters aren't above calling in the middle of the night to catch you off guard. Let me handle them."

Landis assented. Losing himself in the nighttime view across the river, his glance skimmed the soccer fields near the head of Roosevelt Island. The city lights, seemingly more numerous than stars, outlined the grid of Queens streets and glowed in distant apartment windows. Above the city, airplane landing lights slowly swung into position as evening arrivals stacked up for LaGuardia. Tonight, all these lights together, all the lights in the world, could not push back the overwhelming dark.

"Can you sleep?" O'Hanlon asked. "Rest?"

Landis had never been more exhausted. But sleep? How could he be unconscious during any part of this day, his wife and son's last? Twelve hours ago, six hours ago, they were with him, in the world.

"I can stay," O'Hanlon said. He laid a hand on Landis's back and followed his friend's gaze, which had dropped to the street thirty-three stories below.

"Not necessary. Thanks." Landis read O'Hanlon's

mind. "I couldn't do that, Colm. Charleston and Ty aren't ready."

Chapter 14

Saturday morning O'Hanlon and Silk arrived at Landis's apartment early. Though he'd barely slept, he was already up and dressed, again wearing that too-heavy-for-June sweater.

Silk was listening to the messages that came in overnight when Landis's phone buzzed with a new call. Silk listened a moment, then pressed the phone to his leg so the caller couldn't hear him. "Yusuf Zardari asks if you'd like memorial contributions to go to the Peace and Understanding project."

"*He's* rabbitty quick," O'Hanlon muttered, draping his jacket on the back of a dining chair, alongside Silk's.

"You *will* need a charity for the obituary." When Silk didn't get an answer, he said, "Want to think about it?"

It was easiest to agree, and Marjorie would have approved. "Tell him yes."

"Get the exact name and address, and make sure they'll be tax-deductible," O'Hanlon said.

Silk wrote down the information and listened, then muted the call. "He wonders about Hawk. Peace and Understanding for him also?"

"Jesus!" Landis grabbed a handful of hair. "I don't know." The irony didn't escape him that lack of understanding had contributed to these deaths, and his sluggish brain couldn't produce a suitable alternative. What *was*

Hawk interested in? Whales, AIDS, starving artists? He needed time to think. Time he didn't have.

O'Hanlon spoke up. "I'd say no to that. It makes sense for Marjorie, but there's reasons not to be too cozy with this guy. A."

Silk gave him a quizzical look, but let it pass.

"OK. No," Landis said.

Silk ended the call. "We'll have to think of a charity, though. How about Hawk's architecture school? Universities are set up for it. Should be easy to arrange."

"Good," Landis said. "Fine." Landis knew the dean, found his number in a membership directory, and spoke with him briefly. Deshondra would negotiate the particulars with the development office. Done.

In all, they worked through a crushing list of details, interrupted by calls from Landis's friends and a cousin of Marjorie's. These decisions paved the way for Silk's media strategy. He would put Landis's view of the tragedies on the record and allude to past events, in the hope of avoiding new revelations dripping out, one at a time. At 6 p.m., Silk released the following:

> *Saturday, June 11 -- Statement by Archer Landis, principal of the Landis + Porter architectural firm:*
> *Last evening my family suffered tragic accidents that took the lives of my wife Marjorie and our son Hawkins. Everyone who knew Marjorie recognized her generous spirit and commitment to improving our world. Hawk's career in architecture had only begun. They both leave much undone that they would have accomplished with creativity and passion. The Landis + Porter family has proved itself resilient in difficult times, and I am confident our firm will stay strong, despite the*

> *personal loss to me, to our loved ones, and to the*
> *many friends Marjorie and Hawk leave behind.*

The statement continued with details of funeral arrangements and the suggestions regarding memorial contributions. Reading it over, Landis hesitated where it said "Hawk's career." It was a last-minute change Silk had made, because when they rehearsed, the original wording—"my son's career"—stuck in Landis's throat.

Over the next few days, Landis repeated this statement to various members of the news media. Every time, the weakness of the words struck him. They could neither convey what he felt nor stop the journalists' stories from raising painful connections and speculations.

ℰↃℰↃ

No matter how difficult Landis's next few days, eventually they staggered into the past tense. The funerals—where Detectives Fowler and Gennaro were a discreet presence—the condolences, the dealing with Marjorie's family and the sorting of her papers for Zardari (Deshondra took care of that), the media probing, and the settling of financial affairs with help from O'Hanlon's office blurred behind him, details seen through a fog. The first day of summer approached.

The police investigation was mercifully short. After viewing the security camera's record, city prosecutors agreed with Landis's statement that Marjorie and Hawk's deaths were unintentional. Pressed by a few reporters, they alluded to Hawk's mental instability. JTTF investigators Friend and Wojcik twice dropped in on Landis at home, plaguing him with long, redundant lists of questions about Julia's associates and past activities that he couldn't answer and had no patience for. After they left, he skipped dinner and went to bed.

Hawk's confession lurked at the edge of Landis's thoughts always. He'd brought Hawk and Julia together, unknowingly creating the connection that led to her death. If the resultant guilt and pain could be pounded out with exercise, the miles he put in on the treadmill in the basement of his apartment building would have done it. He would have preferred to enjoy the dawdling summer twilight, jogging up to Gracie Mansion and back, but Fowler and O'Hanlon cautioned against it. He might still be a target. Not that he especially cared. He'd lost weight, and, on his six-foot frame, he was as rangy as he'd been in his early twenties, collegiate tennis champion and returning Vietnam vet. It was, he thought, the body Marjorie had fallen in love with, not his more recent self, padded with supposed success.

Misery clinging to him like his own shadow led Landis to consult a psychiatrist for the first time in his life.

"It can be hard to walk in a big man's footsteps," the psychiatrist said. "Perhaps, up to the end, what he wanted was for you to notice him."

"Right." Understanding why it happened was not the same as understanding his responsibility for it.

"Mr. Landis, this is the classic dilemma in father-son relationships, and most of us are strong enough to resolve it. If your son could not—which is probably not surprising, given his apparent instability—that isn't your doing. The problem was his reaction to the father-son dynamic. *His* reaction. Don't blame yourself."

"We—I—should have helped him."

"I understand he had a lot of help in his teen years."

But was it enough?

As Landis left the doctor's office, he thought of his own father, living in the house his eight-year-old son designed, and the stream of fatherly encouragement and support he'd provided. Had he done as much for Hawk? Or tried to? Marjorie's last words absolving Hawk laid the blame right at his own feet. He wished...*No, no point in that.*

ᴄ⌒ᴄ⌒ɔ

Landis had been barely present at work, even when he was in the office for an hour or two. Then L + P suffered a significant setback. The Burj Maktoum commission went to BLK. This massive project would have distracted his staff from the recent tragedies. Ty Geller, especially, was bitterly disappointed and slammed around the office, taking out his frustration on the desks and chairs.

Landis tried to focus him on getting the security team off the ground. To mollify him, and because he didn't have the energy to contribute anything himself, he acceded to all Ty's suggestions. They hired a landscape architect who could help in both site selection and protection—shrubs, plantings, and water features instead of bollards—and Ty persuaded a brilliant structural engineer to leave L + P's Chicago office and join them in Manhattan.

Geller also requested a security expert—one with no architectural training. "An outsider who won't unconsciously reflect our constraints. A profiler," he said. His perfect candidate would understand motive and see opportunity.

Geller and his colleagues vetted candidates and conducted initial interviews. One day, near the end of the month, he arrived in Landis's office carrying two folders. "These are the best," he said, "and both are unconventional."

"That's what you're looking for, right?"

"We've sure learned what we *don't* want. These two have impressive, but different strengths. We could work with either one. Hard to say which might be better."

Landis held out his hand for the folders. "Tell me about

them."

"The one on top is a security analyst for the General Services Administration. His division oversees the thousands of buildings where the federal government leases space. The job's given him exposure to all kinds of buildings and situations. Most were never designed to withstand any kind of attack and aren't easy to secure. His wife's a lawyer, and her firm is transferring her to its New York office. That's why he's looking."

Landis opened the second folder. "This one?"

"Very interesting. Army background. She's worked on security at bases in Europe and the Middle East for twelve years. Not physical security, per se. Threat analysis. Her tour is ending, and she has two young children now. So she wants out of the military."

Landis studied the woman's résumé, which included a B.A. in psychology from Princeton. "Invite them in. Let's talk to them."

Watching Geller leave, he wondered what Terry would think of the shadowy, disjointed world their crisp lines and polished surfaces had become.

⊘∂⊘

When he was at the office, Landis could try to immerse himself in work, but in the early morning and late at night, he couldn't escape the emptiness of his apartment. He still couldn't get warm there, and he'd pulled his winter sweaters and vests out of storage.

He had the treadmill, and his friends made a point of getting him out. He appreciated it and he hoped they knew it, even when he lost the conversational thread. Irving Davidoff took him to a Yankees game and launched a tour of the city's kosher delis, Theo Gregg had him on the tennis court twice a week, with dinner at the clubhouse afterward, and twice, Colm and Jeannie O'Hanlon invited him to a family picnic on Sunday. But eventually, he'd be thanking them, saying, "I have to go back to the apartment." He'd stopped calling it home.

The memory of Julia's apartment, saturated in color, made his own surroundings starker. He couldn't deny she had made him feel younger—young. She was a supportive friend, a superb creative colleague, and an invigorating lover. She was all about possibilities, possibilities that he could be more than he was, better. Her absence was like losing that better self, like losing the sun. When he lost Marjorie, though, he lost the moon. Untethered, floating and drifting, nothing to regulate the tides within or light the darkness. He wouldn't have guessed he could miss her so much.

The truth was, he'd loved both women. Still did. Acknowledging that felt shabby, improbable, self-justifying, a convenient rationalization. He had wanted it all and been left with nothing. It felt like what he deserved.

One empty evening, he surveyed Hawk's room, trying to resign himself to a permanent state of ambivalence about that boy—the enormity of his confession versus the mitigating factor of his mental imbalance. Hawk might have pulled his life together, with therapy and medication—people did that—or his dark moods and strange behavior could have been the first phase of a long downward slide. One Marjorie very likely blamed on him. He had to get out of there; the place was sucking the life out of him.

In that moment, he decided he really should see the Brussels site. He'd make the trip, alone.

Chapter 15

The L + P leadership team advised Landis to go ahead with the firm's annual family picnic. They counted on a display of positive staff energy to outweigh the awkwardness. Recent events naturally affected them, they needed to bond again. The Manhattan office had already lost a couple of young architects. It was a coincidence of timing in one case, but the other one said flatly that recent events "make my wife too nervous." He wouldn't look Landis in the eye as he said it.

"I'll be back from Brussels in time to help with any last-minute preparations, if you need me," he told Deshondra, knowing she didn't. He tossed the keys to the beach house on her desk. "Enjoy the house while I'm gone, if you want to." Seeing her doubtful expression, he added, "Check up on the cleaners. Whether they've made up the beds, aired the place out, evicted the mice, dead or alive."

"Sure it's not an intrusion?" Warming to the idea, her face shone delightedly.

"I haven't been out there all year. It's a help."

She handed him a stack of papers. "Last-minute trip stuff. Don't forget, Ty's two candidates are coming in this morning."

"Great. I'm looking forward to meeting them."

Those meetings went well. In the end, he and Ty agreed to make offers to them both. Former GSA analyst Harry

Stavrakis and U.S. Army veteran Brett Marx became the sixth and seventh members of Geller's security team.

The last item on his morning's "must-do" list was to call Fowler and tell him where he'd be for the next few days.

"You didn't need to call. You aren't under any restraint from us."

"Better to check. What about the JTTF?"

"Who knows? Sure, give them a heads up. While you're on the line, I need to stop by."

഑ഏ഑

Ed Fowler sat across from him, drinking cheap diner coffee from a blue-and-white paper cup and eating an everything bagel. "A couple of interesting things. We've been checking into your son's confession, and it's bogus. I'm sorry it took so long, but since he's—passed on—it wasn't top priority."

"I don't get what you're saying," Landis said.

"Hawkins had an alibi for the evening Ms. Said was killed. We thought his mother was his only alibi, the two of them there at the apartment. Weak. But a messenger brought Mrs. Landis a package in the critical time period. The doorman signed for it and took it up. Your son was there. They talked. She was there too. They weren't down in my precinct shooting people."

Fowler continued to talk, and Landis stopped listening, trying to absorb the significance of Hawk's alibi and the way the detective had tactfully dismissed the possibility Marjorie could have shot Julia.

The alibi was good news, but it destroyed Landis's carefully constructed scenario of how Julia died. True, his rationale for why Hawk killed her—unstable, jealous, vengeful—never made more than superficial sense, and it required relentless mental energy to shore it up into a solid wall of conviction. But now that wall had collapsed, crushing Landis's fragile understanding of his recent tragedies.

He ran a fingernail along a shallow groove in the table's wood grain, making it deeper, trying to assemble these new facts and his scanty psychological insights into a fresh narrative that could explain who Hawk had been.

Fowler added, "You should know, too, that the toxicology tests came back. Your son had a high amount of methylphenidate in his body."

"He had what?" This sounded important. Landis strained to refocus.

"Methylphenidate."

"Never heard of it."

"It's a prescription drug marketed by Orvadis, for one. It treats ADHD."

"How is this relevant? Hawk wasn't on meds."

"Especially at high doses, it can have side effects. Anger, paranoia." A slight pause. "Hallucinations."

Would all this please fucking stop?

"Also, muscle twitches, vomiting?" Fowler asked.

Landis remembered the awkward dinners when Hawk rushed from the table. "Yeah. A time or two. But…"

"We didn't find any in the apartment. Something to keep in mind." Fowler's expression was almost kindly. "It could explain a few things."

Landis breathed through his mouth, deeply. "You mean, like why he came in here that afternoon raging? And why he must have said or done something at the apartment to alarm Marjorie and make her follow him?" He sounded skeptical.

"This will be hard to wrap your mind around. It changes things."

"Meaning?" He was scarring the tabletop.

"You've been able to lay the blame for what happened—to Alia Said, to your wife, even to yourself—at your son's door, on his emotional problems. Now you can't."

Landis crossed his arms and pulled away from the table. "You've gone all pop psychology on me." Without that wall behind which he'd stashed his grief and anger, he'd have to pick them up again. Take possession. He wasn't sure he could.

"I'm serious. Time and again I see people who can't give up their theories about who's to blame for a crime. They hang on for dear life. Now we know Hawk didn't kill Alia, and I doubt he took a shot at you. If he wasn't taking this drug for an attention disorder, why take it at all? We asked ourselves that. That got us thinking. Possibly—probably—he didn't *know* he was taking it. It isn't like the side effects were pleasant."

"And so—?"

"And so, I called your son's doctor. The name you gave me a while ago. He never prescribed it, and he sure couldn't explain why the tox report found it, especially in way over a normally prescribed amount."

"Hawk was mentally unstable, remember? Who knows what he took. Or why."

"You'll want to let go of that."

Landis thought the detective was on the verge of reaching his hand across the table, but he didn't.

"Don't keep making him guilty," Fowler said. "He wasn't."

Confusion and relief warred in Landis's mind, with confusion winning. Facts and combinations of facts spun like a slot machine on overdrive. After a long pause, he said, "Who'd do that? To Hawk? God knows, he was prone to anger. He was erratic. Giving him a big dose of a psychoactive drug was as good as killing him."

"Maybe so."

"What does that make the person who drugged him?

Accessory? Murderer?"

Fowler spread his hands wide, palms up. "We have to find the culprit first. It would be someone who knew Hawk, had access to him over time. One of his friends, a work colleague, a barista at a Starbucks he frequented."

"His friends? His friends taught him to shoot, he said. But that was in Europe."

"Can you give me a list?"

"No idea. They could have been Phi Beta Kappa or graduates of Riker's."

"Then I'll take his cell phone when you can give it to me. Plus his laptop. I'm sorry. Until we found the methylphenidate, we had no idea our investigation would move in this direction."

Maybe Landis's whirling brain had come up three bells. "What do you call that, that grandiose thing? 'Delusions of grandeur.' Is that why Hawk confessed? It was all going on up here." He tapped his temple, and his head filled with a thought that had eluded him while Fowler talked. "But if Hawk didn't shoot at me, who did?"

"That's the million-dollar question. It's another reason I stopped by, to warn you to be careful. It's probably best you do get away a few days, while we keep digging. And one more thing, we've pulled down our tape and given the landlord access to Alia Said's apartment. Maybe now he'll shut up. He wants to repaint and rent it for August."

"What about her things?"

"You want the phony Velázquez? Gennaro's got it in the precinct evidence room."

"No, of course not." A fake artwork? In his apartment? He hesitated. "On second thought, yeah. I'll take it."

Fowler consulted his notebook. "Alia Said's parents will be in the city next Saturday to look the place over and talk to the movers. They may keep her stuff, or it may all go to Goodwill. Gennaro will check with them about the painting. The copy. Whatever. My guess is they'll let you have it. The whole Spanish-identity thing threw them for a loop."

"Can you—" Landis flushed.

"Can I what?"

"Nothing. Tell Gennaro I do want that Velázquez."

Just in time, Landis had stopped himself from asking whether Fowler could get rid of the bloody chaise longue before Julia's parents came. It had been upside down when he went back for the box, and Fowler didn't know he'd been at the apartment right after the murder, had seen the seeping blood and Julia's sightless stare. He'd deal with the building super about that. Fowler left, and Landis considered how the parents' arrival opened an opportunity he hadn't expected to have.

He straightened the papers on his desk while he waited for a phone in Dearborn, Michigan, to be answered. It was a call he knew Julia would be glad he made. And it served his purposes very well.

ഇരു

O'Hanlon volunteered to call the JTTF about the Brussels trip. Landis had other business in Midtown and stopped by the lawyer's office to be on hand. A few minutes early, he sat down to wait and flipped through a magazine. There in full color was a pharmaceutical ad with a familiar slogan that had never before prompted a second thought "Neurostim (Methylphenidate) changes everything." Exactly what Fowler had said. He tossed the magazine onto the table. *Fucking understatement.*

O'Hanlon opened his office door a few minutes later and invited Landis inside. Agent Friend asked for details about where he'd be staying in Brussels and when he'd be back.

This call should not be necessary, Landis fumed, while O'Hanlon provided the information. He wrote down the name and number of the Brussels legal attaché's office—the legat—for Landis to call if his plans changed.

"We'll never know what they're up to, so let it be," O'Hanlon said when he hung up. "Take the number, call them if you need to. At least over there, you're out of harm's way."

Chapter 16

L andis scanned his suite in the Sofitel Brussels, noting its comfortable, contemporary vibe—high-ceilings, large windows, bathroom the size of a Manhattan studio apartment, and ample desk in the living room. *Best of all, no ghosts.*

On his first morning in the city, a Monday, he ate breakfast in a café near the hotel and walked the three blocks to the Schuman roundabout, turning onto the Rue de la Loi to reach the station. As Charleston's schematic indicated, it was conveniently positioned between two of the EU's most important buildings. On the north side of the street and occupying an irregular block, was the X-shaped, glass-walled Berlaymont building, headquarters of the executive staff—some three thousand people. On the south was the Justus Lipsius building, which Landis's cheat sheet told him housed the Council of the European Union. It was another modern structure that, although not as tall as the Berlaymont, included vertical stone elements—granite, Landis observed—that in his view, gave the design an oppressive heaviness. Another thirty-two hundred people or more worked there.

He spent the morning circling the station in ever-wider orbits, absorbing the neighborhood rhythms. He watched where people went. Whether they chose to walk to their offices above ground or to use the underground passageways, a decision that might be made differently in wet weather. He observed how many needed cabs or waited at bus stops, how traffic moved. In the afternoon, he found a seat inside the station and, throughout the evening rush, noted how the station design served its users.

Did commuters choose trains or the Metro? Where did they meet up—was it easy to find a rendezvous spot? Did people in cellphone trance have a place to talk, out of the streams of hurrying people? He watched for confused faces and backtracking, noted where the most popular vendors were placed, and sketched the human traffic flow.

If the thousands of office workers who used Schuman Station knew who he was and the impact his firm's work would have on their daily commute, they might have been more interested in him. When L + P's work was done and a new tunnel under construction was complete, many more people would use that station. Charleston Lee and his team had to get it right.

Fighting the crowds morning and night were a few reverse commuters, the people who lived in the old-fashioned apartment buildings nearby. These included mothers with children and the elderly going shopping or visiting.

He also studied the scene with his firm's new security awareness. Any one of the thousands of people passing through could be a terrorist, or mentally unstable. *Or taking massive amounts of methylphenidate.* That thought flitted like a shadow across his consciousness whenever his mind turned a corner.

Vulnerabilities were easy to spot. A businessman with an unusually large briefcase. A woman's too-innocent-looking shopping bag. *Hellooo, Kitty.* That man, sausage-fat and sweating, with the voluminous untucked shirt. Was something hidden under there? Was that stringy-haired teenager really pregnant?

Not helpful. Wrong questions.

Potential opportunities were everywhere. What Landis + Porter had to consider was whether anything in its design made violent acts more likely, whether its emphasis on openness made it too easy to slip into a tunnel and plant explosives, whether the new glass roof was a tempting target. Or, would the openness of the plan, the daylight everywhere, make a would-be bomber feel exposed? L + P's design must not only make it harder to carry out some deadly purpose; design psychology had to make it *seem* harder too.

He rubbed his neatly barbered beard, a gesture that had become a habit in recent weeks, assessing.

On Tuesday, he reversed his schedule. He camped out at the station in the morning; in the afternoon, he traversed the neighborhood. In the early evening, he finished poring over various reports and analyses, checking their conclusions against his own observations.

Charleston Lee had arranged dinner for him with a key official from Belgium's ministry of transportation and mobility, Jean-Marc Meert, and by dinnertime Tuesday, Landis had a long list of questions for him.

Despite the steady downpour, he walked the few blocks to the restaurant and arrived damp and disordered. Meert arrived shortly thereafter, looking as if he'd come straight from his tailor. Prematurely gray hair, unwrinkled gray suit, pale-gray shirt, and, Landis immediately concluded, gray man, except for the surprisingly incongruous taxi-yellow necktie.

Their small talk was awkward, so as soon as they ordered dinner, Landis began his questions. He asked Meert whether his department had any new thinking about the Schuman site since the proposal stage.

"Charleston Lee thinks the station should try to"—the man struggled for the English word—"*rebalance* attention, space allotted, between the train and Metro—"

Landis broke in. "I know what Charleston thinks. I'm asking what *you* think."

The man played with his silverware, aligning the pieces with military precision. His water and wine glasses were in perfect position as well, while Landis's had broken ranks. He nudged his water glass toward its proper place, listening to Meert's noncommittal answers to question after question.

Landis tossed him a softball. "I suppose Schuman will always be a busy station, located in the European District and so close to the E.U. buildings. With the teardowns, we can enlarge it a bit to accommodate future growth."

Meert's hands trembled as he made another minute adjustment in the placement of the knives and forks.

Landis pretended not to notice. "Do you agree?"

"But of course. The renovated Schuman will most assuredly continue to be an important transportation asset."

That wasn't a response. It might have been, if it had come immediately, but the delay created uncertainty where there shouldn't have been any.

Landis squinted across the table at Meert's closed expression. He wondered whether the man had heard gossip about Marjorie and Hawk's deaths. It was the most significant event in his life, but that didn't mean the news had crossed the Atlantic. Charleston wouldn't have talked about it, he was sure, but if the man had heard somehow, perhaps that accounted for his odd combination of reticence and agitation.

Landis made a benign remark about the trials of air travel, a reliable topic of conversation between strangers. Instead of responding, the Belgian's attention darted around the restaurant.

What the hell. Not trying. At all. No "How was your trip, Mr. Landis?" No "Where are you staying?" No "Is this your first trip to Brussels?"

"Yes, I suppose so," Meert stammered at last.

Conversation stalled. Landis couldn't bring himself to ask whether Meert had a wife and kids. Pets. Too desperate. Anyway, for him, "wife and kids" was dangerous ground for small talk. Occasionally, when his mind relaxed for a few seconds, he forgot. It had done so while Meert delivered one of his formulaic non-answers, and he'd imagined describing this painful encounter to Marjorie. She would have especially enjoyed the egg-yolk tie.

Their dinners arrived. While Landis racked his brain for a way to break the silence, the pool of sauce on his plate acquired a dull sheen of congealing fat. He sighed, picked up his fork, and settled in to eat. When the waiter cleared the plates, the Belgian's side of the tablecloth was pristine, but a rough outline of scattered crumbs revealed where Landis's bread plate had sat, and a drop of wine had traveled down the bowl and stem of his glass and made a short purplish arc on the whiteness. He shuddered.

"Nice meal," Landis said, aware of his grudging tone. "Are you having salad or dessert?"

"Me? No." The man's fingers clutched the edge of the table as if someone might try to jerk the cloth away.

"Me neither." Landis signaled the waiter for the bill. "Haven't adjusted to the time change."

God, that was lame.

The Belgian made a feeble gesture related to paying for his meal, but Landis waved him off. "No, this is on Landis + Porter. Put your wallet away." The perfect smoothness of the man's shirt, the precise knot in the garish tie, the manicured nails, every hair in place. Landis couldn't wait to be free of him. With a guilty start, he realized he'd forgotten the man's name.

They shook hands at the restaurant door, under their black umbrellas, and departed in different directions. Landis took a roundabout way to his hotel, down a narrow one-way street, in order to pass a patisserie he'd found and finish his dinner alone.

At the counter, he ordered expresso and a napoleon and sat at a table near the window. A previous patron had left the *International Herald Tribune.* The rich pastry cream, cool and melting in his mouth, soothed his disordered temper. He sipped the expresso, grateful to be alone, and glanced out the rain-streaked window. Across the street, from between the cars and half in shadow, Moert or Meert or whatever the guy's name was, stared at him.

What the hell.

The man quickly dipped his umbrella. Despite the murky light, there was no mistaking that necktie. Landis shook the newspaper and loaded another forkful, taking his time, as if he'd seen nothing. His eyes were pointed toward the newspaper, but he was no longer reading it. No way could he chalk up Meert's appearance to coincidence. The man had followed him despite the downpour and was waiting to follow him again. If he wanted to tell Landis something, he could have done so over dinner. Or he could cross the street, step into the pastry shop, and talk to him now. Or wait for him at his hotel. Since he hadn't done any of those things, something else was afoot. Landis finished his last few bites.

He'd left his cell phone in the safe in his hotel room, so he couldn't call for help, but whom would he call, anyway? What kind of help? If the man was going to follow him in this downpour, he could damn well stand out there a goddamn long time and get goddamn good and wet. He took his time finishing the coffee and the newspaper.

Chapter 17

Not ten minutes later, from under the patisserie's dripping awning, Landis debated which way to walk. Meert had disappeared, and the mostly residential street appeared deserted. To the left, the block began at a broad avenue, where there was a steady swish of passing cars. The street at the other end was the shortest way back to his hotel, but less traveled. Landis turned toward the busier avenue.

He popped his umbrella open. He'd walked only a few paces when an engine coughed to life behind him. No surprise there. He side-stepped into an unlit apartment building alcove and watched a small car, black or navy blue, pull out of a parking place, its taillights zipping down the one-way street away from him. At the corner was another one-way street, and the car had to turn right.

If the driver circled the block, the car would be back in moments, headed straight toward him. Landis reversed direction, jogging past the pastry shop. When he reached the foot of the block he turned left, where it couldn't follow. The rain came harder now, hammering on his umbrella and obscuring details. Ahead was another sheltering doorway. He ducked into it and watched the corner.

Before long, a small dark car did arrive at the corner and pause. Within a block or two, there must be scores of cars exactly like that, he reassured himself. *Wait and see.* The car waited too. He cautiously peered down the sidewalk, drawing back when the passenger-side door opened. A man jumped out. He glanced up and down the street, then faced Landis's direction.

That awful tie. The universal color for caution. OK, message received.

Meert ducked into the car again, and it drove away. Landis emerged and made a wide circuit that at last brought him to the door of his hotel on Place Jourdan. A long walk usually cleared his head. Not tonight. From outside the hotel, he scanned the lobby. Other than staff, it was empty.

He picked up several messages from the front desk and read them in the elevator. The first was from Charleston, checking to see how the dinner had gone. *Suspicious?* He chided himself. Of everyone he knew, Charleston Lee was the least likely to be involved in anything sinister. The other message was from someone whose name he didn't recognize, Sam Beatty.

He retrieved his cell phone from the safe in his room. As he loosened his tie and unbuttoned his collar, he listened to a message from Deshondra. She'd taken the day off and was at the beach house. Though she said "everything looked OK," her tone suggested otherwise. The service had been to the house and made up the beds—no mice. Then she said she hoped she hadn't exceeded her authority, but was having the locks changed. Everything at the office was fine, fine. Have a good time.

He called immediately. She apologized for worrying him and tried to breeze past any problem, but he persisted. "Changing the locks?"

She took an audible breath. "Somebody broke the lock on the back door and damaged the doorframe."

"Did they trash the place?" His sigh ended with a faint groan. One more catastrophe, even such a minor one, might finish him.

"No. But I had a feeling somebody's been inside, you know? Besides the cleaners? It's weird, but I don't think anything's missing."

He never left much in the cottage to steal. Vandalism, gaping holes in the drywall, clogged plumbing—these were his main concerns. "Let the insurance know. They may pay for some of it."

"I called them already. And the police sent a guy out, but he wasn't too interested? He said it happens a lot. Now I'm waiting for the locksmith."

"You did everything right. Thanks. Are you OK out there?"

"Oh, sure. My roommates are coming out in time for dinner. We'll be fine. Ty came with me earlier."

There's a strapping fellow. He hadn't pictured them as a couple. Probably they weren't. He waited, and she continued, "There was a picture book he saw last summer and wanted to borrow? Something about vernacular architecture."

While Deshondra described the pair of uneventful work days since he'd been gone, he again glanced at the messages the clerk had handed him.

"Is Charleston in the office this afternoon, do you know?"

"He's not here. In New York." She stumbled. "Uh, he's there. In Brussels? You haven't seen him? He flew over last night."

"Oh, I do have a message from him. Sorry." Charleston's message omitted a key detail. Now he was anxious to get off the phone. "Thank you for taking care of everything."

Why would Charleston come to Brussels without telling him? Had he wanted to warn Meert to keep quiet about something? Was that why the man was so nervous? *Stop. Charleston's no schemer. Don't start mistrusting everybody*. Surely that shouldn't be the lesson from his recent tragedies.

Housekeeping had drawn the suite's heavy draperies. He undressed and lay on the bed a long time, his mind in high gear, going over events of the past few weeks. When June began, work preoccupied him, as always, and the affair with Julia filled most other thoughts. Marjorie wasn't approachable—overloaded, he thought—which in a way was a blessing, and Hawk, well, that was a mess. But when it all ended in tragedy three times over, he blamed himself. Somewhere in the tangle of those relationships, he must have missed something. Must *be* missing something.

He was wrong about the ghosts. He'd brought them with him.

Marjorie and Julia, the women he loved. Sometimes, like now, lying uneasy on a hotel bed, their absence felt more tangible than their presence had been. He felt lighter in the bed without Marjorie alongside him, her barely perceptible gravity pulling him toward her. He hadn't had thirty years of nights with Julia. Thirty nights, maybe. Parts of thirty nights. At times the loss of the two of them merged overwhelmingly, smothering him in black grief. Thinking about Hawk's death prompted a different kind of sadness, sealed in its own capsule, an aching, unresolved lump behind his breastbone.

He got up to use the toilet. He could traipse around the inky mudflats of his psyche all night, but regret accomplished nothing. It didn't find Julia's killer, it didn't find who shot at him, it didn't reveal who had given Hawk the drug, the methyl-whatever. It didn't find out *why*. These were his tasks, and he would have to fight his way back to air and light to accomplish them.

Chapter 18

In Wednesday's fragile early morning sunshine, Landis strode toward Schuman Station, stepping around leftover puddles. The menace of the previous night lifted with the steam rising from still-damp streets.

The unfortunate dinner with Meert had lain in his stomach like a paving stone, and the thought of a plate of eggs and sausages repulsed him. A coffee and roll would do it. He stopped at a café across from the station and took a seat by the window to watch how pedestrians approached and departed the station. A previous patron had left the morning paper on the tiny marble-topped table, and, since Landis's French wasn't good, he shoved it aside. A man at the next table asked a question and pointed at the paper. Guessing his meaning, Landis gestured for him to take it.

In a few minutes he finished the roll, and as he rose to leave, the man noisily turned a page. Over his shoulder, Landis saw the dramatic headline *Meurtre!* He didn't need French to guess what that meant, and underneath was a photo of a wide-eyed, dour Meert, with the subhead: *fonctionnaire…Mobilité et Transports.*

"Oh my god!" He leaned in for a closer look. The man turned his head, and their noses nearly collided.

"*Excusez-moi.*" Landis pulled away.

The man rattled the paper, asking if Landis wanted it.

"No, no," he said, backing away. "*Merci.*"

He muttered another apology and dashed across the street to a newspaper kiosk. He fumbled out the coins to buy *La Libre Belgique*. *Why kill someone so bland—so seemingly inconsequential? So...odd?*

He had a French-English dictionary in his hotel room. The first word he looked up was *meurtre*, the word from the headline. Yes, indeed: *murder*. He blazed through the main words in the rest of the story, which as yet held few details.

As he numbly stared at the photograph of Meert, the phone rang. Sam Beatty, who'd left him a message the night before, was on the line. In a faint foreign accent, he said, "Thank you for taking my call. I know you are a busy man. I have something for you and would like to bring it to you at your hotel."

"What is it?"

"I'll explain in person. It relates to the Schuman Station. You'll find it interesting."

"Can't you simply tell me?"

"You need to see it. It won't take long. I can be at the Sofitel in twenty minutes. Your room number?"

This didn't sit right. Landis gave his room number, throwing in an extra digit. "All right. See you soon."

Landis pulled out the sheet O'Hanlon had given him with the name and phone number of the Brussels FBI legat and clipped Beatty's phone message to it. He stuffed them into his jacket pocket, grabbed his passport, room key, and cell phone and hurried to the door of the suite, going back to retrieve his iPad and the newspaper. He dashed to the stairs and made a clattering descent to the ground floor. He ducked into the lobby gift shop where he could watch the hotel entrance from behind a tall display of Belgian chocolates.

At this hour, briefcase-toting guests were mostly leaving for appointments. The few arrivals were families. An overdressed woman entered carrying a fluffy white dog. At exactly ten-thirty, a quartet of men in their thirties strode in. Their jeans and polo shirts revealed time spent at the gym. Despite the casual dress, they looked excessively neat. *Like Meert.*

The way they glanced around, on the lookout, he was sure they were "Beatty." They angled toward the bank of elevators. The fake room number would slow them down, but he didn't have much time. He slipped out a side entrance. There was a line at the taxis, people leaving for the airport, meeting appointments, each person politely waiting to climb into a cab until the one at the head of the line drove away and the next cab pulled up. *Not New York, for damn sure.*

At the head of the line was a French woman with an astonishing amount of luggage, which the bellman and her driver, between them, had difficulty loading to her satisfaction. At last her cab sped off, but two more people dawdled in front of him. The first was a businessman, who'd been amused at the woman's antics. "*Mon dieu!*" He laughed to his driver as he climbed inside. They departed, and the next vehicle crept forward.

Landis had his eyes on the hotel door. Before the elderly gentleman ahead of him could maneuver his cane into the cab, two of the tidy young men burst out of the hotel.

They saw him.

Against protocol, he flung open the door of the second cab and commanded, "American Embassy." In the time it took the startled driver to respond, the two men reached the cab. One grabbed for the door handle. "Now!" Landis shouted, and the driver wheeled around the car in front. The man holding on stumbled, and the door swung open a foot or so. Landis reached over and slammed it shut. He collapsed into the seat. Through the rear window, he saw the two men standing in the hotel apron, hands on hips, watching the cab's escape, while the elderly man's cab had not yet begun to move.

In five minutes, they pulled up in front of the collection of buildings that was a little piece of the U.S.A. in the European capital. The Stars and Stripes snapped in the morning breeze. From the forecourt of the building that housed the FBI legat, he called O'Hanlon.

"D'you know what time it is, man?" O'Hanlon asked. By the time Landis explained his situation, the lawyer was fully awake. "Jesus Christ, I can't let you out of my sight a bleedin' minute. Should I send Carlos over?"

"Not necessary. I hope. Do you remember which FBI agent you talked to before I came? In case I need to establish my *bona fides*? Was it Friend?"

"Yeh. Roger Friend."

"OK. Thanks. I'll let you know how this goes."

"You know, I can talk to one of my partners on the criminal side, whenever you give the word. The firm has a few lads with international connections too. In case we need them." O'Hanlon paused.

"Criminal? God, I hope not."

"You said murder, or am I fogged?"

"Right. Yes, looks like it."

O'Hanlon swore. "Arch, really, how are you doing over there? You sound knackered."

Landis snorted. He was sure O'Hanlon could hear the worry roughening his voice. "Same as at home. One foot in front of the other. All I can do."

"Mind you don't step in something."

⁊⁊⁊

Roger Friend's name proved the key to getting past the legat's security desk. The Brussels FBI agent, who introduced himself as Lepore, listened to Landis's tale of the dinner and skimmed the newspaper story laid in front of him.

"You don't know where he was going after he left you?"

"He didn't say, though I know where he went. He followed me."

"Why?"

"No idea. But he was standing in the rain outside the pastry shop, and I saw him again in the street when I started back to the hotel."

"Time?"

"Nine-thirty, a few minutes after."

Lepore bent over his desk and reread part of the newspaper account.

Landis continued, "So, I'll give this information to the Brussels police, but I thought I'd talk to you first."

"Why?"

"Something's off here. First, he followed me, then when I got to the hotel, I had some messages"—Landis pulled them out of his pocket—"including one from a stranger named Sam Beatty."

He recounted how Beatty was insistent on coming to the hotel and how he knew where Landis was staying before he'd told him. Lepore stared at Landis throughout his recitation, eyebrows raised, looking unconvinced.

"Can you describe the four men?"

Landis did.

Lepore tapped his pen, but hadn't written anything. "May I see that?" He held his hand out for the message slip, and Landis pushed it across the desk, attached to the sheet with the FBI contact information. "Why do you have this?" Lepore asked, tapping the sheet.

"Unrelated. I think."

"Let me decide."

Landis summed up the JTTF interest in the death of one of his associates and their pursuit of a possible terrorism link. "As far as I know, they haven't found anything," he said. He gave Roger Friend's name and ended with "NYPD is in charge of the murder investigation."

"The Brussels police don't need to know all this." Lepore clasped his hands in front of him. "Not yet. Remind me why you're in Brussels."

Landis pulled out a business card and laid it on the desk. "I'm an architect. My firm is redesigning the Schuman train and Metro station. My associate who died, Julia Fernández—that is, Alia Said—worked a bit on that project."

"When are you going back to New York?"

"Tomorrow."

"Change hotels. The Hotel Alexandre is close to the station. Though you might be more inconspicuous at the Holiday Inn."

"I'll do that."

Lepore picked up the phone and dialed an extension. "Jeff, who was that Brussels detective you worked with a few months back? You have his number?" He wrote on the back of a business card. "Euro district, right?…Thanks."

He handed the card to Landis, saying, "Get in touch with this police detective. He works the European Zone. If you run into any problems, which I doubt you will, call me."

Landis could imagine a lot of problems. Plus a lot of questions he wouldn't be able to answer. He shook hands with Lepore and left. Out on the street, it struck him that the agent hadn't agreed to do anything.

"It's a mystery whether he'll follow up," he complained to O'Hanlon. "Detective Fowler at least hinted where the investigation was going. And at least I knew there *was* one."

"Bloody FBI," O'Hanlon said. "Close to the chest, man. If they tell you anything, you can believe there's a reason. One you might not like. So, Arch, change hotels."

൚൚

The Belgian police detective whom he next told his story repeated that advice. Landis decided to take it, because when he returned to his suite at the Sofitel, he couldn't help wondering whether someone had been there. *Like Deshondra felt at the beach house.*

Were his belongings slightly out of place? Hadn't he left his briefcase open? Had someone rearranged his pens? Frustrated, he couldn't remember how he'd left things. The bed was unmade, so housekeeping hadn't done the shifting, if there was any. Nothing was missing. Was something added? Some kind of listening device? A tracker? People were following him all over the city. He didn't know who or why, but whoever they were, they might try technology to make their job easier. He'd have to make it harder.

Yawning and stretching in front of the window like someone about to take an early afternoon nap, he closed the draperies. He turned up the television volume to cover incidental noise and lifted his suitcase from the closet. He examined all the pockets and sides for anything small and hard that might be a listening device or a GPS tracker.

He gave equal attention to his clothing, pinching the seams and waistbands, the cuffs of his trousers, making sure the buttons of his shirts all matched. *What movie was that in again?* He managed to chuckle at his ridiculous melding of Hollywood tradecraft and desperate common sense.

He gave his briefcase the same careful examination. Its lining and strap were smooth, no lumps, nothing but papers in the pockets. The fake hilarity of a game show masked the rattle of his pencils when he zipped them into their case. He unscrewed the barrel of his fountain pen and examined it with the LED flashlight on his key chain. Empty. A hotel ballpoint was mixed in with his stuff. He left it on the table.

In the bathroom, he squinted at his toiletries. Was a bug small enough to be shoved into a tube of toothpaste? Dropped into a white plastic bottle of shampoo? Would the thing work, surrounded by goo? Nothing in the bathroom was irreplaceable. He left it all.

He zipped the suitcase closed so slowly it was noiseless and carried it to the door. The television audience laughed uproariously, and he added a radio discussion program to the mix. Low voices. Confusion. *But is anyone listening?* He waited for the commercials, and when their music blared, he eased open the door and stepped into the hall. He hung the "do not disturb" sign on the handle to keep the maid out for a while at least and quietly closed the door. Then he set down the suitcase with its squeaking wheel and rolled it to the elevator.

Chapter 19

The anonymity the Holiday Inn offered made up for its considerably reduced quantum of cool. The lobby, white as the bare bones it was, contained a sundries shop that supplied Landis with a toothbrush, toothpaste, and other basics. Once in his room—a "spare room" in every sense—he reported his changed location to the police detective, as requested, and called O'Hanlon with his new location.

"Classy," O'Hanlon said.

"Yeah, well." Landis glanced out the window at the blank wall opposite and the narrow alley that led to the forecourt of Schuman Station. "Oddly, I'm more comfortable being closer to the station, after all the time I've spent there."

"Home away from home? Pitiful, that."

"You said it."

"I hope you're not thinking it offers an escape?" O'Hanlon went on. "Arch, whoever might be interested in you knows the area better than you do, not denying your massive powers of observation."

"*If* anyone is."

"How long d'you need to stay? Remind me why you can't do a legger right now? Airport's, what? Twenty minutes away?"

"Not far, but nasty traffic. As it happens, the Schuman

project will fix that. So, my plan was to check in with a few people, show the flag, see how other parts of the project are progressing, muddle all the acronyms, and fly home tomorrow afternoon. Now, though…"

"Now?"

"It bothers me that Charleston arrived unannounced. Why hasn't he called again?" Passing his free hand over the rough bedspread, Landis found a spot that once upon a time had been something sticky. He rubbed his fingers together and frowned.

"Why aren't you calling him?"

"Good question. Call it instinct. His visit makes me uneasy. Like I'm not supposed to know he's here. And I wouldn't have, if I hadn't talked to Deshondra. Why *is* he here? Who's he meeting? The same people I plan to see? Christ's sake, we have to at least *look* like we have our act together."

"And do you?"

"I wonder if—"

A sharp knock startled him. Every muscle in his body tightened, and through gritted teeth, he told O'Hanlon, "Hold on."

When had he become so cautious? He was used to striding across a room, master of any situation. Now he approached the door timidly and to the side, conscious of how flimsy it was—barely a barrier at all—and listened for voices in the hall. Before, he never bothered with the peephole, but now he did. It gave a clear view of the man wearing a sport coat and open-necked shirt leaning against the opposite wall. The livid birthmark on the right side of his face, like someone had drawn the outline of a rose and filled it in with purple crayon, was unmistakable.

Landis let the man in, excused himself, and said to O'Hanlon, "The Brussels detective I spoke with is here."

"Right. Keep in touch. Remember, I've got help if you

need it." O'Hanlon sounded very far away.

"Not necessary. Not yet. But thanks." Landis ended the call and gestured for the detective—de Smet, Landis remembered—to take the room's only chair, a skimpy wood one he pulled out from the desk, leaving Landis to perch on the bed again. The room was small, and with the two of them, it shrank further.

Earlier, at the police station, de Smet listened carefully to Landis's story, making numerous notes. He didn't have Fowler's easy openness, but he was polite, concerned, and brought Landis a much-needed mug of coffee.

"I apologize for disturbing your call."

Landis waved a hand. De Smet's stilted English was slow, but it was miles ahead of Landis's French.

"I see you did change the hotel, as I recommended."

You and the FBI and O'Hanlon. International consensus. "Good advice." Landis's eyes were repeatedly drawn to the port-wine mark on de Smet's cheek, and, embarrassed, his glance flicked around, trying to find other places to land.

"Since we spoke I have talked with the detective investigating Jean-Marc Meert's death." De Smet tapped the back of his head. "A heavy blow. Our newspaper was hasty calling it murder. Yes, he had a fatal blow to the head. Yes, someone put his body in a bin behind Schuman Station. It might be murder, but we will not be sure until we learn how he was injured and why his body was put there. His death arrived at our attention quickly because a, um, *clochard*— a homeless person—was doing the bins for food. He told one of our officers inside the station. The body was completely clothed, except it had no shoes. The officer reports the shoes of the homeless man, however, were in excellent condition." The corners of de Smet's mouth quivered.

What about that unholy yellow tie? Landis studied his own expensive shoes.

"The wallet was present, with the identification, but empty of cash and credit cards."

"You're sure it was Meert?"

"His, um, 'partner,' you Americans say, identified the body."

"Can you tell me if you have any theories?"

"I might, but we don't. The detectives have talked to the…partner, but nothing appeared, as to motive. Today they go to Meert's place of work. In a day or two, information may emerge from our laboratory."

Nada. Running on empty.

"While we are waiting for that, I have a few points to ask of you," de Smet said.

"Of course."

"Again tell me why you came to me?"

Landis repeated that the FBI had given him de Smet's name.

"So you visited your FBI before coming to the Belgian police? Can you remind me why?"

"As I mentioned, I was worried because the man—Meert—followed me the night before. When I found out he was murdered, I didn't know what to think. Possibly, I was—am—in danger too. Then the strange phone call and the men at the hotel."

De Smet asked him to repeat that information. Then he sat thinking about all this long enough to make Landis wonder what was on his mind. Something. "But why Meert?" the detective finally asked.

"Beats me." *Ouch.* "I mean, I don't know."

"The driver of the dark car, you did not see that one?"

"No. It was late and raining hard." Bucketing, O'Hanlon would have said. He wished O'Hanlon were there right now, to help him deal with this man. This marked man. *Or am I the marked one?*

"Number plate?"

"Not that either." Landis shifted on the bed.

"We will talk to the hotel again about the four men," de Smet sounded doubtful. "Unless you can tell me more than you have already."

"I haven't thought of anything else. I saw them for only a minute or two. The bellman helping with the cabs saw at least two of them."

De Smet reached into a pocket and pulled out the business card Landis had given him. "I reviewed the website of your company, Landis plus Porter. Very impressive."

Landis's eyes narrowed. This conversation was headed somewhere.

"You and your firm have appeared many times in the newspapers lately. Violent deaths seem to seek you out."

Landis hesitated before saying, "I'm under no restraint from the police."

"Yes, you *are* free to travel…" He let the sentence dangle, as if he were about to add "for the moment," then said, "yet these cases remain under investigation, if I am correct."

"Yes. In part." Landis picked at the crease in his trousers as he crossed his legs, trying to hide his growing discomfort.

"To me, this is all very curious. You come to Brussels and again within a short time, someone—a public official with whom you have dined—is dead. Very strange."

Landis needed a drink of water. Whiskey would be better.

"How long are you stopping in Brussels?" de Smet asked.

"I plan to fly back to New York tomorrow."

"Speak to me before you go, please. New questions may grow."

"I will." Landis cleared his throat.

"You'll call me if you see any of those men again, the

ones from the hotel? Or if you feel unsafe for any reason? Call me, not my friends at the FBI."

"Count on it."

From the doorway, de Smet said, "Detective Fowler of the NYPD said you have cooperated with him. For the most part. I hope you will do the same with me."

"You talked to Ed Fowler?"

"But of course."

"How'd you get his name?"

"Your American newspapers cover the crimes very thoroughly," he held Landis's gaze, "as to details."

Chapter 20

Landis's cell phone rang a few minutes after three, Brussels time. Deshondra checking in. He had to be grateful someone cared enough to keep tabs on him. He wouldn't want that job. "How was your day at the beach?" he asked.

"Awesome. The beach was perfect. We had a great dinner too."

"Everything under control out there?"

"Absolutely. I left keys to the new locks on your desk."

"Thanks. I'm glad you enjoyed it. Have you heard from Charleston? I haven't talked to him yet."

"That's weird? Oh, wait. Here he is, coming in the door." She sounded as surprised as Landis was, and he heard her say, "It's the boss."

Landis wrote Lee's name, the date and the time, on the quadrille pad in front of him.

"Hello?" Charleston's voice was tentative.

"Charleston! Where have you been? I thought you were here in Brussels."

"I'm here, sir."

I got that. "Deshondra said you flew over Monday night."

"She did?"

"Have I got that wrong?"

"Well," he stumbled, "I did come over, thinking we

could hook up for some of the meetings. But, on the flight, I had second thoughts. I should have checked with you first. Then, when I couldn't reach you by phone, I decided the trip was a mistake and I flew back to New York this morning. I wanted to be helpful, but..."

What's he hiding? "It isn't like you to be so impulsive." Landis let him off the hook. "Some kind of mix-up." *An expensive one.* He'd get the story from Deshondra later. Come to think of it, she hadn't wasted any time letting him know Charleston had done something suspicious. *Forget it, your paranoia is showing.*

Landis continued. "You know your man Meert—you arranged our dinner?"

"Jean-Marc? Sure."

"He's dead. The newspaper says he was murdered late Tuesday night."

"Murdered?"

"He was very odd at dinner. I couldn't pry any information out of him. Afterwards, he..." Landis stopped.

"Murdered?"

"I'm told somebody split his skull open."

Charleston seemed to have difficulty focusing. If the news hadn't shocked him, he was giving a good impression it had. He made a few rambling comments about Meert, and Landis cut him off. "We'll have to see what the police here come up with." He went over the names of the people he still planned to see, courtesy calls, and asked Charleston to give them a heads up. "You OK to do that?"

"Yes, sir."

"You'll run the staff meeting today? I'll be in the office Friday. If anyone needs to reach me before then, have them call my cell, not the Sofitel."

"Yes, sir. Will do."

"Put Deshondra on, please."

Over the phone he couldn't see the two of them, their

body language. So he didn't probe. The tarnished trust in everyone, his closest colleagues included, pained him. He questioned motives and actions that in the past would barely have registered, made worse by the curtain of grief that fuzzed his thoughts. He regretted this, but not as much as he regretted how oblivious he'd been, which had left him and the people around him so vulnerable. O'Hanlon's word.

To end the conversation on a positive note, he said to Deshondra, "Getting good picnic ideas from your colleagues?"

"Mojitos are definitely in. No pies this year. Too messy. Salt caramel brownies instead? Charleston's idea. Doug's bringing a volleyball net? Arch, I called the Sofitel first, before I got you on your cell. Why'd you change hotels? Where are you?"

"See you Friday." Innocent questions, probably.

ఇఞఇ

The rest of Landis's Brussels meetings went well. He and the Belgian engineers walked the future job site and studied it from every angle. The express rail network's new Schuman-Josaphat tunnel was taking shape underneath the existing auto tunnel, and the project director led him on a tour of the underground work. L + P's plans would complement the ongoing projects nicely.

Mid-day Thursday, he stopped into the police station on Boulevard Clovis and asked for Detective de Smet. The detective led him to chairs in the nearby public waiting area. Landis knew then he had nothing important to discuss or ask.

"I'm going home this afternoon. You have my card if you need to reach me in New York."

"That probably will not be necessary."

Landis interpreted this to mean de Smet had another suspect. *Thank God.*

De Smet asked, "How was the rest of your visit? Tranquil?"

It took Landis a few seconds. "Uneventful. Yes."

"Then *bon voyage!*" The detective held out his hand.

ℰↄℰↄ

For Landis, the flight home closed a chapter. All summer the police and the JTTF had pushed him to stop trusting Julia. In the face of their unrelenting suspicion, as much as he hated to admit it, he did have doubts—especially about whether she might have undermined her principal project, Schuman Station.

He'd never forgive himself for abandoning her body, but this second betrayal—his diminished trust in her—gnawed at his confidence in his own judgment. Now, though, he'd worked it out. Yes, she reinvented her history; yes, she was a Muslim. Neither of those facts were points in her disfavor. They didn't prove a damn thing. He stared out the window at the mesmerizing sameness of ocean and muttered to himself, "Those bastards are completely off-base."

The man next to him shifted in the wide leather seat. "Did you say something?"

"I just solved a crime. In my mind."

The man looked intrigued, raised an eyebrow.

"I know who *didn't* do something. That's important too. To me."

"I hear you. I hate spinning my wheels." Seeing no more information was coming, the man went back to reading the *Times*.

The awful picture in Landis's mind of people fleeing the station in every direction, of mangled train cars and shattered bodies, would be unbearable if a leak from Landis + Porter's office made it possible. Now he'd seen the site for himself, the many schematics of the station footprint, the tunnel, the transit plan. His Brussels connections had pulled up every bit of it on their laptops from public websites. His firm's work would be added to that repository. Unwittingly, the websites proved Julia's innocence. Terrorists didn't need a spy in his office. Whatever information they might want about Schuman Station was already at their fingertips. Enough of it, at any rate.

With its new terrorism team, Landis + Porter was moving well beyond the risk of leaks. His firm would proactively, aggressively design security into its projects. Satisfied his professional house was truly in order, Landis devoted his attention to his personal priorities—discovering who killed Julia and understanding what happened to Hawk and, by extension, Marjorie. O'Hanlon and maybe Fowler would add "staying alive" to that list.

Chapter 21

The JTTF's obsessive secrecy constantly frustrated Landis. To learn anything at all about why Julia and Hawk died, he was relying on Fowler. Back in the office Friday morning, Landis called the detective first thing, scrounging for crumbs from JTTF's table. The man's discouraged sigh whistled into the phone.

"I don't know. They seem to have a theory, but…" Fowler's thought disappeared into a fog of uncertainty. "We've checked out your son's friends, from the phone and email traffic. He knew a lot of people, guys mostly, but wasn't close to any of them, as far as we can tell. I sent the phone and laptop back to your office."

"Come to think of it, I don't remember meeting any of Hawk's friends at the funeral." Naturally, he hadn't been in top form, but he was pretty sure of this.

"I'll see you tomorrow afternoon then."

"Saturday?"

"At Alia Said's apartment. Chang got the OK about the painting, by the way. It's yours."

∽∾∾

Passengers from a dozen flights, including one from De-troit, jammed LaGuardia's hallways and funneled out of the secured area. Landis waited a few feet beyond the last TSA post, holding a sign it turned out he didn't need. He hadn't known quite what to expect, but he identified Julia's parents at once. The mother was the model for her daughter, thirty years on, except she wore her hair short, keeping it out of her face with dark glasses pushed to the top of her head. The father had Julia's efficient assurance, guiding his wife through the crowd. They wore Western dress, and Landis was embarrassed that he was relieved about that.

When he'd telephoned them and offered his assistance on this difficult visit, her father at first declined, but as the conversation proceeded, he agreed to Landis's help and now seemed grateful to have it. Landis guided them through baggage claim, taking the mother's roller bag, and to a hired car waiting by the curb. He directed the driver to one of the more restrained new hotels south of Midtown, a short distance from their daughter's apartment.

Working all Friday afternoon and well past midnight, Landis had used his position as the Saids' unofficial escort to gain access to the apartment to "organize things" for them. Really, to spend a few last hours there, alone, taking the place apart, book by book and cushion by cushion, searching for any kind of overlooked clue as to what happened to their daughter.

With the added efficiency achieved by cash changing hands, the building superintendent helped him move the damaged chaise and blood-stained rug to the alley. Landis kept the windows open while he worked, and the last of the terrible smell dissipated. The rearranged furniture now looked more like an antiques showroom than the home where their daughter had built an unknown, unknowable life. He hoped that would make their visit easier. He took down the large portraits, and stacked them facing a wall. She'd told him they were her ancestors, but they probably weren't, and they might upset her parents. It was busywork, but there was enough of it to keep him on task.

Although he was looking for clues to her death, he also wished he'd find insights into her life. Why had she taken on a false identity? Faked the letter from his friend? What was the point? It had to be more than getting the job; she had good training, a good eye, charm. She could have landed a job without any—he reached for the right word—*deception.*

He pored over her papers, shook out her books, and tipped all the upholstered furniture to probe the black muslin linings underneath. He checked the undersides of drawers, felt the hems of the draperies, and rolled up the rugs to study the floors.

Wrangling the furniture into rows and stacking the artworks erased a little of Julia's strong presence. Not entirely, though. When he opened a dresser drawer and found her paprika-red hair clip, he broke down. And when the ghost of her Spanish perfume floated out of the bedroom closet, he fled the room until he could steady himself.

He'd rebuffed Deshondra's insistent offer of help. But she had sent over a few flat-pack boxes for Julia's parents to use and offered to make arrangements with a moving company for the big pieces and a charity shop for any leftovers. In this manner, the carefully chosen furniture and ornaments that defined a particular life would scatter. Landis packed a large shoebox with a few things he couldn't part with, including the hair clip. Her parents wouldn't miss them and never needed to know they existed. Arriving home in the early hours of the morning, he put that box at the top of his bedroom closet for safekeeping.

Walking with them from the hotel to their daughter's apartment on Saturday, Landis described the neighborhood and pointed out L + P's office building. Without directly saying so, he was showing them Alia had made good choices—a modest effort to make them feel better about the choices they couldn't understand. All the while, Dr. and Mrs. Said held their words to themselves. Landis sensed the mother was choking on everything she couldn't bring herself to say. In their company, he thought of Julia as Alia for the first time, and the shift unnerved him.

They declined the apartment building's elevator and climbed the one flight of stairs. The building super followed, chattering as they approached the apartment door. He brushed past to open the door and made helpful sounds as he jiggled the key. All this officious commotion was unnecessary, as Landis had a key, but the super may have hoped there'd be a tip in it.

"Here we are," he said. He glanced over his shoulder, taking in the Saids' brokenhearted expressions. Any intention he had of assisting them evaporated. He flung the door wide and fled down the hall.

Landis walked ahead and pressed the light switch. Although the drapes were open, trees shaded the windows. It did look like a furniture showroom. He'd been successful in that, but not in staving off their grief.

Alia's mother gazed empty-eyed at the furniture, the framed art stacked against the crimson walls, the matador suit in its case, the "family treasures" gathered onto tables.

"I don't understand," she whispered. She was talking about the apartment, yet she meant so much more. "They told us she used another name, a Spanish name. But all this?"

"No one understands," Landis said. The apartment was oppressive, not only from the July heat. "I'll turn on the air-conditioning."

They meandered about the room, unsure what to do next. Landis said, "Detective Fowler is coming later today to meet you in person. Probably not with any new information."

"The only news—" Alia's father halted to clear his

throat. "What we want him to tell us is that this is all a mistake. That our beautiful daughter is alive and coming home to us. This—" he waved his arm to take in the apartment—"this *stuff*, we don't care about. We don't care who killed her. I hope never to see the face of the man who took her from us." He sank to a velvet-covered chaise.

"Why, though? Don't you care *why* she was—?" Landis asked.

"No. Not really." His voice held no spark. "We thought we'd escaped the violence," he said. "My brothers...my wife's fanatical uncle..." His thought trailed off.

From his phone conversations with Dr. Said, Landis knew Alia had two brothers. "What about your sons? Have you thought whether they might—whether there is—" He didn't know how to finish his sentence, either.

"Whether they are in danger? They are not. They have nothing to do with this world."

Landis didn't know which world the man meant. Certainly they weren't involved with Alia's Spanish myth. Beyond that, the father might have meant they inhabited an Islamic world of their own. Or rejected it. Or he could have simply meant New York.

Alia's mother sat at the dining table, head in her hands, weeping. The father gestured for them to leave the room, and Landis walked with him toward the closed bedroom door. Entering Alia's bedroom in her father's company was uncomfortable, and he wished he could have avoided it.

Memories of Julia crowded the room's every corner, and Landis tried to see it through her father's eyes. This brought the sudden, surprising realization that the two of them were about the same age. Landis withdrew several steps in the direction of the door, remembered the weeping woman in the other room, and reversed himself. He avoided Said's eyes and sidled down the wall opposite the window.

"Here's the closet," he said. He raised his hand and let if fall. "A walk-in."

"Are you a father?" Said asked.

"No." That was the easiest answer, though not suffi-cient. "My son died. Three weeks ago. Shortly after..." He pressed his lips tight against the more complete answer: *Shortly after your daughter was murdered, I killed my son. He said he shot her, but he didn't. I'd be lying if I said I was much of a father, as my wife used her dying words to remind me.*

"I am very sorry." Alia's father rested his hand on Lan-dis's arm.

In the living room, Alia's mother dabbed her eyes with a handkerchief. "Let's get it over with," she said to her hus-band.

Going through Alia's belongings took longer than they expected. Numerous times they stopped and puzzled over how a particular thing related to their daughter. Landis found himself recounting Alia's versions of the history of these items, when he could. Although all three of them rec-ognized these stories as fiction, they recreated an imagina-tion, a life. If Landis's familiarity with Alia's stories struck them as strange, they didn't say so. After a point they seemed grateful to hear them.

Pieces of Alia's stories made sense. "That's what your Uncle Fouad did with his trunks!" her mother said, when Landis showed how Alia had used them as tables. "He trav-eled all over the world." And "Alia loved Spain. We took the family on a tour when she was fifteen, and she went back for a vacation after University."

"Before she moved to New York," her father said.

Alia's father shook his head and went to console his wife, weeping again.

Landis gave them a minute, then, looking around, said, "That's probably when she bought many of these things. It would be hard to find them here."

"I am surprised she used her legacy in this way, to create this world," said her mother.

"Her legacy?" Landis had wondered how Julia afforded the apartment, but had never asked.

"From her grandmothers. It was quite substantial."

"Look at these combs." Her father picked up a shadow box lined with burgundy velvet and showed his wife. "You framed your wedding jewelry like this."

Gradually, Alia's life in New York became less foreign. Despite living a fantasy, the ties to her family persisted and reconnected them to her. Also gradually, Landis fitted the pieces of Julia into the frame of Alia, and the two pictures slid into a single image.

"There's these." Landis laid his hand on top of a stack of spiral-bound sketchbooks. "Sketches. Partly to do with her work at the firm."

He moved aside, keenly watching her mother riffle through the top one. Her sigh contained a gallery of memories. She looked into Landis's face. "Would you like to have these?"

"I would." His eyelids fluttered. "Very much."

"Please. They're yours. Our home is filled with her drawings. From when we knew her."

By the time Detective Fowler arrived, the Saids had decided not to keep any of Alia's foreign objects, her New York clothing, her dishes and flatware. Mrs. Said found a scarf and a few pieces of jewelry she wanted, but she'd tuck these in her suitcase. The boxes Deshondra had sent weren't needed.

Fowler reviewed the case with them. He'd kept the Saids up-to-date on the investigation and, as Landis predicted, offered no new information. Leaning against a wall across the room, staying out of it, he watched and experienced anew the depth of their shared loss. Fowler didn't mention

Alia's presumed relationship with Landis or Hawk's false confession. There was no point.

∞∞∞

Landis left the Saids at their hotel and walked to the office. Though it was early evening on a weekend, Ty Geller was at his workroom table. Soon Landis heard him on the stairway.

"Coming to the picnic tomorrow?" he asked, when Geller appeared in the doorway.

"Wouldn't miss it. I haven't been to the beach all summer."

Odd. "You went out with Deshondra, didn't you?"

"Oh, yeah. I did." Ty stumbled. "That was going on an errand, not 'going to the beach.'" He added, "Our two new hires will be there. They start work next week, and I invited them."

"Good thinking. I'll look forward to seeing them again."

After the younger man left, Landis stopped rearranging his papers to stare at nothing. Geller's explanation for his misstatement made sense. He must have meant no towels, no umbrella, no sunscreen. *No big deal. Maybe.*

Mostly, his thoughts were filled with the Saids, the pain he silently shared with them. Finding out who killed their daughter, his son, was the most important thing in his life now, but he hadn't the vaguest idea how to go about it or what might be required of him. What he did know was the search would be the hardest thing he'd ever done. And he'd be doing it, if he had to, forever.

Chapter 22

Y ou're early," Landis said, when Deshondra and her roommates arrived at the beach house Sunday morning.

"We came to help," said Deshondra, just as her roommate said, "to beat the traffic." With the caterers commandeering the kitchen, once the trio of long-legged young women had fluffed sofa pillows and carried a few more chairs out to the deck, they pulled on swimsuits and wrapped themselves in bright pareos. Hands steadying their floppy hats, they wandered down to the ocean.

From the top of the dunes, Landis watched them slather sunscreen on each other's backs. At moments like this, he missed Marjorie badly. The beach house had been her idea, but they'd shared its many pleasures.

It would be a healing day for his staff. Julia's murder, then the two episodes of violence in their own office, the second so horribly tragic, all flew out of the "stuff you hear about" pigeonhole. Not this summer. Now few associates worked late or came in on weekends. Landis didn't read too much into that. It was summer, after all. A busy fall lay ahead.

By eleven, the other guests were trickling in, and soon children's shrieks filled the air, as the ocean pulled them toward the mild surf. Kids raced their dads to the water, their skinny young legs churning. Pale-skinned mothers followed, city women who worked and spent their days basking in the fluorescent light of law firms and public relations offices. They carried straw bags and beach chairs and arranged themselves sociably under Landis's striped umbrellas. The new staff members, the additions to his security team, joined the volleyball game with laughter, cheers, and wicked serves. Team players.

Counting the Manhattan and Westchester staffs and their families, plus the other people who made it a "corporate family" picnic—like Colm O'Hanlon and his wife and daughters—nearly two hundred people assembled to enjoy this perfect bite of summer's goodness. Terry Porter had the idea for the first annual picnic and would have been in the thick of it.

Landis presided at the deck, ready to greet latecomers. It had been a good idea to go ahead with this event. Minor awkward moments occurred as guests arrived, wives he'd seen most recently at the funerals giving him a quick kiss on the cheek and murmuring how glad they were to see him, "You OK?" The squeeze on the arm, his noncommittal replies.

The caterers had set up coolers filled with ice, sodas, and beer halfway to the beach beyond a scrubby line of bayberry bushes. Deshondra was there now, grabbing a soda. She waved.

"Aren't you coming down?" she hollered.

"Water's too cold for me," he said and saluted her with a longneck. The bottle wasn't his, it was an empty he'd picked up to wave around and appear convivial.

He went into the house, again inspecting the new lock and running his fingers over the repairs to the doorframe. The fresh wood needed a coat of stain, and its pale flash drew his glance every time he went inside. His guests were all down at the water, or so he thought, but voices came from the front porch, and he drifted in that direction.

A woman murmured, "You have to tell him."

"I can't. He won't understand. *You* don't understand," the man said in what sounded like Charleston Lee's drawl.

"Julia told you to do it." She put a bitter emphasis on the name.

"Leave Julia out of it."

"Believe me, I'd like to. You're the one who keeps bringing her up."

"I didn't mention her."

"I know what you're thinking."

Silence, then the man continued. "Please, not now."

What's that all about? One of the caterers called to him from the kitchen. By the time he sorted her out, whoever had been on the porch was gone.

The caterers carried the food out, and the guests swarmed up over the dunes, trailing sand. Towel-wrapped kids with seawater-plastered hair shivered in the shade while moms fixed plates for them. The men parked sweating beers under their arms so they could hold their plates in one hand and use the other to pile up the clam and oyster shells they emptied. They schmoozed each other and the old-timers manning the shucking station, two kinds of clams and three kinds of oysters on mountains of crushed ice.

Landis stepped into the house to grab another bag of ice from the freezer and startled Charleston, alone in the kitchen. "Looks like they've taken everything out," the young man said, reddened, and laughed.

"Looks like it," Landis said, inspecting the empty countertops. *What are you doing here?* He recalled the overheard conversation. "Do you need anything?"

"Oh, no. Just checking to see whether I could help."

"Anything bothering you?"

"No, not at all. It's a great time. The kids are loving it. A great day." Lee paused. "It must be hard for you with, without—"

"Without Marjorie?" Landis hoisted the bag of ice to his shoulder. "Everything is hard without her. She would have loved all this."

He delivered the ice and took up a spot at the deck rail to enjoy the scene. Adults sat at long picnic tables, some perched on the railing, and they jammed the steps to the beach path. Children sat cross-legged on the deck or on towels in the sand. Laughter and conversation crowded the air.

Marjorie knew the kids' names and remembered where the spouses worked. She'd flow through the crowd like water, taking used plates, talking to children, leaving cheerful faces in her wake. In his guests' lingering glances and the thoughtful expressions before they remembered to smile at him, he sensed they missed her too. As if by unspoken agreement, they appeared determined to enjoy the day and each other, for his benefit as well as their own. He stared out to sea, grateful.

O'Hanlon came to stand beside him. "Great craic, Arch," he said, "thanks for inviting us. The wife could hardly drag those girls out of the water."

"I should have been coming out here, not hanging around the apartment all summer. It's really—" A noise erupted behind them, and a boy of about seven vomited on the deck.

Christ. Now what?

"I'll grab the hose. Be cleared up in a right minute," O'Hanlon said loudly, to the people quick-stepping aside. For Landis's ears he added, "The Dad's scarlet," as the boy's father disengaged from a knot of men, muttering apologies.

Landis said something supportive and patted the father reassuringly on the back.

Before O'Hanlon could put the hose away, two more

children were sick. "Power of suggestion," he said, looking around at the hovering crowd. A few adults swayed, hands on stomachs. Within seconds, a woman ran into the big rented restroom, covering her mouth, and another vomited into a bayberry.

"We've got a problem here, man," O'Hanlon said. He glanced warily at the shuckers, idle now.

"My neighbor's a doctor. I'll call him," Landis said, his jaw clenched. He strode into the house.

"My stomach hurts," a child wailed in the sudden silence.

∾∾

Aaron Katz came at once, dressed in flamingo-patterned shorts, pink shirt, and sandals that revealed toes gnarly as twigs. But he carried his doctor's bag. His cheerful, bustling manner reassured the parents, and he enlisted them in spreading dry beach towels on the shady side of the deck, far from the food. He laid the growing number of his patients on them.

"We'll get answers," he announced, holding up a hand. "But we won't get ahead of ourselves."

Landis tried to think what to say to the parents, but the words wouldn't come. O'Hanlon pulled him into action. They brought up a cooler, and, as more people became ill, Katz encouraged them to sip cold water or suck on ice chips. If they felt sick again, they should use the bushes on that side of the house.

"It's our vomitorium," he told Landis gleefully.

While Landis handed out water bottles, Katz shooed unaffected guests away like pigeons, encouraging them to go down to the beach and let the sick ones rest. A half-hour passed with no additions to the improvised sick bay. No one was worse. The tension in the parents' faces eased, slightly, though the young patients continued to groan. Landis sat to the side, watching, hardly blinking, not knowing what to think. The shouts and squeals of happy children down at the beach rebuked him. Somehow, he'd spoiled the day.

"Should we take her home?" the father of one of the sick children asked. His younger son looked up at him, face crumbling.

"You'll be immobilized in traffic," Katz said. "Here we can keep an eye out, make sure the worst is over." He clapped his hand on the man's shoulder. "Take this young man for a swim. Your daughter will be fine."

The caterers backed well away from the display of food, only about half gone. No one else touched it now. The shuckers shuffled uneasily in a puddle of melted ice.

Katz motioned Landis to join him in a far corner of the deck, where they would have some privacy. He pulled his phone out of a pocket and called his wife. "Get Tony Palmieri's home number from my book, Myrna, please?" He punched in a new number, and as he waited, he threw an arm around Landis's shoulder and kept it there. "County epidemiologist," he told Landis, who studied the tracks of drying sand on the deck, the furrow between his eyebrows deepening.

"Tony! Aaron Katz here. How's your holiday?" He listened. "Then I'm sorry to tell you it's about to end. We've got a tricky episode here in my neighborhood. A picnic that ended with nineteen people down—a ten percent case rate. Twelve kids and seven adults. None of them serious enough for the hospital, but a couple of kids are damn green. I've got my eye on them. We're rehydrating." He paused to listen. "A boat? You can send it as a precaution, but right now I don't think we'll need it."

Again he listened. "Right, it could be food borne. They had a caterer in, a raw bar—that's why my people never eat that stuff. Could be a problem in the water, of course. They spent the day in and around the ocean. I don't think so, though, or more would be sick. You people check that all the time, right? That's what we pay you for…I've got them vomiting into the bushes so you'll have something to work with. Oh, and Tony, about the adults? All women, all on the small side."

Katz met Landis's eyes and gave his shoulder a squeeze, saying into the phone, "Got it. Food into refrigeration. Don't clean up the kitchen."

"I think they already have," Landis said.

"Too late, maybe," Katz said into the phone. "But we'll save the trash. When will your boys be out?" A pause. "What about the shuckers?"

He listened to a lengthy response. "One thing, Tony. It doesn't quite look like food poisoning to me. Other than the obvious—headache, vomiting, bloating—the symptoms don't line up. Be sure your guys test for a full range of toxins…Deliberate? How the hell should I know? Tony, thanks."

He ended the call. "You heard all that?" He repeated the epidemiologist's instructions, anyway: "The shuckers can go, but they should hang onto the unopened shellfish until the testing is done. Tomorrow or the next day. Keep it on ice. Don't clean up. Counters, sink, nothing. Get the names of the shuckers and all the catering people who were at the house."

"Will do," Landis said. "But boat?"

"Tony will ask the Marine Bureau to send one. It's the fastest way out of here if one of them takes a turn."

"What did you mean, 'deliberate?' Here?" Landis perched on the deck rail, watched by his guests. "These people count on me. Their kids—"

"Wait for the test results. I'm going back to my patients." Katz's upbeat manner hadn't changed, but his searching black eyes were serious. He removed his arm from Landis's shoulder and bounded across the deck.

O'Hanlon came alongside. "Looks like he has it well in hand."

"Could be." Landis kept his voice low and shoved his hands in his pockets. "He thinks it was deliberate."

"You're slaggin' me, man."

"They'll test for everything."

Chapter 23

In the next twenty-four hours, information dripped out of the health department like a faucet that leaked only when Landis's attention was elsewhere, which was not very often. O'Hanlon stayed with him at the beach house. They ate take-out and stayed out of the way of Tony Palmieri's people. The police dusted for fingerprints.

That's optimistic, Landis thought, observing the sooty residue on the kitchen surfaces, grimy evidence of a fruitless search for clues. Tuesday morning, the cleaning service would be allowed into the house, and the last remnants of the picnic would be gone. But the mental image of wives and children moaning and shivering on the deck was not so easily erased.

A long walk or two or five on the beach might help him wrap his head around what had happened. He was worried about the impact on the firm. The picnic—intended to rally his troops—had turned into a disaster. He'd probably lose people soon. *The looks on the parents' faces.*

O'Hanlon nixed any beach walks, saying they were too dangerous. Landis had to stay put. They both kept an eye on the boat traffic offshore, wondering whether a sniper was out there on the water. One thing Landis did know for certain, being around him put people at risk. Including that oddball Belgian, Meert.

The threats were so varied, so unpredictable. Where

would the next one come from? What form would it take? He couldn't protect the people around him, much less himself.

Despite the holiday, Palmieri made an appointment for Monday afternoon and said he'd bring a detective from the Suffolk County Police Department and an officer from the Marine Bureau, which handled routine police work around the island.

Detective Vincent Tremonti's initial questions reviewed old ground—the beach house break-in, the new locks, visits by Landis and others. The Marine Bureau officer, a woman named Wu, said break-ins of weekend houses were common on the island, though usually televisions and electronics went missing.

"We don't keep anything like that out here," Landis said. "They emptied my liquor cabinet is all. Tequila. Scotch. The good stuff. Some vodka."

Palmieri described his interviews with the shuckers and the catering staff. They'd accounted for every item of food served and every ingredient in it. The seafood tested clean. All the other food came prepared from the caterer's own kitchen, finished on-site with the dressings and condiments they brought with them, with one exception.

The dessert chef finishing the salt caramel-topped brownies wanted to add a last-minute decorative sprinkle, but the salad-maker at the other end of the prep line had the caterers' shaker. So she grabbed the sea salt from Landis's counter, surprised by how fine it was—"more like popcorn salt, really," she complained—before piling the brownies on a tray. When Palmieri examined the leftover food, some brownies were missing.

Dr. Katz's quick queries of the sick guests had also pointed toward the brownies, and detailed interviews regarding what everyone ate and drank revealed they were one of the few foods the victims had consumed that other guests hadn't. The physical reaction was so swift, they became sick before most guests tried the desserts.

The health department's initial tests confirmed Katz's suspicion the cases weren't run-of-the-mill food poisonings. Other brownies from the same batch, set aside for a different party, were fine. Something had contaminated the picnic brownies, and Landis's saltshaker was the likely source.

"You think it was intentional?" Landis asked. "How could anybody endanger children that way? What the hell is wrong with people?" A headache like a heavy cloud pressed on his brain. Why were they serving brownies this year anyway? Deshondra had mentioned them. Hadn't she said they were Charleston's idea? And hadn't he thought, typical Southerner, suggesting something sweet? He'd never completely recovered from his first glass of sweet iced tea. The headache was blasting full-bore now.

Tremonti said, "It could be the kids weren't the target at all. How long has that saltshaker been there?"

"No idea. I don't spend much time in the kitchen." The muscles around Landis's mouth stretched and clenched, unable to settle on a single expression.

"So the break-in, let's go back to that a minute," Wu said. "Maybe it wasn't to take something, but to bring something in. The saltshaker."

He answered more calmly. "Well, if so, it must have happened between the time the cleaning service came in late May to get the place ready for summer—they would have noticed the broken lock—and when I went to Brussels," Landis said. "Because I was over there when Deshondra discovered it. She reported it to the police." He looked to them, as if it was their turn to speak.

"Deshondra is—?"

"My receptionist." Landis gave them his business card and Deshondra's full name. "She and her roommates spent a little time out here after the door was fixed."

"That was when?"

Landis rubbed his beard, concentrating. "Last week."

"When did the cleaning service come?"

"The week before Memorial Day."

"My boys would have taken the report on the break-in," Wu said. That this tiny woman would have "boys"—whom he pictured as strapping police officers—struck Landis as comical, but he was beyond chuckling. "I'll check on it," she said.

"So your receptionist could have left the salt behind, easy," Tremonti said.

"Deshondra? Not a chance. She's—Not a chance."

"Then why didn't she and her friends get sick? Everybody uses salt."

"I don't know." Landis studied his hands, remembering his odd encounter with Charleston Lee in the kitchen and the porch conversation he'd overheard. *Are we all going to be suspects?* He muttered, "At least they can't blame this on Hawk."

Tremonti raised an eyebrow. "Meaning?"

"You talk to Ed Fowler yet?" O'Hanlon asked. "Manhattan South murder squad?"

"No. Should I?"

"He can explain everything," O'Hanlon said.

"Oh, no he can't," Landis said. "Less and less, in fact."

"I'd rather hear it from you," Tremonti said.

Landis's exhalation had a catch in it and O'Hanlon grabbed his shoulder. "Let me," he said. "You chime in."

"Hit the gas," Tremonti said, flipping a page in his notebook.

"This is the third attack on Archer Landis—that we're sure of—this summer. He was shot and wounded in his office in early June, and later that month, his son Hawkins—Hawk—threatened him with a handgun. Unfortunately, a third person surprised Hawk and was shot instead. My client tried to stop him, but—"

"Wait a minute, was this the man and his mother who were killed in Manhattan, a couple weeks back?"

"Yes. Self-defense on Arch's part."

"I remember that." Tremonti's eyes widened. "Ed Fowler worked the case?" He made a note.

"He did. The M.E. says Hawkins had a right massive dose of a paranoia-inducing prescription medication in his system at the time, but nobody knows how he got it."

"Hunh. So what is it you're not 'sure of'?"

"Arch went to Belgium on company business recently, and one night he was stalked by a business acquaintance he met casually. Later that night, the man was murdered."

Landis spoke up. "Then someone I didn't know tried to make an appointment with me at my hotel. I reported this to the Brussels police and the Brussels FBI office."

Tremonti stopped writing. "FBI?"

"Yeah." Landis sounded bitter. "We've got the supposed top minds in law enforcement on this case and they can't put the pieces together. Why are these things happening? Why has my life blown up in my face? My wife, my son? Who's behind it? I'm plenty fed up with it, believe me." Landis pressed his hands together between his knees to stop the shaking. Hearing these recent events laid out, one by one—it was *not* a new normal, it was terrifying.

"There's a drop more to it," O'Hanlon said. "Arch's company, Landis + Porter, had on staff a woman the Joint Terrorism Task Force has been investigating." Tremonti would hear about that angle from Fowler anyway. "As far as we know, they've not found a dog's hair of proof of anything against her."

"She's not talking?" Tremonti asked.

"She's dead. Shot to death June second by person or persons unknown."

Tremonti put down his pen and took a deep breath.

"It's been one helluva month," O'Hanlon said. "The important point is that my client is a grieving husband and father who deserves some peace. He's not a suspect in any of this. Here or in Belgium."

Tremonti picked up his pen, saying, "No doubt you've been asked if you have any enemies, people who would be—"

"Following me all over the world and trying to kill me, murdering my associates, and poisoning my son? Now my guests? No, I don't." The words were strong, but Landis's voice shook. "Yet it's happening."

"So, who do you think is doing all this?"

"I'd feel a lot safer if I knew how to answer that question."

Palmieri, the epidemiologist, pursed his lips. "That's interesting. You said 'poisoning my son.' Criminals who use guns and criminals who use poison are typically very different kinds of people, aren't they, Vince, am I right?"

"Yeah," Tremonti said. "Usually."

"Could this *be* terrorism then?" Palmieri asked.

"Unlikely," said Wu. "Terrorists would have gone for a big media splash. Otherwise, what's the point? This stayed pretty quiet."

"Means to some other end, maybe," Landis said. "What was it? What was in the salt?"

"Could have been a lot of things. The lab's not finished testing," Palmieri said.

"I'll save you some time. Check for a drug called methylphenidate."

❧

On Tuesday, Landis was back in his office, anxious to be a reassuring presence. Remembering Detective

Tremonti's suspicions, he told Deshondra to expect a call about the visits she and her friends made to the beach house.

"Did you eat at the beach house?" he asked, trying to sound off-hand.

"Noooo. We ate out! My roommate even made us eat breakfast at Starbucks, so she could flirt with the barista. Super-cute brother."

"You never cooked?"

"At the beach?" She laughed, handing him a stack of phone messages.

"Right." While they went to restaurants, the poisoned salt waited on the kitchen counter.

But was it waiting for his picnic guests? Or for him?

Chapter 24

U p in his office, Landis resisted the temptation to check whether his desk chair was booby-trapped, to believe every piece of mail might release clouds of ricin or that innocent rolls of blueprints might hide a pipe bomb. He did glance under the chair, but then pushed it toward the table and sat. He sifted through his morning messages until he found one from O'Hanlon's investigator.

He scheduled Carlos for one o'clock and called a staff meeting for ten, at which he was generous in his apologies and encouragement. Although no long-term health damage had been done, he acknowledged the frayed nerves.

"We've been through so much," he said. The pain in his voice revealed how much more he'd been through than anyone else. "We'll get past this. Together."

He told them the epidemiologists had pinpointed the brownies as the source of the problem. Everyone who hadn't eaten them visibly relaxed. He assured them that the public health authorities were analyzing the "problem," he termed it, rather than the more ominous "toxic substance" or even worse, "poison." He didn't mention the police, and he didn't say they—and he—suspected the act was deliberate.

Later, O'Hanlon called to give him a pep talk.

"They trusted me, Colm. How long will it take to get that back?"

"They can't think this was your fault. *You* can't think that."

"I don't think it. I feel it. What did I do or not do that let all this happen? Was it the affair with Julia? Was it not keeping better track of Hawk and his friends? Was it assuming the picnic would be safe? Every person I hire comes trailing histories and a cloud of relationships. Was something there I should have seen?"

"There's a limit to what you're responsible for, Arch."

"Practically speaking, I know that, but in my bones...different story. What did I miss?"

"Carlos will be talking to you about that. Hang in."

ಌಲಌ

Carlos was barely recognizable behind a neat black beard, his muscular body dressed simply—jeans and white dress shirt—with an embroidered *taqiyah* on his head. A man who fit in anywhere in a multicultural society, distinctive only because of the supreme confidence with which he carried himself.

Nicely played.

Deshondra glanced up, saw Landis nod, and told Carlos to go on upstairs, following his departure with interest.

"Impressive," Landis said when Carlos entered the office, gesturing toward his own short beard.

"I stopped shaving after we met last month. Thought the beard might come in handy before all this was over," Carlos said. "Too bad it's summer. Itches like a sonofabitch."

"Tell me about it."

Carlos had spent part of June in Dearborn, Alia Said's home town and home to the Arab American National Museum. He settled into the museum's library, posing as a freelance journalist researching Little Syria, an area of Lower Manhattan that had disappeared some sixty years before. The helpful library staff introduced him to a few people who led him deeper and deeper into Dearborn's Arab American community.

"With those librarians bird-dogging me, I had to write everything up for my supposed editor. I haven't done stuff like that since college. Footnotes, for Christ's sake."

Landis made a commiserating noise. "So? What did you learn?"

"About the Syrians? Plenty." Carlos rubbed his thumb and forefinger over his beard. "Thanks be to Allah, that part was interesting. About Alia Said, also a lot. There's an Arab-English newspaper there, and I found several stories that mentioned her, along with other people from some anti-media demonstrations a few years back."

"O'Hanlon said she'd been involved in something like that."

"I met one of the protesters casually, and through him, a few of the others. They had a lot of passion back then, but as soon as they got jobs, they were out of it. I'm sure they're not terrorists, and they're actually not that religious. We went out drinking a couple of times. Religion never came up."

"That's it?"

"I told them my office in New York is near World Trade, to see their reactions. One said, 'That's fucked up,' and the others agreed. I said, 'What happened makes life difficult for us,' but they think it doesn't affect them out in Michigan as much as it would in New York, right 'where it went down,' one said."

"Poor choice of words."

"They're young guys with good educations, and a couple do have solid jobs. Looking to get married. Buy a new car. Not in that order."

"Sounds like Detroit, all right. They weren't playing you?"

Carlos shook his head. "Not on their guard at all. Through them I met Alia's older brother. He's intense. Working for Ford Motor Company. Focused like a laser on moving up in the engineering department and which projects he should attach himself to so he can get his boss's attention. While we were talking, the younger brother showed up. He isn't serious about anything. He's got his car, his perfect teeth, and from what I could tell, about six girls on a string. He's no revolutionary, either.

"All three of them—Alia too—did get arrested once, in that half-assed demonstration. The police rounded up everybody, it sounds like. The cops threatened them with a night in jail, but their parents sprung them right away, and the charges were dropped. The Saids obviously have plenty of money, but, from what I heard, they're not tight with the community because the wife isn't Lebanese, like the father."

"She isn't?" Alia's mother had looked the part. Dark eyes and hair, olive skin.

"She's Israeli."

"You're kidding."

Carlos shook his head. "It's why they came here. They couldn't live in either country, not comfortably. Another reason the sons aren't militant. They'd have to pick sides."

Landis took a moment, adjusting to this new information, like the click of an optometrist's lens when the writing on the wall snaps into focus. Now if only he could read it. "Wow," he said under his breath.

"I asked them if they had any other brothers and sisters, and the older one said 'no,' and cut his brother a look, so I dropped it. Later, one of the other guys quietly told me they had a sister, but she moved to New York and died 'mysteriously,' he said, and the family wouldn't talk about it. Too upset. I tried to get information about Alia out of him, but he didn't know much. When he knew her, she stuck to her books and her art classes. The arrest at the demonstration was an anomaly."

"About that," Landis thought out loud, "could that be how the FBI got her fingerprints?"

"Possibly. Might be why they had the roundup in the first place, to collect prints. Who knows?"

"Did any of them have suspicions about Alia's death? Or hints about who might have murdered her?"

"That totally isn't their world. They're more like your people"—Carlos glanced at the busy associates working below—"than guys on the fringe of society, who'd have the kinds of connections we're thinking about."

Carlos pulled out his phone. "Oh, and Alia did have a real interest in architecture. Going way back. The museum's resource center had a portfolio of her drawings from high school. Won a prize."

"God, I'd love to see that. She had such an intuitive vision." His words trailed off.

"No problem. I took pictures." Carlos swiped the screen of his phone, found the place he was looking for, and handed the phone to Landis. "Can I get a coffee or something?"

"Deshondra will show you," Landis said, absorbed in the photos.

Carlos withdrew, letting Landis scroll through the pictures in private. They showed precisely rendered cornices and carved stone embellishments, fanciful drawings of building facades, a layout of what Alia had titled "The Perfect Park." He rubbed his forehead, missing her every bit as much as the first day after the murder.

After a while, Carlos came upstairs again, carrying a can of Red Bull. "That Deshondra is a piece of work. Great smile, lots of questions."

"She's a gem." Landis pushed the phone across the table. "So what's your bottom line?"

"If Alia Said was linked to terrorist assassins, she didn't find them in Michigan."

Chapter 25

Here's something to look into." Landis handed Carlos the package from Fowler containing Hawk's laptop and cell phone. "Somebody fed Hawk that drug. NYPD has checked out the people they found on here. I'd like you to do it too."

Carlos set his empty can on the table and took the package. "Let's take a walk." Carlos checked the street before motioning to Landis to join him. The two men turned south onto Broadway, busy with pedestrians.

"You asked me to look into your two lead associates, and I've been working on it."

"I take it you found something."

"Maybe. Charleston Lee is married, wife's pregnant, neighbors don't hear any quarreling. They live in a good building across from Prospect Park—nice enough apartment, but small."

All this Landis knew. "His family has money."

"Had money. They're one of the fine old Southern families who've needed to learn to hustle. Lee's sisters married reasonably well and moved out of town. California and Houston. The parents aren't counting on them. Everything is on Charleston's head."

"You talked to them?"

"Yeah. I flew down to South Carolina and interviewed them. The father's heavy into Confederate history, and I said I was working on a magazine story."

"Looking like that?"

"Without the *taqiyah*, I'm a Civil War reenactor."

Landis's laugh caught the attention of a woman collecting cans. Her arms buried in a trash bag, she glared at them.

"The house was full of ancestors' portraits and antiques, but don't look too close. It'll crumble down around them before long."

"From what you're saying, Charleston has to make good."

"Yeah. He needs money, big time."

"He never let on."

Carlos shrugged. "His parents think he's got it made. They mentioned the Schuman Station project—not by name, but 'a big train station in Europe.' What's interesting is, when Lee was over there last year, apparently he met up with Hawk."

Landis stopped walking. "You're kidding. I never knew that."

"What the dad said was that Charleston met the boss's son and was too smart to let that opportunity go to waste. He winked at me."

Landis chewed on this information. "It must have been when we first got the commission. Hawk was still in Europe then. Neither of them mentioned it."

"Then that other thing, the lightning Brussels trip. I watched the security camera DVD several times, and I didn't see any suspicious looks pass between him and Deshondra. Granted, his behavior was odd, evasive. I'd have to show my hand to dig deeper."

"Let it go then." Landis tried to imagine Charleston and Hawk together. Friends? Had Lee been positioning himself in case Hawk took over the firm someday? Maybe much sooner than expected, if he were out of the way? He couldn't believe that.

They stepped into a coffee shop, ordered tuna sandwiches, and took seats in a back booth, Carlos facing the door.

"So, the other one," Carlos said. "Ty Geller."

"Well, Ty. *He's* ambitious."

"They're both ambitious. Geller doesn't hide it," Carlos said. "From all I can pick up, he's very proud of working for L + P, very excited about his new assignment—but vague about the particulars. He's running the security design team, right?"

"Yeah."

"Well, then, vagueness is good."

The counterman appeared with the sandwiches and refilled their coffee cups. When he left, Carlos continued. "Not much family—an aunt upstate. No close friends. Not in touch with the people he went to school with. Granted, most of them settled in Michigan, but a few are here in New York. They never hear from him. No girlfriend. Boyfriend, either, for that matter."

"So how does he fill his free time?"

"He goes to the gym several nights a week. Occasionally to a bar afterwards. On weekends—in summer, anyway—he has a boat down in Jersey he takes out into Raritan Bay. Cleaning the boat up, maintaining it. That's the weekend. People where he moors it say he's not very social."

"I'd forgotten about the boat."

"A boat is a demanding mistress."

"Hmm." Landis watched the steam rising off his cup.

"He has debts. Long-term school loans, the boat. He lives—as you probably know—on Twenty-Third near Ninth. Also small, but what isn't?"

Landis set the sandwich down. "The Michigan connection. Anything to that?"

"Geller's from the western part of the state. On Lake

Michigan. Detroit and Dearborn are east. Out where he's from, people orient to Chicago. He *could* have met Alia's older brother in Ann Arbor, because they overlapped a semester, but I doubt it. There's 40,000 students there. I got in touch with a couple of his former classmates, and they say he spent his time in the computer lab and schmoozing the faculty."

"Did they like him? Was he popular?"

"I'd have to say no, though they certainly remember him." Carlos drank some coffee. "You told me that when he came to New York he worked for Fanning Lord Andreessen for a year? I looked into it, and he left bad blood there. No one's talking. Smells to me like lawyers.

"To sum up, he's out there, floating free, Arch. He puts up a good front, but he has no safety net at all."

While Landis pondered this, Carlos hit him again.

"And Deshondra, your other most-trusted?"

Landis listened reluctantly, eyes closed, shaking his head. Surely she was the one completely reliable person in the mix.

"Possible problems there," Carlos said. "You knew she was abandoned? Lived in foster homes? Not all of them what you'd call supportive. Or safe."

"You're kidding."

"L + P's probably the most stable situation she's ever been in. That's a lot of baggage, and her past may try to sneak up on her."

"But…she's so…normal. She has lots of friends, a couple of sisters."

"Those aren't biological sisters."

"She's a rock, Carlos."

"Is she past all that? I hope so. She seems like a straight arrow, I give you that. And her roommates are all clean. Or is she a superb actress?" Carlos checked his phone. "I've gotta run. Before I go, I'm sending an address to your phone. You'll want to check it out."

Chapter 26

The address Carlos texted wasn't far, and Landis was curious. Here he'd thought they were aimlessly wandering the streets of lower Manhattan, while Carlos must have been guiding them toward this destination all along.

The risk of walking alone through the city streets flitted through his mind, but he took a good look around, saw no one paying any attention to him. Nobody would be lying in wait for him here, so far outside his usual precincts. Nothing to worry about.

The disturbing information from Carlos, however, did demand attention. The people his work relied on most— Charleston, Ty, Deshondra, and before that, Julia—had their own problems, which he'd stayed blithely unaware of, as long as he could get what L + P needed—what *he* needed—from them. What kind of friend and mentor was he, who ignored such important dimensions of their lives? They weren't robot brains attached to flesh and bones.

He found the address: "Connoisseur's Games and Puzzles," with a neatly hand-lettered sign stuck in the lower corner of the window reading "Puzzle Boxes from Around the World." The shop was dimly lit and dusty. Its labyrinthine layout was a puzzle in itself.

He walked past vintage chess sets whose pawns had been inched forward, customers' tentative opening moves, perhaps. Beyond a display of wooden board games and old jigsaw puzzles hung a sign like the one in the window.

The glass case held boxes of many types: roughly carved wooden boxes from Romania, meticulously decorated Japanese boxes, and, on the middle shelf, a few Moroccan boxes with the same Moorish-style mosaics as Julia's. The shopkeeper approached, explaining as he came near that the Japanese boxes were the trickiest. To open the most complicated ones required more than a hundred moves. Landis's heart sank.

"I'm interested in these Moroccan ones."

"Beautiful, but not so devilish."

"I have one similar to that"—he pointed to a box in the rear of the case, wishing he actually *did* still have it—"and I don't know how to open it." He showed the man the photo he'd taken that terrible day, the box sitting on his table, before he wrapped it.

"Similar, yes. I can show you." When he lifted the box, underneath was a folded piece of paper with the instructions diagrammed.

"I understand your method," Landis said.

"Foolproof," the man said, "unless I mix them up. Most of these Moroccan boxes use similar tricks." He moved a side panel that enabled another panel to move, and soon—after about a dozen steps—the top slid off, revealing a small compartment.

"Looks easy when you know what you're doing," Landis said. "Could you open that other one?"

After the man opened several of the Moroccan boxes, Landis had the general idea. "I'll take that one," he said, pointing to the one that looked most like Julia's. "The instructions come with it, right?"

The man laughed. "I could put them inside for you..."

Landis left the shop, pleased, but to open Julia's box, he'd have to find it. He saw it as in the photograph, sitting on a large sheet of paper, waiting to be wrapped. Then swaddled and taped. Then on Deshondra's desk. Then gone. But if it ever came back to him…

∞∞∞

That evening, Landis and his buddy Irv Davidoff were tucking into another deli dinner—three-decker sandwiches and cream sodas. Staying close to Irv and Phil and Theo and Colm had been his only rudder in the last month, and Landis appreciated these friends afresh. They were different from him. Not because they had their families, but because they weren't betrayers. They had their integrity, their souls intact. He tried to remember what that felt like.

"You're quiet this evening," Landis said.

"OK, I confess. I'm watching the Yankees over your shoulder. I had tickets for tonight's game."

"Oh, hey. You shouldn't have given that up."

"You kidding? There I'm one of ten thousand fans. With you, it's one-on-one. Anyway they're losing."

"Who're they playing?" Arch craned around to look at the screen.

"Seattle, for chrissakes. Glad I'm here. Better for my blood pressure." Davidoff signaled the counterman for another soda. "I've been deciding whether to tell you something, and I've decided I will."

"I won't like it."

"You won't."

Landis waited, in no hurry to hear bad news.

"Word on the street is, well, not *on* the street, under the street, under the subway system, so fucking under it's halfway to China. But word is, your big Dubai project—"

"Burj Maktoum?"

"Yep. The competitive bidding process was a sham. The whole thing was wired. BLK got it through some *goniff* kickback scheme. Can't prove it, though, of course."

Landis closed his eyes. L + P needed that job. Needed it for staff morale, needed it to test the security team, needed it to become winners again. The money was the least of it. It would have made several careers. The furrows between his eyebrows were like chasms.

"Goddammit," Landis said. "I can't turn around these days without running into that guy."

"Word is," Davidoff cleared his throat, "to put it bluntly, Arch, he sees blood in the water and wants to move in for the kill."

Irv always took the high road. Coming from him, this warning was much more than idle gossip.

Landis blew out a lungful of air. "It's possible he will lure away some good people too. They loved that project. They really looked forward to working on it—had some great ideas—god*dammit*!"

"The leaders in Dubai aren't fools. If they see Karsch is in over his head, L + P may yet end up with it. A little baksheesh doesn't trouble them, but we know Karsch cuts corners—don't object, Arch, you know he does—and nobody will tolerate a hundred and fifty stories crashing to the sidewalk."

"There's laws against littering."

"Maybe somebody should remind him of that." Davidoff slapped Landis on the back. "He has some talented people. They might pull it off. Though I'm told he got off on the wrong foot. The client doesn't like him."

"They've got plenty of company."

"I suspect this story isn't over yet." Davidoff signaled the bow-tied waiter to bring the check. "On me, bud."

୧∽୧

In Hawk's room was an unopened carton of his

belongings, sent over by BLK. Landis hadn't had the heart to open it. But when he set the new puzzle box in the circle of light from his desk lamp, he had a sudden thought. Since his son apparently was the fake messenger who took Julia's box, maybe it was in that carton.

Maybe I've had it all along.

The carton sat in the middle of the floor like an accusation. He sliced open the tape and found Julia's box right on top—its white paper wrapping gleaming. It seemed like a hundred years ago, he'd written in bold black letters "For Pickup." He folded the carton shut, grateful he didn't have to rummage any deeper.

Landis stripped the wrapping, bits of tape sticking to his wool vest. He studied the instructions and opened the new box several times, until he got the hang of it. Then he picked up Julia's.

"Don't be fucking impossible," he muttered, and he wasn't sure whether he meant the box or whatever might be inside. Worse, he feared it might be empty. Smashing the damn thing with a hammer probably made the most sense, but it had been Julia's and seemed precious to her, so to him as well.

As he followed the instructions' pattern, parts of the box moved slightly, and internal adjustments made muffled clicks. When he reached what should be the final step, he took a deep breath and pressed the likely spot. Nothing happened. He contemplated the box. His hands trembled.

He reread the instructions and started again. He was engaged in a bizarre version of the child's game where the player has five pictures and must guess what a sixth picture would be: Car, truck, truck, car, truck…? He pressed a different spot.

Truck.

The box opened. So smoothly and easily it was hard to believe it had ever resisted him. Inside, a piece of thin paper, folded small. With trembling fingers, Landis picked it out, then examined the red velvet lining and rotated the box in every direction, confirming it held no more secrets.

Only this.

The hand pressing the paper to his chest was damp. When he unfolded it, he saw it was a letter in Julia's neat printing and the familiar blue-green ink. A strangled sound escaped his throat. He read quickly:

If you're reading this, I am probably dead. This box always intrigued you, and I knew you'd work out how to open it. It was the safest place for this message. Landis flushed. Her confidence in him was misplaced. He hadn't thought of the box before Hawk's little game, and without Carlos and that shopkeeper, he wouldn't have solved it.

I've told you a lot of lies, you must know by now. But I didn't lie about loving you. Most of all, I love the way your mind works—creative, all-encompassing, strong. I'm afraid you'll try to put that mind to finding out who killed me. Don't, Arch, please. The one comfort, as I think about my likely very short future, is that you will survive, that your spirit will inhabit many beautiful buildings yet to be dreamed of.

I hope you have my sketchbooks. If any of my ideas work their way into future L + P designs, those buildings—and this will sound foolish, I know, and I apologize—they will be the children we could never have. Please stay alive and keep that possibility real.

The irrational and vicious men I've offended won't hesitate to kill you too, if they believe you are trying to find them. I could never tell you about them, not before, not now, and not after I'm gone, because of the risk to you. This is me, dear Arch, coming back from the grave and begging you to let it be. Your Julia.

He reread the letter, more slowly this time. Lips moving, wetted by tears. When he reached the end, he traced her

name with a finger. She had loved him unto death and beyond. He hadn't known how difficult that was for her, the
fears she fought, the secrets she kept to protect him. After
she died, he repeatedly let her down. He didn't summon
help. He doubted her motives. He questioned her devotion.
Her words rekindled more than his love, they fired an un-
quenchable rage against her killers.

The phone rang. Caller ID said Yusuf Zardari.

*What the hell...*He laid the letter face down and answered gruffly.

"I'm sorry to call so late," Zardari said.

Always the apology, then the ask.

"As you know, Mr. Landis, the time for the gala is near-
ing, and I hope you will attend. We will be paying tribute
to Marjorie."

Landis had no intention of attending the gala. He'd
long-ago distributed the tickets for the two tables L + P had
bought to associates eager for a fancy evening out.

Now, hearing Zardari's unctuous voice, his first thought
was, how much is this going to cost me? He didn't be-
grudge the amount. Whatever it was, Marjorie deserved it.
If only the man didn't make his skin crawl.

"Also, someone desires to meet you," Zardari said, not
without a touch of slyness. Landis still expected to hear a
dollar figure. "Yes. Tamara Dagan. She's a—"

"I know who she is." He'd talked to her a time or two
after his project at Ben-Gurion University, and she told him
about the positive response to the new buildings. He'd forgotten her name was on Marjorie's seating charts.

"You know her? Interesting."

If Zardari was waiting for elaboration, he didn't get it.

"Well," Zardari said, after a moment. "She saw Marjorie's name as head of the planning committee and our note
about...her loss...and asked about you. May I give her
your telephone number?"

"Have her phone the office. I appreciate the invitation, Zardari, but you'll have to celebrate without me. My people will be there. Thanks for the call." He hung up. He'd been rude but he didn't care. Zardari understood rejection perfectly well and, in Landis's experience, took exquisite care to ignore it.

Chapter 27

That night, Landis dreamed about Julia. She sat at a desk or table, writing with absolute concentration. He watched over her shoulder as her pen skimmed the page, the message dissolving before he could read it. Yet he sensed how desperate she was to communicate, words streaming out of her in looping ribbons. He watched her fold the writing—a letter?—and reach for the puzzle box, bracelets coiling her wrists like snakes.

When he woke, his unease lingered as he stumbled to the bathroom. The way Julia's hand had grasped the box was the exact way his own hand had taken it, in its white disguise, from the carton of Hawk's things. That big cardboard box he was so reluctant to touch.

What else is in there?

The methylphenidate hadn't been in the apartment when the police searched after Hawk's death. *Is it here now? In the carton?*

No way could he fall back to sleep. The bedside clock read four-thirty. Early, but not impossibly early, he told himself. Not like three, that desolate hour that burns sleep like kindling and leaves a morning taste of ashes. Four-thirty, he could manage.

He switched on Hawk's desk lamp and upended the box, spilling its contents onto the bed. A windbreaker. He patted the pockets, empty, folded it, and put it in the bottom of the box. A couple of notebooks. A few early pages contained sketches; most were blank. Into the box. A trio of dirty coffee mugs. A rubber-banded packet of BLK business cards bearing Hawk's name.

Trash those.

Some of Hawk's Landis + Porter business cards. That was unexpected. Landis put one of them in the breast pocket of his pajamas. Tossed the rest.

A few books purloined from the L + P library and the copy of *A Pattern Language* Marjorie had given Hawk for his last birthday.

Keep.

After that, a pick-up-stix pile of pens and pencils.

Hawk hadn't left much at BLK, if this was all of it. Landis had hoped for an old-fashioned address book, a rolodex.

What did it mean that he hadn't found the methylphenidate? That somebody slipped it to him? If he *had* found it, what would that have meant? That Hawk took it knowingly? Or that it was supposed to look as if he did? Landis was glad the drug wasn't there. Those new questions were too complicated.

He gathered up the pencils rolling toward him where he sat on the bed. Put the bunch of them in the desk drawer. Grabbed the pens. Landis scowled to see an L + P pen among them. A slender, ineffective spy, telling him nothing about Hawk's time at BLK. Who'd befriended him. Or betrayed him. A couple of BLK pens, into the trash. Another pen, stamped with the name of Yusuf Zardari's organization, pinched from Marjorie's desk. One that looked like a pen but, cap off, revealed itself to be a screwdriver. A nice weight to it. Handy. He set it aside to take to the office.

He regarded the patch of wall Hawk would have faced as he sat at his desk. If only it were a screen on which he could replay whatever pictures had tormented his son's mind. After a while, he shook his head to clear it of these gloomy musings. He made a list of everything he had to do that day, and the weary reality of how long that list was settled on him.

ᥰᥱᥰ

Already a little rumpled in the heat, Detective Fowler came by the office around ten that morning, without an appointment and without Gennaro. Landis pushed aside the proposal he was reviewing.

Fowler said, "Suffolk County called about the picnic, and it's their case, but the background might help me out. Where's the pattern here? You've stumbled from one disaster to another, starting with Alia Said's murder."

"Before that. I'd say the disasters started with Terry Porter's death three years ago."

Fowler closed his eyes a few seconds, as if unwilling to add another possible crime to his full plate. "At least that Brussels detective, de Smet, keeps me in the loop. He says your contact there," he pulled out a notebook, "Meert, lived in kind of a sketchy area called Molenbeek. Apparently it's a bit of an urban terrorism breeding ground."

"Molenbeek? Never heard of it." The thought flew into his mind that perhaps L + P should give up the Shuman project. Pay the penalty. They didn't need any more echoes of terrorism.

"Hope you don't. They watch the area closely. Through a couple of embedded undercovers, they soon figured out terrorism wasn't the issue with Meert. He was gay—"

"So de Smet said. Hinted."

"Yeah, well, apparently Meert was pretty much in the closet, at least at work, but his partner was a big gay rights advocate. Apparently his activism made Meert anxious. Though in this day and age—"

They were interrupted by Deshondra bringing coffee and a tray of danish.

To Fowler, she said, "Thanks for bringing the danish. They look great." She set a cup in front of the detective. "My boss is keeping you busy."

"I'm always busy, unfortunately," he said, grabbing a bear claw.

She waited, as if to see whether he'd say more, awkwardly stretching the pause.

"Thanks, Deshondra," Landis said. "She's a mind-reader." He reached for a cup.

She laughed and left them.

Fowler continued. "Apparently, the partner's fellow militants didn't like Meert. They thought he was overly cautious, always putting on the brakes, always trying to get them to be nonconfrontational. Add to that, they didn't like him working on the train station project. Destroying their heritage, like you said."

"Enough to kill him?"

Fowler shrugged. He took three packets of sugar and stirred them in. "If I've learned one thing, it's don't try logic in an emotional situation."

"OK, so that's why Meert was killed, but why'd he follow *me*? And who tried to come to my room?"

"De Smet didn't speculate. They're checking out the number on the phone message you got."

"At least they don't suspect me of murdering him."

"Well, if they find the murder weapon, I imagine they'll test it for your DNA too."

"*My* DNA? How the hell—?"

"He give you a cup of coffee?"

"Yeah, sure."

"And you just thought he was a hospitable guy." Fowler grinned. "So, about the picnic. Tell me."

Landis did. When he finished, Fowler put his hands on

his thighs, elbows out, like a man about to make a pronouncement. "Landis," he said. "You're keeping police all over New York and in two countries tied up in knots. Cut us a break." A trace of sympathy lit the detective's eyes.

Fowler likes working this case, Landis thought. At least it offers a clean place to sit, and there's usually food. Beats investigating a back-alley mugging gone wrong. "I'll bear that in mind, detective. By the way, I went through the carton from Hawk's office last night. No methylphenidate. No anything, really. Jacket, books, notebooks—mostly empty—a couple of coffee mugs, drawing pencils, pens. Screwdriver." He'd been rolling the screwdriver-pen between his thumb and forefinger.

"That one of them?" Fowler said, and as Landis nodded, "let me see it." He studied the tool's black barrel and pointed to the logo. "Know what company that is?"

Landis shook his head.

He found the screwdriver inside. "Clever."

"Keep it."

"For now. You said coffee mugs? Clean?"

"They didn't bother."

"Give me them too. For the lab. Take a page from de Smet's book."

"Sure," Landis said, sitting forward. He hadn't thought of that. "They're at the apartment. I'll bring them to the station tomorrow. Thanks."

Fowler put his notebook and the screwdriver in a jacket pocket. "Oh, and I brought your painting. That 'Velázquez.' Your receptionist has it. What's her name? Deshondra?"

Landis nodded. "Thanks. I'm glad to get it."

They shook hands.

Landis was confident Fowler was doing all he could. Too bad it wasn't enough. And too bad their comfortable relationship would shatter if Fowler learned how much he'd covered up, hadn't shared.

Fowler passed Deshondra on the stairs, bringing phone messages. Mostly from friends. Phil confirming lunch on Friday. Theo scheduling a tennis date. And Tamara Dagan suggesting dinner.

Chapter 28

When Tamara Dagan picked up the phone, she sounded breathless. "Oh, it's you! This minute I walked in. New York's a fantastic walking city."

Her slight accent brought her into immediate focus, and he said, "The best."

"Archer, Mr. Zardari told me about your wife's death. I am so very sorry. How are you?"

"Holding on, I guess. Some days better than others."

She was slow to reply. "I do understand. In Israel many people have lost family. Such sudden wounds take time…" He heard a catch in her voice.

"I know, Tamara. Thankfully, I have plenty of work. What about you?"

"Still teaching. I don't know why I was invited to this thing. But it's expenses-paid, and I've never been to New York before. I hope it will be more than a bunch of people who like to hear themselves talk. Intractable positions and irreconcilable differences. We've had enough of that. Sometimes I could scream."

Landis chuckled. Prickly as ever. "Let me take you to dinner. What's convenient?"

"The gala is Saturday night. Will you be there?"

"Afraid not."

"The wrap-up is Monday morning, and I fly out early

Tuesday."

"I'll pick you up at your hotel about seven Monday evening. Will that give you enough time to say goodbye to your conference people?"

"Oh, yes. I won't be speaking to most of them by then, anyway."

He guessed that might be true.

"Though I wish I had a chance to see your office," she said. "The birthplace of all those fantastic ideas."

"Now you're being sarcastic."

"Not at all. I liked your ideas. Now that our buildings are built—" her voice softened "—I told you. We love them."

"I'd like to take the credit, but a building is a shell. A fancy shell, sometimes. A purposeful and well-designed shell, usually. It's the people who live and work inside that bring it to life."

"Don't be modest. Your smart design makes that possible."

This pleased him more than he would have expected. Looking at his display wall, he saw a lot he'd like to show her. "Give a call if you have a hole in your schedule, and you can cab over. The sessions are at Cooper Union, right? It's very close."

"On Sunday we start at one. Oh, but you won't be in the office at the weekend."

"I'm always here. Come by about nine-thirty. I'll show you the office, and we'll have brunch." He wouldn't mind seeing her twice. She was good company. "You'll make your one o'clock, no problem." He gave the address.

"How great! See you then," she said. "Shalom."

⁂

On Sunday morning, he met her on the street, and they

exchanged quick self-conscious pecks on both cheeks. She pulled back to study his beard. "Different," she said.

"How was the gala?" He let them into the building.

"Really lovely. Fun too. They kept the speeches to a minimum." In the elevator she said, "There was a tribute to your wife, you know."

"Zardari said there would be."

"And you didn't go."

"Couldn't," he said, opening the door to L + P's office. Hard as he tried to distract himself, every time he walked inside, he saw them lying there. The soaked carpeting, the hole in Marjorie's chest, the surprise in Hawk's eyes. "I couldn't."

The tall windows of the associates' workroom let in the day's brightness, and they climbed the spiral stairs to his office. "Up here, this is the bird's-eye view."

"Oh my god, I didn't know you did all of these." Tamara slowly toured the display wall, the fingers of her right hand skimming the rough brick. When they'd met a decade before, she was in her mid-thirties. She was as lively and as beautiful as he remembered, and those memories were vivid. She wore her long black hair in a neat twist now, but back then it flew around them like strands of silk as they walked the proposed building site. He shifted in his chair.

"We keep busy. I had a partner for a long time, and some of these designs were mainly Terry's. The best ones." Soon she'd reach his childhood drawing, and he'd have to explain. God, that was a half-century ago now. He needed to take that thing down and put it in a drawer. Or burn it.

She inhaled sharply and stopped, not alongside a rendering of one of L + P's signature skyscrapers, but by an eight-by-ten photo from the previous year's holiday party.

"Oh," she said, and her hand came up to touch the glass.

"What?"

She glanced his way, tears magnifying her dark eyes.

"What?" He prepared to move toward her.

"It's Alia," she said, and he stopped. She pointed to Julia clowning between Charleston and Ty, reaching up to put a silly hat on Ty, and Charleston draping a string of lights over her shoulders. The two men were laughing, which they hadn't done much lately. Not around him. He remembered that evening well. He'd been happy too, then.

"Julia." Her name floated out of him.

"Alia. My niece."

His stomach did a flip, and he slowly lowered himself into his chair. "Maybe you'd better explain."

She brought the picture with her to the table and sat opposite him. "I sent her to you. Indirectly. She's my older sister's daughter."

Landis struggled to absorb this information. "I met your sister when she and Dr. Said came to New York to go through Julia's—Alia's—apartment."

"I know. She said you were very kind. Very helpful. Thank you for that." She paused. "You know, she's married to a Lebanese. They met in Madrid, as students. You met him. Wonderful man. You understand, they can't live in Israel, and it was too dangerous in Beirut, especially when the kids were young, so they moved to the States."

Exactly as Carlos said. "Settled in Dearborn."

"They did well there. Very well. They missed home, though, as people do. When the kids were ready to go to college Alia proposed going to the American University in Beirut. They looked into it, talked to all their friends remaining in the city. She won a scholarship. It was—briefly—a rather stable period there. After the Syrians left, and the war ended."

"It's a fine school. Especially in our field."

"They tried to persuade her brother to go with her, but he was determined to go to the University of Michigan to study automotive engineering. He was never interested in anything else."

Carlos learned that too.

"So David's and my daughter went with her. Well, of course, she wasn't exactly *with* her. Because of Chaya's Israeli citizenship, she wouldn't be allowed into Lebanon, so she went to the University of Cyprus. They have a Department of History and Archaeology, and that's what she wanted to study. It's a cheap flight from Beirut, and Alia spent many weekends there.

"Chaya is two years older than Alia. With the mandatory military service, they were entering college at the same time. It worked out. They loved each other dearly. Those were happy years, studying, the frequent visits. Like sisters. Closer."

Landis grunted. "Not so much sibling rivalry."

She gazed out his tall windows, but he sensed what she saw lay in the realm of memory. "Maybe. Then, a few weeks before graduation, David and I met them in Nicosia. Chaya wanted to show us the archaeological dig she worked on. The trip was perfect! Being good parents, we tried to pin the girls down about their plans, but they refused to think about anything beyond exams and freedom." Again, her attention drifted. "As if their whole lives were going to change. As they certainly did."

One night during that visit, as they walked along the beach at Coral Bay, Tamara told Alia she knew—had met—a famous New York architect and could introduce her, if she wished. Alia looked Landis up online and was intrigued. But she asked her aunt not to intervene.

"Alia said most firmly, 'I'll do it myself! Don't tell him anything about me.' She'd had a stomach-full of rich Arab kids and politically connected people pulling strings. Chaya tried to say how important good contacts are, but once Alia set her mind to something…" Tamara sniffed. "She was very happy working here, you know. I'm only saying this now, because…her secrets, whatever they were…this Julia thing…"

She hadn't known about the change in identity until after Alia was killed and her distraught sister tried to explain. But couldn't.

She fished in her handbag and came up with a tissue and a photograph. "Here they are." She handed him the picture.

Julia and her cousin had draped their arms around each other, faces pressed together, grinning for the camera. Two young women ready to embark on an adventure. "They're both so beautiful," he murmured.

"Who's that?" she asked. He glanced up, confused. She pointed down into the associates' bull pen.

Charleston was roaming among the workstations.

"One of the staff," Landis said. "Long hours."

Charleston stopped at Julia's former station, placed his hands on the back of her chair, and bowed his head. He remained like that for so long that Tamara finally said, "That's strange."

"Really." He handed back the picture. "Your daughter and Julia look so alike. More like sisters than cousins, as you said." When he first saw Julia's mother at the airport, he knew her immediately. He thought it was because she was an older version of Julia, but now he could see she also bore an echo of Tamara. Until this moment, he hadn't recognized that resemblance in Julia, but it may have been part of why he'd immediately liked her.

"It's in the genes."

Genes like conquistadors, Julia had said. He pressed his lips together and looked away. Now Charleston sat at his own desk on the far side of the room, his back to them, the computer screen blue-white, his right leg jittering.

Landis sensed there was more to the story about the girls' visit, but didn't know how to resume what was obviously a difficult conversation. He reached across the table and squeezed Tamara's arm. "Let's have brunch." The cloudless morning might lift their spirits. At least such brilliantly clear mornings used to do that for him. When he was young. Before 9/11.

Charleston heard them on the stairs, and Landis called a hello. The younger man stiffened and whirled his chair around. He stopped mid-greeting as his gaze flew to Tamara. He could have only a shadowed view of her, standing in the darkest part of the office and across the full width of the room, and he jumped up and reached out, hand in midair. His expression was haunted, like he needed sleep. The three of them stood suspended until Charleston came to himself and pulled his hand back, fist against his chest.

He sees Julia.

How had Charleston immediately perceived what he had not? Landis broke the moment with a wave and pulled Tamara away.

Chapter 29

Y our man acted strangely," Tamara said, as they settled at an outdoor table with a view to Union Square Park, coolly shaded by a line of Japanese pagoda trees.

"Something got into him." He hesitated. "For a second there, I believe he thought you were Alia."

"Oh my god. Maybe so."

He studied the menu, recommended the eggs Florentine with applewood smoked bacon, "if you eat bacon?" She did. They ordered coffee and mimosas.

"Champagne at breakfast?" She arched her eyebrows.

"Best way to start the day." After a moment, he gently prompted her. "The girls did finish school, after your Cyprus visit?"

Landis supposed she took a while to answer because talking about her murdered niece was so painful. "Yes, they finished. Chaya graduated with honors. Alia won a special award from her department. I'm sorry, I forget the particulars. We couldn't go to her graduation, of course."

That sounded familiar. In the Middle East, his people were always running up against some implacable security consideration.

"Then they flew to Spain, to the Costa del Sol, for a Mediterranean vacation. A graduation treat, they said, part of the diaspora of their school friends."

"Alia was good at making friends. One of her strong points." He hoped Tamara would tell him more about her, but each sentence seemed a struggle.

"In school, she hung around with a large group of students. One or two would come to Cyprus with her, sometimes, so Chaya eventually met most of them. They all were excited about each other's plans. But after graduation, they scattered to their home cities in Egypt and Turkey, to Europe for jobs, a couple of them moving to the States."

"Quite an international group."

"Alia's best friend went home to Kuala Lumpur. She and Chaya planned to visit him in a couple of years. He's in your field—an architect."

The waiter interrupted with their drinks as she fumbled in her handbag for her phone. She quickly swiped through photos and handed it to him. "Here they are. The girls are with Merari Swee. The architect. And these are pictures Alia sent, with all her friends. Merari is on the right." She pushed her chair back with a screech and stood unsteadily. Landis half-rose. "Please excuse me. Ladies room."

In her absence, he perused the pictures of the students, pictures Alia had sent her aunt. Pleasant-looking young people at an outdoor café, squinting into the sun in front of a modern university building, sitting under a tree with their sunglasses off, providing a clearer look at their faces. He messaged the pictures to himself and on his own phone made a note: "Merari Swee." When Tamara returned, her eyes were damply red. Her phone was alongside her plate, and he was stirring his black coffee.

"I enjoy Spain myself," he said. "The Costa del Sol is a mess, brutal traffic, but the rest of the country—beautiful."

"They didn't stay at the beach for long. They relocated to Seville. Doing what, we weren't sure."

"You know Alia worked for me under an assumed name. A Spanish name."

She nodded. "My sister doesn't understand it."

"And her apartment was decorated with Spanish-style art and objects."

"She told me."

"That could be why they went to a historic town like Seville. Outfitting her for her new life."

"Until their old life intruded. They ran into friends from school—from Alia's 'gang,' she said—and were getting together with them one evening." Tamara took a huge gulp of water. "While we were talking, I heard her doorbell. 'Here they are now,' she said, and said good night. I didn't know it was the last time I might ever speak with her."

"The last time you'd speak with her? Almost a year ago?" He struggled to keep his voice calm while his thoughts raced. "What do you mean? The ways kids travel around—or—you don't—no, Tamara—"

Her face reddening, she gave a panicked glance around the crowded restaurant terrace. She rested her forehead in her hand, and Landis saw a tear hit the tablecloth. After a while she recovered enough to say, in a low voice, "She's been missing for ten months. We don't know where she is. Or if—" He reached both arms across the table and took her elbows in his hands. The waiter arrived, balancing their hot plates. Landis gave him a glare that sent him back to the kitchen.

She shuddered, keeping her head down. "I have to stop doing this," she said. "But when I talk about her—forgive me, please." He held on tight until her shaking subsided, then released one arm to push her water glass closer. She reached for the mimosa.

When she was able to raise her head, she apologized again. "Seeing Alia's picture and where she worked and people who knew her…"

"I shouldn't have taken you there—"

"You didn't know, and I wanted to see."

They sat silently, recovering their composure. The waiter, seeing his chance, rushed away and soon plopped their plates in front of them.

"It looks very nice." She stared at the meal as if she'd never seen food before.

"Here. Have a croissant. We can't keep drinking coffee and champagne on an empty stomach."

She tore the croissant in two and laid half on the edge of her plate.

"Try to eat something," he said. "Afterwards, we can take a walk."

The waiter, glancing at their untouched plates, asked, "How's everything tasting?"

⌒⌒⌒

They sat on a park bench near the statue of George Washington on his horse, Tamara with her legs curled under her and Landis with his arms stretched across the back of the bench.

"What's been done to find her? Being done?"

"The Israeli authorities say they are working with the Spanish police, but one lost girl seems not to interest them that much."

"What about the media? Haven't they drummed up any interest?"

"They don't know about it, and we've been warned not to tell them. In fact, we've been told not to interfere in any way, not to draw attention. It might be dangerous. David couldn't stand the lack of information and flew over, anyway. He went to the girls' apartment building and talked to the neighbors himself. The people there remembered them, vaguely, and said they disappeared one night near the end of the summer."

"But Julia came here. What did she say happened?"

"She said she and Chaya shipped her stuff over, and she got on a plane to Madrid and then to New York. The next day Chaya was coming home to Israel. This was the middle of September. She never heard from Chaya again."

"You're sure?"

Tamara made a gesture of frustration.

"Who were these friends they met up with?"

"We don't know. Alia's story was never quite right. The timeline. A couple of weeks unaccounted for. She said they were traveling around, it was the end of summer, they were finishing their vacation. We went over it and over it with her on the phone, and so did my sister. For months we begged her to tell us anything that might help. The calls distressed her as much as they did us. I know she loved Chaya and was as worried as we were, but she said she didn't know where to find her."

Julia had never spoken to Landis about any of this. Every new fact about her subtracted from what he thought he knew. He feared that by the time he learned it all, she would have disappeared entirely.

"We thought—we think—the most hopeful explanation is that Chaya ran off with someone, maybe married. The police have floated this theory. We think it's why they're not looking so hard. She's an adult. But perhaps she thinks we wouldn't approve. That doesn't make sense, because we're the most liberal parents we know. Though, maybe—"

He felt for her, going around in circles. Second-guessing herself. He knew what that was like. "You think she swore Julia to secrecy, something like that?"

"I don't know. We were desperate. 'Tell us,' I screamed at her one night on the telephone, and she said, 'I know nothing.' She kept crying and repeating, 'I know nothing.' The next thing we knew, she was murdered."

Landis struggled to make sense of it. His Julia was—he

thought—so compassionate. He couldn't believe she'd willingly let her family suffer. Or abandon her beloved cousin.

"At that point, we lost all hope. We loved Alia like a second daughter. My sister felt the same about Chaya…it was too much. David and I dropped everything to be in Detroit for the funeral. What a miserable time. Both our beautiful daughters gone, and we'll never know why."

"How's David handling it?"

"Heartbroken. He buries himself in his work and tries not to think. But she is all either of us do think about, every day. It's like black hole, sucking everything inside, all our thoughts, all our plans for the future, everything. I was so grateful for the invitation to this conference, to get away for a few days."

"And now I'm making you relive it." The pressure of tears was building behind his eyes. "This is terrible. I can't imagine how the two of you…"

"Archer, I'm telling you this because I think you *can* imagine it. Mr. Zardari told me how your wife died. Your son. You also have suffered much."

He murmured an acknowledgement, not trusting himself to speak.

"We never got a ransom demand and nobody claimed 'credit,' which convinced the Israeli security people Chaya had gone off willingly."

And, though she didn't say it, they hadn't found her body, Landis thought.

"For their part, when the Spanish police realized the cousin Chaya had been with went to school in Lebanon, their attitude changed immediately," Tamara said. "They thought 'terrorists,' but the Israeli security people dismissed that. Their eyes and ears had picked up nothing."

This last theory elicited a bitter laugh from Landis.

"When we pressed them to do more, the Spanish

authorities said, 'You'll put her in danger,' and naturally we are terrified of that. David and I have called them again and again. They rarely take our calls, and they never contact us. Once they made the terrorist connection, Chaya went into the black hole too, as far as they are concerned. Wait, they say, wait.

"So we've also lost most of our friends now. They always ask about her, and we couldn't talk about it any longer. It was easier to cut our ties. David wants to go back to Seville, but the authorities keep saying no. I'm afraid he'll go anyway. In December, we hired a private investigator. He went. He found no more than David had."

They sat silently in shade, the late-morning sun warming the air. She folded her shawl and stuffed it in her bag. Kids circled the statue at a run, yelling, and the pedestrian traffic picked up. Soon they'd need to share their bench.

At last, he spoke. "What life throws at you…situations…totally unprepared." He took her hand. "I would fix it if I could. All of it." His mind was spinning in too many directions at once, and he wasn't making sense, so he stopped talking.

"I know. Me too."

He checked his watch. "We'd better get you down there. It's about eight blocks. You're OK to walk?"

She uncurled her legs. "Good to go, as Alia would say."

Chapter 30

He left Tamara Dagan at Cooper Union. "You know," he told her, "this college is a symbol of independent thinking."

"In that case, I should fit in well."

They laughed. Although he regarded Tamara warmly, her troubling news weighed on him. If only there was some way he could help. He'd lost Julia, but was Chaya, at least, recoverable?

Back in the office, he powered up his computer and set to work. It didn't take long, visiting Malaysian architecture firms' websites, to find where Merari Swee had landed. He sent a restrained message to Swee's office email address.

Hello, Mr. Swee—

I understand you were friends at university with Alia Said and Chaya Dagan. Ms. Said worked for me and was a talented young architect. I'd like to speak with you about your friends. Is there a time and number it would be convenient for me to call? Thank you very much.

His email signature made clear who he was. Landis + Porter was an important firm, even on the other side of the world. The unwritten rules of the guild of architects guaranteed he'd receive a response. The ping sounded almost immediately.

Call now. I'm at home. Midnight here. There was the number.

Ready or not, he was in.

At first, Merari Swee was guarded. Then Landis made reference to Alia's early drawings, the ones Carlos had shown him, and his voice picked up energy.

"She drew all the time! I didn't know she went to work for you," he said.

"She used a different name here in New York."

"Why?"

"Beats me."

"How's she doing? Great, I bet."

So, he didn't know. The few stories in the trades had been written about Julia Fernández—about her being hired, about her death. Landis's awkward explanation ended with "and that's not all, I'm afraid."

Swee anticipated him: "What about Chaya? Where's Chaya now? They were mates." He spoke in a rush, and the phone picked up his ragged breath. In the background, a glass clinked, and water ran.

When he finished, Swee said, "That's fucked, man."

"It is. A truly awful situation. I called you because Chaya's mother remembered your name. I thought her friends might know something. Have the police talked to you about Chaya at all?"

"No, man. Why would anyone hurt either one of them? It doesn't make sense."

"Did they have boyfriends or politics—were they involved in anything like that?"

"We were too busy. And that would have been dangerous. You know, Lebanon. We had our friends and stayed close to campus. I was pissed Chaya didn't stay in touch. Alia did, but she never mentioned Chaya, even though I asked. Then a couple of months ago, she stopped answering my emails." He made a choking sound. "If there's anything I can do—"

"There is, actually. Chaya's mother had pictures of the

friends that hung out together in Beirut. You, Chaya, Alia, and a bunch of other people. If you could identify them for me? Then I could get in touch, find out if anyone else knows anything—can give a hint of what might have happened, where Chaya might be?"

"And she's been missing how long?" His voice lifted with incredulity.

"Since September. I know it's a long time." Landis said softly, "Her parents need to know. Friends too."

Swee exhaled. "I get that. Yeah."

He gave Landis his personal email address and soon they were looking at the photos together, Landis taking notes. Swee identified the dozen students in the pictures easily and knew where most were now. None of them had gone to Spain, as far as he knew. He stumbled coming up with the names of three young men wearing black jeans and white shirts in each of the pictures.

"They were always with us the last year. Not students. Locals. I forget how they hooked up with us. They didn't talk much. Always smiling. They always had cigarettes to share, and they bought coffee for everybody."

In each picture they sat close to Alia. Swee didn't remark on it; perhaps he didn't notice. Landis asked, "Did they date the students?"

"Those guys? No, man. Alia and Chaya were way out of their class. They liked to get Alia talking about America, though. Like they couldn't imagine anyone actually going there."

"Did they seem all right to you?"

"What do you mean? They were, I don't know, guys."

"OK. Thanks. You've been a great help."

"Sure. But I don't understand. Why are you doing this? Why aren't the police looking for Chaya?"

"The Spanish police tried. No results. For them, it's a cold case, and the answer could be anywhere in the world."

"What about whoever killed Alia?"

"The New York police have done a lot. They've run out of leads too. She was on her way to becoming a fine architect. I have to do right by her." Landis glanced at the computer clock. "I've kept you a long time, and I sincerely appreciate your help. May I ask one more question?"

"No problem. I never go to bed before three."

Landis shuddered, remembering his own late nights. "When Juli—Alia was coming to the States she shipped her stuff ahead, possibly to someone in New York. Do you have any idea who that might have been?"

"In New York? I think so. We had a guest lecturer in the engineering department one semester. He hung around with us, and he and Alia were friends, though I think he wanted more. He asked her to go with him to the States. She told him school came first. They stayed on good terms, though, I'm pretty sure." Swee provided the name.

"You've been tremendously helpful. If you think of anything else—anything—"

"I'll be in touch."

Landis stared at the photo on the screen until the faces were burned in his memory and tapped a message to O'Hanlon. "I need Carlos a while longer." *He can go places and talk to people I can't.*

Chapter 31

Monday, July 11, Landis sat in on the full security team's first meeting. They took over the conference room next to the one where Landis had been shot. Although the room could comfortably accommodate about fifteen people, the team's strong personalities filled it corner-to-corner. Brett Marx set the tone by lowering the window shades and flicking on the overhead lights. One of the architects protested, saying something about "natural light," but Geller intervened.

"She's right," he said. "We have to think differently."

"Develop our paranoia?"

"To the max," Marx said. She spoke in a firm, crisp voice. When she handed out card keys, they noticed the new electronic lock on the conference room door. The door was new, steel-clad, replacing the lightweight hollow-core. These upgrades had barely registered when they walked in, Landis could tell. Now they unconsciously sat up a little straighter.

Landis glanced at the closed shades and was glad of them, glad they hid the sniper's post behind the black windows of the empty office across the way. The team wasn't there to provide security for him, or for the Landis + Porter office, but they had skills, and there was no predicting when they might be needed. Alluding to recent events, he said, "The message is simply that we have to be alert, on the road and here at home."

"Especially here," Marx said. "Home is where people let down their guard."

Geller circulated a printout of the firm's current projects in locations around the world, a sentence or two describing each. Nearly twenty major projects and more than twice that many smaller ones, each provisionally categorized as low, medium, or high risk. They would spend the next few weeks traveling to many of those high-risk sites. Someone suggested they also visit selected projects by other firms, such as the new U.S. embassy being built in London, to see how the designers balanced the opposing goals of security and openness. The discussion well under way, Landis left them to their planning.

Reporting to him later in the day, Geller said the group would use the rest of July and to test his quick-and-dirty risk assessments. Some effort would go into medium-risk projects, but the most intensive focus would be on the projects likely to end up in the highest-risk group, with Schuman Station at the top of the list.

"The team?" Landis asked, pleased to hear the excitement in his voice. Maybe his disappointment over the lost commission for Burj Maktoum was abating.

"They're great. They were taken aback by what Brett said about the need for security in our own workplace, but by the end of the meeting, they got it."

"How is Brett? She's the dark horse."

"She's a good hire. So's Harry. We'll go into September strong."

"This team can put L + P miles ahead of the competition. You'll have to be at your best. Smart, fast, and diplomatic, Ty." Landis's greatest concern about the project was Geller's leadership. "No running roughshod over our colleagues' work. They'll make the design decisions, and you'll help them achieve their vision, but with security."

"I get it."

Landis examined Geller over the top of his reading glasses. He wasn't sure he *did* get it, or wouldn't be carried away by enthusiasm for his new role. "Don't make enemies, Ty. It's a small world." He thought of the few truly troublesome people he had known. What started those divisions, anyway? Trivial slights Landis didn't really remember and certainly never took seriously. Ty Geller's abrasiveness, by contrast, was more calculated, more immediate, and considerably less forgettable.

ಬಂಬಂ

In the afternoon Carlos appeared. He'd tracked down the students Merari Swee identified, one leading to the next, given them the bad news, and probed for more information.

"As far as I could tell, they don't know a damn thing," Carlos said. "No one was evasive, like they were covering up anything. The ones who'd met Chaya were genuinely shocked she'd gone missing. Several of the men are married now and clearly not to her. Wedding pictures on Facebook. The whole deal."

"Any of them in Spain a year ago?"

"I didn't exactly ask for an alibi, but I double-checked where they said they were around that time." He shook his head. "No Spain."

"So when Chaya told her mother they'd met up with people from Alia's old gang, it wasn't any of the students you talked to. You're sure?"

"Oh yeah. So that leaves—"

"What we thought. The three who weren't students. Local Beirut guys?"

Carlos pulled out his notebook.

Like Swee, the others couldn't recall how the three

young men became part of their group. They weren't offensive, nor did they add much. "Social parasites," one of the women students called them. She'd observed how they attached themselves to Alia. Loosely. No pressure, but always close by, listening and smiling. "I don't think Alia really noticed them all that much," she said.

"Pull up one of those photos," Carlos asked. "Let's take a look."

On his computer screen, Landis enlarged the portion of the photo with the three men in it.

Carlos pointed. "The guy on the left, behind Alia, the one with the glasses, that's Mohammed Fakih. Next to him, the heavy-set one, that's Mohammed Mosallam, and on the right, with the wild hair, Amin Chehab. One of the students was from Beirut and knew their last names. Yes, they're locals. He's still in Beirut and hasn't seen them for months, maybe not since graduation. When they weren't around— rarely, I gather—the students called them Mo, Mo and Curly."

Landis snorted. "The Three Stooges? You're kidding. They didn't have jobs? Weren't in school elsewhere?"

"No visible means of support."

Landis studied the men's faces. "Now we need to find three fairly nondescript guys. Like dust on the road."

"Under a microscope, even dust particles have distinctive characteristics. I've put out feelers."

"Great. Great work. Thanks, Carlos."

Carlos also tracked down the guest lecturer Swee had mentioned. On the pretense of asking about a "former Landis + Porter employee," he'd learned the man gladly stored Alia's belongings shipped from Spain. She picked them up in late September and promised to call as soon as she unpacked, but never did.

"He's a sad sack. I didn't have the heart to tell him what happened," Carlos said.

"Just as well. And Hawk's contacts?"

"Next on my agenda."

Chapter 32

Monday evening, when Tamara Dagan let him into her hotel room, a half-packed suitcase lay open on the bed.

"Are you ready for dinner? I have a car." He eyed her elegant stilettos.

"Starving."

The car and driver awaited them under the hotel portico, and ten minutes later stopped in front of a nondescript office building that housed Landis's club, a members-only sanctuary with memorable food, excellent wine, and unparalleled views. The security guard waved and buzzed them in. They rode up in an old-fashioned elevator that had only two buttons: L and 48. From that cramped space they stepped into the openness of the club's main dining room with its wide ribbon of windows, the lights of Manhattan sparkling in the pink twilight.

The maître d' led them to a window table, eloquently describing the virtues of the club's new pastry chef.

"An amazing view," Tamara said. She looked beautiful in the subdued light of the table's dark-shaded lamp. So much like Julia. A sense of loss nearly overwhelmed him.

"I never get tired of it," he responded, grateful for the distraction of a waiter bringing a bucket of ice and champagne to the table. Landis examined the label and said, "Perfect, thank you."

"How was the conference?" he asked, as the waiter eased the cork from the bottle with a subtle pop.

"I thought I would scream," she said, keeping her voice low. "These smug 'experts' gave the same tired old arguments they've made for years. They could have, as you Americans say, phoned it in. Zardari was so polite to everyone, no matter how stubborn they were. I wanted to wring his neck. What was the point?"

He snorted. All too well he understood her frustration with the obsequious Zardari.

"Archer, the best part was the gala. A couple of lively young people joined my table"—Landis remembered Marjorie planning those seating arrangements—"but the old farts wouldn't listen to them at all."

"Sorry to hear it." His wife would have been so disappointed.

"It's OK. I have everyone's contact information. That list was worth the trip."

Her sly smile made him laugh. She'd use it too.

ඏඏඏ

Landis relaxed on the small sofa in Tamara's hotel room while she finished packing. When she closed the latches, he said, "Come sit by me."

She did. He took her hand. "I talked to Merari Swee yesterday," he said.

Her eyelids, sleepy until that moment, flew open. "Why? What did he say? The Spanish police said Chaya's friends know nothing."

"I hate to tell you this, but the police never talked to him. That might be a place to start looking."

She drew away from him a few inches. "We're not supposed to interfere. They said we might put her in danger. They frightened David."

Landis considered this. "Are they actively trying to find Julia?"

"We don't believe so."

"Well, then, maybe I can help. I know I'm out of my depth and it's an incredible long shot, but I have an investigator who is very discreet. Lots of people won't talk to the police, you know. Maybe they'd talk to us. I would be more than careful. I understand the stakes. The chance I'd ruffle any waters seems terribly remote. But it's your call."

She stared at the ceiling. "The months are passing. What could you do?"

Landis didn't admit he'd jumped the gun and had Carlos already working on it. "We'll talk to the students whose names Swee gave me. That can't hurt anything." He didn't mention the three Lebanese men, the hangers-on.

"I have to discuss this with David."

"Of course. Do that. Like I said, we probably won't come up with anything. But now that we have those names and know the police didn't talk to all of them, anyway, it would be a shame not to check them out."

There was a pause. "I know why you're doing this. You called her Julia a moment ago. Not Chaya. You're doing this for her."

"I did? That's strange." He put his hand on her chin and turned her face to his. "I guess I haven't stopped searching for the real Julia. This is for both of them."

There was a longer pause. "Did you sleep with her?" Tamara's black eyes locked on his, an expression he knew so well.

Unexpected tears spilled down his cheeks. "I loved her."

Tamara pulled her hand away—he expected her to give him a shove—but instead she wrapped her arms around him and pulled him close. For a few minutes, they both cried.

Tamara whispered in his ear, "Then I'll tell you this.

Alia said she'd found someone in New York. She said it was complicated. And she said it felt wrong when we were all so unhappy. Archer, she loved you too."

❧❧❧

Hours later, Landis startled awake when a door slammed across the hall. The lights were off in the hotel room's sitting area, and he lay folded up on the sofa, a pillow under his head. He'd fallen asleep and slept so soundly, he couldn't figure out where he was until he saw Tamara in the next room, dressed in white shirt and slacks, her hair done up, ready for the day.

"Good morning." He sat up. "I'm surprised I'm still here."

She opened the drapes, and morning greeted them. "Thinking about what we were thinking about last night exhausted us both. Your jacket's on the back of a chair at least, but your trousers will need to be pressed."

He compared his rumpled clothing to her crisp appearance. "You're so tan."

"I can't help noticing you are a ghost. I thought you have a beach house."

"That's another story. I haven't made it out there much this summer." It was Marjorie's house and for him, lately and indelibly, another crime scene.

"I talked to David while you slept. He's at his wits' end and ready to try anything. He says go ahead. And thanks."

"We'll do our very, very best." He picked up her name tag from atop a pile of conference materials. They needed a lighter mood. "Your name has nothing but a's in it," he said.

"Tamara always wants a banana."

"What?"

"A game my sister and I used to play. Phrases with all

a's. Goofy stuff."

"Chaya, too. Chaya Dagan."

"She and Alia played it all the time." She stepped into the bathroom and came out again carrying a cosmetics bag. "I'm through in there. Feel free," she gestured to the open bathroom door. "Room service will deliver our breakfast any minute." As he slipped past her, she squeezed his arm. "Thank you, Archer, for what you are trying to do."

Chapter 33

I'll miss her.

Beyond the barriers, Tamara entered the maw of airport security. They'd been good company for each other. They didn't have to explain their sudden faraway looks, how they lived at the ragged edge of emotional exhaustion, their closeness a product of painful circumstances and the limited time available to them.

Now she was showing her passport to a uniformed TSA man, and now she was in another line. That hair smelling like a field in flower, that straight spine, that echo of Julia. She banged down two plastic bins and efficiently loaded them—suit jacket, scarf, carry-ons—slipped off her sandals, and sought his face in the crowd. She waved, a last time, over the heads of the shuffling line of passengers.

෴

The car waited, and he asked the driver to take him home. He needed a shower, more coffee. The car's window was a screen on which he replayed last night's conversation. When the driver stopped in front of his building, he felt like he'd arrived from some far distant place.

The doorman greeted him cheerily, and the elevator gave its familiar rattle, but when he emerged on the top floor, his apartment door wasn't quite shut. He set his satchel down gently and took a few deep breaths. He swung the door open and left it that way, ready for a hasty exit.

He pulled his phone out of his pocket, thinking to call the police. But it wouldn't be Fowler who came. It would be new officers. More questions. More explanations. All unsatisfactory.

Find out if something's wrong before jumping into that mess again.

Light pouring through the windows revealed the living-dining room looking as it always did, full of empty. He stretched his head forward, straining to detect the slightest noise. Nothing. His heart rate slowed to a trot, as his eyes inventoried the furniture, the few ornaments, the Miró.

Everything in place. Except…except the phony Veláz-quez. It hadn't hung in the room long, so he didn't imme-diately miss it. *Damn!* He'd been so glad to have it, a last memento of Julia. Valuable only to him. Had someone taken it? Were they still in the apartment? His jaw worked, grinding his teeth. He'd have to find out.

He pulled open the door to the coat closet. Not as full as it used to be, without Marjorie's elegant coats and Hawk's bomber jackets. A slithering noise and an umbrella crashed to the floor, taking his tennis racket with it. He left them lying there. He sidled along the right-hand wall to the kitchen doorway. The refrigerator buzzed, the tap dripped. He stepped inside. No one.

The Velázquez lay face down behind one of the curving white sofas, its kraft paper backing torn away. *Looking for something.* An ordinary thief would have taken the Miró. This was about Julia. Her "irrational and vicious men" on the prowl.

He glanced around the room again. At least the apart-ment hadn't been trashed.

When he reached the wide hallway leading to the

bedrooms, he paused. Ahead were five closed doors—
didn't I leave some of them open?—and many places to
hide. Doors to his office and the master bedroom were on
the right. The hall bathroom door was straight ahead. On
the left, doors to Hawk's room and the guest room.

Again he debated calling the police. *No. This is my
home, goddammit.*

He crept to the first door on the left. The guest room
would be of no interest to an intruder, except as a hiding
place. He turned the knob and pushed the door open. This
was the one room in the apartment that didn't have a wall
of windows, and it was dark. A man stood there. A jolt of
adrenalin shot through him. He caught his breath. It was
him, his own reflection. Marjorie, doing what she could
with this windowless room, had gone overboard with full-
length mirrors. The closet held only a few hangers that
chimed when he brushed them. One room down.

Next on the left, Hawk's room. The doorknob slipped in
his sweaty palm. This room was bright. Bright and empty,
like the closet. Someone had been here, though. The wastebasket lay on its side, Hawk's business cards scattered on
the carpet like losers' betting slips. A baseball bat pulled
from the closet lay half off the bed.

In the hallway, he stared at the three remaining doors.
He stepped into Hawk's room again, grabbed the bat.

Towels and guest paraphernalia occupied their usual
places in the hall bathroom as far as he could tell. When
was he last in there? Months ago. He moved on to his bedroom. Through the closed door he heard a strange low
whistling. He put his ear to the door. The noise was too
steady to be human. The intruder might be in there, but he
wasn't making that noise. He tightened his grip on the bat
and used it to push the door open.

The room appeared undisturbed. Morning sun exposed
every corner. He took his time checking the bathroom and

closets, careful to notice one particular shoebox that sat in its place on a high closet shelf. He looked under the bed and patted the huddled ranks of draperies.

The whistling was the wind. Thirty-three stories up, wind was moving around and through a perfectly round hole that pierced one of the windows. The hole was the size a small-caliber bullet might make. It was low, like someone had taken that shot from the bed, had lain right there on Landis's navy blue dupioni silk duvet. He studied the pillows, looking for the dent of a head, a hair.

Forensics. He straightened. The bullet hole was a warning. *Surplus to requirements.*

Only one room left. He hugged the wall as he moved to his office door, clutching the bat. The dark venetian blinds were drawn, blocking the sun, and the desk lamp was switched on. In its perfect circle of light sat the box he had bought downtown, the near-copy of Julia's, smashed to pieces. Whoever had done the smashing was gone. Landis threw aside the bat.

Several of his books had been swiped onto the floor and lay in disarray. His dictionary of the meaning of flowers— the one Julia had borrowed—rested spine up, pages splayed. A torn fragment of newsprint had fallen from the book, and he bent to retrieve it. A convenient bookmark, probably. The scrap contained something hastily scribbled in the top margin. Julia's handwriting, her trademark peacock blue ink.

His uninvited guest had definitely been looking for something. If it was Julia's box, that was locked up in his desk at the office, and if it was her letter, that was safely in his wallet. *Was it this scrap? Doesn't look like much.* He backed out of the office, not touching anything else, and retrieved his satchel from the hall. He left the door open. He'd never destroy fingerprints again. Except, he corrected, he'd needed that bat.

cɔɛɔ

Fowler covered a different part of the city, but Landis called him anyway. He picked up. Anger propelled his rapid explanation.

"Yeah, well, you're talking 19th Precinct up there. They run a different operation. The 10th and the 13th, where your office is, different story. Our cases cross over all the time, so no problem. I'll call it in, but they'll be in charge. If I can come up there without stepping on too many toes, expect me in a half-hour."

Fowler, the Suffolk County sheriff's people, the JTTF, now another NYPD precinct team, not to mention de Smet and the FBI over in Brussels—it was a struggle to remember who knew what, who cared about what. The police would inevitably ask what the intruder was looking for. "I don't know" would be a handy answer that happened to be true.

He pulled out Julia's letter and opened it on his knee. The familiar writing, the urgent message. Thank god he'd kept it with him, not lying on his desk. If the intruder was searching for this letter, he could have saved himself the trouble. It was for Landis; it was personal.

The doodling on the newspaper scrap looked as if Julia had started some kind of message. There was an A, crossed out, then "Spin Trifchy." Or was it "Trifoly," the three-leafed plant that inspired classic trifoil decorations. A beautiful design element. Perfect for Schuman Station, which linked three modes of transportation—rail, subway, and surface. Had she been seeking design inspiration in his much-used dictionary of flowers?

He put the letter and the torn scrap in his wallet as the elevator doors opened.

A pair of nattily dressed detectives rapped on the door

and walked inside. They glanced around the spacious main living area, looking right past Landis, and only when they'd given the room a good once-over did their gaze rest on him.

"Detective Morales and Detective Salvo." Jerking his thumb over his shoulder, the young-looking man gestured to his even younger partner.

They let you handle firearms? Landis was tempted to ask, suddenly feeling his age. The younger detective chewed gum.

"What happened here?" Morales asked.

Landis was describing how he'd found the door ajar when Fowler walked in. The buffed and tailored men of the 19th contrasted sharply with Fowler's rumpled downtown affect. Fowler pushed the knot of his tie up to a more ceremonial level and stuck out his right hand. "Ed Fowler, Manhattan South." They shook with an obvious lack of enthusiasm.

"Morales."

"Salvo." The gum cracked.

Landis, assessing the uneasy dynamic, spoke up. "So, when I got here around nine-thirty this morning, the front door wasn't completely closed. I searched the apartment"—he caught Fowler's eye and shrugged slightly—"and didn't find anything missing. But a few things are wrong. The painting on the floor behind the couch there." He pointed, and the young detectives strode over to look. "The Velázquez," he muttered to Fowler. The other two swiveled toward him. "A fake." They crouched over the picture, not touching it. Salvo pulled out a ballpoint and lifted the torn paper backing a few inches to peer underneath.

"Looking for something," Morales said. He sounded bored.

"If so, I don't know what," Landis said. "My son's room

had been searched. I can show you." He led them down the hall. "There was a baseball bat on the bed, I picked it up to carry with me."

They gave the debris on the floor a cursory glance. "Where's your son now?"

Landis and Fowler exchanged glances. This would get complicated.

"Mr. Landis's son is dead," Fowler said. "This is the case from earlier this summer when the son went to the father's office downtown with a gun, accidentally shot his mother, and died when his father"—he made a restrained gesture toward Landis—"tried to defend her."

"Oh yeah," Salvo said. "Kid went ape-shit. I remember."

"That's your case?" Morales asked Fowler. "That's why you're here?"

"Yes. Mr. Landis is leading a public safety officers' full employment campaign. There've been two other attempts on his life this summer. At his office downtown and out on Long Island." He had their attention now, and their interest grew when Landis showed them the bullet hole in the bedroom window, and its position. While the three cops dissected the shot in technical terms, Landis's thoughts focused on how creepy it was, how danger circled him closer and closer, and how powerless he was to avoid it.

The smashed box also interested them. In the shadowy room, Salvo tripped over the bat.

"I dropped it when I saw the box. I thought it might have been used to..." Landis made a chopping motion.

"We'll get the crime scene guys out here to dust for prints and check that duvet."

"But you said you found the bat in the kid's room," Morales said, looking at Landis for confirmation. "So somebody used it, then put it back. Uncommon neat."

"Where'd that box come from?" Fowler asked casually.

Only Landis knew what he was really asking.

"Tribeca. A puzzle store." Landis pulled out his wallet and produced the receipt from the week before, a corner of Julia's letter peeking out. Fowler appeared satisfied. Landis hoped he wouldn't visit the store and talk to the owner, who might remember Landis and his claim to have another box like it. He fidgeted with the receipt. He could always say her parents let him keep the box. But if Fowler asked them—

"So you discovered the break-in when you came home this morning." Morales broke into Landis's spiraling thoughts. "When were you here last?"

"I left for a dinner engagement about seven yesterday evening and ended up spending the night...elsewhere." Fowler's eyes were on him. The other two didn't care.

"Who else has been in the apartment?"

"The maid comes once a week. Fridays. She works for management, so she'll be somewhere in the building. Friends come occasionally."

"Any visitors since Friday?"

"No. Except—" Landis gestured toward the desk and the bat lying on the floor.

"Searching for something. Definitely," Morales said, peering at the shattered pieces of the box. "Any idea what?"

"As I said, not a clue." Fowler's eyes hadn't left him. He had the irrational desire to check whether Julia's letter was glowing.

Chapter 34

The Tuesday afternoon client conferences faded in and out of Landis's awareness like a bad cell phone connection. Watching Charleston lead the discussions, Landis couldn't stop wondering about him and Hawk—the two of them meeting in Europe and neither mentioning it—and the peculiar behavior he and Tamara witnessed. Steady Charleston Lee had revealed an unpredictable streak.

The apartment break-in hijacked the largest chunk of his thoughts. As far as he could tell, the intruder had zeroed in on two specific things, the painting and the box, both of which linked to Julia. Sitting in the conference room, waiting for the day's final meeting, he ran his finger around the collar of his shirt, too loose. He'd lost weight.

The facility development rep for a national bank arrived to discuss a design template for new branch offices across the country. He dealt his business cards around the table. His name was Maxwell Sandman. Landis recalled the business cards scattered around Hawk's wastebasket. What did that mean? Anything? The intruder left a calling card too—the bullet through the bedroom window.

Landis wrote Sandman's name at the top of his pad and, leaning back in his chair, pulled the pad into his lap and doodled. "Max Sandman has a bank." "Max Sandman wants a branch bank." Julia and Chaya's game.

એઝએ

At O'Hanlon's suggestion, Landis met him and Carlos in the six o'clock office. He found them in their usual booth, tipped to their location by a server setting down three foaming pints of Guinness. He slipped in facing them and, between pulls on his mug, brought them up to speed.

"What were they looking for, d'you think?" O'Hanlon asked.

Landis shook his head. "Something to do with Julia, though, for sure. Oh, and thanks to Carlos's lead, I got the puzzle box open. There was a letter inside. To me." Landis took it out of his wallet, and the newspaper scrap came with it. He unfolded the letter and lightly passed his hand over it a few times to smooth it. He slid it across to the two men who read carefully. "Are you not thinking you should heed her warning?" O'Hanlon said. "Especially after this morning?"

"I can't, can I? Now there's Chaya to consider too."

"Her mum still in town?"

"She flew to Detroit this morning. Before you ask, I spent last night in her hotel room. On the sofa. Alone. Good thing I did, or I'd have been home when somebody barged in to shoot up the place."

"You'll be safe there?"

"The building manager's installing a more secure doors on the apartment today. New locks. Trying to find out how the intruder got past the doorman. He's plenty pissed about that window."

"Whacking expensive piece of glass, that. Meanwhile, though, Carlos may have a line on your visitors."

"Mo, Mo, and Curly did travel to Spain last summer," Carlos said, "putting them there at the time Chaya disappeared. My contact didn't find a record of Amin Chehab leaving Spain, but the other two came here. Landed at JFK

May thirtieth. Memorial Day. Three days before Alia was shot."

"Are they still here then?" O'Hanlon asked.

"Judging by the condition of my apartment, I'd say yes," Landis said.

"We don't know for certain it was them, though, do we? Any number of people could be tied up in raggedy ends of your situation."

Carlos consulted his notes. "They came on Lebanese passports with tourist visas they got in Spain. At JFK, Homeland Security gave them a four-month I-94, and they haven't left, not with those documents."

"You're sure it was them?" Landis asked.

"Documents passed muster at JFK."

When their burgers arrived, Landis returned Julia's letter to his wallet and placed the torn scrap of newsprint on the table.

"What's that?"

"Doodles. Not sure what they mean, if anything. This was in a book Julia borrowed. Her handwriting. I thought maybe it was a logo idea. But if it was, she hadn't shared it with her team yet.

O'Hanlon wiped his fingers and reached for the scrap. "If it was important, wouldn't she have put it where you could find it?"

"In a way, she did. I use that dictionary a lot. It was on top of a stack of books in her apartment."

"It's scribbled, not like the letter," Carlos said. "She wrote this quickly. On the first paper she could find." He turned it over. "Torn from a copy of the *New York Times*."

Landis pulled on his short beard, letting the implications of what Carlos said sink in. "In a hurry? Too bad there's no date." Perversely, he was half-glad. The date might confirm what he was thinking, that this was one of the last things Julia did before...But if it was, it was a message of utmost importance to her. And therefore, to him.

"Part of a news story there. I can figure out the date easy enough," Carlos said.

Landis screwed up his mouth and studied the few letters. The crossed-out "A," then *Spin trifchy.* "Means nothing to me."

At least it meant nothing until well into his third Guinness. The three man were discussing their tennis game, Landis lamenting the neglect of his, when he broke off mid-sentence and said, "Spain." He pulled out a pen, and amended Julia's message with a few well-placed letters. "The crossed-out 'A'—it isn't a mistake, it's the key."

"Spain, Tarifa, Chaya," Landis muttered. Aloud he said, "Chaya is in Tarifa, or was the last Julia knew. I'm sure of it," he said.

"Tarifa?" O'Hanlon asked.

"Far southern tip of Spain, close to Morocco," Carlos said.

"Never heard of it."

"It's small," Landis said. "Maybe twenty-thousand people, not counting tourists."

"Take your word for it. But why write that in code? With no explanation? You'd never heard of Chaya until a few days ago."

"Maybe she thought if I found out about Chaya—I do know Chaya's mother after all—this would point to her. Maybe there wasn't time to explain."

She'd had too much confidence in him. It was sheer luck he'd figured it out, that he'd found the note in the first place. *Stop. You did. Some bad things haven't happened.*

"She could have put it in her letter, spelled the whole thing out, not make you guess," Carlos said.

"I don't know," O'Hanlon said. "The letter was the full shilling. A love letter to Arch. A simple message. When she wrote it, she might have thought she had time to solve the Chaya problem. Then she didn't."

"She wrote it in code—" Landis spoke slowly, struggling to work out an explanation "—so whoever found it would know it was important. And if someone found it who didn't recognize it as code, like the Moes, they'd disregard it."

He pulled out his phone and checked the calendar. The rest of the week was jammed, despite his sense business was slow. "I can leave for Tarifa Friday night. Meanwhile, Carlos, can you look into a couple of things for me?"

"Whoa, whoa, whoa. Why are *you* going?" O'Hanlon asked. "Send Carlos. At least take him with you. He *hablas* the *español*. A good man in a fight too. Face it, Arch— you're a genius, but with your white hair and beard and— call it what it is—*pasty* complexion, you'll be as obvious as balls on a cow. Southern Spain? No way, *amigo*."

Landis fumed and muttered, but there was every reason to take Carlos and no good reason not to. This was a search for Chaya, not his personal quest to find Julia's killers. Two people could work faster than one. "OK," he said.

"Your pal Fowler should get a heads up."

"Fowler's not interested in Chaya. If Carlos and I find out anything that bears on Alia's death here, I'll tell him. I promise. But not in advance. He'd slow me down. So would the JTTF. We'll leave and be back before they know we're gone. No reason to think they're tracking me that closely. Is there?"

O'Hanlon shook his head. Carlos was absorbed with his phone, checking flights. "Would you make our reservations?" Landis asked. "They shouldn't go through Deshondra, my office." That caused raised eyebrows on the other side of the booth.

Landis's pen tapped out its own code on the table. If Julia had known where Chaya was, why hadn't she told anyone, why hadn't she helped Chaya's desperate parents?

Answers only led to more complicated questions.

Flying to Spain, he told himself, was an impressive exercise in optimism. It presumed they might actually find Chaya. And second, that finding her wouldn't put her in more danger. And third, that she would come away with them. Despite the improbability of success, he was determined to find out what happened to her. He had to try—for a broken-hearted Tamara and for Julia, who'd loved Chaya like a sister. And for the sliver of a chance he could save one young woman, having let another so precious slip from his grasp.

Chapter 35

Designer, businessman, mentor—Landis enjoyed all aspects of his work, except one: dealing with personnel problems. Landis + Porter had a vice-president in the White Plains office who oversaw local human resources directors in each of its far-flung locations. Jill Nisley was the local director for Manhattan and White Plains and on Fridays, she trekked to the smaller downtown office to handle any matters needing in-person attention.

On this Friday, he saw her greet Deshondra, open the front door again to shake the rain off her umbrella, and step back inside to change her shoes—a conscientious, tidy woman of about forty-five. She looked up at his office, caught his eye and waved, and he motioned for her to come up.

"Does it rain every time you come?" he greeted her.

"No, of course not. Sometimes it snows. And then the train is late."

Deshondra followed behind her with coffee, and they moved papers aside to sit at his table. "How's Travis?" he asked. Nisley's son had been one of the first children sickened at the staff picnic.

"He's fine. At camp for the rest of the month. They don't let the kids call home for a week, but since he'd been sick, they let us talk to him last night. His complaints are right in sync with his older brothers'. Totally normal."

"Glad to hear it."

"Remember what we talked about last week? Mass defection? I'm not hearing it. I think the staff is more puzzled and sad then worried." Nisley glanced down at the associates' bull pen, only a few workstations empty. "A couple of them may be nosing around for new opportunities, as at any time, but for the most part, I don't think they're going anywhere."

"I hope you're right." The worry loitering in the background of his thoughts showed in his voice. "Being a little shorthanded puts pressure on everyone else. Ty and Charleston have really had to pick up the slack."

"Burj Maktoum?"

"That was a disappointment. Don't believe anyone but Ty took it personally. He really wanted to take the lead there."

She pulled a leather portfolio from her large handbag. "How are Brett and Harry working out? I enjoyed giving them their orientation. Very interesting people."

"Seem to be fine." He tapped the tabletop. "OK, whatcha got?"

At the top of her agenda was a position that might be opening in White Plains. "Lynette's baby is due in October. She'll get the usual four months' leave. But if she decides she's not coming back, she'll let us know so we can recruit."

"She should do what's right for her family, but tell her I hope she'll stay with us, if she can swing it."

Nisley stopped writing and studied him, eyebrows raised.

"I've been reminded lately how we aren't doing enough for women in our profession," Landis said. "Unless we can stamp out the biological imperative, we have to get better at this, Jill. When you talk to Lynette, be flexible."

She wrote herself a long note. "I'll take a look at our

parental leave policy and talk it over with my colleagues. Maybe it needs to be updated. Part-time an option?"

"Why not? Everyone who leaves us takes institutional memory with them."

She closed her portfolio and folded her hands on top. "There is one issue?" she said, in a tip-toeing way that told him bad news was coming.

His full attention on her, Nisley said, "Ty Geller and the security team. I think the White Plains people understand the need for it? From what I hear, people in the other offices also like it. And they get the whole 'learning organization' thing." She drew in a breath.

"But?"

"People say Ty is throwing his weight around. When the other members of the team visit us, everything's fine. No complaints. It's Ty. He rubs them the wrong way."

"He has a bit of an ego, I know that."

"Don't they all? A few people worry he'll mess up their client relationships. Coming in so heavy-handed."

Landis rubbed his forehead, hard. "I'll talk to him."

"They've seen him with you. They know he doesn't act like that when you're around."

"I'll talk to him."

ᏋᏗᏋᏗ

As it happened, he had a briefing scheduled with the security team that afternoon. The H.R. director could have scripted it. In the early part of the meeting Geller deferred to Landis, then took charge of reporting from his group. A general and his troops. If L + P had snagged the Burj Maktoum project, Geller would have had the lead on both it and the security team. He would have had his hands full and maybe would have managed the team with a lighter touch. Maybe.

After watching Geller control the meeting for a few minutes, Landis broke in. "You're moving forward nicely on the technical side, and I hope you're bringing the rest of the staff along with you. The security imperative is something everyone has to own. Think of yourselves as teachers, not overseers."

Members of the team expressed agreement. Geller's face reddened, and he fumbled with the papers in front of him. Landis guessed he'd heard much the same thing from them. He hadn't listened.

Landis continued. "It's good tactics. We need their cooperation. If we incite resistance, it will slow us down and, worse, the job won't get done." This was about as tactful as he could muster.

"Cooperation has been outstanding," Geller protested, but Landis observed how the others sat stoically. No meaningful glances. No surprise.

Geller stared at his notepad as Landis asked each of the others to update him on their findings of the past three days. When they were finished, he engaged Geller. "The team's doing great. Exactly what I'd hoped for. More, actually. You've been on the road yourself?"

"I've gone out with different team members. They already reported what we've been telling them."

What we've been learning, Landis silently amended.

Deshondra sent Landis a message on his phone. "Your three o'clock is here."

"New client—an office building rehab in downtown Kansas City. They're not looking for a lot of new construction, they hope to preserve the shell. Harry, you did a lot of that with GSA, right? Sit in with us, see what you think on the security angle. Great work, everyone. Ty, my meeting should be over by four-thirty. Stop by the office, would you?"

❧❧❧

After his guest left, Landis touched base with his friend Phil Prinz. Upbeat as always, Prinz got him laughing, momentarily forgetting the impending conversation with Geller. But when the younger man appeared in the doorway, he cut the call short.

He would prefer to put this meeting off—forever, if he could. Since that wasn't possible, he wanted it behind them. He shifted papers from one stack to another, many with notes attached guiding staff on how to follow up during his trip to Spain. Geller drummed on the tabletop, waiting for Landis to finish.

Don't let him get under your skin.

"Good meeting today," Landis said. "Your team seems on top of things. What do you think?"

"They're doing OK."

Surprised at this lack of enthusiasm, Landis probed. "Any problems?"

"Not really." Geller gazed at the sky above the buildings across the street. "What you said about 'inciting resistance,' where did that come from?"

"I meant we'll bring people along sooner if they come willingly."

"Did someone actually tell you that? They were talking about me, weren't they?"

"It isn't a big deal, Ty, unless you make it one. It's a caution. Any time people are asked to work differently, there's pushback. We can't let it solidify into opposition. It has to be handled."

"You saying I'm not handling it?"

"No, I did not." Landis answered more sharply than he intended. The conversation was going exactly the way he'd feared. He had to end it before he said something he'd regret. "People's perceptions can be tricky. We may have to overcompensate. Now, I have to get ready for a dinner meeting." He gathered and shuffled his papers again, but Geller didn't move.

"Has the team been talking to you?"

"No, actually." Landis slapped the papers on the table. "But I hope you're being a leader and not merely doling out orders. Everyone on that team is at least as talented as you are." Too late. He couldn't erase those words. "In their own fields," he amended.

"So put one of them in charge."

The trust between them was dissolving. He willed himself not to make an angry retort. "Take a long walk, Ty. Cool off. You're in charge. You have a great team. Feel good about it. Now, I have to finish up a few things."

Geller sat another minute, not moving, then darted down the stairs. From above, Landis saw him fly out the front door, without a jacket or umbrella, Deshondra staring after him.

Chapter 36

As the plane rose out of New York's air space late Friday evening, the issue weighing on Landis most was Geller's state of mind. He'd called him from the airport and left a supportive message—not an apology, but an unmistakable statement of confidence. *He'll get over it and be fine, if only because it's in his best interest to do so.* A "voicemail full" alert interrupted his good-bye. It might be a while before Ty would hear his reassurances.

As the air miles piled up behind him, he succumbed to the comforts of first class and cleared his thoughts of L + P business. In the morning, he'd have a few hours' layover in London before his flight to Gibraltar. Carlos would meet him at the Gibraltar airport, where they'd pick up a rental car. They'd arrive in Tarifa late Saturday afternoon. Then they'd do the impossible. He didn't dwell on the difficulties. *We'll find her.*

⁂

Hotel Poniente, squeezed into a narrow street in the middle of the old part of town, had only seventeen rooms. Carlos had rented a two-bedroom suite, newly constructed on the hotel roof, thereby becoming a sixth floor. The suite was alone up there, and to reach it, they used a private elevator that barely held the two of them. The bedrooms were connected by a living room, and the indoor space occupied about a third of the roof. The rest was fitted out as a private patio, partly shaded by a wood awning, with lounge chairs and an umbrella table. Six-foot cypresses in terracotta pots stood sentry in the patio corners.

Landis admired the view from the patio's back wall—a pixilation of roofs leading to the sea. Across the water, the mountainous coast of Morocco loomed, no more than twelve miles away.

The boy who brought up their bags pointed out one of these mountains, Jebel Musa. "One Pillar of Hercules," he said in heavily accented English, "like your American money," a subject he mentioned with enthusiasm.

"What?" Landis looked to Carlos.

"The dollar sign is supposedly based on the old Spanish reals." He explained that the reals bore the Spanish coat of arms—two pillars, symbolizing the Pillars of Hercules, and an S-shaped banner curving around them. "Or so they say." To the boy, Carlos spoke in Spanish. "Then you won't mind taking a couple of these. We haven't been to the cash machine yet." He handed over four single dollars, and the grinning boy disappeared.

"What was the other pillar of Hercules?" Landis asked, gazing distractedly at the peaks. Africa was so close.

"Gibraltar." Carlos examined the suite more carefully now, checking out the bedrooms, each of which had its own bathroom. Back in the living room, he grabbed his bag and carry-on, taking them into the bedroom on the right. This gave Landis the larger room on the left, and he moved his bag into it.

Carlos examined the locks on the sliding doors, and pushed one of them open. The two men walked the patio's waist-high perimeter wall and returned to the living room.

"Well?" Landis asked.

"The private elevator's a bonus. We can switch it off at night, though someone can still get up here using the stairs. The patio's the problem. Too easy to jump onto from one of these other roofs. The locks on the sliding doors are crap. As expected."

"If aesthetics were the only consideration, I'd say it's perfect." Landis stood in the patio doorway, the sea breeze riffling his silver hair. The July sun was strong, but the temperature was in the low seventies. *Perfect indeed.*

"Mind if I leave you here for an hour, while I go to the ATM and pick up a few things?"

"Go ahead. I'll unpack."

ⅇⅉⅇⅉ

Landis changed into a loose, open-weave blue shirt and white linen pants. He sat under the patio awning, sketching the jumble of rooftops. Here and there among them appeared church domes, a candy-striped bell tower, and bursts of palm fronds. The crenellated walls of an ancient castle overlooked the Mediterranean.

"Here's how we'll work it," Carlos said, dragging a lounge chair close, and stretching out in the sun. "We keep that elevator locked, except when we're using it. When we come back to the hotel at night, I'll unlock the elevator and come up first, make sure the suite and patio are clear, then send it down for you. Don't call it. Wait. Then we'll lock it again overnight."

"Aren't we being overly cautious?"

"They've tried to kill you, man. If they find out you're here, they might try again. It would be much less risky for them here, believe me. Let's be optimistic. Say we find Chaya. We bring her here. It's too late then to work out a security plan. We have to be ready for *any*thing, with our gear and in our heads."

Landis thought about this. "What about these doors?" He looked over his shoulder at the expanse of glass behind him and the three sets of sliding doors, two in the living area and one in his bedroom. Carlos's windows were on the side of the hotel, and beneath them was a six-story drop. And, because it had the sliding glass doors, Landis's room had no windows.

"Come inside a minute."

They sat on the sofa, Carlos's canvas carry-on and a shopping bag on the floor at his feet. "Fact is, we can't stop a determined intruder from getting onto the patio from one of those adjoining roofs. But we can know he's there, and we can slow him down. Then this will stop him." Carlos pulled a Glock 36 from the small of his back. "Had to declare this for the flight. Brutal paperwork."

"But can you have it *here*?"

"With the letter in my possession, yes. I stopped by the police station to declare it. More paperwork. But Spain isn't *Tejas*, and I doubt our guys will be armed."

Landis almost asked "*What* letter?" but thought better of it. A heavy-lifting letter, he supposed.

Carlos brought out the contents of the carry-on, each item carefully wrapped and stowed under straps. He showed Landis a plastic rectangle resembling a car's key fob, with a long loop cord. "At night, we hang this on the fire stairs access out in the hall. We can't lock that, obviously, but if anyone fiddles with the knob, the alarm goes off."

He gestured to the room's large overstuffed chair and ottoman. "At night, we wedge these between the sofa and front door. It would be another labor of Hercules to move all that."

From his duffel, he pulled out a box the size of two thick paperbacks lashed together. "I knew about the patio doors so I brought this kit. Wireless motion detectors. Don't go

out there at night without turning them off. Use this remote." He handed Landis a remote and showed him how to
use it. He put a second remote in his shirt pocket. "Batteries
already inside."

"Leave the patio doors open?"

"Sure, if you want to. Those locks won't slow anybody
down. You might as well enjoy the breeze. If the motion
detector alarms don't scare him off and he gets as far as the
doors, he'll find these." He checked to be sure Landis was
paying attention. "Trip wire flashbangs. Blinding light,
huge—I mean fucking *huge*—noise. Smoke. He won't
know what hit him, and by the time he sees he's OK, it's
too late."

"They let you fly with those?"

"I have a buddy with the Royal Gibraltar Regiment and
paid him a visit on my way in. He says these are a new type,
less dangerous, but just as effective as the kind you may be
familiar with.

Landis didn't say so, but he wasn't familiar with any of
this stuff.

"And he gave me a mod kit for trip-wiring them. 'Quite
off the books,' he says. But that way, we don't have to
worry about throwing them. Also picked up these." He
pulled out two more boxes, and handed one to Landis.
"There's three balls inside. Switch them on like this"—he
demonstrated—"then toss them on the floor in the direction
of the break-in. They roll around flashing. Harmless, but a
total distraction."

"Jesus." The vision of noise, smoke, and flashing lights
stirred uncomfortable memories of nighttime sapper at-
tacks. Grenades flying. Searchlights sweeping the camp
perimeter until the Viet Cong machine-gunned them out.
He pulled his brain forward four-plus decades.

"Let's look at your room," Carlos said.

As they entered, the patio slider occupied the right-hand

wall, the long wall opposite them had the bed. The bathroom and closet doors were along the left wall. A bedside table, a heavily cushioned rattan chair with matching ottoman and a standing lamp for reading filled the space between the bed and the expanse of glass.

"OK, Arch. Any of this stuff goes off—any of it—you roll off the bed that way"—Carlos pointed toward the closet side—"and keep the bed between you and the sliding door. Nobody will get that far in. But you can't be charging into the living room through the smoke while I'm coming the other way with my gun out. Because I *will* shoot. Got it?"

Landis's picture of himself didn't include huddling behind a hotel bed. But how would he react if he was scared? "Shouldn't I have a gun?"

"You done much shooting?"

"Not since Vietnam."

"There's your answer. You lob these balls toward the door. Add to the confusion. Our first line of defense is the alarms. They may be enough to scare him off. At least give him second thoughts. Then the flashbangs will disable him, momentarily. I'm armed. And we won't be confused. We'll know exactly what's happening."

Chapter 37

As soon as I hang these motion sensors we can be out of here."

Too distracted to take up his sketching again after Carlos's demonstration, Landis paced the patio, squinting against the light reflected off the whitewashed buildings. The strong breeze was pleasant, though, and blew a distant train whistle his way.

From the patio's back wall, the roofs of the boxy buildings around the hotel resembled a flat white plain, ornamented here and there with lines of flapping laundry. Chaya might be under one of those roofs. If only he could lift them up like lids and peek inside. That surely would be another labor worthy of Hercules.

Most likely, she isn't under any of them. The sneaking doubt he'd tried to suppress, slipped into his consciousness. For the past week, he'd pushed negative thoughts into the background. Now that he was tired from a day of travel, his optimism flagged.

He turned around and rested against the parapet. "Do you think she's alive?" he asked Carlos.

"Chaya?" Carlos said, peeling the plastic from a motion detector's adhesive strips.

"What if she doesn't want to be found? What if she *has* run off with a guy?"

"From what you've said, that isn't it."

"Right. She wouldn't do that to her family." Landis retreated to the umbrella's shade. "Every day they hold onto her, isn't that risky? If we're right, and it really is Mo, Mo, and Curly behind it, and the two Moes are in the States, then the one who has her—Amin Chehab—is at risk if she's discovered or tries to escape."

"Maybe she's not trying to escape." Carlos finished his work. He moved a lounge chair near Landis. "Too many unknowns."

"Is all this really necessary?" Landis gestured toward Carlos's alarms.

"Let's go over what we do know. First, Julia's murder, three days after the guys land in New York."

"June second." The words even tasted bitter.

"Then you were shot. Or do you think that was Hawk?"

"No. His false confession was…Now I can see how irrational he was. I should have—"

"Don't go there, Arch. When was that?"

"June eighth."

"Hawk and Marjorie died June tenth. Though our guys didn't have anything to do with that."

"Except someone was feeding Hawk that drug. That could have been them."

"Fowler have any theories?" Carlos asked.

"If he does, he's keeping them to himself."

"Right. Next?"

"Next I flew to Brussels toward the end of June, and our liaison guy there, Meert—with that disgusting yellow tie—followed me. Then he was murdered. A group of men tried to visit me in my hotel room. Got in, maybe, maybe not."

"Can those events be connected to our three *hombres*?"

"I suppose, if we thought Schuman Station was their ultimate target. Totally different backgrounds, though. Plus, the Moes and Chehab don't seem that resourceful or connected."

"OK, set Belgium aside. The next incident was the picnic."

"July third." Landis shuddered. "That salt shaker could have been planted anytime between Memorial Day, approximately, and the Brussels trip, when Deshondra discovered the break-in. Waiting for me to go out there."

"Roughly speaking, after they arrived in New York."

"Yeah. Then the break-in at my apartment. They're still in the States, right?"

"As far as we know. If they left, they used other identities."

"That would be expensive."

"So, roughly between early June and mid-July, you've had three near-misses? The shooting at your office, the poisoning, the apartment." Carlos moved his chair to follow the sun. "Four if we count Brussels, and five if we think Hawk was being manipulated into attacking you. Thought that last one is too subtle for the criminals I know."

Landis was mentally turning over alternative theories like cards in a high-stakes game of poker, coming up with a mismatched hand every time. He took a breath. "The big mystery is, why are they interested in me at all? Julia's secrets died with her."

"They don't know that. If she shared them with anyone, that's you. We can bet that whatever they went to the States for, they don't have it yet." Carlos sat forward, leaning on his forearms.

"Some thread must tie it all together, but I don't see it."

"Not yet. Back to your original question. Is Chaya alive? To do our work the next few days, Arch, we have to believe the answer is yes. As for your second question, 'is all this necessary?'" He waved at the installed equipment. "If you tell me where and how they're going to come at you next, I could answer that."

"I hear you."

"O'Hanlon said to keep you safe."

Landis, urging full disclosure, said, "Give it to me straight. How does Hawk fit in, really?"

Carlos grunted. "I've talked to his contacts. Found a few more in Facebook photos. But they all seem no more than club buddies. They drink, they get high, they act foolish. Several said Hawk toned down once he started working. The last few weeks, though, he got bad again. Erratic. They steered clear of him because of it."

"Hunh."

"I asked what he said about you, Arch. To a person they claimed he never discussed his father."

"Hunh."

"Change of subject? Your associate Geller. When you called Friday and said Geller left the office in a huff, I caught up with him at his apartment building. I hung around in the coffee shop on the corner and followed him when he came out. Is there any reason he'd be meeting with BLK?"

Landis's head snapped up. "Ivan Karsch?" *Eating my young again, the bastard.*

"Yeah."

Behind his dark glasses, Landis's eyes narrowed to slits. Turning over cards in his imaginary deck, he'd drawn the joker.

⌀⌀⌀

A big red-and-white hydrofoil churned away across the water as Landis and Carlos watched from the dock. The streets around the harbor teemed with tourists. In mid-August, Tarifa's population swelled to several times normal. Young people descended on the town to enjoy the beaches and the town's legendary wind-surfing. Gray-haired visitors queued at ticket kiosks for tours of the nearby Roman ruins and whale-watching trips.

Landis considered the hydrofoil. "An hour or so to Morocco? What do you think?"

"Unlikely. They couldn't isolate her on the boat, and when they got over there, there's customs and passport control. Her Israeli passport would raise questions."

"Good then. Something to eliminate."

They walked the crooked Calle Sancho IV el Bravo away from the docks, past the toothy walls of the Castillo de Guzmán el Bueno. These strung-along names reminded Landis of how Julia had charmed him by telling him her full name. Sadly, another invention.

Carlos had chosen Hotel Poniente for its location in the old part of town, where most younger tourists and Moroccan service workers, Arab-speakers like Chehab, stayed. It was a semi-luxurious exception to the more typical two- and three-story buildings, jammed with apartments. They walked the district's narrow brick side streets—"couldn't get a VW bug down here!" On some of them, the buildings came right up to the curbs. Landis admired how, no matter how narrow the passage, the buildings' whitewashed exteriors brought in reflected daylight. They crossed a square with a central fountain spitting and gulping lazily. Landis checked his watch. "Seven o'clock. Nowhere near sunset, and I'm starving."

Carlos suggested a main street leading off the square. They soon found a bar that displayed a long chalkboard menu of tapas. They sat outside, sharing a pitcher of sangria, and watched the passing stream of young people, out for a Saturday night on the town. Amidst the laughter and loud talk, they heard many languages.

Landis speared a piece of grilled octopus. "The trouble is—this is delicious!—trouble is, after a while they all look like our guy. Medium height, medium complexion, dark eyes, dark curly hair. Scruffy as hell. Do you think we might see her?"

"He'd keep her out of sight. For all he knows, the police are actively looking."

"Should we talk to them? The cops?"

"They won't help. We're encroaching."

Carlos dug into a plate of sausages and roast peppers. He pointed approvingly with his fork. "Our desk clerk says rents are cheap in the immigrant neighborhood, but you still need money. And the nicer areas, forget it. A person—two people—couldn't stay several months without euros coming in. So I asked where young guys with no papers might work. He said most likely the beach—renting windsurfing gear, selling towels, *helado*. Jobs not monitored closely."

"So we look for him there?"

Carlos shook his head. "While he's there, we look for her here, in the low-rent district. Someone must have seen her. Landlady, maintenance guy, bodega owner, busybody, anyone."

"Unless she's locked in a closet or something."

"That kind of thing is hard to maintain. And people get suspicious. More food being brought in than needed. Feminine supplies. Strange noises. When you know your building well, it's obvious when there's two people tromping around overhead instead of one. You need an isolated place to pull that off, or at least a house of your own. Nothing we know about them from Chaya's friends suggests he can afford that."

Landis regarded the overwhelming number of apartment buildings, the crowds of young people. How had he ever imagined they could do this?

"So the area of interest is fairly circumscribed," Carlos was saying. "That and one other factor persuade me this trip is a good idea. A worthy idea."

"What's that?"

"I followed up on that scrap of paper from the *Times*. Alia's coded note was written on June 2, the day she died. When we speculated it might have been one of the last things she did, we were right. And you were right: It was in code because it was important."

Landis pinched his nose to hold back the tears. Julia's last moments. "Ah, geez."

"Alia wrote it to help us find Chaya, not for any other reason, Arch."

Landis took a deep breath, taking in the redolent smoke from the restaurant's grill. "It's gotten us this far anyway." After a few moments of staring into nothing, he returned to his plate and finished the smoked sardines with guacamole, which, in the interim, had lost all flavor.

Carlos ordered espresso for them. When it arrived, Landis adopted a brighter expression and took a much-folded map out of his pocket. "OK. We'll make a grid of the old town and walk it off." He glanced down the street at the tiers of balconies above every storefront. "Lots of apartments. Show her picture to everyone we see." He repeated Carlos's words. "Someone must have seen her."

"The desk clerk showed me the neighborhood where the Moroccans congregate." Carlos circled a few blocks with his finger. "I don't know, maybe they're not so welcome elsewhere. But that lets us concentrate our efforts where they're most likely to pay off."

"And it's not a huge number of streets, either."

"Arch, say we find her, will she come with us? We're strangers."

"When we find her," Landis said, confidence restored, we say, "'Tamara and Chaya want a banana.' She'll come."

Carlos, in the middle of a long drink from a water bottle, choked and spluttered.

"Trust me."

Chapter 38

From different breakfast outposts on the following three days, the Americans confirmed the desk clerk's advice. Young men who looked as if they'd barely rolled out of bed filtered out of the narrow streets in a shuffling morning migration to the sea. By nine the flow stopped. Carlos would drain his coffee, scrape back the minimalist café chair and say, "Here we go." They worked opposite sides of the same block, Carlos near at hand in case Landis needed his Spanish.

Merari Swee had told Landis that, in Beirut, English was the common language among the students, and the three Arab boys had spoken it, if brokenly. It might be Chaya and her captor's common language. Landis became expert in asking housewives sweeping their doorsteps and gimlet-eyed landladies about any young couple living there—*una joven pareja*—and whether they spoke English. *¿Hablan inglés?* He interrupted busy apartment handymen to show Chaya's photo. He didn't need Carlos to translate the shaking heads.

Three days of this and Landis's initial buoyancy had faded. The difficulty of finding her, the possibility she was no longer in Tarifa, and the worse possibility she was already dead weighed on him. His shoulders drooped. At breakfast, his mood was blacker than his *café solo*. Today was their final push, their last chance. What had begun as a blushingly optimistic quest had succumbed to painful reality.

They'd covered the most likely territory and penetrated the concentric rings of surrounding neighborhoods. On the map they'd marked addresses where they hadn't found anyone to ask. It was their last day, and before evening set in and the workers returned home, they would scout those missing addresses once more. *What will I tell Tamara?* He'd lie down on a railroad track before he'd say anything as foolish as *At least I tried.*

They'd trudged the quiet streets for hours. At the next address, Landis craned his neck to watch the closed balcony shutters. Frustrated and with nothing to lose, he shouted, "Tamara and Chaya want a banana!" He glanced up and down the nearly empty street, but no one seemed to notice the crazy American. He shouted it again. He and Carlos shouted it outside every remaining address.

They were only a few blocks from Hotel Poniente, on a street that held the late afternoon sunlight like a bowl. Flushed and sweating under his straw hat, Landis looked forward to a cold drink at the hotel.

At the next address on their list, clay flowerpots pockmarked the stucco walls. The insistent cheerfulness of scarlet geraniums had become an irritant, and he scowled at the dripping pots. He shouted. The balcony doors were shut, but a hand appeared and moved the curtain slightly. Landis blinked. Had he imagined it? He spoke the phrase loudly again. The balcony door opened a few inches. He definitely didn't imagine that. Heart accelerating, he called the banana phrase a third time, and a woman appeared in the gap between the doors. She was paler and thinner than her picture, with sunken cheeks and disheveled long brown hair. He'd have to be blind to miss the resemblance to her mother and the powerful echo of Julia.

He caught his breath. "We've been looking for you."

She was a few feet above him, but without thinking he stretched a hand toward her. Ever since Tamara told him about Chaya, she'd lived in his imagination—reachable possibly, unreachable probably—but now, confronted with the young woman herself, he was afraid she might be a mirage, the product of wishful thinking.

Carlos trotted up and stopped a dozen feet away, giving them space.

Landis said, "Your mother sent me. I'm Archer Landis. Her architect friend from New York."

Chaya said nothing, but the shutters swung open as she sank to the floor of the tiny balcony, her hands gripping the twisted wrought iron bars so tightly the knuckles knobbed like a spine.

"We've come to take you home." A tear ran down her face, and he added, "We need to move quickly. Will you let us in?"

"I have no home." She pressed her fists against her eyes.

"What do you mean?" Landis said gently. Carlos edged closer.

"My parents won't take me back." Now the tears fell steadily.

"Chaya, that's not true. If someone told you that, it was to convince you to stay. Your parents love you. They're desperate to have you home with them."

"He lied?"

"Of course he did." Landis conducted this entire conversation in a low tone to prevent anyone from overhearing. Nevertheless, Carlos nudged him and with his head indicated a neighboring window where a curtain moved, despite the air's hot stillness at that hour. "They are frantic to find you, but we must act quickly."

After a moment, she whispered, "If I come with you...Alia?"

"Nothing you do can harm your cousin."

❧❦❧

Carlos thought they might have been followed back to the hotel and waited in the lobby a good half-hour to make sure. Meanwhile, Landis installed Chaya in his larger bedroom. Soon they heard bathwater running.

They didn't plan to ask her many questions, at least not at first. Her mental state was too precarious. All that mattered was they had her. Carlos examined her passport. It was valid, but she didn't have the required visa for stays over 90 days. He recommended a trip to the Israeli consular office in Marbella, seventy miles east, for help sorting out the problem. "It's too risky to try to slip her past passport control."

"Then let's get going," Landis said.

"I recommend that we keep her under wraps until after dark, when we're less likely to be seen leaving. Also, in daytime these roads are jammed, and it takes hours to get to Marbella. How about an early dinner, grab a nap, leave around eleven?"

"I would think the less time she's in Tarifa, the better."

"Except that, on that road, we're too exposed. Cars aren't moving, but guys on scooters have no problem, and Chehab may come after us. The airport's in the same direction, so there won't be any mystery about which way we left town. Here we have security, and staying is something they probably wouldn't expect."

The corners of Landis's mouth drooped.

"We need a strategy for handling things at the consular office," Carlos said. "They'll have to consult the Spanish authorities, and there's a potentially massive fine. Tomorrow will be a long day."

Landis's frown took over his entire face.

"Amin *will* look for me," Chaya said from the doorway.

She wore the hotel's white cotton robe and was drying her long hair in a towel.

"Amin Chehab? We've been assuming he's the one with you, but we weren't sure," Landis said.

"Oh, yes. Amin Chehab."

"Is he on his own, or does he have friends?" Carlos asked.

"There's a big gang of them, selling ice cream at the beach. He has one or two guys with him all the time. His Spanish is very bad."

"Will he go to the embassy in Madrid? Or one of the consular offices? Try to head you off?"

"I doubt he'll think of it. He's not too bright."

"Chaya, I have your mother's number here," Landis said. "Shall I call her? Or wait until you're settled up at the consulate?"

A glazed look came into Chaya's eyes, and in slow motion, she walked toward him, her attention fixed on the phone as if she'd only that moment remembered such devices exist. Landis tapped the number and handed it to her. He stepped onto the patio.

Carlos returned to the lobby to settle their bill and order dinner to be brought up at five. He consulted some of the travel guides lying around and found them a hotel in Marbella for the night. Later he recounted for Landis the desk clerk's muttering about the uncivilized early dinner hour, but Carlos was a generous tipper, and his requests weren't problems for long.

They found Chaya curled up on the sofa, her face wet, the phone pressed to her ear. When she saw Landis, she said, "She wants to talk to you." In truth, Tamara Dagan was barely able to speak.

"I know…I know," Landis said. He walked outside to the far end of the patio and stood in the narrow shade of one of the cypresses. "We'll get her to the consulate tomorrow…We won't leave her. She looks good. She looks good…No, we haven't asked for details. She's a little fragile. You understand." Landis could only guess at what Tamara was trying to say. "She asked about Alia. We haven't told her yet. It might be too much. Not until this is over."

Chapter 39

Before they took their naps, Carlos gave instructions. To Chaya he said, "If anything happens, roll off the bed, away from the door, and keep quiet. Don't let him know where you are." She was pale and trembling, and he repeated himself three times. "You have to do it instantly. Automatically. You won't have time to think." He told Landis, camping on the living room sofa, much the same. "Don't stand up unless I call you."

Carlos checked the components of his security apparatus, said "*buenas noches*," and now soft snores emanated from his bedroom. As far as Landis could tell, Chaya also slept. Stretched out on the sofa, he tossed, disturbed by singing and carousing in the street below. The more he told himself he had to get some sleep, the wider awake he felt. Eight o'clock.

It's too light outside, for Christ's sake. He flopped onto his back. The ceiling fan barely stirred the air.

Shortly after ten a terrace alarm blared, shocking him out of a deep sleep. Unbelievable. It was happening.

He rolled off the sofa and wedged himself between it and the coffee table. A thump came from Chaya's room, and Carlos's footsteps pounded toward the living room. They stopped. Landis brought his head above table level. He reached out a shaking hand to grab the balls of light. Carlos's silhouette moved slowly across the living room windows toward the two sets of open doors.

"Arch?"

"Ready," he croaked. A second alarm blasted, doubling noise already so loud he thought he could see the waves of sound.

They'd hoped the alarms would warn Chehab off, but then he wasn't a normal intruder, and they had something he wanted badly. Which door would he pick?

Landis felt about to choke on his own heartbeat. He shoved the table aside to give himself room to breathe. Out on the terrace, shadows darted against the persistent glow of the city. Two of them.

A man raced toward the living room door. Landis remembered Carlos's warning. He squeezed his eyes shut and covered his ears. Yet, when the intruder tripped the flashbang on the door closest to him, the blast was overwhelming. He saw red through his eyelids. It was like a bomb had gone off inside his head.

When he opened his eyes, smoke filled the doorway. He tossed two of the balls, low. They hit the floor flashing unpredictably and rolled toward the patio. In those few seconds of chaos, Carlos grabbed the intruder and threw him hard against the wall.

"Now, Arch!" he yelled. Landis scrambled to his feet. The second flashbang went off outside Chaya's sliding door. It lit the living room like noon. Carlos gut-punched the first man and flung him in Landis's direction. He dashed into Chaya's room.

The man bent over, gasping. Landis seized his shoulders and kneed him in the stomach. He twisted away and rounded on Landis, butting his head into Landis's chest. Landis struggled for air. Hanging onto the man's shirt, he landed a few ineffectual punches with his weaker left arm. He got his left leg between the intruder's legs and jerked. The man stumbled into him, and they both toppled over.

As they fell, Landis propelled himself forward. His chest, now high on the man's body, forced his opponent's head down on the floor. The man reached his arms over his head. He went for Landis's face. Landis tucked his head, and the man got handfuls of hair. He pulled, hard. Landis reared up and broke the man's hold. He came down hard, pinning the man's arms with his own. He tried to head-butt Landis's chin. Landis's teeth cut the inside of his cheek. He tasted blood. The intruder was squirming away underneath him.

Landis gave an exhausted huff and rolled off the man, who immediately rolled onto his stomach. He scrambled up, exactly as Landis hoped he would. As soon as the man was on all fours, Landis leapt onto his back. They crashed to the floor again, the air whooshing out of the younger man. With Landis's greater weight pinning him, he gasped like a fish, trying to regain his breath, nose bleeding profusely.

The air was foggy with smoke. Landis reached over to the coffee table, grabbed the remote control for the alarms, and switched them off. Grunts and thumps came from Chaya's bedroom. Heavy punches connected, each one making Landis wince. Which way was it going? A metal object clunked to the floor. Knife, gun? Whose? Carlos yelled something in Spanish. Handcuffs rattled and snapped.

Someone pounded on the suite door. *"¿Qué pasa? ¡Todo ese ruido! Gerente,"* the manager shouted. *"¿Qué pasa?"*

Landis had his man secured and was struggling to regain his breath. Carlos came into the living room. He tucked his gun under a sofa cushion, yelling. *"¡En un momento!"* He shoved the ottoman out of the way, which allowed the door to open wide enough for the manager to shoulder his way inside. He'd puffed his way up the stairs, and the doorknob alarm was blaring. Carlos slipped past him and switched it off. The hallway's dim light revealed he wore only his boxers.

The night manager bobbed on tiptoes, trying to see into the dark room. *"¿Qué pasa?"* he wheezed, winded from the stairs. He stepped forward, stumbling into Landis and the man on the floor.

"Luz," Landis muttered, one of the few words of Spanish he knew. The manager flipped the switch.

Landis's ears still rang, and he lost part of Carlos's reply. Something along the lines of: "We had visitors. Not unexpected. Give me a minute." He headed into his bedroom.

"¿Quién es?"

Landis studied his captive's face. The wide-open eyes darted every which way. A string of drool stretched from his mouth to the tile, and the blood from his nose made a puddle the size of a saucer. He didn't look like Chehab. The same type, but not the same man. In answer to the manager's question, Landis shrugged.

Carlos came back into the room wearing sweatpants and carrying his wallet. In Spanish, he said, "Call the police on these guys. Tell them to check their papers. I guarantee they'll be considered 'undesirable aliens.'" He handed the man a large bill. "Give us twenty minutes."

The manager shifted in the doorway, unsure whether to stay or go. Carlos brushed past him into the hall and keyed the elevator on. The manager took the hint.

"OK, *amigo*." Carlos pulled out another pair of handcuffs, and Landis moved aside. To Landis, he said, *"Pistolas."* As Landis patted the man down, Carlos retrieved his own gun from under the cushion. They pulled the man to standing, and Carlos marched him through the last of the smoke onto the patio. He recuffed him with his hands behind one of the pillars that supported the awning.

Landis hurried into Chaya's room. Dimly he saw the other intruder handcuffed to a pipe, the front of his shirt spattered with blood. Carlos had put a pillowcase over his head—extra insurance he wouldn't see Chaya. He flipped on the overhead light. Chaya lay on the floor on the far side of the bed, as instructed, squeezed half underneath it, shaking. He put a finger to his lips, helped her to her feet, and walked her into the bathroom. He ran cold water on a towel and handed it to her. He left her there, shutting the bathroom door behind him. For the first time, he realized that, throughout this encounter, he hadn't been afraid.

Carlos released the man from the pipe and held the gun to his head while Landis shoved him out the patio door. Carlos recuffed his hands behind the awning's nearer pillar. The two captives now squatted about ten feet apart.

"They'll be out of action until the police come," he said in a low voice, once they were inside again. Carlos pointed to the intruder's gun, which had slid under the nightstand. "We'll leave that baby for the cops. This turned out to be a two-man job. Good work, Arch."

Landis tapped on the bathroom door and said quietly, "You can come out now." Chaya opened the door, her face damp and eyes red.

"Sorry about that," Carlos said to her, keeping his voice low.

"How did they find us?" Landis asked. "Can we question them? Try to get some answers? I have a lot of questions."

Carlos glanced toward the patio. "Tempting. But, no. Eyes on the prize."

Chaya.

"Frustrating as hell."

"Yeh. Now let's get out of here before the police show. Anything we can't pack up in ten minutes we leave."

Landis whispered to Chaya, "Don't let them hear your

voice, but can you at least get a look at them? I mean a really good look? Is one of them Chehab? They can't see you."

She peeked around the sliding door. The men had slumped to the patio and the nearer one sat cross-legged, his back to them. She whispered. "The far one, I do not know. But the close one, even with his face covered, I recognize his clothing, the scar on his arm, everything. Amin Chehab."

Chapter 40

As soon as they were on the road, Landis called Tamara again. It was nearly midnight in Israel, but he guessed Tamara was nowhere close to sleep. Chaya talked with her a few minutes, then Landis took the phone. He soaked up Tamara's gratitude only a moment before breaking in, "Tamara, there's something we need you to do." That stopped her. "Do you and David have any connections in your Israeli foreign ministry or Shin Bet? Someone who knows Chaya's situation, who knows you, who will listen to your story and call the consulate in Marbella, smooth the way? Chaya's overstayed her visa, and they can help us keep the Spanish authorities from holding her up for days. Best case, we can put her on a plane home tomorrow."

He thought Tamara was quiet because she was trying to think whom to call, but she was making a list, and she soon mentioned seven or eight people. "I thought you'd have ideas," he chuckled. "We'll be at the consulate when it opens at ten here. You and David make those calls."

That task in motion, Landis spent the first hour of the drive decompressing. The alarms, the flashbangs, the smoke, the blows, the now-worsening pain, the dash from the hotel. It was a lot to deal with. He glanced at Chaya, huddled in the back seat, asleep. *Eyes on the prize.*

"Well," he finally said, "*that* was exciting. I hope my

body doesn't need any more adrenalin for a few days…or weeks."

Carlos laughed. "They were young and strong, that's true. Lucky for us, they don't know how to fight. An excellent night's work." He too checked Chaya in the rearview.

She awoke as they approached Marbella, and the two men asked a few questions to help them construct a strategy for the consulate. It was tempting to believe the worst was over, but the implacable machinations of bureaucracy could prevent Chaya's escape as decisively as Chehab would have.

The next morning, remarkably rested, they breakfasted at an outdoor café near the commercial-looking building that housed the consulate. Chaya was pale and brittle thin. He hadn't told her mother that. In his relief at finding her, she looked perfect to him, and Tamara would see her that way too.

They weren't totally unscathed. Carlos had skinned knuckles and a faint discoloration under the tanned skin of his cheekbone. Any other bruises were hidden by his long-sleeved shirt. The still-healing gunshot wound to Landis's left arm throbbed. He was grateful to be right-handed. His ribs were especially colorful, and he couldn't take a deep breath.

Despite everything, here we are. Bruised, bloodied, and ready for our next challenge.

Carlos was their lookout on the street and stayed at the café when Landis and Chaya walked to the consulate. In contrast to what Landis had seen at Israeli embassies in Europe, this office looked low-key and no better protected than a local branch bank. *Interesting.* It was a high-risk target, it must have security, he thought. But there weren't any external signs that would discourage an attack. Inside, at least a body scanner and X ray for handbags and briefcases. Standard stuff. What he could not see interested him more.

Carlos had rehearsed them on what to say. His advice boiled down to "as little as possible, but tell the truth." Chaya should explain she had been held against her will, and Chehab had terrified her with his constant threats. He told her he had people watching her all the time. If she tried to escape, he would know, and he would find her.

To make clear why she hadn't made the attempt anyway, Carlos encouraged her to relate an episode she'd told them in the car. Back in October Chehab borrowed a car and drove her to a deserted area where a half-starved dog was tied up. He beat the dog cruelly, but didn't kill it. Then he dragged her away from the suffering thing, its plaintive whimpering filling her ears. That would be her fate, he said, if she tried to get away. After that, she didn't dare leave their room.

A few minutes before the consulate opened, Landis and Chaya joined a growing cluster of visitors in the building forecourt. People were admitted a few at a time for security screening, then milled in the lobby.

At ten o'clock, by some silent signal, Landis and Chaya were carried forward in the press of people rushing to the elevator. When they reached the consulate's modest waiting room, most of the twenty or so seats were already taken. They signed in and were handed a numbered placard. Eleven. As expected, a long morning ahead. Chaya sat between him and a large family of Hasidim.

After a long delay, the receptionist called number one. Landis gave Chaya's shoulder a squeeze. "We're here. It's good."

The receptionist had called number four when a nicely dressed young man came out and hovered over her desk, asking a question. She pointed to the sign-in sheet. He scanned the attentive faces. "Chaya Dagan," he called.

"Showtime," Landis muttered. Tamara and David had pulled strings. He helped her to the front of the room. Not unexpectedly, the young man gestured for Landis to stay behind, and he didn't press the point. The less friction, the better, although it pained him to watch her walk away. Perhaps no one else would notice how unsteady she was. Immediately, their seats were taken by two of the standees who pointedly ignored him. He took up a spot leaning against the wall next to a single man, an Israeli-American, as it happened, dressed like a student in sandals, cargo shorts, and a faded University of Chicago T-shirt.

Time dragged. New people continued to arrive, keeping the waiting room full. When the receptionist called "Seven," a family of nine people—three adults and six children—vacated an entire row of chairs. Women with babies and old folks needed those chairs, so Landis continued to slump against the wall, the stresses of the last few days catching up with him.

The consulate door opened and a pair of sharp-featured Spaniards in suits strode in.

"Cops," the American muttered.

"You sure?" Landis asked.

"Oh yeah."

They marched to the receptionist's desk and announced themselves. She picked up the phone, and in a moment the same young man who'd fetched Chaya came for them, politely beckoning them to follow.

Now she'll get some tough questions. Landis checked the clock over the front desk. Chaya had been inside more than an hour. He hoped the consular staff believed her story and her parents' calls had bolstered her credibility. Mostly, he hoped the staff backed her up with the police.

He and Carlos had discussed how to engage with the National Police Force. Whatever they thought about her story, the fact was, they hadn't found her. They might want her out of the country quickly to avoid embarrassment. Or it could work the other way. The obscure tenets of machismo might require them to detain her as punishment for making them look bad.

"Or to help them delve into Chehab's activities," Carlos had said.

"Jesus."

Landis leaned one shoulder against the wall and faced the receptionist. After a while, the young man reappeared, glanced around the waiting room, and seeing Landis, flicked his upturned fingers, signaling him to come.

He greeted the young man pleasantly and was led to a cramped conference room where he found Chaya, the two Spanish police inspectors, and three consular officials, one of whom was a translator. Landis took the empty chair next to Chaya, and under the table she pressed a trembling leg against his. Her expression was serious, but her eyes weren't red. She hadn't been crying. She was holding it together.

The inspectors had questions for Landis.

"How did you find her?" the older one asked, but before he could respond the younger one broke in, regarding Landis narrowly, "No, *why* were you looking for her?" These questions came to him via the translator.

He responded in an upbeat tone. He'd expected this one. Keep it simple. "I hired her cousin, and she told me she had a cousin in Tarifa. I've also met Chaya's mother, my employee's aunt, in a professional capacity. She was in New York recently and told me her daughter had gone to Spain, then went missing. She was worried sick. I put two and two together."

"Why didn't you simply tell her mother about Tarifa?"

"In case I was wrong. I couldn't raise her hopes for nothing."

"Why didn't you call us?"

Egos lay all over the table. "That's easy," Landis grinned. "I really didn't think I'd find her. Didn't want to waste your time. Mostly, the trip was a vacation. You know, R and R." He wondered how the translator handled "R and R." "Since I was here, I thought I'd give it a try."

"Even so—" the older detective said.

"How did you find her?" The young one interrupted his partner again.

Landis kept the fidgets in check. No drumming his fingers, fiddling with a pen, tapping his foot. He tried to appear serene and pleasantly thick-headed. "Pure luck." Their maps with addresses checked off and annotated with question marks were in a trash can on a street dozens of miles away. "Chaya's mother had shown me a picture of her, and I was out walking near my hotel and saw her. There she was!" That was the story they'd agreed upon. Keep Carlos out of it, if they could. Keep it simple.

The situation would get dicey if the Tarifa police had filed a report on a pair of recently jailed Moroccans that included the names of two hastily departed American guests of Hotel Poniente. However, the likelihood seemed small that any such report had found its way to these two investigators quite so soon.

Coached by Carlos, the hotel manager was prepared to tell the police his guests had been worried about intruders—the security set-up verified that much. He'd also been asked to say they planned to fly out of the country imminently. If he followed through, the police might assume the Americans would be someone else's problem before long and not bother to mention them in their report at all.

"You've heard her story?" the young investigator asked.

"Yes."

"Do you believe it?" His voice was incredulous.

Landis was a master at projecting total confidence when necessary. He held the man's gaze. "Absolutely."

"What do you know about this man who she says held her captive?"

"Nothing."

"What is the address where she was held?"

"Frankly, I didn't notice the address. It was a narrow street, an alley really, off Mar Rojo? I think I could find it on a map."

The officials muttered between themselves. Landis said, "Of course I understand your interest in finding this man. He kept a foreign national captive, in a tourist center like Tarifa, for how long, Chaya?"

"Ten months," she whispered, staring at the table.

Landis continued, "Ten months. The good news here is that her story may instill some caution in these young tourists. And if this man goes on trial, the whole world will be talking about the risks to young women travelers."

He didn't make it sound like a public relations disaster for Spanish tourism, which it would be, but the muttered consultation between the two detectives rose in pitch. Then they were quiet.

"I can pay her fine, if there is one," Landis said. "I want to get her home, out of your hair, and back with her family."

One of the consular officials spoke up. "We're prepared to expedite that and will have her paperwork ready within the hour."

While the inspectors' long silence dragged on, Landis kept an expression of bland cooperation. *C'mon, do it.* At last, the younger man put his pen in his shirt pocket and snapped his notepad closed. "OK. When is she going?"

"Today, if we can get a flight." Landis locked his fingers together to hide his shaking hands. The Israeli official murmured assent.

After another long pause, the younger police inspector said, "Since, as we agree, she was held in Spain against her will, we will waive the fine." *An olive branch.*

സ്ക്ര

There were surprisingly many ways to fly from nearby Malaga to Tel Aviv, though the itineraries most airlines proposed included absurdly long layovers in convenient locales like Moscow. Landis objected to the idea of Chaya sitting in any airport by herself for hours on end and offered to accompany her, but she refused. As a compromise, they booked her on a Turkish airline that had one relatively brief stopover in Istanbul. Leaving Spain at 6:30 p.m., it would arrive in Israel very early the next morning.

The men would fly to London after Chaya left, then take an overnight flight to New York. With the time difference, Landis would be back in his office late morning.

The pressure finally eased when they could call the Dagans with an actual schedule. Tamara said the Israeli officials also wanted to talk to Chaya—payback for their assistance in extricating her from Spain. "She's up to it," he said. "She was terrific at the consulate and, since then, she hasn't stopped smiling."

By the time all this was settled, airline tickets safely in their possession, and Carlos's gun cleared and secure in his checked duffel, they had time for an early dinner. They found a secluded table in a sleepy airport restaurant. Gratitude and relief shone on Chaya's face, and her companions begged her to stop thanking them.

Chapter 41

They ordered a Spanish meal—fish, potatoes, artichokes—along with a bottle of *rioja*, refreshing after the small plates of salty olives they'd demolished. Landis asked Chaya, "Would you be willing to answer a few questions?"

Chaya met his eyes. "OK."

"You came to Spain with Alia, whom I know as Julia." His use of the present tense was deliberate. Painful too.

"Oh, that identity-switch thing! She went through with it? You know about it?"

"Yes. As I told them at the consulate, I hired her."

"My mom gave Alia your name. How is she? Does she really work for you? Tell me about her. Does she love New York?" The eagerness in her voice made Landis study his plate, suddenly intent on probing for a nonexistent fish bone.

"All in good time. There's lots to tell."

Carlos distracted her by refilling her wine glass. "Good stuff," he said.

Landis asked, "Was Alia in touch with you after she left Spain?"

Anger flashed in her eyes. "They wouldn't let me talk to anyone. We missed each other's birthdays. That's never happened before. In our whole lives."

Landis didn't give her time for the questions he could

see forming. "Shortly before you disappeared, you told your mom you ran into friends from school. That was Amin Chehab and his friends? The two Mohammeds?"

"Here's what happened. We were in Seville—we loved it there. We rented a tiny apartment for the summer. We shopped for stuff for her 'new life,' she called it. The day we found the matador's suit, we were so excited! You've seen it?"

Landis's fork trembled, and he set it down. "Yes I have. Spectacular."

"It was in bad shape, but she had it cleaned and spent evenings repairing it. 'If I put it behind glass, no one will ever know!' she said."

"Why did she do all that? What was the point?"

"You should ask her. I think it was for fun. A fantasy. Not that she was tired of being Alia Said. More that she had a new life ahead of her, she wasn't a student any longer, so why not be a new person? There really was no explanation at first."

"What changed?" Carlos asked.

"It was the guys. One afternoon, we were walking in the university area—there were lots of cheap restaurants along there—and she saw these guys from school, Amin and the other two. They weren't students, but they hung around with her group of friends, she said. So, you know, when she saw these familiar faces, we stopped to talk to them. It was a little awkward, their English wasn't great, but we did OK.

"They offered to walk us home, acting all gentlemanly, but we said no, and we promised to meet them for pizza later that night. I didn't figure it out until later, but they must have followed us, because before dinner, they came to the door and rang the bell. And me, with all my military training. I should have been more suspicious."

The men made supportive noises.

"The evening was OK, though afterward Alia and I decided we didn't need to see them again. But then in the middle of the night there was this loud knocking. Alia opened the door, and it was them. They burst into the apartment and said we had to come with them. Someone from school was in trouble. They were very excited. Worried, we thought."

"Eat your dinner. This can wait."

She took a few bites. "We were half-asleep. It was confusing. We weren't afraid of them. So we pulled on jeans and T-shirts and went with them. They drove us to another apartment, and it was their apartment, and right then we knew we'd made a huge mistake. It didn't occur to us until later how it was not a coincidence they found us in Seville in the first place. We were still kind of in that world, you know? Of school? Our old connections? It seemed natural.

"Once they got us to their apartment, the two Mohammeds went out again, and Amin watched us. He had a gun and said he'd shoot if we screamed or tried to get away. Maybe we should have tried to at that point, before he became such an expert guard dog. The other two came back with all our stuff. They cleaned out our apartment in the middle of the night. Alia was worried about what our landlord would think, you know, skipping out like that. But that was the least of our problems.

"They knew Alia wanted to go back to the States and work in New York, and they heard her talking about Landis + Porter. From what my mother had said about your work for Ben-Gurion University, it was her dream to work for you.

"Then they looked up your firm online and were really excited to see the kinds of projects you do, so they told her she had to go through with it. They expect her to be a spy for them. They'd hung around with the architecture and engineering students long enough to have an idea of what the work was and to believe she can be useful to them. Their plans are sophisticated and very unsophisticated at the same time."

"Useful how? Are they terrorists?"

Chaya rolled her eyes. "They're punks. They aren't hooked up to any organized groups. Nothing like that. They aren't a bit religious, either. Alia said the other Muslim students made fun of them when they weren't around."

"You're sure?"

"They have no imagination and no skills. Back then all they could think of was making names for themselves in that world. It was absurd, the dreams they had. Including hooking up with some guys in New York to make bombs."

"Did they mention any specific targets? Particular buildings? I could name a few."

She shook her head. "Nothing specific. That's what they told Alia to do, figure out what would be possible for them."

Landis poured her a glass of water. "Chaya, eat. I can wait." *I've waited two months, and maybe I don't want to hear this.* Some rough moments lay ahead for her.

She finished most of her plate and placed her fork and knife neatly parallel. "*Gracias.*" She took a drink of the *rioja*. "After Alia understood what they were asking, she smashed a plastic razor and tried to slash her wrists."

I saw those scars. Pictures of them.

Chaya put her hands over her mouth to force back a sob. "They took her to the neighborhood clinic and got her stitched up. They left me with Amin and the gun and told her that if she did or said anything out of line, he would shoot me.

"We had to cook for them, you know. So when we needed food, Fakih took Alia shopping, and I stayed behind. The last thing she would see as she left was me, tied to a chair and a gun to my head. The looks she gave me.

Broken-hearted. She would blow me a kiss."

"How long did this go on?" Landis asked.

"A few weeks, because they were insisting Alia go to New York. As I said, she wanted to work for you very badly, someone who knew her aunt. She told me she would feel safer and not so alone with that invisible connection. She planned very carefully what documents she'd need. She called the university—with Amin listening in and all the time pointing his gun at her, of course—and told them she was changing her name and they should be certain to use only her new one. She *had* to get that job. Thinking about it was her one lifeline.

"We were more and more anxious and unhappy as the time came for us to separate. When we needed to speak privately, we spoke Hebrew. They never realized we could also speak Arabic. We overheard their plans to move me to Tarifa. It was cheaper to live, and they thought they could escape to Morocco in an emergency. Then Alia left.

"They shipped all her Spanish stuff ahead to a man she knew from school, so it was waiting. Her wrists were barely healed, and I gave her my bracelets to cover up the stitches, the scars. When she got to America she was told to say not one word about me. She said she will never for one moment stop seeing me tied to that chair."

How little he'd known Alia. The bright bird in his office. The woman with the licorice hair, the brilliant smile. The hidden scars, the made-up history. The corroding fear. Landis picked up the bottle, Chaya shook her head, and he divided the last of the wine between himself and Carlos.

"Why keep up the masquerade, though? She had to change her name and credentials, everything."

"As I said, it started in fun. But if she has to help them, she doesn't want Alia Said connected to any bad thing like that. Her other persona—Julia—is more, I don't know, un-predictable? Maybe Julia could do what Alia could not, to get me free. She must have, right? Because you're here."

Landis dug his fingers into the midline of his forehead, trying to focus on his questions. He'd expected this to be difficult for her. He hadn't considered how hard it would be for him. Julia had split into two different people again.

"So you were in Tarifa to—?" Carlos interceded.

"I was their maid. Cooking their meals, keeping the apartment clean for the three of them. One of them was with me every minute until the two Mohammeds finally went to New York. After they left, Amin did have to leave me alone during the day, to go to work, but I had no money, and…" The hint of a frown on Chaya's forehead was deepening, as if it was becoming harder to ignore their evasions.

"They knew my Spanish isn't good, and if I tried to tell someone what was going on, they said they'd find out. They said people were watching me. They had a paper saying I was Amin's sister and mentally unstable. I knew the police wouldn't help. They're much more likely to believe a man with a paper than a woman with my crazy story."

She drank some water. "I cried all the time. Worrying about Alia and what my family must be going through. They insisted my family had given up on me. They said they didn't want me back; I was so depressed, I actually believed it." She paused. "I thought, at least Alia is safe. And they didn't beat me or hurt me." She lowered her eyes discreetly. "They were actually in a good mood—excited—last winter. But by April, May, I heard lots of yelling behind closed doors. They weren't getting what they want from Alia. Finally, the two Mohammeds took off. Before they left, they kept telling me if I tried to escape, Amin would let them know, and they'd be in New York. With Alia. They'd kill her for sure."

"Did you try?" Landis asked.

"Of course not!" Her expression went from annoyance to shock, and slowly she laid the palms of her hands on the table. The thin cotton of her shirt trembled with the strength of her heartbeat. "What are you saying? Is—"

Landis reached for her hand. The excruciating pretense had to stop. "Two months ago."

"Two months! Oh, Alia," she wailed. The few people at other tables glanced toward them.

"I'm sorry," Landis said. "So sorry. She was a lovely, wonderful person. Smart. Hard-working. Beautiful." He had to pause. Tears were gathering, and he stared at the ceiling a moment. "Everyone in our office liked and admired her. I miss her every day."

She jerked her hand away and covered her face. They let her cry a few minutes. When she lifted her reddened eyes, she said, "Those bastards! Those stupid bastards."

Landis changed the subject, afraid he'd break down too and afraid it would occur to Chaya that with Alia gone, there had been no reason to keep her alive. He said, "Alia kept her bargain. I didn't know about you until your mother told me ten days ago. She was in New York for a meeting. She and your father tried everything they could to find you. They harassed the Spanish police, your dad went to Seville himself, to your apartment. They hired a private detective. The police told them not to interfere. That they'd put you at risk. It's been...hard."

She sniffled and had trouble speaking. They heard "sorry."

Carlos cleared his throat. "I take it that since they left for New York, you haven't seen the two Mohammeds?"

She shook her head. "I never want to see them again."

Landis squeezed her shoulder. "I'm sorrier than I can ever say."

❦

When time came for Chaya to board her plane, she

hugged the two men, her shoulders trembling. Landis whispered, "*Shalom*," and held her a long moment. At the door to the jetway she gave a final wave. With the tears distorting his vision, she looked just like her mother. Like Julia, leaving him.

Chapter 42

Chaya wasn't Julia, but she was a connection to her. Probably the closest connection possible. The girls had spent their last few years together, they'd spent the Spain vacation and the trauma of the kidnapping together. They were the same age and looked like sisters. And now she was gone too.

Late Thursday morning he arrived at the office, operating in a time zone somewhere mid-Atlantic.

"Welcome home!" Deshondra handed him a pile of messages. "Glad to get these off my desk. Was it fun?"

"Everything worked out great, thanks." *But fun? No. Not exactly.*

"You've got some—" She waved a hand toward his bare forearms, dark marks from his fight with Chehab's pal showing through his tan.

"Bruises? Windsurfing."

"Really? That's way more exciting than here. It's been super-quiet."

"I brought you a present." Landis reached into his satchel and pulled out a package wrapped in glossy white paper with a pink and white polka-dot bow.

"Oh, my god. Thank you, Arch!" She reached for the box. "You didn't have to get me anything," she said, clearly delighted he had. "Should I open it?"

"Sure, go ahead." So many times in the last two months

he'd walked past a shop and, caught off guard by the window display, said to himself, "That scarf would look great on Marjorie," or, "Those look like bracelets Julia would wear," or, "Hawk might enjoy that book," only to be swamped by grief. Deshondra wouldn't know this gift was mostly for him, to show himself he had someone left in his life to give presents to.

She lifted a dainty bottle of perfume from the box. She dabbed on a bit and reached out her arm so he could sniff her wrist. The scent began as light as an armful of spring flowers in a sandalwood box. "Beautiful!" he said. "Don't let the deliverymen spend the day buzzing around you."

She laughed and thanked him extravagantly. "Charleston asked to see you? And Detective Fowler needs to touch base. I told him to stop by about noon? He said it will only take a minute."

Here we go.

కుకు

Fowler arrived shortly, carrying a small white bag and a blue and white cup of Greek diner coffee. He plopped into one of the chairs at Landis's table in a way that made his "only take a minute" sound unlikely. "Glad you got a little vacation. Deshondra says you've been in Spain. That was good?"

"Great."

"Looks like you got some sun. Though you look a little banged up. Tell me, are the Spanish police after you?"

Panic swept through Landis as he remembered the flashbangs, the alarms, the handcuffed men, the nighttime escape to Marbella. Then Fowler's relaxed expression registered.

"Believe it or not, I spent a whole week over there without being arrested once. That's because *la policía* didn't hear my Spanish."

Fowler actually laughed. "I came by to close the books on the Brussels case for you. I talked to de Smoot, de Smits—"

"De Smet."

"—de Smet while you were away. They got a confession out of their gay activists. Apparently Meert's death was an argument gone wrong. He got into a shouting match with a bunch of them. They were pissed he hadn't confronted you like they wanted him to. He was supposed to do it over dinner, but when he didn't, they insisted he follow you. But again, he failed.

"They were in his face and Meert was backing away, tripped, cracked his head open. Died instantly. The case was confusing at first because they moved the body. De Smet said it was raining that night, so some evidence was lost. They're up on charges, and de Smet says there won't be any more problems at your construction site."

"Thanks for that bit of good news. Were they the men who came to my hotel?"

"Yeah. They were planning to confront you themselves, try to intimidate you. But they missed you too. So that's one question answered."

"And they broke into my room?"

"They say no. Were you sure someone had been in there?"

"Not really. Paranoid at that point, actually." This was welcome news, but Landis had more pressing issues on his mind. "Hawk and the drug?"

"Not yet. We're working on a couple of theories."

Landis hesitated. "And Julia? Alia?"

"I don't know what to say about that. I've been putting my head together with the guys from the 19th, and we think the fact your burglars were interested in the phony Velázquez and that box you bought that looked like hers—yeah,

I recognized it—suggests whoever killed her hasn't lost interest in her. Or in you. What do you think?"

"Sounds right to me." Landis frowned, wondering whether to tell Fowler about Chaya. Then he'd know how exactly right it did sound, that Alia had definitely been of interest to terrorists—or rather, to would-be terrorists. He remembered his promise to O'Hanlon to tell Fowler about Chaya. And Carlos's advice: Keep it simple.

"Uh, Ed, while I was in Spain, I talked to Alia's cousin, Chaya. They both graduated from university last year, Alia from Beirut, as you know, and Chaya from a school in Cypress. There were three guys always hanging around Alia's crowd, not students. After graduation, Chaya and Alia learned they were wannabe terrorists. Freelancers. Punks, really, Chaya said. Two of them came to New York at the end of May, a few days before—" he searched for words he wouldn't stumble over "—a few days before all this started. From what Chaya says, that initial theory about Julia trying to get information out of this office was right. Not because she was a terrorist, but because they threatened her. Sounds nuts, doesn't it?"

"Not to me." Fowler drained his cup. "Know what's coming up in less than two months?"

"9/11?"

"Tenth anniversary. You wouldn't believe what we're hearing, the stuff simmering in wackos' brains. So why'd they follow Alia here? She was an American. Why didn't she say something, call us?"

"They had Chaya."

"Holy shit." Fowler stared into his empty cup. "Who is this cousin? Where is she?"

"She's an Israeli citizen. She's home now."

"She didn't say anything before now? When her cousin was murdered?"

Landis sighed. Keeping it simple would be impossible.

"She didn't know. One of them had her up until four days ago." Landis managed to keep a bland expression.

Fowler studied him. "Yet you managed to stay clear of the Spanish police? Good work, Landis."

"The police searched for her when she went missing a year ago, but they gave it up. The Israelis looked for her too, at first, but didn't believe she'd been kidnapped. I thought…I had to try."

"The two that came over after Alia. They're still here? In New York?"

"As you say, the break-in at my apartment suggests they are. My sources—" he winced apologetically "—say they haven't left, at least not using the passports they came in with." He let that sink in. "Doesn't that prove Julia wasn't giving them any information? If they thought she was useful, wouldn't they keep her alive? If they haven't stopped looking for whatever-it-is, isn't that precisely because they didn't get it?

"Or maybe she tried to deal with them," he continued, "saying she had information hidden away, but wouldn't hand it over until they let Chaya go. That explains what they went after in my apartment—Julia's things. As your guys said, they were 'looking for something.'"

"Funny they didn't tear up her apartment the night they shot her. Lots of places to look, as I recall," Fowler said.

"Something spooked them? Afraid someone heard the gunshot? They saw the table set for two? They needed time to think it over? Chaya says they aren't too bright. Once they left the apartment, they couldn't get back in. Seeing Julia's painting and the box at my place must have felt like a gift."

Fowler shook his head. "Maybe they shot her *because* they got what they wanted. They didn't need her any more. But you're right, if they're still nosing around, that suggests they didn't get anything. Or not everything. Of course, it's possible they *did* find what they were looking for in your apartment. Behind the painting, say."

"Maybe. Ed, talking to Chaya convinced me Julia is an innocent victim. I'd been ninety-eight, ninety-nine percent sure. Now I'm a hundred percent. The rest of what Chaya said bears out some information I have."

Fowler was giving him a look that didn't allow holding back.

"I've got names. Photos."

"Goddammit, Landis! You've been holding out on me!"

"Until I talked to Chaya, it was total speculation." He sounded contrite.

"Yeah, well, I get paid to speculate. Begin at the beginning. Though I can see already I'll have to talk to my buddy Wojcik at the JTTF. Goddammit." Fowler pulled out a notebook. "Tell me."

Landis recounted Chaya's story. Chaya and Alia's story. Tamara's visit. None of which touched on his own guilt, sealed in its flaming private compartment.

"What led you to Tarifa, specifically?" Fowler asked.

Landis closed his eyes a moment. He was prepared for this question. "I found a scribbled note in one of the books Alia borrowed. It was all she had time to write."

"And you didn't bring it to us?"

"The message didn't make sense until I talked to Chaya's mother. And the problem was in Spain, involving an Israeli citizen, not here."

Fowler watched Landis closely. "Then you're lucky everything worked out so well."

"Incredibly."

Chapter 43

Fowler's visit had taken up the rest of the morning, and he had other business to deal with, the easy stuff. Ty Geller was high on the list of people he needed to talk to, but Ty was the hard stuff. He would have to wait. He texted Charleston: "Free now. Come on up." Flipping through the mail, he found a letter from Julia's parents. Their thanks for helping with the apartment resurrected that painful day. They didn't mention Alia. They didn't need to.

"Welcome back, sir," Lee said. "How was the vacation? Where were you in Spain? Deshondra wasn't sure."

Was this a reproof? "Tarifa. Worked out well. Wonderful beaches." *So they say.* "How were things here?"

"No problems. Ty and I made a list for you." He waved a printout. "Miami wants a call, but Rolando says it's not urgent."

"OK. Thanks." He folded his hands on the table and waited, looking expectant. Lee's eyes searched for a spot to land. He sat down abruptly, then jumped up again and walked to the wall of photographs. "You took down the awards."

"Weeks ago."

"Oh." He shoved his hands into his pockets.

Landis fidgeted with his pen. He'd hoped this would be quick.

"I see the police were here again," Lee finally said.

Is he making small talk? Or is there a point to this?

"Fowler? He tied up the final threads about your man Jean-Marc Meert's death in Brussels. They've decided—"

"It wasn't my fault!" Lee turned despairingly pale.

"Nobody thought—what do you mean?"

"I *did* see you there. I was going to join you at the restaurant, but you finished sooner than I expected, and I saw you two standing in front. I was on the other side of the street, getting ready to cross over, when a man spoke to Jean-Marc, right in his face, and he started following you. Remember, it was raining? He hadn't seen me. So I followed him."

"I don't get it."

"I—I needed to talk to him, though he was acting so strange. Sneaky. I watched you go into the pastry shop and saw him waiting outside. After a while, he got into a car. Finally you came out. Did you know he was out there?"

"Wearing that tie? How could I miss him?"

Lee paced the office. "I *thought* you knew, because you eluded them rather cleverly. They never noticed me in that downpour."

Neither did I. "What do you mean, you needed to talk to him?"

Lee sat and put his head in his hands. "I was afraid of what he might tell you about me. He'd offered me some money to change the station plans—or to convince you to—so that we didn't tear down the gay rights headquarters after all and...I hadn't exactly said 'no,' yet, but when you said you were going over there, I knew I had to made it clear to him. I couldn't do it. Take his money.

"After you got away, I called him on his cell and told him we needed to talk. He told me to meet him in front of Schuman Station at ten-thirty. So I did, and he walked me around to the side where we're going to pull down those few buildings. Pointed out the important one. I told him we were close to a final design, and I couldn't guarantee anything.

"He was pretty upset, and I asked him why he was following you, and he overreacted. He shoved me, and I
shoved him back—I wasn't thinking, it was reflex, I'm so
sorry—and he slipped on the wet paving stones. I took off.
At the end of the block I looked behind me, and he was
sitting up, but from what you said about a blow to the head,
he must have hurt himself in the fall, and a brain injury
can—" Lee was close to tears. "I panicked and caught that
late flight back to New York."

Landis was too stunned to speak.

"Then you told me he was murdered," Lee continued,
"and I knew I'd gotten L + P in trouble."

Landis waited a minute. "That's it?"

"I've been wanting to tell you, but—"

"Charleston, here's what happened. After you saw him
at the station, Meert met up with some of his associates—
his partner is a big gay activist—and they scuffled, and he
fell and cracked his head open on a curbstone. More than a
bump. It was an accident, and the men have admitted their
part in it. The Belgian police have charged them." He
waited for Lee to meet his eyes. "You're not at fault. But
you should have told me at once when he tried to bribe
you." Getting into a shoving match with a client was not
recommended practice, either, but Landis let that go.

"I know it."

He gave Lee a few minutes to reorder his thoughts. Finally, the younger man said, "You're sure about Meert?"

"Positive. You are absolutely not to blame." He let that
sink in. "Now I have a question. Why didn't you tell me
you'd met Hawk before he came to work here?"

"I'm sorry, sir," Lee said without hesitation. "You know
about that? I met him and a bunch of his friends in Brussels,
by chance. In a bar. It caters to foreigners, Americans.
When I found out who he was, I was kind of bragging, I

guess, about the train station job. Being a lead on it. I thought I'd show him around the station, talk about our plans in a general way. He was an architect. I thought he'd be interested."

"He wasn't."

"I'd only just met him. Or I'd have known." Lee's eyebrows made a quizzical frown. "Sorry."

"I know what he was like." *Now I'm lying. I didn't know that boy at all.*

"Then I was afraid I'd broken confidentiality. We didn't have the commission yet. We thought we were getting it, but we weren't sure. I could have messed the whole thing up. Until that contract was signed, I was worried sick."

"We did get it."

"Yes, sir, but the whole encounter left a bad taste in my mouth. Then when he came to work here, it seemed better to act as if we'd never met. I guess we both thought that." Lee chewed his upper lip. "To tell you the truth, I'm not sure he remembered me. The couple of times we saw each other in Brussels—"

"He was high?"

Barely audibly, Lee said, "Yeah. Very."

Their silence wasn't uncomfortable. They each needed a few minutes to disentangle themselves from regrets and lost possibilities. Then Landis patted the table and said, "I suppose you have things to do, and I have calls to make. About Meert—remember, his death had nothing to do with you."

"Thank you, sir."

"You could do one thing for me, though."

"Of course."

"Go back to your Schuman designs and figure out how we can incorporate the façade of that gay rights building or some other creative memorial in the finished project. Get some input from Meert's activist friends."

"Yes, sir!" Lee's enthusiastic response showed this issue too had weighed on him. He raised his long body out of the chair like a collapsed marionette, strings tightening into action.

As he reached the doorway, Landis attempted one last question. "Out of curiosity, Charleston, did you discuss any of this with Julia?"

"Julia?" The younger man looked confused. "Oh. She said don't worry about Hawk. That he couldn't hurt me. If it was bothering me, she said, I should clear the air with you. It was good advice. My wife told me the same thing. More than once. Julia was a good friend, sir. Her murder…it hit hard." Lee clattered down the spiral staircase.

It hit hard. He could understand that.

Chapter 44

Landis had buried a message slip from Yusuf Zardari at the bottom of the pile on his table, with a muttered, "What's he want now?" but he'd worked his way down to it. Marjorie had liked the man, so he might not be as ridiculous as Landis believed, and out of allegiance to her, he called.

"Oh, Mr. Landis, I am so grateful to hear your voice. I hope you know our gala was a smashing success, and we owe so much appreciation to your late wife. I am desolate you were not there to hear me singing her praises. You received the program I sent? It included a lovely photograph of her."

"Mmm." *Now what?*

"There is only one tiny favor, may I ask of you?" His voice, trembling a bit, made it sound like the favor might not be so tiny.

"What's that, Zardari?"

"I've met two young men who are very interested in architecture. They so badly want to meet a world-famous architect and see where you work and hear all about this important profession. This could be a career path for them."

As Zardari spoke, Landis gradually straightened in his chair and now sat tall and stiff as his old drill sergeant. "Where are they from, if I may ask?"

"Lebanon." There was a noise in the background. "Say 'Morocco.'" And Zardari amended his geography.

Landis spoke slowly but was thinking fast. "Well, I'm sure a meeting can be arranged."

"Perhaps, as they suggest, it should be at a time after working hours, so they don't interrupt. They apologize in advance, but they have a lot of questions for you."

Oh, really? Me too. "Fine, then."

"Thank you so very much, Mr. Landis. This is a great honor for them. I told them you are one of the most illustrious architects in the West. They are very fortunate boys. Is today acceptable?"

Christ's sake. Stop pushing. I need time to plan. "Today? Tomorrow is better. How's tomorrow?"

Muffled voices filled the pause that followed, then Zardari slipped back to him. "Unfortunately, I'm afraid tomorrow doesn't work. They have some jobs, and one of them has an appointment—"

Zardari's voice was urgent. Perhaps he was a partner in their scheming after all. Landis's mind flew over options. "OK. This evening then? Around seven?" *Go ahead, get it over with.* And this time he'd have backup. More muffled consultation.

Zardari came back on the line. "Yes, that will be fine with them."

Landis seethed. *Fine with* Them? "Do they have names?"

"Oh, certainly. I'm so sorry. Their names are—" he was consulting someone again "—their first names are both Mohammed, and their last names are—are hard for Westerners to pronounce."

Doesn't matter. I know who they are. "How did you meet these young up-and-comers, Zardari?" *These killers?*

"They came to my office after the conference. They attended the open sessions and the gala—we filled every seat—and met very interesting people, and thought I might possibly have a few connections"—Zardari's nervous, self-deprecating chuckle made Landis shudder—"who could advise them on their careers. They were especially interested in meeting you, my friend." That clinched it. A lot of prominent architects were at the dinner. He knew. He talked them into buying tickets.

Landis bit back a sharp answer. "You'll come with them?"

"Of course. I would enjoy seeing your offices myself."

I don't think you'll like your reception. "Fine. See you at seven." He ended the call and set the phone down slowly.

Zardari had said something that bothered Landis. In fact, everything he'd said bothered him, but near the end. What was it? They'd gone to the conference. They'd met interesting people. Marjorie might have met them, if she'd...

෴

Landis waited in his office for Carlos and Fowler and Gennaro and Wojcik from the JTTF. It was almost two and he still hadn't eaten. He sent Deshondra out for sandwiches. He had the urge to pace, but he never did that in view of the staff; it would worry them, especially with the NYPD about to arrive.

He ran over his conversations with Tamara. *Oh, my god.* "Some lively young people joined my table," she'd said. Were the young men she sat with her niece's murderers? Her daughter's kidnappers? Did they know who she was? Though they were here and she was safely in Israel, his hands shook as he picked up his phone and scrolled through the directory. What time was it there? Nine-thirty? The home number then.

"David? It's Archer Landis." His voice cracked. "Please, no need to thank me. We were incredibly lucky. How *is* Chaya?...So glad to hear it. Is Tamara there? Well,

David, tell her I called. No, nothing urgent." *How could I say that?* "Well, no, it is, actually. Rather urgent. I need to ask her something. Have her call me tonight."

Chapter 45

Down in the reception area, Fowler, Gennaro, and Wojcik arrived, Carlos right behind them. Deshondra, holding a white shopping bag from the deli near their office, introduced them. Carlos took the bag, and Deshondra hurried toward the staff kitchen to get drinks. Landis finished clearing the round table as the men reached the top of the stairs.

"I see you've met," Landis said. "Carlos works for Colm O'Hanlon's firm. He's the one who made it happen in Tarifa."

Fowler raised an eyebrow. "From what I hear, it sounds like you did some good work there."

Carlos gave a modest grunt.

Landis looked for Wojcik's reaction and got quick acknowledgement.

"Heard about it from Ed," Gennaro said.

"OK, then," Landis said, wondering how OK it really was. He handed around sandwiches and piled bags of chips, fruit, and cookies the size of pancakes in the middle of the table. Deshondra brought a tray of four waters and a Coke—the Coke was for Fowler—and cleared the accumulating cloud of white wrappers. Wojcik handed her ten dollars with a thank-you. Fowler handed her a twenty-and said, "This cover ours?"

"More than, thanks."

As soon as she disappeared down the stairs, Fowler said,

"Thanks for arranging lunch, but tell us."

Landis had said enough about the phone call from Zardari to get them there. Now he gave the details.

"For months, we haven't had a goddamn clue who they were or where to look for them, and now they're going to walk in here this evening?" Wojcik said. "Do they suspect we're onto them?"

"If they got a call from Tarifa, they'll know Chaya was rescued. Do they allow one phone call over there?" Landis asked Carlos.

Carlos finished chewing and wiped his mouth. "Getting ahead of yourself, Arch. Say the two Mohammeds do know Chaya was snatched, they don't know who was behind it. Could have been Israelis, sent by the parents. IDF, Shin Bet. In the hotel room, they never heard us speak English, and Chehab never got a look at you."

"One of the hotel clerks?"

"The reservation was in my name, not yours. We paid cash. The front desk was busy when we checked in, re-member, and they didn't get a photocopy of our passports. For some reason, the copier wasn't working. Later on, after they plugged it in again," Carlos shrugged, "they forgot to ask for them."

Landis chuckled.

"I had to write out our passport information. My pen-manship is pretty bad, but chances are nobody looked at it twice anyway."

Wojcik and Fowler listened, eyebrows raised. "So this is how the other half lives," Wojcik said. Gennaro chuck-led.

Carlos set his sandwich down to tick off another point. "Chehab and his buddy can't be sure we really had Chaya. They never saw or heard her. So while they might think we were unusually well prepared for visitors, and while people might have seen us with a young woman, men take women

to hotels all the time. Not many people in Tarifa could identify Chaya definitely."

"Then why the hell did they try to break into your hotel
room?" Wojcik asked.

"They obviously had some information, or thought they
did," Carlos said, "but after a night in a cold dark cell, people's doubts grow."

"Their whole scheme relied on each woman's determi-
nation not to put the other at risk," Landis said. "I don't
understand why they're coming here tonight, though." He
shoved the last of his sandwich into his mouth and brushed
a few crumbs off his white shirtfront.

"I'd bet they don't know Chaya's free. They're coming
here to keep threatening you until you give them information for their terrorist agenda," Carlos said.

"Which further proves they didn't get what they wanted
from Julia, or at my apartment."

Wojcik said, "We won't know any of this for sure until
we interview them. I like Carlos's theory and hope he's
right. It removes the element of desperation. If they don't
expect you to know who they really are…" He shrugged.

"You mean if they think I'm simply a nice guy, going
along with Zardari's request?"

Landis's phone vibrated and he checked the screen.
"This may be good news." He took the call. "Tamara?
Apologies for this quick call. I have people here in my office. You told me you had a list of the conference at-
tendees? Contact information? Were the students on it?
Like the ones that sat at your table?" He listened to her reply. "Do you have that list with you by any chance?…Well,
do you mind getting it?"

Landis reached for a cookie, caught sight of Carlos's
well-muscled body, and grabbed an apple instead.

"OK. Yes. See if there's a Mohammed"—he looked at
Carlos, who spelled it for him—"Fakih-F-A-K-I-H, or

Mohammed Mosallam....Are there phone numbers for them?"

"Email addresses we can trace too," Wojcik interrupted.

"Phone numbers and emails, both," Landis said. "OK, read them to me?" He jotted the information on his paper plate. "Are those the two who sat with you, by any chance?...No? OK, good." He listened a moment. "I'll call you later—tomorrow—to explain. Many thanks. *Shalom.*" He pushed the plate to the center of the table. "You can find them with this?"

"It may take a while, but the JTTF has resources." Wojcik grabbed the plate and walked away a few feet to place a call. "Well, we know one thing," he said, easing into a chair after a few minutes and laying down his phone. "We know where the hell they'll be at seven."

Landis said, "I'll have to find an excuse to get everyone out of here on time. I'm not sure my people's nerves can take another crisis." He glanced to the bull pen below. *I'm not sure mine can.*

Carlos thought a moment and said, "Tell them I'm doing a security check around five, and the alarms going off will drive them batshit. Do themselves a favor. Leave before I get started."

Wojcik's phone buzzed. "Yeah," he said into it. "OK, thanks, anyway." He shook his head disgustedly. "The Technical Response Unit says these phones are off. Now that we have the numbers, if they do turn them on again, we'll send some code that will let us track them 24/7. But for the moment, we can't. Meanwhile, they'll work on those email addresses."

Fowler studied the bags of chips, as if deciding whether to be tempted. "Is Yusuf Zardari in on it? How'd they know to get in touch with you through him?"

"That guy keeps coming up," Wojcik said.

"They know him. At least they've met him. From the

Peace and Understanding conference and the gala. Zardari organized a tribute to Marjorie," he explained to Wojcik. "So they knew he had a connection to me through her. God, I'm glad I didn't go to that event."

"How'd they connect up with him in the first place?" Fowler asked.

"Marjorie said he was rounding up spare bodies—students—to fill any empty tables. Friend-of-a-friend? Tight community?"

Landis continued. "Zardari said he'd come with them today. That should reveal how involved he is. I never liked him, don't trust him, though Marjorie did. Do I think he's a terrorist or a murderer? No. He doesn't begin to have the guts for that."

"The FBI and then the task force had him on their radar," Fowler reminded him. "Nothing came of it, so far as I know."

Wojcik shrugged. "I was planning to tell Agent Friend about your Tarifa escapade tomorrow. With this going down today, I'll have to brief him by phone, if I can reach him. Mondays the FBI has some kind of afternoon meeting over at Federal Plaza. But we can't wait for them and blow our chance to nab these guys."

"I have an idea or two about that," Carlos said, and to Wojcik, "you may not like them."

"You've got the background, so say your piece. Maybe I'll agree with you, maybe not. In the end, though, we do it my way."

"Got it." Carlos didn't get his back up easily, and he didn't now. "Number one: Arch should make sure all the staff are gone. Check the rest rooms, whatever. He waits until five-thirty to be sure nobody comes back.

"Then he goes out the back way and down the stairs. Gets clear of here. That's a little risky, because there's two of them, and they could split up. My guess is that, if they are watching the building, they'll be watching the front. Mostly because they don't have any reason to think Arch suspects anything.

"I know you'll have your own people and your own equipment, but if you bring too many big guys—strangers—in here, they might notice. If they *have* been watching, they've seen me come and go—and I look like them. I'm not trying to do your job, but I can get in and out without raising suspicion. I come in around six to set up. For one thing, I'll secure that back staircase."

"They won't get that far," Wojcik said.

"Then you won't mind, if I—?"

"Knock yourself out. Not necessary, though."

"Setup won't take more than a few minutes," Carlos said. "By six-thirty, at the latest, your guys and I are ready and waiting."

Wojcik said, "Fine, but then you take off. I'll have plenty of people up here, and more downstairs monitoring the entrances."

"You can't have police loitering around," Landis said. "In this neighborhood? They'll be noticed."

"I'll start moving them into place around six. They'll be plainclothes. Your visitors will never spot them."

"Unless the FBI shows up wearing those fucking jackets," Fowler muttered.

"Not a chance," said Wojcik. "It's going down after five o'clock, right? They'll be 'out on operations.'"

They pawed through the detritus of the lunch. "Deshondra will give you cardkeys so you can get in." Landis brought over a wastebasket and the trash went into it, including Fowler's three empty chip bags and a cookie wrapper.

Chapter 46

Landis gathered the staff mid-afternoon for a quick catch-up. The alarms were being tested after closing, he said, which would be at five that day. When Carlos gave the system an unexpected burp as they were discussing the week's business, no one was inclined to stay late.

"Sorry!" Carlos yelled from the reception area, barely audible to their shocked ears.

Geller took his usual careful notes. Knowing he'd had conversations with BLK, Landis wondered whether the record-keeping was the prelude to betrayal. When the discussion moved to new ideas and prospects, Landis called an adjournment. No point giving Geller more than necessary.

He bounced a stack of papers on the conference room table, evening their edges. "Don't forget. Be out by five. No workers' comp for hearing loss if you hang around!" Laughing, they went back to work.

❧❧❧

Landis had an hour to kill, and he was restless. Between calls he'd read the mail that stacked up while he was in Spain and flipped through a pile of trade magazines. Carlos had gone "shopping." After Tarifa, Landis had a better idea of what that meant. He tried working on a list of things to do *after*.

He wrote "Call Tamara." She and Chaya needed to know the Mohammeds were out of commission. That would lift a cloud from them too. He underlined his note, but couldn't think of anything to add. His immediate priorities depended on the outcome of the evening ahead, and too much treacherous territory lay between now and then. Carlos, Fowler, Wojcik's JTTF resources—they should be able to take care of these two punks, but so much had gone wrong in the last few months. They'd gotten close to him time and again, and they hadn't given up. He balled the non-list and tossed it into the wastebasket.

"Going for a walk," he told Deshondra. She glanced up from her computer screen and waved.

A mile uptown was the New York Public Library where he regularly communed with the stone lions, Patience and Fortitude. If it were possible to channel these attributes, he needed to do it.

A banner out front announced a special exhibit of Near Eastern manuscripts, and the coincidence prompted him to climb the steps for a quick look. The beauty of the illuminated volumes engaged him at once, especially the illustrations of curved and convoluted palaces and fortresses, with their flat-on perspective, their windows and doorways placed to reveal the paintings' message. He admired the minute detail, some of which must have been created with a brush composed of a single hair. His hand curled in his pocket, tense with awareness of the control such stunning work required.

An especially beautiful page drew him in. It depicted the eternal battle between the dragon on the ground and the magnificent bird of prey, the phoenix, hovering overhead. Today that bird was him, he thought, taking the fight to the wicked dragon. The Mohammeds would see it the other way around. He would be the vain phoenix and they would be the dragon bringing light. He chuckled, thinking how artistic ambiguity always worked in the viewer's favor.

Either way, by tomorrow, I'll be rid of those little shits.

Energized, he strode back to the office. His adversaries weren't a dark mythical force. Their past could be known and understood, like Islamic art was known and understood. He'd made them into a featureless foe that could kill Julia, shoot at him, poison his picnic guests—and Hawk—and break into his apartment at will. Adversaries who could do all these things invisibly. Until now. Tonight they'd be out in the open, and their illusions about themselves would come crashing down.

He entered the L + P office shortly after five. Following Carlos's instructions, he checked the kitchen, the men's room, cracked open the ladies' room door and called out. No one. When he climbed the stairs to his own office, he saw Carlos had left a paper shopping bag at the top of the steps. He peeked inside and recognized what Carlos had brought.

Deshondra had deposited a pile of paperwork on his desk. He'd take care of that while he waited to make sure none of the staff returned, then get out himself. Sitting there, though, he was distracted by the sense this was a re-play of the afternoon when he waited for his mysterious visitor, the afternoon when time crawled forward, excruci-atingly slow. Then, at the key moment, when the slightest delay could have averted two tragedies, the seconds rock-eted past. Hawk had no time to recognize his mother before he fired his gun, she had no time to call his name, and Lan-dis had no time to stop Hawk from slipping into the path of the swinging arc of steel, no time to stay his arm, no chance to save his family.

The door buzzer rang, shaking the recollection out of him. His watch said five-thirty. A delivery? Carlos, Fowler, and Wojcik had card keys. If it was his visitors, they were early. Way early. The buzzer sounded again.

Landis speed-dialed Fowler. Voice mail. Carlos. Ditto. The deadly scimitars he'd seen in the Islamic art exhibit flashed in Landis's mind. No, no scimitars. Guns. They'll bring guns. Again, he was unarmed, except for, he told himself, his lion heart and his phoenix wings. The buzzer sounded a third time, and Landis clattered down the spiral stairs shouting "Coming!" As much as he feared letting them in, if it was them, he was more determined they not get away.

Two shadows were visible through the glass panel alongside the door. When he opened it, he managed a slight bow to two scruffy-looking young men, noticing their un-combed hair and wary dark eyes. "Welcome. I'm Archer Landis, please come in. You're early." Keep up the cha-rade. They glanced all around, not focusing on anything yet.

"I see many computers. Many people work here. Where are they?" the skinny one asked Landis, sounding suspi-cious.

"Some of them are out at job sites. It's August, so vaca-tion time. You know 'vacation'?"

"Of course. You are alone?"

"Yes. It's nice and quiet for our talk." *This is inane.*

"Good."

Landis made a show of herding them to the stairs. "Let's go up to my office. Up the stairs, please." His plan was to occupy them, contain them, if he could, until help arrived. As they preceded him up the stairs, he tried to spot their weapons. One of them was getting fat, here in the States, and his white shirt and dark pants looked a couple of sizes too small. If he had a gun, it wasn't tucked in his waistband, next to his spine, where Carlos carried his. The other, also wearing dark pants and a white shirt, was skinny as a tent pole, his loose shirt flapping.

What's underneath there?

They prowled Landis's office, stopping at the photo of Julia. Landis pretended not to notice their interest. "Those pictures are of buildings we've constructed around the world. You might recognize a few, if you've been to Qatar or Saudi Arabia. Would you like something to drink? Can I get you tea or a Coke?"

"Coke," the fat one muttered.

"Yes," the other one said.

Landis went back down the stairs and crossed the open floor below. He wondered whether they were watching him or still staring at the photo of the woman they murdered. He disappeared from their view down the hall and into the kitchen. Looking at Deshondra's bulletin board of staff photos produced physical pain. All those people, that talent, those relationships—all at risk.

He rested his forehead on the cool refrigerator and closed his eyes. If he ran down the hallway and out the emergency door, they would never see his escape. It would be so easy. But when he didn't come back, they'd look for him, and when they found him gone, they'd leave and be in the wind again, warier than ever. He couldn't let that happen. He had to keep up the charade Zardari had put in motion. *Where was he, by the way?* Seeing them looking at Julia's picture and knowing what they'd done to her—he might not win this battle, but he couldn't abandon her to them again.

Chapter 47

L andis grabbed three Cokes from the fridge and clutched them to his chest. The cold penetrated his shirt, all the way to his skin. That sensation of exposure made him think of Julia's last seconds, her wounded chest open to the air. That horrifying memory steadied his resolve. He stepped through the kitchen doorway, never giving the emergency door a glance. When he reached the open space of the associates' workroom, the two Moes were looking down at him. Landis waved. *Little bastards.*

"Where's Mr. Zardari?" he said, puffing from the stairs and the electric tension skittering through his body. He clanked the cans onto the table, one for each of them. "Sit, please." They did.

"Zardari not coming," the heavy-set one said. He popped the top of a Coke.

"Oh, too bad," Landis said. *Can they detect sarcasm?* "Let's see. You're both named Mohammed, right? What do I call you?"

"I'm Fakih," said the skinny one with the glasses, in an unexpectedly high voice—a voice that recalled the singsong outside his office door as he backed against it, blood dripping on the carpet. Fakih pointed to the other. "Call him Mo."

Do they know what happened to Chehab? Is that what brings them here? Or are they running out of time and money living in New York? They're young, not many skills, but they probably don't care about comforts and can live cheap. Five to a room, eight.

"Where are you staying, here in New York?" Landis smiled as if he cared.

"Queens," Fakih said. Astoria, Little Egypt. Directly across the East River from his apartment. They could be watching each other.

"Convenient," Landis said.

"Is OK."

"So, you're interested in architecture careers? Here in the States, or in the Middle East, or—?"

"We do not know," Mo said. "Yet."

"There's certainly a lot of construction in that part of the world. Lots of building." Landis struggled to maintain a pleasant expression. Fakih's eyes were black and alert as a bird's, and his gaze flitted around the office, always landing on him.

He'd remained standing. He couldn't sit at the same table with them. He grabbed the last Coke and strolled to the brick wall. He pointed out various photographs, dragging out his explanations as much as he could, looking for a spark of interest that might reveal what it was they were looking for. As he spoke, he half-turned toward them. He held the Coke out of view and gestured with his free hand, slowly backing along the wall, one photo at a time, toward the stairs and the bag Carlos left.

He pointed to a large photograph. "This apartment building is in Ankara. Thirty stories," the last building he and Terry created together. A few steps to the right. The bag was about ten feet away. He gestured to another set of pictures. "These three are in Doha. Offices, quite a bit taller than the apartment building. The developer for these buildings is very active in the region. Many new projects in the works." A few steps more. He jiggled the Coke back and forth.

"Have you seen any of these buildings in your home country? Which Zardari said is Morocco, right?"

No response. *Liars.*

Landis had an inspiration. "There are a few buildings we recently finished that I don't have pictures of yet. A U.S. embassy in Abu Dhabi," the project Hawk trolled before the FBI. No reaction. "Here in New York, the Coppersmith Building." *BBC?* Again nothing. He jacked up his courage and said, "We're working on a major transit hub in Brussels, Belgium." They stared impassively. "Near the European Union." Nothing.

What the hell DO they want?

He pointed to another photo. "We did some good work in Amman. You can see a few skyscrapers in the background there, but the scale of the city is relatively low, tight to the ground." He took another few steps backward. "There's beautiful stone in that part of the world, and we used it to good advantage here."

Landis was only three feet from the stairway and Carlos's shopping bag now. He heard a click and faced Fakih, taking a step sideways. Less than two feet. Fakih's pistol pointed at his face. "Local materials," he said, faintly.

"Enough," Fakih said. "We do not come for tour."

"Why did you come?"

"Information," Fakih said.

Landis tightened the muscles in his crotch. *You will not piss your pants in front of these boys.*

His accomplishments filled the adjacent wall, testaments to his imagination and skill, to his leadership and creativity, to the multi-million-dollar confidence others had in him. What had they accomplished? They killed a defenseless woman whom he loved. They compromised the mental health of his son. They shot at him, poisoned his staff and their families, broke into his apartment. And they parted Chaya and her parents for almost a year. He shifted his weight to his heels, ready to duck down the stairway, if necessary, and inched closer to the shopping bag.

"What information? About Schuman in Brussels?"

"Who he is? I never hear of him. No."

Obviously not. "Then about the Coppersmith Building? In Midtown Manhattan?"

"You wasting time. We do not care about this building, that building," Fakih waved the gun in the general direction of the wall of photographs. "We want information on what makes building—*ghyr hasin*—"

"—easy to destroy—" Mo put in.

"—and every such building a good target. We don't care what is this building. This is what Alia Said was supposed to tell us." He gestured with the gun toward Julia's photo.

"You killed her."

"When she not giving information. Of course," Mo said, unconcerned, his hands folded across his stomach like an old man. "We come to New York to persuade her."

"Did you shoot at me from across the street over there?"

Fakih grimaced. "That was to scare you. We see we have to come to you for information we need. You must give us it. Before, I shoot to miss, and crap gun almost kill you." His mouth drew down with disgust. "This time I not miss."

Landis's knees shook. He inched sideways, and his pantleg brushed the bag.

"You broke into my apartment?"

"We thought you are there so finally we get what we come for," Fakih said.

"Instead, we find Alia's painting and things. Maybe she hide something for us after all." Mo shook his head. "We make sure."

"We should get information ourselves from start. We should look here. L plus P." Fakih waved the gun toward the open floor below. The racks of file drawers, topped with 3-D models, looked enticing. As Fakih's gaze followed the gun, Landis glanced into the open bag, locating what he would need.

"You sure took your time," Landis said. "You murdered Julia—Alia—in early June but didn't get around to my apartment for six weeks."

"So what?" Fakih said.

"I'm just saying, it sounds more like you're on vacation, living it up here in New York, not on much of a mission." Landis hoped an argument would keep them talking. He had nothing to lose. After all their admissions, he was a dead man.

"What you know?" Mo said. "We are busy. We making contacts in the community. We have some jobs—"

Fakih cut him off. "Where we stay, they have many guns. Shotgun, rifle." He wagged the handgun. "Little ones. We know where they hiding. But we must wait until men all go out. When we are having the gun, we don't find you. Lucky day today."

Fakih muttered a phrase in Arabic that Landis understood as a curse. "Now you tell us what we want. We see these big building go up so fast. They coming down faster."

"Nine-eleven, dude." Mo looked gleeful.

"Where is best place to plant bomb? Elevator shaft? Two or three bomb, different places? How we know? Show us on these pictures or down there"—he gestured to the workroom below—"show us on little buildings."

"Little buildings? You mean the models?"

"Yes, models. Then we can attack buildings anywhere in world."

"Everywhere," Mo said.

"Each building is different. That's not an easy question." *And not one I plan to answer.* "Is that what you asked Julia to do?"

"Yes, but she not do it. Every time she give us papers,

lots of bullshit, but nothing what we need."

"Papers?"

"Papers about buildings never being built," Mo chimed in. "She say, study these papers, so we can read plans for real buildings. A load of big bullshit. We can't understand papers."

"We don't want to study. She should tell us. But she say impossible."

Stalling for time, she was, and now I am too. When was she going to tell me what was going on, so I could help her? It pained him to think how she'd struggled alone.

"She tell you about us?" Fakih asked.

"She never told me anything."

Mo added, "As long as we have her Jew cousin, she is careful."

Landis screwed up his face and shrugged. "You said cousin. What cousin?"

Fakih waved his gun hand. "In Spain. My uncle kept Jew cousin, but after Alia is dead, we tell him kill her too."

Landis had stopped listening, his mind absorbed in visualizing what he had to do. He'd keep trying to get them off their game. But before he could say anything more, Fakih said, "Enough useless talk. Tell us what we need to know. Or we will make you do it."

"Why should I tell you anything! What about my son?" Landis shouted. "Why were you giving him drugs? You killed him!"

Fakih looked to Mo, saying something in Arabic, then, "What the fuck?"

With that brief distraction, Landis popped the top of the shaken Coke and threw it at Fakih's head. The foaming soda spewed into his eyes and down his front. Fakih sputtered, and Landis dropped to the floor in a crouch.

He grabbed a flashbang from Carlos's bag. Rolling to the side, he pulled the pin. He threw it onto the table, the surprise and the Coke spoiling Fakih's hasty aim. Landis clapped his hands over his ears and squeezed his eyes shut. Even though this was a tiny commercial version, not military grade, the flash-bang's percussion felt strong enough to shatter the glass wall. Fakih's second shot also went wild.

The men, dizzy and disoriented, coughed and gasped. As the cloud billowed toward Landis, he took several deep breaths. He covered his mouth and stood. He pulled a can of pepper spray from the bag, stepped closer to the table. Averting his face, he directed the powerful spray toward first Fakih then Mo. Fakih gasped, inhaling a terrifying quantity of the spray. The residue of the flashbang hung in the air as this new cloud spread over them. Fakih folded forward, coughing and choking. The gun fell. Landis grabbed it and threw it behind him. It clattered down the staircase. Fakih's eyes streamed. He was blinded and helpless.

With unexpected agility, Mo leapt over the table and crashed into Landis. Near the floor the air was a little clearer, though both of them were coughing. The suffocating bulk of Mo was on top of him and his airway burned. Landis swung his arm as hard as he could, trying to hit the back of Mo's head with the spray can.

An anguished yell told him he'd reached his mark. He pushed Mo off him and crawled toward the circular stairs, gripping the canister. Mo grabbed his foot, stopping his progress. Landis twisted away, leaving Mo holding his shoe. He crouched at the top of the stairway, where the air was clearer. He and Mo met like sumo wrestlers, when Mo lunged again. They were both knocked onto the stairs. They rolled down a few steps, becoming impossibly jammed in the winding metal.

Landis's neck was pinned against a stairway support. Mo was on top of him, his forearm across Landis's throat.

Pressure from two sides was blocking his airway. He choked, about to pass out. The stairway clanged and the pressure eased, amidst much cursing in Arabic and English.

Landis gasped and opened his eyes to see Fowler standing over them, holding Fakih's gun.

"You OK?" Fowler asked, as a couple of uniforms crowded behind him, helping untangle the two fallen men.

"I wouldn't go up there," Landis huffed, "not without masks. That's Fakih's gun. He may have another one. No Zardari. Thank god you're early."

The gasping and choking upstairs hadn't lessened. At the bottom of the stairs, Wojcik motioned for two men with rifles to move into the workroom and cover Fakih through the windows below. Landis and Mo were standing now, and Fowler told Landis to go down first. Mo followed, an officer behind him, gun drawn. Wojcik and two more men charged past them on the crowded stairway, shouting orders.

At the bottom of the stairs, Landis found Carlos perched quietly on Deshondra's desk.

"Nice," Carlos said. "I'm in my assigned position as observer."

"Good of you to leave me some tools." An officer snapped handcuffs on Mo and took him out to the elevator lobby.

"I came as soon as I got your voicemail then ran into Fowler downstairs. When we got off the elevator, we heard that flashbang and a couple of gunshots. Wojcik and crew bolted up the building stairs just as we reached your door. Sorry I missed the fun."

Landis wheezed. "You can't be everywhere."

Tromping feet descended the stairs. Fakih was handcuffed, with a uniformed officer behind him, gripping his neck, guiding him. His eyes were fiery red, and he coughed and gagged nonstop. Mucus ran down his face onto his shirt. Wojcik came next, followed by Fowler. Both men's eyes were watering.

"Powerful stuff," Wojcik said to Carlos.

"Sometimes you get only one chance."

The police took Fakih out.

Fowler stopped to speak to Landis. "You should know, Zardari's dead. Someone in the building reported gunfire late this afternoon. I sent a couple of uniforms over to check it out, and they found him."

"Christ."

"Yeah, well, at that point, Wojcik's people pinged their phones again, so we knew they were here. When I got your message, we were already on our way. You could say Zardari saved your life."

"Christ."

"Our friends here left a lot of physical evidence in his office. They could risk being sloppy." He pulled a couple of airline tickets out of his pocket. "We found these on Fakih. They planned to leave tomorrow, before we could catch up to them. We can pin Zardari's murder on them easy. And we'll try to match them to that bloody fingerprint from Alia Said's apartment."

Landis pointed to the tickets. "That was a near miss."

"Yep. Your murder would have been their last thumb in the eye of the United States."

Someone yelled, "Elevator's here."

"They told me—" Landis was saying.

Fowler waved him off and walked to the elevator. "Let Wojcik and me interview them, then I'll hear from you. I'm going in with an open mind. They're guilty as hell. That's what it's open to. Arch, you need to decompress."

When the elevator doors closed behind them, Carlos took Landis's arm. "Find your shoe, and let's get out of here. O'Hanlon's six o'clock office is open."

Chapter 48

Here he is!" O'Hanlon gave Landis a bear-hug. "The hero of Tarifa!"

"Please," Landis said, though he couldn't stop the grin. "That's the man, right there." He pointed to Carlos.

"Not how I heard it. Wasn't only dealing with the punks, it was the embassy and immigration cops too. Excellent work there, Arch."

Over the next two hours, in a dozen different ways, Landis said, "I can't believe people build their lives on nothing, then do anything—even murder--to protect it. To protect a fantasy." As the adrenaline of the last few hours burned off, the reality of what those fantasies had cost him darkened his mood.

"Dreams of glory," O'Hanlon said. "Because their rationale is so fucking flimsy, don't they have to protect it with all they've got?"

"I get true believers. In this business, I've met a few. The Moes aren't that. They're self-deluded punks who dressed up their criminality with a phony veneer of religion. To think their half-assed, half-baked scheme could end in…" He choked on his words. "Fakih admitted he took that shot at me. And, the apartment break-in."

"That figures," Carlos said.

"I didn't have a chance to pin them down about everything else."

O'Hanlon ordered another round. "The JTTF has the

lads now. Their goose will be bloody well roasted, we know that."

"Don't forget Fowler," Carlos said. "He's interested in them too."

Landis's thoughts were elsewhere. He said, "They didn't know we rescued Chaya. They said they sent a message to Chehab to kill her. 'The Jew cousin.'"

With effort, Landis pushed himself out of the booth. "Gotta go. I'm running on empty."

"We'll probably never know whether Chehab got that message," Carlos said, while Landis fumbled for his wallet. O'Hanlon waved at him to put it away. "A buddy called over to Tarifa for me, and Chehab and his pal are still in jail. The Spanish police are getting tired of chasing illegal Arab immigrants and delighted with the chance to make an example of them. 'Threw the key into the Strait of Gibraltar,' he says."

He got a weak smile in return.

 senso

Landis hadn't realized how much tension he'd been living under until he stepped into the shower Tuesday morning and let the hot water pound it out of him. He felt a gash on his forehead and saw quite a few bruises on his arms and torso from rolling down the stairs, but these physical hurts barely registered.

He thought about what he had accomplished, despite the odds. Finding the who and why of Julia's murder. And, to his immense gratification, she hadn't betrayed his trust.

Julia must have been so frightened, walking the thinnest tightrope, trying to string these men along to protect Chaya, while keeping L + P's secrets. How long did she think she could keep it up? Especially once they appeared in New York? The JTTF—so paranoid about the impending anniversary of 9/11—tried to paint her as another terrorist. In the end, Landis not only cleared her name, he proved she was a hero. At least to him.

And, he and Carlos had ended Chaya's ordeal. Thinking about her, back home with her grateful family, made him smile.

As he pulled a sport coat and trousers out of the closet, he saw the box from Julia's apartment on the top shelf. Until her murderers were caught, it had felt unlucky to disturb it. He'd reserve that bittersweet experience for tonight.

The phone rang. Fowler sounded tired and pleased. The Moes had admitted to killing Julia—the crime scene photos did them in, he said—and Zardari. Mosallam fingered Fakih for that and for the shots fired at Landis from across the street. "My new friends from the 19th are coming in this morning to ask them about the apartment break-in. They have some physical—hairs, fibers," Fowler said. "We can go for a DNA match. I'm betting we'll get it."

"They told me they did it. What about Hawk and the break-in at the beach house?" Landis was banking on this answer to tie up that last loose end. "The methylphenidate, the poisoned salt?"

Fowler grunted. "They say that wasn't them, and I'm inclined to believe them. It's *nada* compared to what they've already confessed to."

"But—" The escalating tension of his situation had become a way of life. How dysfunctional it was hadn't hit him until he believed it had ended. To be thrust back into that world of constant danger was unbearable.

"Hard to believe it's all over," Fowler said.

But it isn't.

Fowler continued talking. "Zardari kept notes. So we found out what the hell they were doing this whole time. They weren't cooling their heels. Fakih—that 'good Muslim'—got himself a Latina girlfriend and was partying at her apartment. Meanwhile, Mosallam took a job washing dishes at a shish-kabob restaurant. He banked most of his money, and that's what paid for their tickets home."

"Zardari knew all this?"

"Apparently. And apparently he made the call to you to set up their visit under some duress."

Fowler didn't elaborate, and Landis preferred not knowing. "Ah."

Before Landis left for the office, he made his call to Tel Aviv.

೧೧೧

Because the crime scene investigators worked late and let the building cleaners come in at seven in the morning, by the time Landis arrived, the gritty smoke residue was gone. He moved a wastebasket to cover up the bullet hole low in the wall. Rearranging a few pictures hid the other one, and it appeared nothing out of the ordinary had taken place there. He surveyed his team below. After yesterday, confronting Ty Geller would be a welcome diversion, one with somewhat more predictability.

Deshondra came upstairs with the mail. "Mr. Geller in today?" Landis asked.

"A super-important meeting this morning? With the city zoning board staff? Then here all afternoon, according to the schedule."

"I need to talk to him."

"No problem," she said and sniffed. "Smells funny in here. Chemical-ish."

"I don't notice it."

Landis's greater sense of freedom stayed with him. He could think about the work at hand, without devoting most of his attention to the question of who killed Julia and what their next move might be. The game wasn't over, there were Hawk's issues and the picnic to sort out, but he'd knocked a couple of major pieces off the board. Deshondra came up to say she was going to lunch. "Can I bring you something?"

"Chicken Caesar, iced tea, but not if it's sweetened."

"V-8?"

"Perfect."

He pulled out his wallet and handed her a twenty. "Get your own lunch too, and donate the change to petty cash."

"There won't be much."

"That's why it's petty cash." He chuckled, seeing her dubious expression.

"Ty called. He'll be in about one."

"OK, and I've got Ben Silk, O'Hanlon, and Carlos coming at three. We'll need a conference room." This wouldn't be a meeting for the fishbowl of his office. He glanced at the associates working below. "Send up Mr. Miller."

"The new guy?"

"Please."

e/ɔe/ɔ

L + P's newest hire, Kent Miller, hurried up the stairs, evidently puzzled about why the new boss would ask to talk with him one-on-one.

Landis put him at ease. "I have a project for you." He gestured to the brick wall. "I used to keep L + P's awards over there, but I like the staff photos better. Could you design a cabinet for our awards? With room for more, of course," he smiled. "Deshondra can show you what we have. I'd like it to be down below—you pick the best spot—where everyone can see them. They're not *my* awards, they belong to all of us."

"Well, sure," the young man acted surprised and pleased at this unexpected assignment.

"If you have questions, Charleston can advise you. He knows about this. Come back to me with a plan when you have it."

After Miller left, Landis studied the security team's interim report on the projects they'd examined so far. Their assessment of Schuman Station was ongoing. He ate the salad Deshondra brought him, scattering parmesan flakes over the pages. She called up to tell him Ty was back. "Tell him ten minutes."

Ten minutes later exactly, Geller arrived upstairs. Usually, he strode in and sat without hesitating, but today Landis had to invite him in. He sat stiffly in the chair, and the chill in his demeanor crept across the table like an ice fog.

"I've been reading the report from your team." Landis brushed a few last flakes of cheese off the report's black cover. "Very interesting. How do you think it's going?"

"Slow. They have a lot to learn. At least they seem thorough." He sounded barely engaged. He gazed out across the associates' bullpen, avoiding Landis's gaze.

"It's a unique opportunity." Landis dragged a morsel of bait across the conversational flow. "None of the other major firms have a unit like this."

"So far."

Don't like the sound of that.

Apparently, a confrontation was inevitable. No point pussyfooting. "I hear you've been meeting with BLK."

Geller's head snapped around, and he glared at Landis. "So what?"

"I'm disappointed."

"Your son went to work for them."

Landis stopped the harsh retort—"but he was irrational"—that immediately came to mind. Instead, he took a deep breath and let the words out slowly. "My son was not a senior associate in this firm, a gifted designer in whom I have entrusted an activity I believe is vital to our future." He tapped the report.

"It hasn't felt like that lately."

"Do you mean our conversation before I went to Spain?"

"Exactly."

"I saw trouble on the horizon, and I needed to address it, needed you to address it before it got out of hand. That's all. As I told you the next day."

"You told me?"

"Yes. In the message I left."

"What message?"

Landis took another deep breath. This was why people found Geller difficult. He didn't meet you half-way. "On your phone."

"I never got a message from you."

No point arguing that one. "Well, I wish you had. What I said was that I'm absolutely confident you can figure out how to lead the security team in a way that builds partnerships with your colleagues in the firm. In the process you will make L + P the nation's—possibly the world's—leader in security-conscious design. We need both. Good design, that's everyone's job; and strong security, that's your team's job." Landis put an extra note of sincerity into his voice. "Let me put it this way, Ty. You're too smart to fuck this up."

Geller sat unmoving, but gradually, the angry set of his jaw relaxed.

"You're not going to fire me?"

"Of course not. What gave you that idea?"

"Karsch said—" He stopped. "He offered me the chance to work on Burj Maktoum. I really wanted that."

"I know you did. You put your heart into it."

"I met with him a couple of times and with his team. There was something about the way they acted—not pleased, but smug and a little guilty—it bothered me."

"The job was wired. They didn't snatch it away from us honestly."

"I figured as much." Geller's voice was quiet and filled with more than one brand of disappointment. "I knew I might be looking for a new job soon, but I couldn't work with them."

"Ivan Karsch has his own agenda, and he is always at the top of it. Always. Always and forever. Remember that, and you'll get along with him fine. Mostly. Maybe."

"So you didn't tell him you were planning to let me go?"

"I haven't spoken to him, except in passing, in months. I can't stop you from talking to him or anybody, but, Ty, he's poison." The minute he heard himself say the words, something clicked into place. He wanted Geller to leave. He needed to think.

He patted the report in front of him. "You and your security team aren't engaged in an intellectual exercise here; you are safeguarding the future users of our projects, the people who bring our buildings to life, people we'll never know. Care about them as you go about your work, do it with sensitivity, and everything will be fine, more than fine."

Slowly, Geller reached his right hand across the table.

Chapter 49

L andis dug out the phone number for Tony Palmieri. He and the Suffolk County epidemiologist hadn't been in touch lately. First there was Tamara's visit, then the apartment break-in, then the trip to Tarifa, then...

"I can only deal with six crises at once," he muttered, punching in the number. He and Palmieri exchanged pleasantries, then Landis said, "Did you track down what made my guests sick?"

"Didn't I call you about that?" Papers rustled in the background. "No, guess I didn't. Sorry. It took a while, the usual summer backlog. It was what you said, though. Methylphenidate."

"I was afraid of that," Landis said, more to himself than to Palmieri.

"You know it, right? ADD drug? Has side effects in large amounts. That's why the kids were so susceptible. Their systems couldn't handle it."

"I was afraid of that."

"You're repeating yourself." Palmieri was cheerful.

"Yeah, I know. Though something may finally be making sense."

"Whatever it is, the Sheriff's Office is handling it now. Keep Vince in the loop."

"Sure, sure. Tony, thanks."

എൃ

Carlos and O'Hanlon. The PR consultant, Ben Silk. A lot of troubled waters lay behind them, with more chop ahead, Landis thought. Silk arrived first, followed by Carlos. He was clean-shaven again. The Tarifa sun had tanned him, and his newly exposed jaw was oddly pale. Landis introduced Carlos, saying, "Salvador Carlos, and, believe me, he *is* a 'savior.' I know that much Spanish."

"I understand you pulled off an awesome coup in Spain." Silk shook Carlos's hand. "Brave work."

"I train for it," Carlos said. "Arch was the brave one. But yesterday? All him. One hundred percent."

O'Hanlon strode into the conference room, as excited as his red hair. "Did you congratulate him?" he asked Silk. "He got the murdering bastards. Harassing our fair city's most brilliant architect," O'Hanlon winked at Silk. "An effing relief to one and all."

Landis responded to Silk's questioning expression. "The prosecutor is charging them today. There's a media briefing scheduled, putting us back in the news, maybe."

"Count on it," Silk said. "The media played Julia's death as long as they could. They'll be delighted to strike up the band again." He laid a hand on Landis's arm. "They'll bring up Marjorie and Hawk too."

"I know it." A few more hard miles ahead.

"Bloody shame," O'Hanlon muttered. "But if it weren't for Ben, it would be worse."

"I know that too. Much worse." Landis gave Ben a forceful nod.

"They'll think they're clever for making the connection," Silk said, setting up his laptop. "I'll draft a statement from you as head of the firm, not you as father and widower. Short and relieved."

"What are they charging them with, exactly?" O'Hanlon

asked.

"Julia's murder and Zardari's. The shot at me. The apartment break-in. That's what they've admitted to. And the police have forensics to back up everything. Partial fingerprint on the toilet seat in Julia's apartment."

"Nice find, that," O'Hanlon said.

"They left the seat up."

"Filthy buggers. Serves 'em right. Sounds like they need a good lawyer. Saint Brigid be praised, I'm not available."

"Saint Brigid?" Silk asked.

"Patron saint of fugitives."

Silk laughed. "Here's what I expect the story will be. Two Muslims waltzed into the country, got themselves guns, and ran around New York shooting people. The failure of our nation's security systems. Once again."

"Holy mother of god." O'Hanlon's voice filled with disgust.

"It's a shame they're Muslim," Landis said.

"Why so?" Silk stopped typing.

"It makes the narrative too easy. Puts them in a pigeonhole with the true believers. Which they were not. All the media need to hear is 'Muslim' and they won't look any deeper."

"What the hell. Why should they?" O'Hanlon asked.

Landis said, "I don't have any sympathy for them, don't get me wrong. But I've been thinking how easily Julia became a target of suspicion. The story shouldn't be 'Two Muslim terrorists blah, blah, blah.'

"Maybe it would be different if they came out of a fanatical wing of Islam and that's what motivated them. But these jokers used religion as an excuse. They were in it for themselves, for the supposed glory. For the thrill of anarchy.

"The story should be that *these two individuals* came to our country hoping to cause trouble, but with no clear or specific plan. They got hold of guns—too easily in my opinion—killed my associate, shot at me, murdered a peace-loving man who helped them, then tried to finish me off. These two guys. Not some political or religious abstraction."

"You're right, Arch," Silk said, taking his hands off his keyboard. "Absolutely. Lots of Muslims in this world. All of them have their own stories. As a Jew, I should be the first to object to stereotyping. We won't do that in our statement. What the prosecutor does, and the JTTF, and the media, well, that's out of our control. If I can, I'll put in a word. Their names alone, though—"

"Right." Landis thanked him, and said, "Since we're all here, I'd like to pick your brains about the other thing. The one very loose end."

Carlos pulled out his notebook.

"We know Hawk was hostile and erratic in his last few weeks. I don't deny he had long-standing issues with me, and, yeah, a lot of that was my fault. I'm not saying everything was great between us before, but there was a definite escalation."

"It's always tough when a kid follows you into your career," Silk said.

"Yeah." Landis stared at the ceiling long enough to make the others uneasy, but they waited him out. He'd never told them what Marjorie had said to him at the end, how she'd started to tell him what a useless father he was. She surely wouldn't have said that, if she'd known those would be her last words to him. He'd come to believe she was trying to get Hawk's attention by taking his side, trying to make him stop a minute, to think.

"We know his body was full of methylphenidate, and some of its side effects are anger, paranoia, delusions—they're not totally positive about that last one, because most people don't react that way—but most people aren't exposed to the heavy dose Hawk was. On top of his other issues. He also had a physical side effect. Nausea. He had to leave the dinner table more than once to be sick. Marjorie blamed me, said I was pressuring him."

"What is this stuff, anyway?" Silk asked.

"Methylphenidate helps people with ADHD. Also narcolepsy. Neither of which Hawk had. So why was he taking it? In such large amounts?"

"He wasn't 'taking' it," Carlos said. "Somebody fed it to him."

"But how would they get it into him?" Silk asked.

Landis had given this question much thought. "Through his coffee. Hawk drank coffee by the gallon. Lots of sugar. I thought too much caffeine explained why he was so jumpy and irritable. But maybe it wasn't the caffeine. Maybe it was the sugar. And if sugar can be doctored—"

"So can salt," O'Hanlon said. "The picnic."

"Bingo. I talked to the Suffolk County epidemiologist today, and their guys finally pinpointed the problem. Methylphenidate. He said if a person ingests small amounts over a longer period, there's one set of side-effects. They're especially risky for somebody like Hawk with prior mental health problems. But when a person gets a big dose all at once, like at the picnic, there's the rapid onset of nausea, vomiting—everything we saw."

"You've lost me," Silk said. "How'd this happen again?"

"When Deshondra found the beach house broken into, she thought nothing was taken. She was right. But something was added. A saltshaker full of the stuff. Intended for me, I suppose. Then I didn't go out there until the picnic. I—" He didn't need to explain.

Ben Silk gave a worried cough. "We've kept the beach house fiasco quiet so far, not attached to you, Arch. Do we have to bring it up now? Is it connected to—" he waved at his computer screen.

"Doesn't seem to be," Landis said. "But I'm close to clearing up everything."

Carlos said, "What if the break-in was a fake? Could Deshondra have staged it, left the doctored saltshaker herself? She had access to Hawk here for as long as he worked at L + P."

A rap on the conference door, and Deshondra came in, bringing a tray of coffee and sodas. "Pick-me-up?" She beamed.

Carlos watched her closely, as the men murmured their thanks and shifted around to take a mug or grab a can of Coke.

O'Hanlon spoke up, grinning. "Do you treat all the staff this way? Feeding their caffeine habits? You're a dangerous woman."

She held the empty tray down at her side like an oversized tambourine. "Those guys out there? Never. They can get their own." She laughed. "I bring coffee to Arch because he forgets to take a break, and next thing you know, he has a raging headache."

"That happened once. Twice."

"Twice was enough." She tapped the tray against her leg.

"Her genius is knowing what I need before I do."

Deshondra laughed again as she left the room. Carlos made sure she was out of earshot before closing the door.

"I can't believe it's her," Landis said. "When she found the beach house break-in, Ty was with her."

"She says she doesn't take drinks to the staff. Could she have gotten it to Hawk another way?" Carlos asked.

"Carlos, it wasn't Deshondra. I admit I went through a phase where I didn't trust anyone, but that's over. I *choose* to trust her."

"That's grand, Arch. I hope you're right." O'Hanlon

said.

"Here's how I see it. Carlos told me last week that my associate, Ty Geller, had been meeting with BLK. Hawk must have done the same. He can't have phoned Ivan Karsch on a Friday and said, 'I want to come work for you. Starting Monday.' They must've had at least a few conversations. Over a couple of weeks. Being hospitable, they could have offered him coffee. Anyone at BLK could have doctored it."

"Just like that bloody man to court your boy," O'Hanlon said. "But how can we know for sure?"

"BLK packed up Hawk's dirty coffee mugs with the rest of his stuff. I gave them to Fowler, and he sent them to the lab before Tarifa."

"*Who* at BLK packed them up?" Carlos asked.

Landis stared at him long enough for the question's implications to sink in. "Now that's an interesting question. You're thinking they could have left out anything incriminating?"

Carlos shrugged. "Or maybe they didn't know some of the items might *be* incriminating."

"I hope all this doesn't come out," Silk fretted. "It will make Landis + Porter sound like *The Sopranos*."

"Too much speculation. Let me give Fowler a ring, see if he has that report. Then we can settle this," Landis said.

Silk was reading his screen, muttering, "Maybe I can get a reporter to ask how Zardari ties in? The irony of the 'peace and understanding' leader being murdered. They might focus on that."

"Fowler's probably busy preparing for the briefing," Landis said, speed-dialing him anyway.

Fowler did pick up and, in response to Landis's question said, "I think that report came in, but—" Fowler paused. "I have to get ready for this thing. Can I hand you off to Gennaro?"

When Landis repeated his question to Gennaro, the detective said, "Yeah, hang on. It's here. Somewhere." There was a longer pause. "I'll call you back."

Landis set the phone down and continued putting the pieces in order. "So at the picnic, when the caterers were hurrying to finish up, and the dessert chef needed sea salt for the brownies, she grabbed the shaker sitting there. That's another reason it couldn't have been Deshondra. She wouldn't have taken the chance her friends and their kids would get sick. She would have retrieved that shaker, hidden it. She was there early. She had plenty of opportunity."

"How does this sound?" Silk read them the draft statement. Short and simple.

"I don't hear any problems," O'Hanlon said.

"It's good. Thanks," Landis said, as his phone buzzed.

The detective's booming voice announced himself. "Gennaro. Gave Fowler a look at the tox report first. He says the two of you should talk about it. The lab tested three coffee mugs." It sounded like he was reading. "They checked DNA acquired from the rims of the mugs to make sure Hawkins Landis had used them, and it matched what they had on file from the mur—from his death...and they analyzed the dregs by—you don't care about all this scientific shit—and found coffee residue...and they give numbers here. I can't read them, but they found a 'significant and unusual' amount of metha—meth-elp-hen-I-date."

"Methylphenidate."

"You said it. Something else too: stevia."

"Thank you, detective."

"Wait. Fowler wants a word."

Fowler came on the phone. "Are you coming to the briefing?"

"One second." Landis queried Silk. "The briefing? Should I go?"

Silk shook his head, and pointed his thumb at himself.

"No. Ben Silk will be there for me. And Colm O'Hanlon."

"Tell them five-thirty, downtown. We need to talk about how to handle those tox findings."

"Of course."

Landis set the phone down and looked at his colleagues. "Well, that's settled. Hawk's DNA and methylphenidate in the mugs, along with something called stevia."

"Interesting," Silk said. "Some of our food industry clients use stevia as a sugar-substitute. It's more than a hundred times sweeter than sugar."

"So what you're spooning into your coffee could be a lot of drug for the same amount of sweetness," O'Hanlon said. "That clinches it then, right? Not Deshondra?"

"Not Deshondra," Carlos said.

Silk ejected his flash drive, saying, "Good, because I need her to print out copies of the statement." He opened the conference room door and they all looked past him, to Deshondra at her desk, effusively greeting the Fed Ex delivery woman.

Chapter 50

Because he thought he knew all of it now, Landis immediately disregarded caution. While he'd prefer to meet Ivan Karsch on neutral ground, he was determined to put this confrontation behind him, tactics be damned.

He strode the twenty-five blocks to the BLK office hoping to clear his head, and arrived a few minutes before seven. Be ready for anything, Carlos would have told him. Be mentally loose.

BLK occupied the 26th floor of a building at 47th and Second Avenue. The building was quiet at this time of day. The diplomats who leased most of the other offices had already departed. Several young architects waited in the BLK lobby for a down elevator. The bad blood between Landis and their boss was no secret, and they didn't hide their surprise when the doors slid open and he stepped out. He recognized one of the young men from Karsch's Burj Maktoum team and greeted him by name.

"Ivan in?" Landis asked.

"He's here." The man pointed toward the empty receptionist's desk, the half-wall behind it blocking any view of the office layout. Hostile territory. Landis fixed the young man with an expectant gaze.

"Here, I'll let you in," he said and swiped a card that unlocked the glass doors. "Uh, turn left, go to the end of the hall, turn right, and he's in the corner office at the end."

"Thanks," Landis said.

As the glass doors closed, a voice said, "*Yes*, that's Archer Landis. He *killed* his s—"

That left a chill in the air. It wouldn't matter what opinion they'd formed of Hawk in his short time working there, normal people don't expect violence in their midst.

Karsch's desk angled across the corner where floor-to-ceiling windows met—dizzyingly huge expanses of glass divided every six feet by narrow metal frames. A glance in one direction gave a view of the United Nations, and in the other, Midtown's skyscrapers. Low black cabinets topped with bookcases lined the other two walls.

While Landis's blond wood, glass, and brick office cantilevered toward the associates' light-filled workroom, connecting him with his colleagues, the corner layout of Karsch's office and its sleek black and gray décor was cold, isolating. The man himself sat behind a massive black box of a desk which rested on a subtle six-inch platform, giving him height. He looked like a spider in his lair, arms reaching across, signing the stack of papers in front of him. He didn't look up.

"Good evening, Landis. I heard you were on your way to me," his slight Russian accent more pronounced at the end of the day. One of the men from the elevator must have called. Of course. His associates would have done the same.

"If you want to talk, sit." Karsch indicated the chairs facing the desk. Landis strode to the desk and leaned on it, fingers splayed. In an odd gesture, he reached into his inside jacket pocket. Karsch stiffened. He exhaled when Landis's hand emerged empty and adjusted the jacket's lapels.

"Should I congratulate you on the Burj Maktoum job?" Landis said. "Or will it sink you?"

"We will handle it beautifully." Karsch resumed signing, his ballpoint pen steady.

"I mean when word gets out about how you got the job. Payoffs, I hear."

"Then you hear wrong." Karsch put his feet up on the desk, giving Landis a close-up of the soles of his shoes. "I suspect you're making that up—but such rumors hardly compare to the mayhem surrounding L + P this summer."

"Now you're trying to poach my people," Landis said, his temper cooled by an icicle of contempt.

"If you mean Mr. Geller, he came to me." Karsch attempted to convey an injured innocence, but his glittering amber eyes betrayed him.

"And my son?"

"The same." He pointed at Landis with the pen. "I am very sorry about young Hawkins. It's sad when a young person is lost to any kind of—tragic mistake."

"My son was a troubled and erratic young man. Mostly the result of the chemicals someone was feeding him. Someone in this office. You." He said the words slowly, emphatically, as if they contained all the bitter history between them.

"Me? Why would I do that?" Karsch sounded barely interested.

"Hawk—and Ty too—gave you chances you otherwise wouldn't have had. To mine Ty's good ideas. To destabilize my family life, to distract me from my firm's work. Does it matter *why* you did it?"

"Bullshit, Landis. You are a valued professional colleague."

"Now *I* say 'bullshit.' The police have plenty of evidence." Landis gripped the edge of the desk.

Karsch shrugged. "Evidence? I doubt that. How could they? I've done nothing wrong. I certainly haven't barged into your private office flinging accusations and—do I detect?—threats." On the desk was a big knife—a Russian hunting knife with an eight-inch blade, its bone handle inlaid with running deer. Karsch picked it up and ran his fingers along its back, testing the point. "Violence surrounds you like a nasty smell, my friend, and you would like it to rub off on me." His laugh was an ugly sound and he said, "Do not try to dirty me with your shit."

"Methylphenidate, Karsch."

"What? What is that?" Karsch took an envelope from a pile of mail on his desk and used the knife to slit it open. Very neatly.

"It's the drug you put into Hawk's coffee. In large doses, it makes susceptible people hostile, delusional. What'd you do, put it in the sugar? Give him his own personal sugar bowl? Hawk always took at least two sugars. Two sugars and a big dose of a paranoia-inducing drug."

Karsch didn't reply. He tossed the knife onto the desk, where it skidded, coming to rest by a stack of memo pads. The pads bore the familiar logo of a pharmaceutical company and a few words, easy to read upside-down for a man like Landis, who'd spent his life around drawings and plans, showing them, sharing them.

"What about the beach house? Was that your plan to get me too? Heart palpitations, grieving for my son and wife, suicidal, maybe? Instead you made nineteen people sick— people who have never done you any harm. A dozen of them, kids."

Karsch shrugged again. "I heard about that ill-fated picnic on the news. They said food poisoning. So that was yours? It's a miracle anyone will work for you, Landis. Shootings at your office"—he hoisted one arm stiffly, as if in a sling—"your associates murdered, their children poisoned. With salt!" He laughed.

"You bastard. You got one of your Brighton Beach cronies to do it."

"What is your problem? None of this has anything to do with me."

"You're trying to destroy me—my business. You've already destroyed my family."

"Oh, please." Karsch slouched in his chair, eyes half-closed, and said, "I *am* sorry about Marjorie. Such a lovely woman."

"You barely knew her."

"You're wrong. Marjorie and I..." He sighed and smiled, a lizard's expression.

Knowing Karsch was baiting him didn't stop the fire that shot from Landis's chest all the way to his fingertips. When Marjorie first met his fellow architecture students, she was so young, a sorority girl. Sweater sets and pearls. Naïve, but weren't they both dangerously innocent? "What do you mean?"

Karsch swiveled his chair to gaze at the U.N. building. Fiery clouds, backlit by the setting sun, reflected on its glass exterior like flaming ghosts. "A long time ago, sadly."

Leaning over the desk, his throat tight, Landis repeated, "What are you talking about?"

"Before you were married. Marjorie and I...I met her when you brought her to a party at—you know, your friend from Yale." Karsch pretended not to remember the name of Oskar Chuikov, one of the most prominent architects of the twentieth century. "I wasn't invited of course. An acquaintance brought me. You and your pals wouldn't even speak to me, your fellow-student. But that's of no importance. You were busy cajoling Chuikov so he'd recommend you for the fellowship. Your gold-plated ticket. It should have gone to me, you know. A fellow Russian. So while you were engaged in stealing my future, I looked for Marjorie. Alas, she only wanted to talk about you. She loved your mind, you know."

"Oh really? I rather thought it was my heart."

"Arch, Arch. You never showed your heart to

Marjorie."

This struck a little too close to home. It was Julia who'd taught him to risk exposing his feelings. "What would you know about it?"

"Marjorie went for a walk in the garden, alone, in the dark. I learned a lot about women's hearts, and other things, that night."

"Are you hinting you had sex with her? With Marjorie?" The strength of his disbelief made him laugh.

"Hinting?" His tone was crafty, calculating.

Landis couldn't look at that horrible face. He walked to the window and, with absolute conviction, said, "I don't believe it."

"When she was young, a cunt like rose petals," Karsch sighed.

Landis gripped the window frame and took slow breaths. At that moment, he could kill Ivan Karsch. But he had to stay in control. He wasn't finished.

"She wasn't really willing," Karsch continued, "but I think she enjoyed it in the end."

"You raped her."

"No, not rape. I'd call it irresistible persuasion. Very soon, you were going to marry her. I *might* not have another chance."

Landis had seen autopsied bodies, the gruesome Y-shaped wound that exposed all a person's insides. This was how it felt to experience that while living. "I don't believe any of this."

"Don't be a prig. You certainly didn't resist her carnal charms. You two must have been fucking like rabbits, she got pregnant so quick."

An awful thought flamed in Landis's mind. He tried to ignore it. "I don't believe it. I don't believe you had sex with Marjorie."

Karsch laughed. "The fact is, Arch, I've fucked all your

women." At his best, he was an ugly man, but in the lurid light of sunset streaming down Manhattan's east-west streets, he looked like a grinning troll.

Chapter 51

Fists clenching and unclenching, Landis backed to the far side of the room, putting a heavily cushioned black leather sofa between them. "What the hell are you talking about?" He was off-kilter now, playing defense when he'd expected to quarterback this conversation.

Landis had loved two women, heart and soul. Karsch had never loved anyone but himself. He saw Julia's face, her long dark hair tumbling around her, and shuddered at the thought of Karsch touching her. Had he? Surely not. How would he have known about her? Still, if he had known, he would use that information. Was he going to throw Julia in his face?

Instead, Karsch veered in an unexpected direction. "All these years, I have followed behind you, picking up crumbs. That's over." He tried signing another document, but the pen wouldn't write. He threw it at the wall in disgust and it sprang apart, plastic and metal bits scattering. "I suppose all your pens work too."

He came to the front of his desk and half-sat on it, ankles crossed. He reached behind him to pick up the knife again, in a pretense of cleaning a fingernail. "Terry was a lively one," he continued in his sly tone. "A couple of drinks and she became positively amorous. I had to fight her off."

"Terry Porter could never have gone for you. She hated your work, she hated your ethics, she thought you were scum."

"Maybe so, but she liked what she found in here." Karsch reached down and rattled his privates. "We were at a conference in Saranac Lake. I walked her to her cabin after dinner, and, you know…she wanted me to come inside. I know she did. Such a tragedy she died the next day."

Landis trembled. Vile though Karsch was, he'd never connected him with Terry's death. "You arranged it."

"Archer, my friend. You have a suspicious mind. I admit she did promise to ruin me. She called me a sexual pervert. But I say it was consensual."

"You killed her."

Karsch laughed. "I did not *kill* her. Perhaps I created circumstances under which her Jag might crash on that treacherous road, if she hit the brake pedal hard enough to finish rupturing the hoses. *If* she did, perhaps I knew where she would likely lose control and where the car would end up. Merely out of curiosity I might have waited at the bottom of the precipice.

"When her car somersaulted down, the rocks tore up the underside, and obliterated much evidence."

"You set the car on fire." Landis's whole body shook. He backed up to steady himself against the bookshelves. *Hang on. Let him talk.*

"Fluids leak and spill in a crash like that. They hit a hot engine. Those magnesium components? Very dramatic, how magnesium reacts to fire. But don't worry. Terry was dead by that time. At least she was unconscious. Possibly."

As Karsch's words sank in, Landis's stomach churned. He thought he might vomit. He grabbed the bookshelf to steady himself. Through clenched teeth he said, "I don't believe one word of it. You're making it up to avoid the subject."

"What subject? Making what up? Get ahold of yourself. We're laying it all out here."

"The main subject. Methylphenidate."

"You keep harping on that goddamn drug."

And you keep baiting me. Why? The question rang in Landis's head like a bell. Then he answered it. *You want me to attack you. Then you can finish me off and claim self-defense. That's why you're telling me all this. You plan to kill me.*

The weapon was right there in Karsch's hand. He was playing with it. With him. Landis crossed his arms, took a breath, swallowed hard. If he played Karsch's game, he'd be dead. Karsch was right. *Get ahold of yourself.*

Karsch scanned him through narrowed eyes, searching for weaknesses. After a crackling silence he said, "Face it, Landis. You are done. Your business. Your family. Now all these wild accusations? You're as crazy as your kid."

Here we go. My big play. "Not *my* kid, Ivan." Landis could have used more time to think this through. He never expected the discussion to end up here, yet his voice was so much calmer than he would have thought possible. He'd moved into a zone of bottomless hate. "*Your* kid. Hawk was your son, not mine."

"No way." Karsch chuckled, full of bluster.

"Marjorie must have been pregnant when we married. Barely. Then Hawk arrived, a big healthy baby, a few weeks 'early.' *Your* son."

Karsch paused a moment before responding, and when he repeated his "No way," he barked the words.

"No wonder he didn't look like me. People said he reminded them of one of Marjorie's grandfathers, but I couldn't see it."

"You *are* crazy." The words half-disappeared in a growl as he pushed off from the desk.

"You said it yourself: 'It's so sad when a young person is lost to a tragic mistake.'"

Karsch's face blackened. Knife clenched in his hand, he charged. He swooped around the end of the sofa. Landis, taller and in better shape, easily vaulted it, keeping it between them. Karsch tried leaping it himself, and the knife ripped the leather. Pale foam erupted from the torn cushion.

Landis braced himself against a bookcase as Karsch roared toward him, his right arm raised to strike. "I'll kill you, you son of a bitch." At the last second, Landis feinted. Karsch, husky as a bear but not as agile, crashed into the bookcase. Already pivoting, Landis crushed Karsch's face against the books and held it there.

Karsch let loose a stream of Russian through lips distorted by the pressure of Landis's palm. The hand with the knife waved wildly, trying to bury the long blade in any part of Landis's body and caught him in the right thigh.

Landis's leg reflexively jerked away, and he held onto Karsch only by leaning his shoulder heavily into him. Blood wet his pantleg. He twisted his lower body out of Karsch's reach. That made it harder to catch Karsch's arm, each wild gesture closer to doing further damage. He focused on mashing the Russian's face into the bookshelf and waited for the flailing arm to come to him. It was slowing, as Karsch tired and struggled for breath. Finally, he grabbed Karsch's wrist and jerked the arm up hard behind his back, much farther than it could comfortably go. The knife fell to the floor. Landis kicked it away.

"I've made a lot of mistakes," Landis panted into the man's ear, pivoting again so that his entire body weight pinned Karsch in place, "but I've never played in your league." A rush of brain chemicals masked the pain, but the loss of blood was weakening him. He pressed harder on Karsch's back.

"You? Mistakes?" Karsch's voice was muffled. "You were the perfect one. Always held up as the example. Ha!" Karsch's head moved slightly sideways. "Convinced you're better than me." His spit had darkened the rusty leather spine of the book in front of him.

"No, Ivan."

"You were a little shit, finagling your way into every advantage. While I worked my ass off. My parents starved to send me to school, but you grabbed that fellowship away from me."

"It was a competition, Ivan. You lost," Landis said softly in his ear.

"My brother could never go to college. Did you know that? Our parents couldn't afford another one. His only prospects were in dealing drugs, and it killed him. That's blood on your hands, you—"

Landis increased the pressure. "You're crazy."

The Russian growled, "So what are you after now? Revenge?"

Landis kicked the back of Karsch's right knee, and he collapsed on that side. His chin caught a shelf and he yelped. He kicked back with his left leg and connected with Landis's shin. Landis jerked up on Karsch's arm again as the Russian put all his remaining strength into twisting from Landis's grasp. He kicked the back of Karsch's left knee. Karsch slid toward the floor, scraping his face against the books, his chin bouncing off the shelves until he came to a stop, kneeling in front of the bottom cabinets.

Landis grabbed Karsch's hair, pulled his head back, and bent over him. "Not revenge, Ivan," he whispered in his ear. "Absolution." He smashed Karsch's face into the cabinet. Once for Marjorie, once for Hawk, and three times for Terry Porter.

Chapter 52

Landis was pulling Karsch's head up after that third blow when Fowler and Gennaro arrived, followed by two uniformed officers. Karsch blinked a few times, tried to stand up, and collapsed. His nose was broken, his face was scuffed up, and his shoulder would be sore for weeks, but, considering the damage Landis wanted to inflict on him, he got off easy.

Landis sat on the floor across the room, leaning against a window, trying to stay conscious despite the loss of blood and mounting pain from the wound in his leg. His gaze remained glued on his adversary.

Fowler knelt beside him and whispered, "Goddammit, Landis. I told you I needed to talk to you about that lab report. And about him." He jerked a thumb toward Karsch.

"Not in so many words," Landis muttered.

Karsch's eyes glinted. He lifted a shaky arm and stabbed his finger toward Landis. In a hoarse voice, he said, "This man attacked me. I want him arrested."

"I'm guessing he'll call it self-defense. And you're looking at Assault One." Fowler pulled an evidence bag out of his coat and wagged it at Karsch. The knife was inside. "Your prints will be on this, right?"

"Of course they fucking are! It's from my desk."

A pair of emergency medical technicians crowded through the doorway.

Fowler motioned toward Landis. "He's first. Loss of

blood."

They knelt beside Landis and cut off his pant leg. The pain as they probed the wound was like a red-hot dagger and he bit his lip against it. They applied a pressure bandage and gave him a shot of morphine.

"Does he need the hospital?" Fowler asked.

"Need eyes on that, sure."

Karsch, for now not the center of attention, yelled some creative accusations. "He attacked me! It's his word against mine."

"You think so, jerkoff?" Gennaro said.

"Of course!" He panted like a dog.

"Except for the voice recording," Fowler said.

Landis fumbled in his inside jacket pocket and pulled out his phone. "I downloaded a new app for that. Amazing pickup."

"We listened to your whole conversation in the car on the way up here," Fowler said. "Most enlightening."

Karsch sealed his lips, as if to let not one more word escape. Then he grunted, his body shaking with anger, "Not admissible!"

"You a lawyer?" Gennaro asked. "One-party consent here in New York. You're toast."

To Landis, Fowler said, "When your call came in, and I figured what was happening, we hopped in a car. I contacted the 17th. They've got a bad domestic on Park tying up the Homicide Squad and gave me the green light to deal with this. We don't have to wait for them, we can take Mr. Karsch into custody right now. He's going to the hospital too, though, right?" he asked the EMTs.

"Oh, yeah. Let us give him a once-over first."

After a few minutes' examination, during which Karsch emitted groans of agony, the lead EMT said to Fowler, "Shoulder strain. They'll give him a sling for that. Not much to do for his face. He doesn't need stitches, and the nose will take care of itself. The bleeding's about stopped. He says he was briefly unconscious, so the neurologists will take a look. His pupils are OK, though, and he says he's not dizzy."

To the police officers at the door, Fowler said, "Help the man up. Put him in your car, and follow the EMTs to Mount Sinai." Karsch yelped when they pulled him up without regard for his strained shoulder.

"Can you walk?" an EMT asked. "We've got a stretcher."

With both hands, Karsch made shoving gestures and staggered toward the door. Gennaro provided hands-on encouragement from behind. From the hall, he yelled back at Landis. "You won't get away with this."

"Shut up," Gennaro said.

Landis, head back against the cool pane of the window, let the relief the morphine provided take hold. "Well?" he asked Fowler.

"I think we've got him. The Essex County sheriff will be itching to interview him about Terry Porter's death. I'm pretty sure the prosecutor will give us the go-ahead on the arrest for the assault on you. The other stuff will be more complicated, but we'll see. Why were you so sure about the methylphenidate?"

Landis pointed to Karsch's desk and said, "Check out that stack of notepads. See the logo? You noticed it on that screwdriver pen. It's for Orvadis, the company that makes methylphenidate under a trade name—Neurostim—the drug that 'changes everything.' BLK is designing their new headquarters."

"How'd you know that?"

"Found out yesterday, when I was catching up on the trades, waiting for the two Mohammeds. Knowing Ivan, he sniffed out a weak link there and cut a deal to get the stuff in bulk. I mean we're only talking about, what, half a pound, a quarter? A little goes a very long way. The pills you buy are mostly filler."

"Hunh."

"What clinched it was when he laughed about the people at the picnic being poisoned by salt. The press briefings and news coverage hadn't mentioned that detail. Neither did I. He knew it already."

"Gennaro should be able to track down the weak link at Orvadis using his light touch. Let's go," Fowler motioned the EMTs to bring the stretcher. "You'll be in the clear on the assault, though Karsch may raise a stink. I'll put the audio on a loop and give him headphones."

Walking to the elevator behind Landis's stretcher, Fowler said, "Not any of my business, but you've evened up the scales, Arch. And then some. It's time to cut yourself a break. What happened here, it's a lot to handle."

ల♋ల

When the hospital released him to go home the next day, Landis called O'Hanlon from the cab and gave him the broad strokes of the evening's events.

"McSweeney's!" O'Hanlon said. "I can open my six o'clock office early today."

"Thanks, Colm. Not today. I need to go home."

"Soon, then. I can't believe you finally nailed that bastard."

"Yeah. It was so much worse than I ever believed it could be. I'll tell you about it sometime. But right now…"

"Got it. When you have a chance, talk to Ben. He put a bug in the ear of a couple of reporters at the briefing— 'Where'd these guys get the guns?'—and their questions mostly steered clear of you. Landis + Porter doesn't seem to be a major part of the story so far."

"That's great." Landis felt like a balloon with a slow

leak.

"Some idjit from Homeland Security—ICE—was there and made a statement so confusing it grabbed most of the reporters' attention."

"Figures."

"I'll touch base with the JTTF. Their issues should be wrapped up. They may have questions about Spain. I doubt it, though."

"Right. Hey, look, my cab's dropping me off now." In fact, the cab was several blocks south of the apartment, but Landis couldn't talk any more. There'd been too much talk the night before.

"OK, I'll let you go. Congratulations, Arch. This whole bleedin mess is behind you now. At last."

"Right. Colm? Thanks for everything."

∽∾∽

The view through the open draperies of his bedroom window provided snapshots of other apartments, other lives. He hoped they were filled with normal people unburdened by terrible secrets. Like Julia's. Like Marjorie's. Like his own. He could think about that secret now with less pain than before. He'd done Julia wrong. He'd uncovered wrong. And in whatever ways open to him, which were not the ways he would have chosen, he'd fixed it.

Marjorie had never trusted him with her big secret. Maybe she hadn't been sure herself. But then, maybe that's what she meant at the end, gasping, "It's not Hawk's fault. It's…" His own guilt about Hawk made him think she meant the fault was his. He prayed she hadn't thought it was hers. His tears came, thinking of the pain Marjorie had lived with, while he'd never made her believe she could tell him about Karsch. He'd done so much wrong there.

Maybe this explained why he and Hawk never fit

together. In his heart, he did believe the awful man was Hawk's biological father. What was the phrase? Intimate strangers. He wiped away more tears. Yet, what did it matter? *He was* my *son, biology be damned.*

Two boats passed on the river, shimmering in the gray water. The swimming pool in John Jay Park glowed turquoise among the trees. Traffic on FDR Drive flowed, full of purpose, in both directions. People trading places.

The release of tension and the ache in his leg left him shaky. He filled an empty carton with the sweaters he'd been wearing. He'd leave them downstairs for the dry cleaners. One more thing to do. He reached high in the bedroom closet for the shoebox of Julia's things and took it to a chair. He hadn't allowed himself to look inside until her murder was solved. That was sorted out now, and so much more. Chaya. Hawk. Terry. Marjorie.

He removed the box lid and found Julia's paprika-colored hair clip on top. The sight of it brought her back to him full force, and the tears returned. Underneath he found a scarf that bore her scent, and he breathed into it. She had her massive dose of pain too. Her awful fears.

Underneath was the sketchbook she kept at her bedside. Sometimes, he came awake and found her drawing in it— ideas, plans for buildings, rooms. One of those sketches was of him, head on the pillow, sleepy eyes watching her. Now he laid it on the night table, open to that page, and rested a hand on the drawing—their fleeting moment she'd tried to keep forever.

∽∾∽∾

The next morning, Landis finally shaved, surprised to see in the mirror how thin his face had become. The hairs of his short beard swirled in the water from the tap and slid down the drain. He put on a new shirt and his pale linen suit. Although the day would be warm, he wore a tie.

At the shoeshine stand around the corner, his tan oxfords received a good polish. He stopped at the florist's shop down the block and bought two dozen roses of such a pale pink they were nearly white and a dozen stems of asphodel lilies, the flower of regret. He retrieved his car from the garage and drove to Greenwich, making his way to Putnam Cemetery, through its stone gates and along the drive to the stand of trees where Marjorie and Hawk were buried.

He limped across the lawn to Marjorie's grave and knelt there a long time. He talked about justice and merciless timing. About head versus heart. He learned the heart lesson too late, he admitted, but he'd learned it. He told her everything, especially how he loved her. Then and now and his whole life to come. The roses blushed softly, and their perfume tinged the air.

At his son's grave, he laid out the lilies one by one, asking for forgiveness with the careful placement of each flower. A dozen ways, and more, he'd let this boy down, whoever's genes he carried.

The July sun was directly overhead, warming him. He took off his jacket and folded it over his arm. The distant hooting of a train whistle announced the journeys of people he would never meet, but who might someday know one of his buildings. They could live and work in them, happier and safer because of decisions he made. He was committed to doing for them what he hadn't done for the people he loved. It was a commitment that gave him the strength to go on.

THE END

About the Author

(c) Robin Resch Studio

Vicki Weisfeld's short stories have appeared in leading mystery magazines, including Ellery Queen, Sherlock Holmes, and Black Cat. Find her work also in a variety of anthologies: Busted: Arresting Stories from the Beat, Seascapes: Best New England Crime Stories, Murder Among Friends, Passport to Murder, The Best Laid Plans, Quoth the Raven, and Sherlock Holmes in the Realms of Edgar Allan Poe. She's a member of Sisters in Crime, Mystery Writers of America, the Short Mystery Fiction Society, which awarded "Breadcrumbs" a best short story Derringer in 2017, and the Public Safety Writers Association, which gave a similar award to "Who They Are Now" in 2020. She's a reviewer of New Jersey theater for TheFrontRowCenter.com and crime/mystery/thriller fiction for the UK website, crimefictionlover.com. Online: www.vweisfeld.com